WORDS I SHOULD HAVE SAID

LOWCOUNTRY LOVE STORIES
BOOK 1

STEPHANIE LYNN BELLIS

Edited by
SABRINA GRIMALDI

Cover Design by
ANNIE HIGHT

STEPHANIE LYNN BELLIS

"One day, years from now, you'll see her in a coffee shop surrounded by notebooks, and you'll hope that you're in them somewhere."

To whoever wrote that Tumblr post that I found as a teenager, and to everyone who wished to become her too. This is for you.

A NOTE TO MY READERS

Words I Should Have Said contains frequent and explicit sexual content. On the next page, I have included a "DICKtionary," that denotes the specific pages/chapters where this content is prevalent, should you choose to skip over them.

I would also like to include a content warning for the discussion of the mistreatment of people within the LGBTQIA+ community. While this is not a main focus of the story, I recognize that it is a very sensitive topic for some readers.

DICK-TIONARY

Though it will mean compromising some of the character development, I understand that open door sex scenes aren't everyone's cup of tea. Or, if you're like me, you might want to flip back to those chapters later. Either way, I have listed them below for your convenience:

- Chapter 3: pages 26-34
- Chapter 9: page 102
- Chapter 10: page 109
- Chapter 20: pages 207- 209
- Chapter 24: pages 237-242
- Chapter 25: pages 250-251
- Chapter 32: pages 312-317
- Chapter 42: pages 383-386
- Chapter 43: pages 387-390

PLAYLIST

Landslide (Live) from *The Dance* 1997 by Fleetwood Mac
hate to be lame by Lizzy McAlpine
Suddenly Okay by Blake Rose
Where'd All the Time Go? by Dr. Dog
Mess It Up by Gracie Abrams
bad idea right? by Olivia Rodrigo
Never Let Go by Blake Rose
False Confidence by Noah Kahan
Cate's Brother by Maisie Peters
Not Strong Enough by boygenius
august by Taylor Swift
Nobody Knows by GUNNAR
Nonsense by Sabrina Carpenter
Use Me by Blake Rose
Old Me by 5 Seconds of Summer
Ribs by Lorde
It Was Always You by Daisy Jones
No Hands by Waka Flocka Flame (ft. Roscoe Dash & Wale)
Trojans by Atlas Genius
Growing Sideways by Noah Kahan
Movie by Blake Rose
Beat This Summer by Brad Paisley
don't break my... by Kenzie Cait
Afterglow by Taylor Swift
Dancing With Our Hands Tied by Taylor Swift
illicit affairs by Taylor Swift
Teeth (Live from The Vault) by 5 Seconds of Summer
Carolina by Harry Styles

Put a Little Love On Me by Niall Horan
Blank Me by Hastings
Serial Monogamist by Ashe
Sex On Fire by Kings of Leon
False God by Taylor Swift
Island In The Sun by Weezer
Late Night Talking by Harry Styles
Wildflower by 5 Seconds of Summer

WORDS I SHOULD HAVE SAID

1

STAY MAD—HE DOESN'T DESERVE YOUR TEARS

Rosie:

"You know who you are, you have a solid career path, and I still have no idea who I am. I feel like I'm playing catch up, like I'm wasting your time. You deserve to be with someone who knows what they want in life," Justin rambled through the phone.

"No. You don't get to make this about what I deserve. But I will sure as hell make it about what *you* deserve, which is actually having to face the guilt you're so desperately trying to avoid," Rosie pressed back, swerving her car into the nearest parking lot.

Shouldn't she be crying? Hurting? Her two-year relationship was suddenly crumbling beneath her grasp. Even so, all she could manage to feel was unadulterated rage. It was a good thing she'd pulled over; no one should be legally allowed to operate a motor vehicle while fantasizing about running their boyfriend—ex-boyfriend?—over with it.

"Rosie, I—"

"You know what I think? I think that rather than work to

change the things you don't like about your life, you take the easy way out. Telling me that I *deserve better* is a copout to convince yourself that breaking up with me is the right decision so that you can assuage your guilt."

"Rosie, this hurts me just as much as—" Justin tried again.

"And maybe you're right. Maybe I do deserve better than the way you've treated me, but if you genuinely cared about me, you would do something about it. You'd change. You'd be better. Treat me better. Treat *yourself* better—"

"Rosie, please—"

"Please what? You've clearly known you weren't willing to change for a while now, yet you strung me along anyway because it was easier than being honest with yourself about the fact that you have done absolutely jack shit to figure out what you want in life. You don't want to feel like you're playing 'catch up' to me?' Simple. Stop existing. Start living instead. Goodbye, Justin."

Rosie clicked 'end' before Justin could get another word in, and the line went dead. She half expected him to immediately call her back, to insist that he explain his decision; then again, Rosie hadn't expected him to break up with her just now, so could she really gauge his intentions as well as she'd thought?

Three days ago, on the last night of their trip to California, Rosie had suspicions that Justin might propose. Whenever people had asked if Justin was 'the one,' she'd always answered with a confident 'of course!' But, in the quiet hours of the night, when she really stopped to let herself think about it, Rosie hadn't been so sure. Justin wasn't perfect, but she had spent the last two years of her life investing in a relationship with him, and that had to count for something, right?

Having turned twenty-seven a few months ago, Rosie had started to fall into the mentality of most women her age: thinking that she'd fucked up somewhere along the way if she didn't have a ring on her finger by thirty. And if Justin was offering, who would she be to deny him? But now, she was sitting alone in her car, parked halfway between her house and Justin's with absolutely nothing to show for the past two years of her life.

She supposed Justin had been wanting this for a while but didn't have the guts to be honest with her. That would have taken ambition, which he'd never had. He'd pushed back whenever Rosie had ever suggested he start school, find a job that actually made him happy rather than one that paid the bills *without* a college degree, or buy a house instead of continuing to rent that same shitty apartment with the damn faucet that just would not stop leaking.

Rosie had continuously attributed all of these things to his lack of a healthy family model. His parents didn't communicate with each other, they didn't push him, or really bother to do much more than tell him he wasn't good enough. But Justin was twenty-seven, and her excuses for him really didn't cut it anymore. At least she could see that now; better late than never she guessed.

The only good thing about the way Justin had gone about breaking up with her was that she could cling to the intense anger it made her feel rather than wallowing in pain. Thinking she was safe in the privacy of her own car, Rosie let out a guttural scream. Much to her dismay, a middle-aged woman and her two children chose that exact moment to walk by her car with their cart full of groceries. Pulling her knees up to her chest, Rosie shrunk down into the driver's seat trying to disappear. Couldn't the universe just let her have this one moment?

Rosie couldn't stop herself from replaying the past few months of her relationship with Justin in her head and wondering at what point he'd decided he wanted out, how long he'd sat there and strung her along because of his own fear. She felt betrayed, like she'd had the rug ripped out from underneath her. And she didn't care if it made her a bad person, but, right now, she just wanted Justin to feel that same sense of betrayal. Focusing on that was easier than focusing on the hurt.

Rosie dialed Noah, who picked up on the first ring.

"Hey, babes! Aren't you supposed to be on your way to dinner with Justin?" Noah inquired in her usual light-hearted tone.

Noah Langley, one of Rosie's two best friends, never took life too seriously and never planned more than a day ahead. She was the perfect person for Rosie to call right now, considering Rosie planned on showing up at Noah's doorstep in about twenty minutes.

"Considering he just broke up with me, over the fucking phone nonetheless," she laughed as the words spilled out because what the fuck else was she supposed to do, "I'm hoping to be on my way to your apartment for a movie night," Rosie half-asked, half-stated.

"Fucking *coward*," Noah scoffed. "Of course, you can come over. I'll have wine waiting in your favorite glass. See you soon! Love you always!"

"Love you most," Rosie responded gratefully before putting her car in drive and heading for Noah's apartment.

She would have called Elena, her other best friend, but she knew Elena's not-so-little brother was with her tonight —Elena's not-so-little brother, Callum Costello, who just so happened to be Rosie's former go-to friend with benefits. There wasn't much she could count on Callum for, but she could definitely count on him to say yes to a hookup. That meant that being around Callum right now was dangerous territory considering all Rosie wanted at the moment was for Justin to feel betrayed too, wanted to get even. Thus, she didn't trust herself not to do something impulsive around Callum. Like fuck him.

Of course, Rosie was going to tell Elena what had happened with Justin tonight, but she wanted to explain everything in person, sans Callum and the rest of Elena's family. Rosie had met Elena during their freshman year of high school when Elena's family moved to Charleston and they'd been inseparable ever since. As a side-effect of her friendship with Elena, Rosie had also known Callum for over a decade now, having grown up with him as she'd spent most of her life at the Costello's house.

Being that he wasn't even a full year younger than Elena (Elena and Callum were Irish Twins), Callum was always hanging out with Rosie and Elena. There was an attraction between him and Rosie from day one, an attraction that they very quickly began to explore; but as great as that attraction had been, Rosie had never let it grow into anything more. Callum was the guy you went to when you were in the mood for a good time, not when you wanted anything to do with a relationship.

Of all the people she could have chosen to hook up with repeatedly, Callum was a messy choice, but there was just something that felt inevitable about ending up back in bed with him so many times over the years. And there *was* something to the level of comfort Rosie felt with Callum. Years and years of on-and-off hooking up will do that, not to mention the whole seeing Callum at every Costello family event she'd been to over the years aspect of things.

Rosie typed out a quick text to Elena before setting her

phone in the console of her car and pulling back out onto the main road toward Noah's apartment complex.

> Rosie: Long story short: Justin broke up with me before our dinner plans tonight. Brunch tomorrow?

Elena's face popped up on Rosie's phone screen not even a minute later.

Rosie answered the phone call with a muttered, "Hi."

"I will drive to his apartment and slash a hole in every single one of his tires right now. Just say the word," Elena huffed rather than saying hello.

"I'm sorry, I thought I dialed Elena? My nonviolent best friend?" Rosie said sarcastically. "And aren't you at family dinner?" Rosie asked.

"Yeah, but you're the priority right now. Want to come over here? Or I can leave and come to you?" Elena responded earnestly.

Rosie knew she was serious. Elena would drop everything to be there for her.

"No, it's okay. I'm on my way to Noah's for a wine and movie night. But let's get brunch tomorrow?"

"Absolutely. Over Easy around ten?" Elena suggested.

Over Easy was their favorite local brunch place. They had the best breakfast plates and served bottomless mimosas on the weekends.

"Sounds good. I'll see you then," Rosie answered.

"Uh-uh. You're not about to hang up the phone without at least giving me the gist of what happened," Elena demanded.

"Justin called me when I was on the way to his place to go to dinner tonight as we planned. He said he 'didn't know who he was or what he wanted out of life,' and that he 'felt like he was playing catch up and wasting my time,'" Rosie explained.

"He broke up with you *over the phone*? After *two years*?" Elena sounded dumbfounded.

"Yep."

"Fuck. Him."

"That's what got me into this situation in the first place."

"Are you alright to drive to Noah's?"

"Yeah. I'm honestly too angry to be sad right now."

"Promise?" Elena asked.

"Promise," Rosie answered.

"Okay, well I'll see you tomorrow at ten. Order the entire menu if you want—my treat."

"I love you for that," Rosie laughed. A small laugh, but a laugh nonetheless.

"I love you too. And Rosie?" Elena paused.

"Yeah?"

"Stay mad. He doesn't deserve your tears," Elena said before hanging up.

Rosie parked in front of Noah's building and walked up to her second-floor apartment. When she got to the door, she didn't bother knocking. She knew it would be unlocked—it always was. Noah claimed that it was 'a fuck you to the patriarchy that told her that, as a woman, she should live in fear.' That was the way Noah lived every aspect of her life, and Rosie loved her for it.

Rosie had just barely crossed the threshold into the apartment when Noah's arms flung around her and pulled her into a hug. Rosie laughed as tears stung her eyes.

"Oh *hell* no, you're not going to sit here and cry over a

boy who was too much of a goddamn coward to end things between you in person," Noah said into Rosie's shoulder.

What Noah was lacking in height, she made up for in personality.

Rosie squeezed Noah even harder. She wasn't crying because she was sad, but because she was so vehemently angry. She wasn't sure what she could do about it, which made her feel helpless, which had led to the tears.

"I'm not sad, I'm *angry*. I feel betrayed," she explained to Noah.

"Okay, well that's good. I can work with anger," Noah replied with a smirk on her face as she disappeared around the corner to pour them each a glass of wine.

"Why are you smirking? What are you thinking?" Rosie called after her.

"Wine first. Go sit, I'll bring your glass to you," Noah winked.

Rosie knew better than to argue with Noah and did as she was told, going to sit on her green velvet couch. She couldn't help but be flooded with memories of all the late-night conversations she and Noah had had on that couch. It was like a comforting wave of nostalgia, blanketing Rosie in a hug.

Noah quickly returned from the kitchen, her nearly waist-length black hair falling over the tattoo sleeve that ran from her forearm all the way up the skin of her shoulder to her collarbone.

Noah was a tattoo artist and was always letting coworkers ink something cool onto her skin, which was how she'd ended up with the vast array of pieces on her arm that somehow formed a cohesive sleeve. Among them were countless American traditional motifs from other artists at her shop (Rosie's favorites were the dagger and serpent), a pair of cherubs, a few floral pieces that wove seamlessly amongst the rest, a luna moth, a mermaid, and a spider all done in variants of black and gray. The bold black lines were made extra striking in contrast to Noah's pale coloring.

Despite being only four foot eleven, Noah's appearance still managed to appear incredibly intimidating to people who didn't know better. Rosie was one of the people who knew better, having met Noah at summer camp in middle school. They'd been assigned to the same cabin: Cabin #9899 for sixth-grade girls. A week into camp, prank wars began. Noah pitched the idea to steal a ketchup bottle from the mess hall, throw a few opened tampons into an empty pizza box, and squirt the ketchup onto them to 'deliver' to the boys' cabin. That was the moment Rosie knew that she and Noah were meant to be best friends. They'd spent every second of the rest of that summer attached at the hip.

Being districted for two different middle schools did nothing to wane their friendship; every Friday night, Rosie and Noah had sleepovers. And much to Rosie and Noah's delight, the Board of Education redrew the school zones the summer before their freshman year of high school, leaving them zoned for the same school for the first time. Rosie still remembers the day the announcement was made—it was better than Christmas.

Freshman year was also the year that Rosie met Elena; they were both in Ninth Grade Honors Lit together and had bonded over a mutual disdain for the fact that every novel listed on the syllabus was written by some old, white man. Honors American Lit the following year was slightly improved if you believed that, though F. Scott Fitzgerald was the name printed on the cover of *The Great Gatsby*, it was really written by his wife, Zelda. And Rosie and Elena were both team Zelda because, honestly, what man could write such flowery prose?

The first time Rosie mentioned Noah in a conversation with Elena, she was reminded of the fact that most people found her intimidating. She couldn't remember Elena's exact wording, but it was something along the lines of "that girl looks like she could have me on my ass in five seconds flat."

Although Noah looked bitchy and standoffish, she was one of the most affectionate and loyal people Rosie knew. Had proven that loyalty when Rosie came out as bisexual during their junior year of high school.

Half of the girls in their grade slowly stopped inviting her to sleepovers; they never explained why, but Rosie knew. For every sleepover Rosie didn't get invited to, Noah had been there. Not long after that, Rosie decided to introduce the two people she loved the most to each other. Once Elena realized that Noah wasn't nearly as scary as she looked, the two of them began to love each other just as fiercely as they each loved Rosie; so from that summer on, it had been Rosie, Noah, and Elena against the world.

Rosie had gotten to return the support Noah had shown her when Noah came out as pansexual during their freshman year of college. Living in a dorm with a communal bathroom as a queer woman wasn't always easy. People tended to assume that because someone was attracted to multiple genders it automatically meant they were attracted to *everyone* of said genders. No amount of analogous 'well, you're attracted to men, but you aren't attracted to *every* man you see, are you?' questioning ever seemed to be enough to assuage them. If you were queer and lived in a 'female' dorm, you'd be seen as a predator by at least half of the residents regardless of the efforts you made. Even so, Rosie and

Noah had gotten through that like they'd gotten through everything else: together.

Though Elena wasn't queer, she was a proud ally and would go down swinging to defend and protect her friends. Massive strides have been taken for LGBTQIA+ rights, but the world could still be full of hate. While Rosie was grateful that her parents hadn't disowned her for being queer—not everyone was so fortunate—the place where she felt the safest was with her chosen family. Noah and Elena didn't just accept Rosie, they celebrated every facet of who she was.

"So, why the smirk?" Rosie prompted Noah as she sat down, a glass of wine in each hand.

"Right now all you can focus on is making Justin feel the same sense of betrayal he made you feel, right?" Noah said, hitting the nail on the head.

"Am I that transparent?"

"Have you forgotten that I've been your best friend for almost two decades? I know how that pretty mind of yours works, babe," Noah said lovingly.

"You have a point. Does that make me a bad person? Wanting him to hurt the way he hurt me?" Rosie asked hesitantly, not really sure if she wanted the answer.

"It makes you human. And if that's what it takes to keep yourself from breaking down, then that's what you focus on. *Justin* caused this hurt, and now he gets to deal with it however it manifests itself in you. It's *his* problem, not yours," Noah said definitively.

"Damn, Noh," Rosie replied, using the nickname she'd had for Noah since that year they met at summer camp. "When did you get so wise?"

"I've always been this wise, thank you very much," Noah crossed her arms sarcastically.

"How would I even do that? *He* left *me*, I have no power over him," Rosie thought aloud.

"Are you kidding me? Right now, Justin is probably sitting on his couch thinking about how he would deny you if you asked for him back. He expects you to sit around in mourning."

"And how does that help me, exactly?"

"Because he *expects* you to sit around mourning, Rosie. Anything less would hurt his ego."

"So?" Rosie asked, still not understanding where Noah was going with this.

"So, you do the opposite. If Justin saw you with someone else immediately after he ended things with you, he would understand how deep his betrayal cut you," Noah explained.

Rosie took a big sip of her wine. She had to admit, Noah had a point. Suddenly, a familiar face popped into her mind: Callum.

Justin had always worried about Rosie being around Callum as often as she was. She supposed his worries weren't unfounded; he'd known her history with Callum. Still, she would never have done anything to betray her relationship with Justin and had never given him a reason to doubt her.

Oddly enough, Justin had never spared a shred of concern over her relationship with Noah. Not that there was concern to be had. They were inseparable, would always be inseparable, but there had never been any romantic feelings between the two of them. Noah and Rosie were soulmates in the most platonic sense of the word. Not that it mattered anymore, but, if the roles had been reversed, Rosie would have at least *clarified* that there was nothing else going on. It was as if Justin forgot she was bisexual just because she was dating him. As if an entire facet of her identity ceased to exist solely because of her choice of partner at the time.

All signs pointed to Callum being the perfect point of insecurity to fuck with Justin. She could go over to Elena's parent's house right now, take a picture with Callum in it, and post it to her Instagram story for Justin to see, but that wouldn't be good enough. She needed to make sure Justin only interpreted the picture the way she intended. The way she knew would hurt him just as deeply as he'd hurt her.

She needed a picture of her and Callum alone, preferably at his apartment. That would send a message without any room for speculation. But did she trust herself to go over there without actually doing what the picture would imply? She wasn't sure. Truthfully, she wasn't sure she *wanted* to stop herself. Looking down, she realized she'd emptied her glass of wine.

"You're suspiciously quiet. What are you thinking?" Noah raised her eyebrows.

"I think I know the perfect person for this, but I'm not sure it would end up being just an innocent means to get back at Justin," Rosie admitted what she'd been thinking out loud.

"What's stopping you?" Noah asked.

"I just," Rosie hung her head in her hands. "I feel like sleeping with someone else so soon is wrong. It feels like blatant disrespect for the relationship I had with Justin," she muttered.

"Nope. I'm stopping that train of thought before it even leaves the station. Justin clearly had no respect for your relationship considering he didn't even end it in person like a decent human being, so fuck that mentality," Noah stated bluntly.

When Rosie didn't say anything, Noah continued,

"Forget about right and wrong. What do *you* want, my precious Rosemary June?" Noah asked genuinely.

"I... I just don't want Justin to be the last person to have touched me. Not after the way he betrayed me," Rosie sighed.

"Then there's your answer," Noah said plainly. "Maybe there's some credibility in that whole 'the best way to get over someone is to get under someone else' mentality after all."

Yeah, there was her answer. Whether she liked it or not.

2

SOMETIMES, DOING THE RIGHT THING MEANS LOOKING LIKE AN ASS

Callum:

CALLUM WAS HELPING HAYDEN, his oldest sister Lydia's husband, clean up after dinner at his parents' house when he overheard Elena telling their mom that Rosie's boyfriend had dumped her, over the phone no less. He strained to hear the details of what Elena was telling their mom, trying to glean as much as he could without having to actually ask about Rosie himself.

"You gonna let me dry that plate, or are you gonna rinse it until Elena stops talking to your mom?" Hayden elbowed Callum in the ribs.

"I wasn't eavesdropping if that's what you're insinuating," Callum responded, sounding a lot less nonchalant than he'd intended, considering that's exactly what he'd been doing. "I just zoned out."

"Sure," Hayden replied sarcastically.

Callum raised his eyebrows in Hayden's direction.

"Dude, everyone in this family knows about your history with Rosie. She's suddenly single after two years, and you're gonna pretend your ears *didn't* just perk up like a dog begging for a treat?"

"I think you're forgetting that *I'm* not single," Callum retorted.

"Please, we both know that you're not serious about her. And you've only been dating, what, a month?" Hayden asked.

"Ish," Callum answered.

"Do you even know the exact date?" Hayden pressed.

He didn't. Fuck, Hayden was reading him to filth.

"I—no," he admitted. "I don't."

"That's what I thought," Hayden replied sarcastically, looking satisfied with himself. "You barely talk about her, and I don't remember the last time you actually volunteered to help with dishes at family dinner. Seems to me like you just wanted space from her."

Olivia, Callum's girlfriend, was nice enough, and the sex was good. Even so, whether Callum had thought about it consciously or not, Hayden was right. By volunteering to do the dishes, he got a few minutes of space from Olivia, who was currently in the living room with the rest of Callum's family. And though he didn't have any experience with long-term relationships, Callum was pretty sure that wasn't exactly a good sign.

"All things aside, just because she's single doesn't mean anything. She's probably upset, and the last thing on her mind is jumping back into bed with me."

Callum handed the last plate to Hayden and dried his hands on the towel next to the sink.

"But what if it wasn't? The last thing on her mind, I mean," Hayden teased as he slipped the plate into the dishwasher and walked out of the kitchen, back toward the living room to rejoin the rest of the family.

With one hand braced on the counter, Callum ran his fingers through his hair.

But what if it wasn't?

Fuck if Callum knew. It's not like the fact that she had been in a relationship had stopped his attraction to her, and the fact that they'd slept together before didn't exactly help, considering he could rely on his memories rather than his imagination to know that she was even more beautiful when she was naked with her legs spread for him.

Putting those thoughts aside, Callum walked down the hallway that took him back toward the living room.

"Is it time for dessert, yet?" Harper, the youngest Costello sibling, asked as he sat down on the couch next to Olivia.

"The boys *just* finished cleaning up from dinner, honey," their mom laughed.

"Yeah, but the apple pie isn't gonna eat itself," Harper glanced toward the kitchen.

"Then go fix yourself some, but only if you bring me back a slice," their mom said and winked in Harper's direction as she headed for the kitchen.

His conversation with Hayden in the kitchen had apparently fucked with him because Callum couldn't help but notice the way all the other couples were sitting in comparison to the way he was sitting next to Olivia. His dad's arm was propped on the couch behind his mom's shoulders. Lydia, his oldest sister, sat on the floor between Hayden's legs, propped comfortably against his chest as they both watched their five-year-old daughter, Willow, playing on the floor. Cole, Elena's fiancé, had his arm wrapped around her waist, Elena's fingers intertwined with his where their hands met. And Callum sat plainly next to Olivia, their knees just barely touching. The only other people in the room who weren't cuddled up to their partner were Layla and Liam, Callum's nineteen-year-old sister and twenty-three-year-old brother, both of whom didn't currently have a partner.

Callum was a grown, twenty-six-year-old man; he wasn't afraid to show affection around his family. He just didn't have the desire for those casually affectionate touches like everyone else around him seemed to. But that was something to evaluate later, he decided.

"I'm gonna grab another glass of wine, want me to bring you anything?" Olivia asked, pulling Callum from his thoughts.

"Nah, I've already had a few beers," he answered. "But thank you."

As Olivia was leaving the room, Callum heard Elena mutter, "I wonder if I should just go meet her at Noah's," to their mom.

Callum was no Prince Charming himself, but come on? Who ended a several-year relationship over the phone? Rosie's asshole ex, apparently.

With Olivia out of the room, he let down his guard enough to ask, "what happened with Rosie and Justin? Weren't they just on a trip together like last week?"

Callum didn't need confirmation that Rosie had been on a trip with Justin; he'd seen her posts on Instagram.

"He told her that he 'didn't know who he was or what he wanted out of life.' Honestly, I think he just felt like he needed some sort of change in his life, but wasn't willing to put in any effort to actually *make* a change. Hence the breakup—little effort, major change," Elena rolled her eyes. "He's an idiot though if he thinks this is actually going to give him the sense of fulfillment he's clearly looking for. Rosie was the only person in his life who bothered to push him."

"What are we talking about?" Olivia asked as she walked back into the living room, taking back her spot next to Callum on the couch.

Unlike Callum, however, she sat close enough that Callum could feel the body heat rippling off her.

"Rosie's boyfriend of two years dumped her over the phone, like the cowardly ass that he is," Elena answered, saving Callum from having to explain why he was a part of this conversation.

It wasn't that Olivia didn't know *who* Rosie was... it was that she just happened to be missing a few *very* compromising bits of information about Callum's history with her. After what amount of time was it appropriate to tell your current girlfriend that you've been on and off fuck buddies with your sister's best friend for the better part of the last decade? As far as he was concerned, that had to be at least a three-months-in kind of conversation. And until tonight, Rosie had been off the market anyway, so it's not like telling Olivia even made a difference.

"God, men are the worst," Olivia chimed in, pulling Callum from his thoughts.

He must have looked startled because she quickly traced her fingers along his arm and added, "not you, babe."

If Callum was being honest with himself, Justin had always *seemed* nice enough; he just didn't seem like the person for Rosie. Rosie was bold, independent, driven, someone who grabbed life by the balls and took what she wanted... but Callum was definitely not going to think about Rosie and balls in the same sentence. Absolutely not, because that would take him on a trip down memory lane which was wildly inappropriate considering who sat next to him.

Olivia. He should think about Olivia. His perfectly nice

girlfriend. See? Not thinking about Rosie.

"You feeling okay, babe?" he heard Olivia mutter in his ear. "You're flushed."

Fuck, he really needed to get himself in check.

"Yeah, I guess those beers are starting to catch up to me," he nervously chuckled. "Do you mind driving us back to my apartment?"

Lie. He wasn't nervous, he was turned on as all hell at the memory of hearing Rosie moan his name. At least he wouldn't have to deal with the war that was keeping his dick in his pants at the sight of Rosie tonight, not in person anyway... but he'd definitely be seeing her when he gripped his cock in the shower later. Because there was absolutely no way that he would be sleeping with Olivia while he was so preoccupied with thoughts of Rosie. He wasn't that much of an asshole. To say that he was fucked would be an understatement.

After leaving his parents' house, Callum and Olivia went back to his apartment to watch a movie. He had just sat down on the couch next to her when his phone buzzed in his pocket. Of all the names he'd expected to see pop up, Rosie's didn't even rank.

She had *just* been broken up with. She had to be sad, hurting. Why the hell would she be texting him of all people? Suddenly, Hayden's earlier words drifted back to him.

But what if it wasn't? The last thing on her mind, I mean.

He swiped his phone to read the text, careful to avoid tilting the phone at an angle that Olivia would be able to see. *Just in case,* he told himself.

Words I Should Have Said

> Rosie: You busy?

He was busy. However, he couldn't deny that he was intrigued by her text. Maybe Rosie just wanted to talk? Although talking between them had only ever gone in one direction, their mouths too preoccupied with other things to hold a conversation... He decided to hear her out and see what she wanted. Maybe there was some merit to Hayden's words after all...

> Callum: What's up?

He added a second text in an attempt to sound more sympathetic.

> Callum: I heard about Justin. I'm sorry.

> Rosie: I'm not.

Okay, so she definitely wasn't texting him because she was sad and needed someone to talk to. She had Elena and Noah for that anyway. Callum had always known the ins and outs of her life, but only due to the forced proximity of their adolescence, not because he was a great listener or anything.

Which meant... was she about to ask what he thought she was about to ask? There was no way, not this quickly after the breakup at least. Right?

But if she was...

> Rosie: His way of breaking up with me was gaslighting me into thinking it was my idea, that I 'deserved better.'

> Callum: What an ass.
>
> Callum: Sorry. Too soon?

> Rosie: Actually, no. Noah told me that the best way to get over him was to get under someone else...

Callum was pretty sure he'd stopped breathing.

> Rosie: Which brings me to my reason for texting you.

Fuck. So she *was* seeking him out to hook up, and everyone knew that angry sex was always hotter. Just because Rosie wasn't angry with him didn't mean she couldn't take it out on him. And God, did Callum want her to. His cock hardened in anticipation, pressing against his pants.

Honestly, it made sense that she'd ask him. He was familiar, and he'd had the past ten years to learn her body, to learn exactly where to touch her to elicit those pretty little moans he loved so much. From their awkward first time together as teenagers to trusting each other enough to explore their kinks, Callum and Rosie had developed a level of comfortability that was hard to find. Given that dynamic, sex between the two of them was guaranteed to be good for them both, and things wouldn't be awkward afterward because they'd already slept together more times over the years than they could even begin to count.

That just left him to deal with the issue of Olivia. They'd only been together for a little over a month, and, yeah, Callum didn't see it going anywhere. He'd only let things go on for this long because dating Olivia meant not having to seek someone out every time he wanted to fuck. Beyond that, they didn't have much in common. Honestly, he could break up with her right now, and not give it a second thought. Olivia would be over it in a day or so, and she'd go on to find someone actually willing to commit long-term. Really, he reasoned, he'd be doing the right thing by breaking things off.

Did that make him an asshole? Probably, but Hayden had been right earlier tonight; the only reason he was staying with Olivia was for the convenience of sex. Sex with Rosie sounded much more appealing, especially given that she'd been off limits for the past two years, though that certainly hadn't stopped Callum from wanting her. It was probably just the familiarity, but something always drew him back to her.

Callum wouldn't be breaking up with Olivia to be with Rosie; no, the opportunity to fuck Rosie just gave him a reason to do what he'd already been thinking about. At that moment, Callum knew he'd made his decision.

"If you're just going to sit on your phone all night, why am I even here?" Olivia asked next to him.

Normally Callum would have thought of a flirty retort, something along the lines of 'why don't *you* sit on my face instead?' but he knew this was the 'in' he needed to break things off.

"I actually wanted to talk to you about that. About us. I just... don't feel like this is going anywhere."

"Uh?" she stared incredulously.

"Look, I know it's shitty of me to drop it on you like this, but, if we're being honest, we're wasting each other's time. We clearly don't have much in common," he motioned to the space between them on the couch. "If we did, we wouldn't have been sitting in silence for the past ten minutes."

"If you wanna talk about wasting each other's time, then why the hell did you take me to your family dinner with you tonight if you were just planning on breaking up with me afterward?" Olivia challenged.

Shit. Honestly, he'd kept bringing Olivia along to things because it meant that he kept getting to fuck her, but he wasn't about to tell *her* that. He thought back to the casual intimacy that he'd seen between everyone else at family dinner tonight, how they seemed incapable of going without touching, how he didn't feel that way toward Olivia whatsoever. Had never felt that way toward anyone.

"I'd already asked you to come tonight before I decided anything for sure. Seeing Elena with Cole tonight just solidified what I'd been feeling about things between us not heading anywhere long-term. I don't have the craving to be close to people like they seem to crave being close to each other."

There. That was more like it. He still sounded like an ass, but at least he sounded like an ass with some semblance of logic.

"So that's it? It's over? Just like that?"

"I don't know what else to say. I just know that I can't be the kind of partner that every other man in my family seems to be," Callum shrugged. "No point in wasting more of your time. Can't we just leave it at that?"

"Yeah, asshole, we can leave it at that."

With that parting comment, Olivia snatched her keys from his counter and walked out the front door, letting the door slam shut behind her. The moment Callum heard the door close, the thought of Olivia floated from his mind in favor of the memory of Rosie's perfect tits bouncing in his face as she rode him. Yeah, he was absolutely not busy. Not for her. Never for her.

He pulled up her last message again. *Noah told me that the best way to get over him was to get under someone else...* Callum typed his response and hit send.

> Callum: In that case, nah, I'm not busy. I'm always happy to be over you.

Or under you. Or behind you. Inside you.

> Rosie: Wait, are you still dating that girl you brought to family dinner a few weeks ago? Olivia?

> Callum: Nah. We broke things off recently.

Very recently. As in, she just walked out the door five minutes ago recently. He hoped Rosie wouldn't talk to Elena about tonight. At his parents' house. Where he was hours earlier. With Olivia. *Fuck.* Too late, he'd already sent the text.

> Rosie: Thank God.

> Rosie: Can I come over?

If it came down to it, he had the excuse that he broke up with Olivia because he realized he didn't see a future with her like he saw in Elena and Cole tonight. *Not* because the thought of fucking Rosie once was more exciting than the entirety of his relationship with Olivia had been.

> Callum: Fuck yeah, you can. See you in twenty?

> Rosie: See you in twenty.

3

THE BEST WAY TO GET OVER HIM IS TO GET UNDER SOMEONE ELSE

Rosie:

Rosie knocked on the front door before she could talk herself out of it. For fuck's sake, it had only been four hours since she and Justin had broken up. But hey, nothing said "screw you, Justin" quite like fucking the one guy he'd always been jealous of mere hours after he'd broken up with her, right? She intended to make Justin feel betrayed, and she wouldn't deny that this would be an enjoyable way to accomplish that. Knowing Callum, she knew he wouldn't mind posing as her plaything. A quick picture of her thighs on either side of his chest would do just fine. Callum *had said* he'd be happy to be under her.

Callum answered the door quickly, wearing gray sweatpants and a white t-shirt that fit snugly against his muscled torso. Despite the casual attire, he still wore a simple chain around his neck and an array of rings sat on his fingers, except for the middle two on his right hand. It didn't take long for Rosie to figure out why, which had her blushing. Callum was the exact opposite of Justin's clean-cut aesthetic with his black-painted fingernails and inked skin.

As much as she had loved Justin, Callum was definitely more her type—well, aside from the fact that she would never actually consider dating Callum. *Physically*, he was more her type.

He looked her up and down torturously slow. She hadn't bothered to change out of the jade green mini dress she'd intended to wear to dinner; she knew the dress showed off her ass, which just so happened to be one of Callum's favorite things about her.

"Hey, so, how are you doing?" Callum mumbled, visibly showing his attempt at restraint.

"Shhhh, less talking, more stripping," Rosie pulled Callum's body to hers, stepped into his apartment, and shut his front door behind her in one swift motion.

His hands immediately found her waist, pulling her even closer to him. He pressed her back against his front door, trailing a hand up from her hip and tangling it in her long, copper-red hair.

She hadn't felt Callum's lips on hers in the past two years that she'd been with Justin, but she couldn't say she hadn't thought about it. They melted together with ease like it was the most natural thing in the world. Callum ran his tongue across her bottom lip in question, and she parted for him in return. He kissed her without a trace of gentleness; his kisses were rough, greedy, like he couldn't taste enough of her at once. He grabbed a section of her hair in his fist and tugged, deepening the kiss further. Their tongues tangled together, reacquainting themselves with one another.

Rosie separated her mouth from Callum's long enough to greedily grab at the hem of his shirt and pull it over his head. He gazed at her with hungry eyes.

She glanced down at his now-exposed chest, eyeing his tattooed arms and torso. Starting at the base of his left elbow, a snake wound its way up his bicep and onto his collarbone where it eventually wove through the hole of a skull on his chest. Underneath the skull was an American Traditional style banner that read 'Memento Mori.' On his left bicep, he had a depiction of Icarus reaching toward the sun as he fell back down to Earth. Rosie had never asked about the meaning behind that piece in particular, but she knew enough Greek Mythology to recognize the story. Then, slightly hidden by the waist of his sweatpants, a prowling lion done in red ink. Rosie knew that one was a tribute to his zodiac sign: Leo. Fuck, she loved his tattoos, and she had every intention of kissing her way down them until she was on her knees in front of him.

As she began to trail her tongue down his neck, Callum changed direction and backed her into the kitchen island, lifting her legs up and wrapping them around his hips. He carelessly shoved an assortment of mail, keys, and his wallet onto the floor to set her on the island.

Pressing himself against her center, he whispered onto her lips, "uh-uh, baby. As much as I'd love to see your pretty little lips wrapped around my cock, I'm focused on you right now. You had a shitty day. Let me make it better."

All Rosie could manage in response was a moan. Holy hell, she'd forgotten how fucking wet Callum could make her with his words alone. She leaned back into the kiss, taking his lower lip between hers and biting. He groaned and rocked into her again. Swallowing her moan with his lips, he moved his hands over her ass and slowly up her hips and to her breasts.

Slowly, he traced his way down her neck with his tongue, stopping occasionally to bite her skin—not hard enough to hurt her, but hard enough that it threatened to drive her mad if she couldn't get his cock out of his pants in the next thirty seconds.

Callum slipped the thin strap of her dress down her shoulder, revealing her to him.

"Fuck Rosie, I've missed your tits," he groaned against her nipple before sucking it lightly into his mouth.

Tangling her hand in his shoulder-length, curly brown hair, Rosie held him to her breast and whispered, "Callum, I swear to God if you don't get on your knees in the next ten seconds, I'm getting on mine."

"Shut the fuck up and be patient, Rose," he smirked, using the nickname he'd only ever used for her with his head between her legs.

"It's been two years *Costello*, I don't have much patience when it comes to you."

"Then lift your goddamn hips for me so I can take off the thong I know is underneath this dress," he said, nudging her legs farther apart with his own.

"Better," she whispered, lifting her hips up to help him grab the black lace and pull it down her legs.

He didn't bother removing her heels as he discarded the lace onto the floor of his kitchen with his mail. Hooking his arms around her thighs and grabbing her ass, Callum pulled her to the edge of the counter and sank to his knees between her legs. Just as she thought he was about to put his hand where she so desperately needed it, he reached up to grab her wrist. Before she could ask what he was doing, he pulled the hair tie from her wrist and wrapped his long hair into a messy bun. And damn if the image didn't ignite her core. Rosie had always loved watching the women she'd been with tie their hair up to sink to their knees for her and seeing Callum do the same was just as intoxicating.

Rosie grabbed Callum's neck, urging him to touch her.

"Use your words, Rose. Tell me what you want," Callum slowly kissed the insides of her thighs.

"Touch me," she pleaded.

"Do you want to ride my fingers," he kissed the crease between her inner thigh and her pussy, "or my face?"

"Both," she breathed out.

Without hesitation, Callum buried his face between her legs, sliding his tongue up her pussy to circle her clit.

"You taste," he groaned, "just as fucking sweet as I remember," looking up at her as he slid a finger inside her.

She couldn't stop the whimper that fell from her lips.

"Good girl, let me hear how good I'm making you feel," he added another finger then, curling them both as he pumped them in and out with the precision that only someone who knew every inch of her body could do.

Just as he sucked her clit into his mouth, his fingers met that spot inside of her that nearly sent her over the edge. That was a major advantage to the amount of times she'd fucked Callum: he knew *exactly* where and *exactly* how she liked to be touched.

"I can feel you clenching around my fingers, Rose. Ride my face, baby," he encouraged her. "Take what you need from me."

Rosie had never been shy with Callum. Didn't need to. Sexually, she trusted him to do just about anything with her. Hell, they'd been comfortable enough with each other to have experimented with anal sex for the first time before they'd even graduated high school. Even so, she loved the praise, loved the encouragement. She moved against him with reckless abandon, chasing the release she was so close to reaching.

With the slightest scrape of his teeth as he sucked her

clit, Rosie fell over the edge. She was fairly certain she screamed loud enough for his neighbors to hear, but Callum didn't seem to mind, and neither did she.

He didn't break eye contact with her once as he drug his fingers from her pussy and into his mouth, groaning as he licked them clean. Then he stood, kissing her lips so that she could taste herself on his tongue.

Callum:

Callum was nearly in pain from having kept his cock in his pants this whole time, yet it had been worth it to see the look in Rosie's eyes as he licked the taste of her from his fingers. She looked of pure arousal, and he fucking *loved* it.

She wrapped her legs back around him, seeking friction, and let out a breathy plea, "Bedroom. Now."

Fuck, if she kept grinding into him like this he'd come before they ever left this kitchen. Beyond words, Callum replied by lifting her from the countertop by her ass and heading toward the hallway to his bedroom.

Rosie took advantage of his concentration and began kissing her way down his neck, all the while continuing to grind herself against him.

It was the breathy little moan that she let out right into his ear that prompted him to speak, "Rosie, baby, if you keep doing that, I won't make it to the bedroom."

Evidently, Rosie didn't care because the next thing Callum felt was the scrape of her teeth as she tugged on his earlobe. *Jesus. Fuck.* Callum set her down, and Rosie let out a groan of protest before she realized that Callum had only let her go so that he could turn her around, her back to his chest, and bend her over the couch.

Pulling her dress up with his left hand, he reached around Rosie's waist with his right, feeling how drenched she was from the orgasm he'd just wrung from her. She was wet and throbbing for him, which, had he not already been straining against the waistband of his sweatpants for the past ten minutes, would have made his cock even harder.

The moment his fingers entered her pussy, her head fell back against his chest.

He kissed the exposed skin of her neck, and whispered in her ear, "Rose, I need my cock inside you, baby."

She spun around to face him, her chest now pressed to his and her waist to the back of the couch. Grabbing the waistband of his sweatpants, she began to lower herself in front of him. She stared straight into his eyes as she pulled the waistband of his sweatpants down enough to draw his cock out. Gripping it confidently with one hand, she traced her tongue up his shaft. Callum felt his eyes flutter closed at the feeling. Wholly aware of the effect she had on him at even the smallest of touches, she took the head of his cock into her mouth and sucked lightly.

Fucking. Tease.

The knowledge that she wanted his cock in her mouth was almost enough to make him come on the spot, but this was about her. This was about Rosie and her shitty ex and how Callum was going to fuck all of her anger and resentment right out of her. Callum knew how incredible it felt to fuck her mouth, but that wasn't what he needed right now. He needed to feel the warmth of her pussy surrounding him.

"Not inside your mouth, Rose," he breathed out in a moan.

Slipping her mouth from his cock, Rosie teased him, "Then use *your* words, Costello. Tell me what you want."

"Apparently I haven't made myself clear. Tonight is about you, about your pleasure. So be a good girl, bend the fuck over, and let me fuck you until you come around my cock."

"Yes sir," Rosie purred, looking up at him through her lashes.

Very good girl.

"Shit, condom. One second."

Callum quickly walked to his bedroom and grabbed a condom from the drawer of his nightstand. He unwrapped it, slid it down his length, and walked back into the living room.

Grabbing Rosie by the waist, he spun her back around. Keeping one hand on her hip and moving the other up to her neck, he bent her over the couch at the angle he knew would allow him to hit that spot inside her that would have her seeing stars.

He didn't need to touch her pussy to know that it was still dripping for him. He teased her by rubbing the head of his cock against her clit before sliding all the way inside her in one swift thrust.

"Oh fuck," Rosie groaned. "Harder."

Add that to the long list of reasons that Callum loved hooking up with Rosie. Most girls pretended to like it rough, but the second he gave them what they claimed to want, he was 'too aggressive.' Rosie met him stroke for stroke, both literally and figuratively.

Callum thrust into her harder.

She moaned for him. Loudly.

"I know, baby," Callum dug his fingers into her hips and

pounded into her, hard like she'd demanded of him, "I know."

He could already feel his release building. Maybe it was her teasing, maybe it was because he'd not been inside her for two years, but Callum knew it would be soon. He'd be damned if he let himself fall over the edge without taking Rosie with him again, so he slid the hand that had been holding her hip to her clit, and began circling it.

He grabbed a fistful of her hair with the other hand he'd tangled there and pulled hard. She'd asked for rough, and Callum would happily give her what she wanted.

"That's it, baby, look at how well you're taking my cock," he praised.

"Fuck yes," Rosie groaned.

Seeking deeper contact, she pushed back into him as he thrust into her from behind.

"Come for me, Rose."

"Demanding mu—oh *fuck*, Callum I'm coming," Rosie cried.

His name on her lips was his undoing. His thrusts became less and less rhythmic as he released two years' worth of pent-up need into her. He could feel her pussy contracting around him and knew she'd found release too.

As he pulled out of her, she slid her dress back down over her hips. He put his sweatpants back on and walked into the kitchen to get a glass of water for each of them.

As she followed him into the kitchen, she grabbed her panties from his floor, slid them into his pocket, and whispered against his lips, "You can keep these. I wasn't that attached to them anyway."

And with that, the best fuck of Callum's life walked out his front door.

4

BOTTOMLESS MIMOSAS CAN FIX ALMOST ANYTHING

Rosie:

Rosie woke up the next morning feeling a little sore but loving that she did. Not only was Callum bigger, but he knew Rosie's body better than Justin ever had, even though she and Justin had dated for two years. Sex with Justin hadn't been bad by any means, but sex with Callum was simply *more*. Callum gave her exactly what she wanted without hesitation, and he wasn't afraid to be rough with her. Rosie had always preferred hooking up with people who weren't afraid to be dominant; man or woman, dominance was hot. Ceding control to someone who wasn't afraid to take your pleasure was hot. Escaping into the feel of someone else's touch was hot. Fighting someone else for control just to ultimately surrender your body to them? *So fucking hot.*

Although Rosie had gone to Callum's apartment to get back at Justin, all thoughts of her plan had eddied from her mind at the first stroke of Callum's tongue between her legs.

It had turned out that simply sleeping with Callum was enough to satiate her anger. She didn't need Justin to know what she'd done—sleeping with Callum had affirmed in her that Justin didn't deserve to know what she was up to anymore.

Rosie had kept waiting for the tears to inevitably start falling, but all she'd been able to feel since the breakup, discounting her initial feeling of rage, was relief. She hadn't realized it while she was dating Justin, but she had subconsciously made herself smaller so that he wouldn't feel bad about his own lack of ambition. Waking up this morning as an independent woman, she felt relief in being able to take up as much space as she deserved in the world without concern for how it made anyone else feel, and that was intoxicatingly freeing.

Picking up her phone to check the time, Rosie realized that she had both a missed call and several texts from her mom. She didn't even need to read them to guess what they were about; June Dawson wanted to see the ring she assumed to be sitting on Rosie's finger. Rosie was not looking forward to informing her that there not only was no ring but there was no longer a Justin either. Her mom could wait—Rosie absolutely did not have the energy to have that conversation today.

Rosie clicked the new message icon, typing in her younger sister's name. Hazel, Rosie's only sibling, was a junior at Louisiana State University. With their six-year age gap, Hazel was still in middle school when Rosie graduated high school, so there hadn't been much common ground for them to bond over. When Hazel left for college, however, their relationship began to flourish. It turned out that they liked each other far better when they were both adults.

Rosie still only saw Hazel for holidays—LSU wasn't exactly a short drive from Charleston (twelve hours to be exact)—but they texted and FaceTimed enough to keep up with each other's lives. And Rosie knew that if there was one person that would understand her reservations about telling her mom about the breakup, it was Hazel.

> Rosie: How bad do you think mom will take it when I tell her that not only are Justin and I not engaged but that we broke up too?

Rosie hadn't even had the chance to set her phone down before Hazel's response lit up the screen. Though it usually annoyed Rosie, she was currently happy that Hazel seemed to always be on her phone.

> Hazel: Damn
>
> Hazel: And I was really hoping that you getting engaged would get her off my back about my dating life.

Rosie snorted, typing out a response. She knew that Hazel was only teasing her in the name of good old-fashioned sibling bickering; even so, she was grateful for the light-hearted way that Hazel never pressured her into talking about things unless she wanted to.

> Rosie: I'm so sorry to inconvenience you with my breakup. How selfish of me.

> Hazel: Wanna talk about it?

> Rosie: Honestly? Not really.

> Hazel: Well, for what it's worth, I think you can do better than Justin. And mom's just gonna have to deal.

She would. Just as soon as Rosie mustered up the emotional bandwidth to tell her.

> Hazel: Ooh, idea! Want me to post a picture of my new tattoo to distract her??

> Rosie: When did you get a new tattoo??

> Hazel: A few weeks ago. Got it as a twenty-first birthday present to myself. I'll send a pic later.

> Hazel: Hey speaking of, you think Noah will tattoo me when I come home for Thanksgiving break?

> Rosie: Not sure. I'll ask if her books are open.

Remembering the actual reason she'd picked up her phone, Rosie mentally calculated that she had now only had about thirty minutes to get ready before Elena would be at her apartment to pick her up for brunch.

Over Easy was on the nicer side of casual brunch spots —people wore anything from jeans and a cute top to floral sundresses and heels. After trying on a few different outfits, Rosie settled on a blush slip dress with her oversized leather jacket, both of which were two of her favorite thrift finds to date. The slip was just oversized enough to accommodate the food baby she intended to have by the end of her meal. She grabbed her platform Chelsea Doc Martens from the closet. They were the most comfortable shoes she owned, and, as far as she was concerned, matched absolutely everything in her closet.

She took a quick picture of herself in the mirror and sent it to Elena to make sure she wasn't too overdressed.

> Rosie: Outfit for brunch today?

Elena: Yes, cute!

Elena sent back a picture of her own outfit: a tan, linen jumpsuit with an oversized denim jacket and espadrille sandals. Perfect, they were on the same page. Well, except for the sandals. *Those damn platform sandals had straight bitches in a chokehold.*

Rosie was looking forward to bottomless mimosas, especially since Elena had agreed to pick her up so that she didn't have to worry about driving. Just as she'd finished brushing her teeth and washing her face, another text pinged on Rosie's phone. Elena was on her way, which meant that Rosie had about fifteen minutes to finish getting ready.

She put on a minimal amount of makeup, just enough to give her skin a natural glow, and swiped her copper hair into a low ponytail. She rummaged around her kitchen for her keys, tossing them into her tote bag on the way out the door.

"Damn, you look put together for someone that just got out of a two-year relationship," Elena called through the rolled-down window of her Honda CRV as Rosie walked down the sidewalk that led from her apartment's exterior stairs to the parking lot.

"My sincerest apologies," Rosie pressed a hand to her heart, the picture of an elderly southern woman about to 'bless someone's heart. "Am I supposed to look like I was too depressed to shower?" Rosie tossed back.

"So I take it we're still in the anger stage of the grieving process?" Elena laughed as she unlocked the door for Rosie to climb in.

"Considering he couldn't even be enough of a man to break up with me in person, yeah. And I don't plan on hitting the other stages. Well, except for acceptance," Rosie deadpanned as she opened the passenger-side door.

"Are you going to put me out of my misery and give me the whole story, or do I have to beg?" Elena raised her eyebrows at Rosie.

"Mimosas first," Rosie sidestepped Elena's question, shrinking from her gaze and closing the car door.

She knew that giving Elena the full story also meant telling her about the fact that Rosie had slept with her brother, and she wanted to put it off while she could think of the best way to explain how things had happened. It wasn't as if Elena didn't know about her history with Callum—their entire family pretty much knew in some capacity—but she wasn't sure how Elena would feel about her having slept with Callum so soon after ending things with Justin.

No one in the Costello family had ever given a second thought to Rosie and Callum hooking up because everyone knew it would never turn into anything more. And if there was absolutely no chance that it would ever turn into anything more, then no one needed to worry about Rosie getting hurt. Rosie had the fleeting thought that no one had ever bothered to wonder if Callum, ever the playboy, would get hurt.

Opening Spotify on her phone, Elena clicked shuffle on a playlist titled 'I'd say go to hell, but I never want to see you again,' by someone with the username 'allymazza.' Rosie couldn't help the outright cackle that came out of her.

"Subtle," Rosie snorted.

"What? You said you were too angry to be sad! I was trying to match your energy," Elena exclaimed in defense of herself.

"Fair enough," Rosie managed through her laughter.

The first song that played was Picture to Burn by none other than Taylor Swift. As the chorus led into the second verse, Elena nudged Rosie's arm playfully.

"You know, Miss Swift was really onto something here. I think we should burn all your pictures with Justin," Elena joked.

"As long as you don't accidentally set my apartment on fire in the process. I don't think my neighbors would take too kindly to that," Rosie teased back.

They spent the rest of the drive singing along to various breakup songs. Angry women were amazing lyricists, Rosie concluded. Maybe she should write a song.

Elena parked, and they walked inside. The warm lighting and farmhouse decor created a cozy and inviting atmosphere. Signs hung around the restaurant that said anything from 'If you feed them, they will come,' to 'Life happens, coffee helps.' A bit cliche for Rosie's taste, but the food was good, and, *hello*, bottomless mimosas?

There was only one other person in line at the hostess stand, which hopefully meant the wait wouldn't be long. Considering Rosie's dinner had solely consisted of wine and Callum's lips, she was starving.

"Just two, please," Elena said sweetly, approaching the stand.

"Right this way," the hostess smiled, turning to seat them at their table.

She seated them at a booth near the back of the restaurant. Rosie was grateful for the privacy considering what she was about to tell Elena about.

"Your server should be with you shortly. Enjoy!" the hostess cheerfully exclaimed as she walked back toward the front of the restaurant.

When their server came around, Rosie ordered the Sunny Side Plate and bottomless mimosas. Elena ordered the Cinnamon Roll Pancake Plate with a coffee and one mimosa because she was driving.

"Alright, Rosie, spill."

Rosie relayed the conversation she'd had on the phone with Justin, all his bullshit excuses and attempts at gaslighting her into thinking the breakup was her idea.

"I'm personally waiting for the part of the evening that you're so clearly hesitant to tell me about," Elena crossed her arms.

"I have absolutely *no idea* what you're talking about," Rosie mirrored Elena's posture, very obviously deflecting.

Elena merely raised her eyebrows.

"Ugh fine," Rosie groaned. "After I hung up, I drove to Noah's. We talked things out and came to the conclusion that, at that moment, what I wanted most was for Justin to experience the same level of betrayal that he'd caused me," Rosie continued, attempting to smoothly lead into the fact that she'd hooked up with Callum.

"Oh hell, what did you do?" Elena eyed her from across the table.

"More like *who* did I do," Rosie laughed nervously.

Their server picked that exact moment to return with Elena's coffee and both of their mimosas. Honestly, downing the entire thing before admitting that she'd slept with Callum wouldn't be the worst idea in the world. Rosie started sipping quickly.

"You can just go ahead and bring my next mimosa," Rosie told the server in between gulps.

"Rough week?" their server, Robin, according to the name tag, smiled politely.

"Something like that," Rosie smiled back.

Rosie gulped down the last of her mimosa before looking back up to meet Elena's eyes.

"Rosie..." Elena hesitated, like she knew where Rosie was steering the conversation, but didn't want to admit it out loud.

"Elena..." Rosie knew her face was turning a million shades of red.

Best to rip the bandaid off.

"Callum," she admitted, avoiding eye contact with Elena as his name escaped her lips.

"CALLUM?!" Elena practically screamed.

"Shhhh! Shut the fuck up!" Rosie whisper-yelled at her. "I'm not trying to inform this entire restaurant about my sex life!"

"Sorry! Sorry, it's just," Elena seemed to be choosing her words carefully, "when exactly did this happen?" Elena asked seriously.

"Last night?" Rosie wasn't following Elena's questioning.

"*When* last night, Rosie?"

"I don't know exactly, like ten thirty? I don't see why that —" her words were cut off.

"That. Mother. Fucker."

"What? Are you mad that it happened?" Rosie asked,

trying to understand what was going through Elena's mind. "I know it was soon after the breakup, but you've never cared about us hooking before and... just, please don't be mad at me..."

"I'm not mad at you. Callum, on the other hand," Elena took a deep breath. "Callum, I'd like to drop kick off a cliff," Elena replied.

"Okay, will you please give me a clue as to what the hell is going on? Because I clearly missed a chapter," Rosie pleaded.

Rosie's face was definitely as red as a tomato by this point in the conversation.

"Do you know where Callum was earlier last night?" Elena asked.

"Yeah, family dinner at your parents' house," Rosie answered.

Where the hell was Elena going with this?

"And do you know who he was with at family dinner last night?" Elena pressed.

"Uh, yeah? You? Your family? Why are you asking me this?" Rosie asked.

"Because it seems that Callum conveniently forgot to mention that Olivia, his *girlfriend*, was also at family dinner last night," Elena stated bluntly.

"What the actual fuck? He told me that they broke up," Rosie muttered incredulously.

Actually, his exact words had been 'We broke things off recently.' *Recently*. As in minutes before he'd been inside Rosie? Or was Callum just lying altogether and hadn't even broken up with her?

"Well, then he must have broken up with her less than an hour before you were with him because they left family dinner together around nine," Elena estimated.

"Okay ladies, I have a Sunny Side Plate and a Cinnamon Roll Pancake Plate," Robin said, returning with their food and another mimosa for Rosie.

Setting their plates on the table, Robin asked, "Does everything look alright?"

"Everything looks wonderful, thank you," Elena responded appreciatively, seemingly unbothered despite the conversation she and Rosie had been in the middle of.

"I hope you two enjoy," Robin smiled as she walked away to check on the rest of her tables.

"What exactly did he tell you about Olivia?" Elena asked, returning to the conversation.

"I asked if he was still with her, and he said, and I quote, 'We broke things off recently,' which I guess isn't *technically* a lie," Rosie answered, continuing to sip a little too aggressively on her mimosa.

Gulp was probably a more apt description of the way she was consuming the drink.

She should have told Robin to have a third one waiting.

"I don't doubt that they were broken up. Callum wouldn't cheat, but what he told you is misleading. 'Recently' to any normal person means a few days or weeks, not *minutes*."

"So, essentially, he broke up with his girlfriend just to get with me? That's what I'm taking from this conversation," Rosie processed out loud.

"Yeah, that's pretty much what it seems like."

Fucking great. Maybe, by technicality, Callum hadn't cheated, but that didn't justify his actions. He had intentionally misled Rosie about the timeline of his relationship with Olivia. Rosie bit angrily into her toast; crumbs cascaded down the front of her dress. She didn't even bother to brush them off.

"Hey, uh, do me a favor," Rosie told Elena. "Don't say anything to Callum."

"And why the hell not?" Elena responded defensively.

There was no reason to overcomplicate things. Callum was just being Callum: a fuckboy. When people showed you who they were, who were you to expect anything different?

"I mean, I'm not looking for anything romantic with Callum, *especially* not now," Rosie explained. "And I don't want to make things awkward with your family. He misled me, so I just won't sleep with him ever again. Simple as that."

"Sure. Simple as that," Elena parroted back sarcastically.

5

LITTLE MISS 'MEN CAN ALL FUCK OFF'

Rosie:

WAKING up from what was supposed to be a pre-dinner nap to sleep off the bottomless mimosa hangover, it took Rosie several minutes to register that she'd slept *through* dinner and that it was now dark outside. Rosie blindly ran her hand across her couch in an attempt to find her phone to check the time.

Pulling it out of the crack between the arm and the cushion, Rosie wasn't surprised to see a text from Elena checking on her and offering to come by for dinner. What she *didn't* expect to see was a text from Justin. She clicked on the notification, her heart rate rising.

> Justin: Can'twait see you tonigh, Isa. swear I cnstill taste u

Uh, what the *actual fuck*? And who the *fuck* was *Isa*?

Checking the time stamp on the message, Rosie saw that Justin had sent it at twelve thirty-four in the morning, who, based on the number of spelling errors, was probably pissed drunk and had meant to send it to whoever the hell *Isa* was. He definitely hadn't meant to send the message to Rosie.

She sat up on the couch, rubbing sleep from her eyes. It might have been one forty-seven AM, but Rosie had never felt more awake. She could feel the adrenaline seeping through her veins, the rage she thought she'd quelled reigniting almost immediately.

Knowing she wouldn't be able to sleep until she could set herself at ease, Rosie decided to put on a pot of coffee and try to read through one of the latest manuscript samples she was currently evaluating as an acquisition editor at the publishing house she worked for.

While scooping coffee grounds into the filter, Rosie's head cleared enough for her to sort through what the timeline of Justin's text implied. The message read like it was meant for someone Justin knew well, not someone he'd randomly hooked up with the night they had broken up. After all, he'd called her Isa, which had to be a nickname.

That could only mean... Rosie scrolled up in their text thread, noticing all the seemingly random, late-night texts from Justin. They had all been overly affectionate, compared to his diction at normal hours of the day.

> Justin: I love you so much, Rosie. You know that right?
>
> Justin: Don't deserve you, Rosemary.
>
> Justin: You're an angel, Rosie.

She'd always thought it was sweet, that it was his way of telling her she was the last thing he thought about before closing his eyes at night... but now she couldn't seem to halt the doubt from creeping in: had Justin been cheating on her this whole time? Had he sent all of those texts after fucking

Isa, because he felt guilty? Was that why he had abruptly ended things? Had the guilt become too much?

> Justin: I'm just so lucky. I don't deserve someone as wonderful as you.

Damn right, he didn't. Rosie suddenly felt like throwing up. She already felt betrayed, blind-sighted, but this made her feel deeply ashamed. How could she have been so blind, so stupid?

She called Elena as tears began to slide down her face.

"Hi babe, you okay?" Elena groggily answered the phone.

Her tears turned into full-on sobbing as she barely choked out, "I need you."

"I'm on my way," Elena responded without a second's hesitation.

They had always been like this, Rosie and Elena: willing to drop everything for each other no matter the time, no questions asked.

"I need you to try to breathe for me, okay?" Elena's soothing voice spilled through the phone.

"Okay," Rosie managed through racking sobs.

She had never been more grateful to hear the sound of keys jingling than she did at that moment. The sound meant that she wouldn't have to be alone for much longer. That Elena would wrap Rosie up in her arms, and she could let everything out without fear of being judged. That there were still people in her life who loved her enough to never betray her. To drop everything for her.

"I'll breathe with you, okay? Breathe in."

Rosie could hear Elena's own breath through the phone. She tried to breathe too, but all she could manage was a shallow intake of air.

"Breathe out."

"Again," Elena encouraged. "Deep breath in, deep breath out."

After a few minutes of their breathing in unison, Rosie was calm enough to speak clearly, to offer Elena some explanation for what had prompted the middle-of-the-night breakdown.

"He cheated on me. I don't know for how long."

"Oh, that *asshole!*" Elena raised her voice loud enough that Rosie had to pull the phone back from her ear. "I'm five minutes away. You okay until then? I'm calling for backup."

Backup probably meant Noah and a pint of peanut butter ice cream.

"Yeah, yeah, I think I'm okay now," Rosie reassured her.

"Promise?"

"Promise."

"I love you, Rosemary June Dawson. That jackass never deserved to know you."

"I love you too, Elena soon-to-be Scott," Rosie said, hanging up the phone.

Thirty minutes later, Rosie sat on the couch with Elena, Noah, and a pint of peanut butter ice cream.

"Well, I've never been arrested for assault, but there's a first time for everything," Noah shrugged casually.

Between Noah and Elena, Noah was the more aggressive one. Rosie wouldn't put it past the four-foot-eleven brunette to actually try to swing at Justin; that was how protective she was of her friends.

"You can't get arrested for assault, Noh. Elena would be down a bridesmaid," Rosie laughed.

A small laugh, but a laugh nonetheless. She'd felt better the second her best friends barged through her front door ready to burn the world down to make her feel better.

"Fine, but we are doing something to get back at him, right?" Noah pushed with a more serious tone.

"I think we should try to find out who *Isa* is. Assuming she doesn't know Justin was cheating with her, and, technically, *on* her too I guess," Elena thought aloud. "Doesn't she deserve to know, too?"

"Found her!" Noah exclaimed from the opposite side of the couch. "Well, at least I *think* I found her. Justin follows three people on Instagram with 'Isa' in their username, but only one lives in Charleston."

Rosie shivered. She wasn't sure she wanted to see who her no-longer-secret competition was.

"Want me to look first?" Noah asked, noticing the hesitation in Rosie's body language.

Elena laced her fingers through Rosie's instinctively.

"We'll look together," Elena decided.

Noah passed the phone to Elena, who sat in the middle of the couch. Elena clicked on the profile without a word.

"Well, it's definitely the right 'Isa,'" Rosie laughed incredulously.

Four out of the top six photos on Isabella's account were of her and Justin: Justin with his hands on Isabella's ass on Folly Beach, Isabella as Justin's date at his work's office party that he'd told Rosie was 'employees only,' a selfie of the two of them at some club downtown, them dressed in formal wear posing with champagne glasses on the rooftop of Stars Restaurant with a caption that read, to Rosie's abject horror, 'Celebrating one trip around the sun with the most amazing man! Cheers to the years that are yet to come!'

"Holy *fuck*," Elena muttered.

"Permission to be arrested for assault *now*?" Noah added.

"I don't even…" Rosie trailed off in disbelief. "I spent the past year thinking about *marrying* Justin, while *he* spent the past year with a whole-ass second girlfriend? *Clearly* I wasn't enough for him…" The tears had started falling again, despite Rosie's best efforts to keep them at bay. "Why wasn't I enough?"

Immediately, both Noah's and Elena's arms were around Rosie.

"Look at me," Noah said, cupping Rosie's face in her hand. "You are more than enough, Rosie. Justin is trying to fill a void that he created with his own lack of ambition. Nothing will ever be enough for him until he learns to be enough for himself. You are *not* the problem. Don't you dare let yourself think that, not for a goddamn second," she said in a tone that managed to be simultaneously stern, yet loving.

"The real icing on the cake is that not one, but *two* men have lied to me in the past forty-eight hours. Justin and your asshat of a brother," Rosie turned to look at Elena.

"What happened to Little Miss 'he misled me, so I simply won't sleep with him again?'" Elena asked.

"Yeah, well. I changed my mind. You can officially call me Little Miss 'Men Can All Fuck Off.' And while I'm at it, I might just quit men altogether and go full lesbian."

"Yeah, babe, I don't think it works like that. If it did, I wouldn't still, much to my dismay, be attracted to men," Noah snorted.

Rosie looked over to see that Noah had taken screenshots of Isabella's account and was now selecting them all from her camera roll.

"Uh, Noh? Whatcha doing?" Rosie asked.

"Sending these to Justin with a message telling him to watch his fucking back," Noah said casually. Rosie had been joking when she told Noah not to get herself arrested for assault, but now she was a little worried that there was some merit in her warning.

Ultimately too exhausted to care about stopping her, simply cuddled closer to Elena until the three of them eventually fell asleep on the couch.

6

BARTENDERS DON'T GIVE THE BEST ADVICE—
LESBIANS DO

Callum:

CALLUM KNEW Olivia was angry with him, but he also knew that he had been right about how noncommittal their relationship was since she hadn't bothered to call or text him since she walked out of his apartment two nights ago. He was self-aware enough to realize it was an asshole move, but it was better than being a cheating asshole because there was no way in hell he would've been able to deny Rosie, not after he'd lusted after her from afar for the past two years that she'd been with Justin.

Callum was getting ready to head to Lafayette's for his shift. He'd worked at the bar for the past four years, having worked his way up to managing the place, with the goal of eventually taking over ownership when Henry, the current owner, finally decided it was time to retire. Tonight was Sunday, the slowest night of the week, which meant that Callum would probably get to leave around eleven, giving him enough time to invite a certain redhead over for some more fun...

He hadn't heard anything from Rosie or Elena regarding the timing of his breakup with Olivia, which hopefully meant that Rosie hadn't told Elena what had happened between the two of them. Callum sure as hell wasn't going to ask. He figured he'd eventually have to explain himself, but if he did so after wringing another orgasm or two from Rosie, she'd probably take it a hell of a lot better.

Yeah, he could have been more upfront with Rosie about how recently he'd ended things with Olivia, but it wasn't like he and Rosie would ever be romantically involved. Everyone knew he was allergic to commitment—not because he was afraid of getting hurt, but because no one had ever been interested in him long enough for him to try for anything aside from a casual fling. Well, no one aside from Rosie; but their relationship was purely physical and it wasn't like it could ever be more even *if* Callum had wanted it to be. Which he didn't.

Rosie was his sister's best friend. His own mother loved Rosie as if she were her own daughter. If Callum ever got the wild idea to date her and fucked it all up—which, given his track record with relationships, he was bound to do—his own family would disown him if it meant keeping her. She was too important. So it was a really damned good thing that Callum was only interested in a physical relationship with her, which brought his thoughts back to the issue at hand: convincing Rosie to sleep with him again once she found out about his breakup with Olivia.

Callum reasoned through the events of the night in his head. It wasn't as if Rosie had asked for specifics when she asked if he was still with Olivia. Callum hadn't lied about having broken things off, he'd just been vague about when it had happened. Besides, Rosie had simply been using him as a distraction in the form of a hookup. The rest was semantics.

He pulled out his phone to text her but decided to wait until later that night to keep things casual between them.

Parking in the deck closest to Lafayette's, Callum walked the two blocks to the bar. Unlike Thursday nights through Saturday nights, the streets were practically empty save for the occasional couple moseying down the sidewalk. Callum didn't envy them in the least. It wasn't the idea of committing to one person for the rest of his life that Callum had an issue with, it was closing off the possibility of new experiences that came with that commitment that Callum couldn't imagine for himself.

Walking inside, he immediately felt content. He loved his job, largely due to the atmosphere of Lafayette's. The place felt more homey than any other bar Callum had ever been to. There were no overhead lights; instead, Lafayette's was lit with mismatched chandeliers and light fixtures to create a dim, intimate ambiance. The downstairs level had a bar and a full kitchen, while the upstairs levels branched off into a speakeasy-styled room to the left and a modern terrace to the right, both with their own adjoining rooftops. It sort of felt like the Swiss Family Robinson Treehouse, but for adults, full of alcohol, and not in an actual tree. Okay, so maybe it wasn't really anything like the Swiss Family Robinson Treehouse after all.

Even though he was the bar manager, Callum still insisted on working one regular bartending shift each week so he wouldn't ever lose touch with how it felt to be in the trenches pouring drinks for hours on end. He'd had managers in the past that had been so far removed from the actual bartending aspect of the job that they'd placed entirely unrealistic expectations on their employees. Thus,

Words I Should Have Said

by working alongside the bartenders he managed once a week, Callum would prevent himself from ever becoming that out of touch. Tonight was a bartending shift.

Callum spent the first half of his shift pouring more draft beers and glasses of wine than he could count, but had slowed down significantly after the dinner rush. Checking his phone for the first time in two hours, he saw that it was now nine thirty. Late enough to text Rosie without insinuating anything but a casual hookup.

> Callum: What are you up to later?

> Rosie: What's it to you? I'm not your girlfriend.

Rosie sounded defensive, which meant... Ah fuck—had Rosie talked to Elena after all? He decided to play it cool on the slim chance that she hadn't. Either way, he needed to figure out how salvageable the situation was before he accidentally did anything to make it worse.

> Callum: No, you're not.

> Callum: As of recently, I don't have a girlfriend, which frees up my time for other things... and people.

> Rosie: Speaking of, what's your definition of recently, Callum?

Well, fuck. She'd definitely talked to Elena. He needed to explain himself before Rosie started filling in the blanks herself—any more than she already had.

> Callum: Listen, it's not what it seems. Come over when I get off and let me explain?

And taste you. Callum decided it was best to keep that idea to himself. For now.

> Rosie: Fuck you, Costello.

> Callum: I'd like to, Rose.

> Callum: Kidding, sort of. I do want to explain, but I won't lie and say I don't desperately want to be inside you again too.

Flirting was definitely not helping the situation, but that's the only way Callum knew to talk to Rosie. They flirted, they fucked, and they didn't discuss the repercussions of said flirting and fucking. End of story.

> Rosie: Yeah, well. Not happening again.

Callum sent another text, this one to Lilah, his oldest and closest friend.

> Callum: Hey Lih, come by the bar tonight?

> Callum: Need to sort some shit out.

Callum's family had moved to the lowcountry during the middle of his eighth-grade year, which had made it harder for Callum to make new friends. Callum started hanging with the neighborhood kids, which included Lilah, whose parents lived a few houses down the street.

She was one of the few girls who regularly showed up to the neighborhood's basketball court to actually *play*, not just to watch the boys. At first, he hadn't even realized she *was* a girl; she wore men's athletic shorts, oversized t-shirts, and *always* wore a hat or beanie. One afternoon, she took her hat off to wipe the sweat from her brow, and, to Callum's shock, a thick pile of dirty blonde curls fell loose. None of the other boys seemed to care, and Callum certainly didn't. So, they kept showing up to the court.

Lilah's first words to Callum personally were, "Yo, dude, I'm gonna start calling you Troy Bolton if you can't quit staring at Gabriella over there. We're trying to play a game here."

Who was the Gabriella in question? Rosie, of course. Even back then, he couldn't help but notice her. That was the moment Callum decided that he and Lilah would be great friends, and so they were. Much to his dismay, however, 'Bolton' stuck around instead of a regular nickname.

Halfway through their freshman year of high school, Lilah came out as lesbian. Callum threatened anyone who had anything negative to say about it within an inch of their lives. Not that Lilah needed defending—she was plenty intimidating on her own—but still. He was stupidly protective of her. He couldn't help it. He loved her as much as he loved his own sisters.

Honestly, having Lilah for a best friend hadn't been all that different from having a guy best friend: the two of them had gone through the 'how the hell do I talk to a girl I like?' stage together, shortly followed by the 'what the hell do I *do* with a girl I like?' stage. They went to all the high school sports games together. They played video games. They worked out and went on runs. They went hiking. They called each other on their shit. Plus, Callum kind of got the best of both worlds whenever he needed relationship advice: advice *from* a girl who was *into* girls. He'd hit the best friend jackpot as far as he was concerned.

> Lilah: Olivia? Thought you broke things off with her?
>
> Callum: I did, but I might have also hooked up with someone else right after, who wasn't very happy to find out about the timing of everything.
>
> Lilah: BOLTON
>
> Lilah: Dude...
>
> Callum: Yeah...
>
> Lilah: In my expert opinion, it sounds like you're fucked.
>
> Callum: Not helpful. Just get your ass over here.
>
> Callum: Please <3
>
> Lilah: Alright, alright. Give me ten to get dressed, then I'll head your way.

Callum decided not to respond to Rosie's last message until after he'd talked things out with Lilah. In the meantime, he poured several rounds of shots, made a fuck ton of vodka sodas, and several Old Fashioneds. Finally, around forty minutes later, Lilah strolled into Lafayette's and sat down at one of the bar's high-top chairs wearing her usual: joggers, sneakers, and some sort of graphic t-shirt with her curls piled into what didn't even deserve to be called a messy bunny on top of her head. It was more of a chaotic nest, but, somehow, Lilah managed to pull it off. And, as evidenced by the fact that it was more than a regular occurrence for women to bypass Callum to hit on Lih instead, women loved curly hair.

Lilah was also the sole reason Callum had grown out his

own hair. Years ago, she'd told him that it was 'totally lame' that, just because her best friend was a dude, they couldn't braid each other's hair. Callum ended up loving his hair grown out, and so did women—particularly Rosie. So, as far as he was concerned, any advice from Lilah was good advice.

"So, what the hell did you do that warranted my ass driving down here at ten PM?" Lilah asked rather than greeting Callum with a hello as she hoisted herself onto the wooden barstool.

"In short? Found out Rosie's boyfriend dumped her, broke up with Olivia, then fucked Rosie in the span of about an hour," Callum admitted, laying everything out for Lilah.

Callum and Lilah never kept things from each other; he was comfortable telling her anything without fear of judgment. Lilah would still tell him when he was being a dumbass, but never in a way that made Callum feel ashamed of anything. Most people found it odd that he talked so openly with her about his hookups, but he appreciated her perspective on things. She had firsthand experience in dealing with the complexity of women, so her advice was usually pretty sound. Exhibit A: Women and their love of curly hair.

"Well damn," Lilah chuckled. "I'm gonna need a beer before I'll be mentally prepared to continue this conversation."

Callum popped the top off of an IPA and set it down in front of her.

"Much better," Lilah took a sip from the sea of foam. "So, what's the problem? You didn't cheat on Olivia," Lilah waved the branded glass, prompting Callum to further explain.

"The problem is that Rosie is Elena's best friend, and

Olivia was at family dinner with me, where Elena also was, the night I hooked up with Rosie," Callum explained.

"But Rosie knew you broke up with Olivia before you slept with her, yeah?"

"Yeah, but all I told her was that I'd broken things off 'recently,'" Callum sighed. "I just sort of left out exactly *how* recently. Which was about twenty minutes before Rosie came."

"To your apartment or...?" Lilah teasingly implied, taking a sip of her IPA in an attempt to hide the smug grin on her face.

Callum jokingly shoved her shoulder across the bar, stealing a sip of the IPA while she was distracted.

"Can you be serious for two seconds please?" Callum whispered aggressively. "Besides, I don't think the customers care to hear about me getting my dick wet."

"Okay, okay. Sorry. Do you know for sure that Rosie knows the timeline of that night? Have you asked Elena?"

"Considering the last thing she texted me was that she'd never hook up with me again, I think it's safe to assume she knows. And fuck no, I haven't asked Elena. I don't have a death wish."

"Let me read the conversation," Lilah reached out her hand for Callum's phone.

Callum entered his password, opened to his conversation with Rosie, and handed Lilah his phone. She read through the messages, smirking to herself.

"What could you possibly be smirking about?" Callum prodded her, attempting to snatch his phone back from Lilah's hand, but she dodged him too quickly, spilling a little of her beer on Callum's arm in the process.

"'*I won't lie and say I don't desperately want to be inside you again too,*'" Lilah mockingly read the message off Callum's phone. "Bolton," she snorted.

"I asked you to come to help me fix this, not mock me, Lih."

"Oh come on, you would've laughed so hard you fell off this barstool if you read a text like that from me," Lilah managed to say through her incessant laughter. "I've been pussywhipped more than once, but, dude, that was desperate as hell."

It was a wonder beer wasn't coming out of her nose with how hard Lilah was laughing in between sips.

"Have you *seen* Rosie? Anyone would be desperate as hell, especially after she's been off limits for the past two years."

Callum attempted in defense, but, if he was being honest with himself, it *was* desperate as hell. He couldn't explain what it was about Rosie that had him willing to take whatever she was willing to give him, even if it was just the chance to get on his knees for her.

"Fair enough," Lih shrugged. "Maybe she's just sick of men right now. Hey, you know what?"

This couldn't possibly be good—mischief was written all over her face.

"Maybe *I* should shoot my shot," she stared at Callum with a shit-eating grin on her face.

"Fuck off. Rosie's off limits," Callum declared, a bit more aggressively than he'd intended.

Knowing he had absolutely zero justification for his statement, he said the one thing he knew would make Lilah drop the subject immediately.

"Besides, we both know you were always more interested in Noah," Callum crossed his arms defiantly.

Years ago, Lilah and Noah had made out at a high school

house party during Seven Minutes in Heaven, and Lilah had refused to discuss it ever since. Noah hadn't come out as pansexual until college, so maybe Lilah not talking about it was a respect thing? Either way, they'd both come out of that room looking ruffled, and Callum wasn't an idiot. They definitely would have done more than make out had they been left alone for longer than seven minutes.

Lilah steered the subject back to his current problem: Rosie being pissed at him.

"Question—she already said she isn't interested in hearing an explanation from you, so why not just leave it be?"

"Because, in my twenty-six years of fucking around, I have never had sex that came anywhere close to being as good as sex with Rosie is. I've had ten years to learn *exactly* where to touch her, how to touch her. It's intoxicating," Callum admitted.

"Well, then you need to find a way to make her hear what you have to say," Lilah said, like it was some novel idea that Callum hadn't already thought of.

"Yeah, no shit, but how the hell am I supposed to do that if she won't even talk to me?" Callum asked.

"You said it yourself: she's *Elena's* best friend. You know, Elena, your sister who is getting *married* in a few weeks, whose wedding party both of you happen to be in..." Lilah pointed out with a smug half-smile etched on her face. "Do I need to continue?"

"Which means, she won't have a choice but to listen to me when we're stuck in the same beach house for the weekend."

"Exactly," Lilah gestured with a wave of her glass. "I was wondering how long that was gonna take you."

"How the hell did I not think about that?" Callum sighed, grabbing the IPA from Lilah and taking a long sip.

"Because you're too preoccupied with *desperately wanting to be inside her again*," Lilah shoved Callum's arm jokingly, taking the IPA back from him. "Plus, you're a man. You were already at an evolutionary disadvantage."

"I *was* planning not to charge you for the beer, but, just for that, you can pay," Callum teased, holding his hand out as if to take Lilah's card from her.

"I'm not paying for shit. If it weren't for me, you'd still be sitting here trying to figure out how to make her talk to you," Lilah teased back.

"Fair point. It's on the house."

"How generous of you," Lilah said sarcastically.

She tipped the IPA bottle all the way up, draining it of its last drops, "Alright, I'm gonna head out and let you finish your side work."

"Hey, all jokes aside, thanks for coming tonight," Callum expressed his gratitude.

Lilah reached her arm across the bar, laying a hand on Callum's bicep, and squeezing gently, lovingly, "you know I'm always here, Callum."

"Lowcountry court for life?" Callum asked, holding out his pinky to her across the bar.

That was their thing. Never goodbye. Always lowcountry court. Always a reminder of their roots. Of what brought them into each other's lives all those years ago.

"Lowcountry court for life, Bolton," Lilah repeated back, looping her pinky in his. "Hey, are we still on for going to that axe-throwing place next week?" Lilah called over her shoulder on the way out.

"For sure," Callum confirmed.

As the front door closed behind Lilah, Callum pulled his phone back out, rereading the last text Rosie had sent him.

Yeah well. Not happening again.

He decided to cut the flirtiness, settling instead on a straightforward response that he hoped would be enough to persuade Rosie to listen to him.

> Callum: It doesn't have to. I still want a chance to explain.

7

C'EST LA VIE

Rosie:

The incessant cry of Rosie's alarm clock broke the peaceful sleep she'd been in the middle of at the early hour of seven AM Monday morning. She was already contemplating how many times she could feasibly hit snooze without being late to work. Yes, she was still going to work, because the world carried on even when your own life was falling to shit.

Dragging herself, begrudgingly, from the comfort of her blankets was a feat in itself. She deserved a medal. Rosie pulled the crewneck she'd discarded at the edge of her bed last night over herself and trudged to the bathroom to brush her teeth and wash her face. In between being broken up with, sleeping with Callum, figuring out that Justin had been cheating on her for a year *and* that Callum had lied to her about when he and Olivia broke up, she'd had little time to sleep. And damn, was it evident as she flipped on the light; she quickly realized that there was not enough concealer in the world to hide the dark circles under her eyes.

C'est la vie.

Rosie would have called out of work, taken a mental health day, if she didn't truly love her job so much. How could she not? She got paid to work with romance authors and bring their stories to the world. Even reading samples of potential manuscripts on her own time was enjoyable. So, despite the early wake-up call, the work week ahead was a welcome distraction for Rosie. She was more than ready to think about the problems of fictional characters instead of her own.

Fortunately, the dress code at Rosie's publishing house was business casual, with a heavy emphasis on the casual, which meant that putting an outfit together required little to no effort from Rosie. She perused her closet, deciding on a pair of slightly oversized black and gray striped trousers, a black short-sleeved bodysuit, and a red and black plaid sweater vest from her favorite thrift store.

When she was young, Rosie learned that one of the cardinal rules of fashion was not to mix patterns; Rosie had instead chosen to do the exact opposite and embrace the concept. Growing up and feeling like your existence is the human equivalent of pattern mixing will do that to a person. If she was dating a man, people assumed her bisexuality was a 'phase,' but if she dated a woman they assumed she was just a lesbian. No matter who she fell in love with, she was never the right fit. It had taken her years to accept that she was bisexual, but no amount of self-acceptance would prevent her from being constantly invalidated by the world.

Thus, thrifting had become one of Rosie's favorite ways to express herself; she'd spend hours between racks of clothing, running her fingers across each item with care, waiting for a hidden gem to present itself. By the time she'd turned seventeen, her closet was filled with clothing anywhere from the '70s to the 2010s. By the time she graduated college, roughly ninety percent of the clothing she owned were pieces she'd thrifted at some point over the last decade.

Yet, as exciting as finding a rare piece or the item you'd been searching for for months, the thing Rosie loved most about thrifting was that each and every piece was like a mirror to the way Rosie felt: different. Amongst the messy racks that never seemed to end, she felt seen and understood. Despite the chaos, despite the hours and the patience it took to find what you were looking for, despite the imperfections, there were still people who wanted those unique pieces. Which gave Rosie hope that one day someone might want her too—chaos, effort, imperfections and all.

After putting the entire outfit on and looking it over in the mirror, Rosie nodded to herself in approval. Slipping on her 8053 Doc Martens, she mentally ticked off what else she needed to accomplish before heading out the door. She double-checked the work bag she'd packed last night: Laptop? Check. Charger? Check. Planner? Check. Kindle, notebook, annotation kit, lip stain, and wallet? Check.

All that was left to do was swipe on a minimal amount of makeup and do something with her hair. Checking the time on her phone—seven twenty-four—she realized she had plenty of time to brew a pot of coffee while she contemplated what that something would be. Her office had a full espresso bar, but Rosie refused to leave her apartment without at least eight ounces of coffee in her system.

One day, in her dream home, Rosie would love to have an entire coffee bar setup complete with a cafe-grade espresso machine. She blamed her years of barista experience. There was just something so comforting about the clank of the portafilter when it hooked into the espresso machine, the whirring of the steam wand that almost sounded like a kiss as it frothed the milk. Rosie wanted to fill her home with those comforting sounds.

Rosie settled on putting her hair into a messy bun as it would save her enough time to read a chapter or two while she drank her morning coffee. She was currently reading a fake-dating rom-com about a billionaire who had (sort of) accidentally told a client he was engaged to his pregnant fiancé in an attempt to close a deal. The problem? He didn't have so much as a girlfriend, let alone a *pregnant fiancé*. Conveniently, he found someone willing to be his fake fiancé when he ran into her on a walk in his neighborhood trying to find a potential rich husband. Rosie knew it would be a five-star read when the male love interest suggested they talk over the terms of their deal at a Chipotle of all places. C'mon, who wasn't a whore for Chipotle?

After drinking her coffee, then pouring more for the drive through downtown into Mount Pleasant, Rosie headed to work. Though her commute was nearly forty-five minutes with traffic, she really didn't mind it. It was the perfect amount of time to listen to a solid playlist or several chapters of an audiobook. Plus, she got to drive over the new bridge, which was two and a half miles of the most beautiful scenery. Rosie could have done a lot worse as far as work commutes were concerned.

"Morning, Nora!" Rosie greeted the front desk clerk as she walked inside her office building.

"Rosemary! How was your weekend? You had that big dinner with your boyfriend, right?" Nora inquired.

Shit. Trauma-dumping on her coworker first thing in the morning was definitely not a thing Rosie should do. The last seventy-two hours of her life had been such a fucking whirlwind that it honestly felt like the breakup had happened weeks ago. She had no idea how to even begin to answer Nora.

"Yeah, we um," Rosie tried to think of the best way to respond that would invite the least amount of questions.

Nora was always well-intended; yet, she was old enough to be Rosie's grandmother, which meant that she often offered unsolicited advice in the spirit of elderly wisdom.

"We did. But, we actually decided to break things off. We're just both in such different stages of life, yanno?"

That was a vast understatement, but Rosie didn't want to open herself to any line of questioning that would require her to explain how she'd gone from thinking she was about to be engaged to sleeping with her best friend's brother. For the first time in two years.

Luckily, Nora was perceptive enough to grasp that Rosie wasn't in the mood to rehash her weekend, offering a polite, "Well, it was his loss, baby."

"Thanks, Nora," Rosie smiled softly as she headed for the elevator.

Because Rosie's office was on the fourth floor of their building, she had a decent view of the sky over Shem Creek. In the winter, when the sun set early in the afternoon, she got to watch the blue sky melt into rich hues of orange, pink, and red as she finished up her tasks at the end of the workday.

Before Rosie could begin to unpack her things at her desk, Isla was rounding the corner, headed straight for Rosie.

Isla did developmental and copy editing at their publishing house, so she and Rosie often got to work together to see projects through. As acquisition editor, Rosie passed manuscripts on to either Isla or one of the other developmental editors.

"What's this I hear about you and Justin breaking up?" Isla raised her eyebrows dramatically as she approached Rosie's desk.

Isla was wearing a flowy yellow sundress that contrasted beautifully with the ebony of her skin. As always, her eye makeup perfectly matched the color of her outfit: today, Isla had gone for yellow eyeliner with tiny sun rays branching off the wing. Rosie applauded anyone who could put on eyeliner, let alone draw a perfect wing before breakfast.

"Jeez, Is," Rosie laughed, "I'm not sure whether to be terrified or impressed that I've been here for less than ten minutes and you already managed to find out."

"I expected you to come in this morning with a rock on your finger. When you didn't, I asked Nora what she knew," Isla shrugged.

"Fucking Nora," Rosie rolled her eyes with affection. "She may seem like the sweet, innocent office grandma, but she has more shit on the employees here than anyone, huh?"

"That she does," Isla laughed. "Worked in my favor though."

"Uh-huh."

"So?" Isla pressed, obviously trying to pry the details out of Rosie without seeming insensitive.

"So?" Rosie parroted back, pretending she wasn't going to tell Isla.

"Let's go downstairs to grab a coffee—you can tell me what the hell happened on the way," Isla grabbed her arm, dragging her back toward the elevators.

The espresso bar was on the second level of the office building and was free for all employees.

"Let me at least check my calendar—I don't know what time any of my meetings are this week!"

"Cover design meeting at ten, nothing before that. Plenty of time," Isla sing-songed.

"How do you—" Rosie started to ask.

"Checked the staff-wide calendar already," Isla explained. "Now, out with it."

Rosie relayed an abridged version of her weekend to Isla, sans explicit details. Though Isla would likely pry them out of her later, they were currently within earshot of everyone else waiting in line for coffee.

"*Please* tell me you have a picture of this hot brother," Isla sighed dramatically.

Rosie took out her phone to pull up Callum's Instagram profile. Isla grabbed it out of her hand before she could even choose a picture to show her.

"Holy *fuck,* this man is hot!" Isla exclaimed.

"Shh!" Rosie slapped her arm jokingly, "But, yeah, I know," she chuckled. Then, whispering, added, "Why do you think I jumped his bones?"

"Does he have any other siblings?" Isla asked while continuing to scroll down Callum's profile.

"Lydia, the oldest Costello, is married. You know Elena, and Callum is off-limits," Rosie tried to hide her smirk at the fact that she'd essentially called dibs. "And there's Liam, but he's only twenty-three."

Isla groaned, "How much of an age gap would qualify me as a cougar?"

"I'd say at least ten years," Rosie snorted. "You're safely away from cougar territory at six years."

"Good morning, Rosie! Sixteen ounce Americano black?" Nolan, the barista asked cheerfully as she and Isla approached the counter.

"If I ever order anything else, you'll know something is incredibly wrong," Rosie answered, smiling back.

Though he had nothing to do with the actual publishing process, Nolan was still technically employed by the company and had worked as a barista in their building's cafe for the past two years.

"And what can I make for *you* this morning, Isla?"

"Mmm, make me something hot with matcha, please."

Unlike Rosie, Isla never ordered the same thing twice. She always gave Nolan an ingredient or flavor and told him whether she wanted the drink hot or iced; beyond that, Nolan got creative license to make whatever concoction that came to mind that morning.

"Thanks, Nol!" Rosie shouted as they headed toward the pickup station.

At the cover design meeting, Rosie's team had approved the cutest cartoon-style cover for a rom-com that was set to release in a few months. It was a sapphic, enemies-to-lovers novel about two women planning a wedding between their respective best friends. The forced proximity of wedding planning forces them to acknowledge that attraction has no regard for hate. Over the course of the planning process, they fall in love—duh.

Rosie had been the one to read the initial chapters that had been sent in for this manuscript and had been looking forward to its release day ever since. There was such a lack of sapphic romance in the traditionally published world. And, as a queer woman herself, she was always excited to help put those stories into the hands of readers.

After the meeting, she answered a shit ton of emails, got back to several authors about future acquisitions, visited Nolan for another Americano, and organized her desk.

Finally, five o'clock rolled around. She was happy to be back at work, but she was fucking tired. This weekend had worn her out, both physically and emotionally.

All the way from her office, down the elevator, and into the parking lot, she dreaded the inevitable: informing her mom that she and Justin had split. She knew her mom would be disappointed—not necessarily in Rosie, but in the fact that she would no longer get to make a fuss about her daughter's engagement to her friends.

Opening her text thread with her mom, Rosie again ignored the unanswered questions about her big dinner with Justin and instead clicked "call," wanting to get it over with. Her mom answered on the second ring.

"Rosie! I've been trying to get a hold of you all weekend. Shouldn't you be FaceTiming me?" her mom asked without even a trace of subtlety.

"Not for any reason I'm aware of."

Rosie knew what her mom was implying. She just didn't want to be the one to say it. Like everyone else, Rosie's mom had expected her to come back from her trip with Justin with a ring on her finger.

"Don't you have something to show me? Something shiny perhaps?"

"Sorry to disappoint, but no. I have absolutely nothing to show you," Rosie sighed.

She wasn't sure if she should even bother to tell her mom about Justin cheating; she and her mom weren't all that close. It wasn't that they had a bad relationship, but Rosie had always felt a bit like her mom cared more about the *image* of having a daughter than her daughters themselves. Rosie's engagement would just be another thing for her mom to brag to her friends about.

"Oh, honey," her mom's tone shifted to one of dismay. "What happened?"

"He ended things over the phone. Said I deserved better," Rosie offered the bare minimum of explanation. She was tired of rehashing the conversation.

"I can tell you're not in the mood to go into detail," her mom said. "I'm here for you when you're ready."

The words sounded kind and sincere, but Rosie knew it was just a formality. That it was just her mom's polite way of keeping things surface-level, the way it had always been between them. Sure, there wasn't room for conflict when you kept people at arm's length, but there wasn't room for much else either. Like comfort, compassion, or support.

"Yeah," Rosie sighed. "Thanks, Mom."

"And honey?"

"Yeah?"

"The right man is out there. You'll find him."

The right *man*. Not the right *person*. Because even though Rosie was out to her family, even though she'd had relationships with women that her mom had been privy to, Rosie marrying a woman just didn't fit with her mom's perfect image of her daughters' lives: the perfect husband, a quaint house with a white-picket-fence and a yard full of kids. Never mind that there were avenues that queer couples could take to start a family.

Though her mom never said it outright, she made her hopes painfully obvious through comments much like the one she'd just made. And her dad was always too busy with work to have a conversation with her about anything that actually mattered. Though Rosie was grateful that her family had accepted the fact that she was queer—she was very aware of how privileged that made her—it still hurt that her family would never revere that part of her identity.

Yet another reason why she loved the Costello family so much: Elena's parents didn't just accept her, they always made a point to make her feel seen for who she was in totality. From the moment she found out that Rosie was bisexual, Mrs. Pammy, Elena and Callum's mom, had always made a point to ask about Rosie's *partners*. Such a small thing, but it had meant the world to Rosie, especially knowing that she'd never hear the word from her own family.

At the end of the day, there was no point in dwelling on things that wouldn't change. She had her chosen family, and they were more than enough. Dealing with things the best way she knew how, Rosie opened the audiobook she was currently listening to and clicked play before peeling out of the parking lot.

8

BACHELORETTE PARTY IDEAS FOR BAD BITCHES

Rosie:

It was girl's night, which meant Noah and Rosie were going out for drinks. Normally, Elena would be going out with them, but she was busy with last-minute wedding stuff. With roughly three weeks until the big day, Elena had officially entered panic mode—not about marrying Cole, but about making sure every detail of her day went just as she had imagined. She'd already had a wedding notebook full of floral arrangement details, the wedding playlist, and everything in between when Rosie had met her at the age of fourteen.

It made all the sense in the world to Rosie that Elena had inevitably become a graphic designer. She'd met Cole through the company she started working for out of college; he was the head of IT. Though he gave no indication of his interest in Elena while they were working together, he asked her out immediately after she started working freelance—something about not dating coworkers—and the rest was history.

Currently, Elena was her own biggest freelance client. She had taken it upon herself to design everything imaginable for her wedding: place cards, the wedding program, the refreshments menu, the list went on and on. Hence her absence from girl's night.

The fact that it would just be Rosie and Noah tonight ended up to their benefit as they still needed to finalize the details of Elena's bachelorette party. After ten minutes of arguing, Noah had finally convinced Rosie that they should plan at Lafayette's on the basis that they wouldn't have to pay for drinks with Callum working. She'd even taken Rosie's phone and texted Callum to ensure that fact.

> Rosie: Heyyyy Noh and I are coming to the bar and you know you wanna give us free drinks. :)

Callum: Hey Noh, give Rosie her phone back. Sure to drinks.

> Rosie: Sorry about Noah. Save our favorite table for us?

Callum: Someone's needy tonight.

> Rosie: Oh whatever.

> Rosie: You can't honestly tell me you wouldn't rather wait on us than a random couple that will order one drink each, and then take up the table space for the next two hours being nauseatingly touchy.

Callum: Fair point. See you in a bit.

No matter what was or wasn't going on between them, Rosie and Callum would always be friends. They'd grown up together just as she and Elena had, and that kind of bond didn't just go away, no matter how complicated it might be at times. Like right now for example: a week ago Callum and Rosie had had insanely hot sex only for Rosie to find out that he'd broken up with his girlfriend an hour before and then decided that she would never, under any circumstances, be hooking up with Callum *ever* again. Emphasis on the 'ever.'

The beauty of Callum and Rosie was that there was no relationship to ruin. Thus, their friendship would simply carry on as usual, sans the 'benefits' part, and, okay fine, maybe with a few petty comments from Rosie.

They took a car downtown from Noah's apartment, Rosie secretly banking on a ride home from Callum so they wouldn't have to pay to catch another ride back. Her favorite part of downtown at night was seeing the Arthur Ravenel Jr. Bridge all lit up. Despite how many times she saw the bridge's lights reflected in the river, she couldn't help but feel an excitement in the air, like anything was possible.

Their Uber driver let them out in front of Lafayette's on Market. Market Street was always lively at this time of night, people bouncing from bar to bar; Callum or no Callum, Lafayette's would always be her favorite bar in the entire city.

Rosie and Noah walked inside, waved to Callum, and headed for the table he'd saved for them on the downstairs level. It was tucked into the corner, making it easier to hear each other without isolating them from the ambiance of the rest of the bar. Callum brought drinks to their table a few minutes later: a Cosmo for Rosie and Rosé for Noah. Rosie surmised that they patronized Lafayette's often enough for Callum to know their go-to's.

The second Callum went back to the bar to serve the

other guests, Noah piped up, "So, does your 'All Men Can Fuck Off' manifesto still apply to Callum?"

"He intentionally left out the details about when he and Olivia broke up just to get in my pants," Rosie stated matter-of-factly, taking a sip of her Cosmo.

"I mean, he did say 'recently,'" Noah shrugged her shoulders.

"Yeah, but recently doesn't usually mean 'less than an hour ago,'" Rosie countered.

"Are you angry because he misled you, or angry because of the actual timeline of events?" Noah asked, twirling her wine glass back and forth by the stem between her thumb and pointer finger.

"I don't know, both? I guess I'm angry because I wouldn't have gone through with it had I known he'd just ended things with Olivia," Rosie reasoned.

"Why not?" Noah pushed.

"Because that's wrong," Rosie responded.

"Wrong like how you fucked him right after ending things with Justin?" Noah stared straight into Rosie's eyes as she said the words.

Rosie took a large sip of her Cosmo to buy herself time to think about how to respond. Noah had a decent point. Rosie *had* hooked up with someone she had history with immediately after ending a relationship. The difference was that Callum hadn't told her how recently things had actually ended between him and Olivia.

"Hm?" Noah prompted Rosie to answer her question, sipping her Rosé with a smirk on her face.

"I didn't hide how recently things ended between Justin and I. Callum did. Besides, Callum dumped Olivia. I *got* dumped. Not the same," she answered, crossing her arms in defiance.

"Babe, if you really cared to know how recently, why didn't you just ask?"

Rosie kept quiet, not wanting to answer. Noah always called things like they were; usually, Rosie loved that about her, but right now it was working against her. She wanted to wipe that smug little smirk off Noah's face. Instead, she took another sip—okay, a gulp—of her Cosmo.

"Or, possibly, did you not ask him to clarify because you wanted him, and 'recently' was good enough to justify that to yourself?"

Noah hit the nail on the head. She smirked at Rosie across the table just in time for Callum to walk back over and ask if they needed another drink. Looking down, Rosie realized that she'd almost downed the entirety of her Cosmo.

"Another round, ladies?" Callum smiled, showing that stupid dimple of his that Rosie suddenly found herself wanting to kiss.

No, she wasn't letting herself go there.

"Mmm, and cheese sticks," Noah answered, smiling and batting her eyes at Callum as if they hadn't just been discussing him before he walked over.

"I'll go put those in for you," Callum called as he headed back toward the bar.

Noah wasted no time jumping back into their earlier conversation as soon as Callum was out of earshot.

"He told you he wanted to explain. Why not just hear him out?" she asked.

"Because it doesn't matter. We aren't dating, we will never be dating. There are plenty of other people he can sleep with."

The words had come out a little more aggressively than

she'd intended. She wasn't quite sure who she was trying to convince: herself or Noah.

Sure, there'd been moments when she had thought about what it would be like to date Callum, but she'd been a naïve teenager then. Sure, there'd been times when she thought she was privy to a side of Callum that no one else got to see, but she quickly realized that it was just part of his natural charisma and that she was far from the only girl to fall for it. He was forthcoming about the fact that he wasn't a relationship guy. Thus, Callum fell firmly into one category for Rosie: friends with benefits. Nothing more. There was no potential relationship to lose. So, why bother hearing him out?

"Rosie, I say this with all the love in my heart: Callum isn't Justin. You don't have to sleep with him again if you don't want to, but don't *not* sleep with him because you're equating him misleading you with Justin's betrayal."

"I'm not equating him with Justin," Rosie defended, rather unconvincingly.

But was she? She thought back through the last few days in her head. She hadn't felt angry with Callum until she'd found out about Justin cheating on her. She'd known that Callum had misled her for an entire day without feeling anything but indifference. Maybe she was equating Callum's actions to Justin's after all.

"I suddenly have to pee," Noah said while scooting out of her side of the booth. "I might be a while, I'm going to reapply my lipstick."

Noah smirked at Rosie as she walked away. Rosie's eyes moved from her to Callum, who was now heading back to their table with their second round of drinks. Convenient time for Noah to have to go to the bathroom. Traitor.

"If you just give me five minutes, I can explain everything, Rosie," Callum muttered, noticing that Noah was walking toward the bathroom, leaving him and Rosie alone together for the first time since they'd slept together a week ago.

"Why do you care? It's not like there aren't a million other girls that would love to get on their knees for you," she deflected from his question.

"Maybe, but none of them would look as pretty on their knees as you," he stared straight into her eyes as the words came out.

Rosie swore she could see something behind those eyes that was more than lust… She swore she could see longing.

"That's too bad seeing as I won't be getting on my knees for you again, Costello," she countered.

"Then let me get on mine for you, *Rose*," he responded.

Rosie looked everywhere but his eyes, afraid he would see just how much his use of that nickname affected her.

When Rosie didn't answer, Callum continued, "I won't quit trying."

With that, he set their drinks on the table, turned, and walked back to the bar.

"Traitor," Rosie fake-coughed as Noah sat back down at their table a few minutes later.

"Oh, hush. I saw him come over to talk to you. Did you hear him out?" she asked eagerly.

"No, but he did tell me that he won't stop trying to get on his knees for me, so there's that," Rosie admitted.

"Has anyone ever told you that you're incredibly stubborn?" Noah kicked Rosie under the table playfully.

"Aw, thanks. That's so sweet of you," Rosie kicked back.

"Okay, down to business. We have a bachelorette party to plan," Noah said definitively.

Rosie was grateful that Noah had steered their conversation away from Callum. She opened her notebook, placing it on the table where she and Noah could read through it together.

<u>*Bachelorette Party Ideas for Bad Bitches*</u>
* Mani/Pedis
* Axe Throwing (because girl boss shit, duh)
* Bar Hopping Across Downtown
* Drink Fish Bowls at Folly Beach
* Escape Room
* Karaoke
* Painting and Wine Night
* Strip Club (?)
* Sunset Booze Cruise
* Drag Show
* Dance Club (could be combined with bar hopping)

All of the bridesmaids would be going out to a nice dinner in downtown Charleston before the real bachelorette party events started so that Harper, the youngest of the Costello siblings and the only sibling under the age of eighteen, would still get to be included in the festivities. Elena's mom had taken care of the reservations, which just left Rosie and Noah to plan to afterparty.

"Hear me out: what if we got Fish Bowls at Folly, then headed to an escape room in downtown and tried to solve it drunk?" Noah could barely get the idea out without snorting.

Rosie couldn't help but start laughing at the idea, too.

Fish Bowls were exactly what they sounded like: literal fish bowls filled with various types of alcohol and garnished with a swirly straw for the ripe price of twenty dollars. It was recommended that two people share one, being that they held 44 oz each. It was pretty much guaranteed to fuck a person up even if they shared with someone else.

"When the hell else would we have a reason to order Fish Bowls? It wouldn't be a bachelorette party if we didn't get at least a little reckless."

Rosie held up her Cosmo in salute.

"Look at that—half of the night planned already. We should quit our jobs and start an event planning service together."

"I happen to like my job, thank you very much," Rosie fake-scoffed at Noah's idea.

"You get paid to read smutty romance manuscripts," Noah rolled her eyes.

"And you get paid to turn people into living canvases," Rosie rolled her eyes back.

"Touché."

Noah reached out to click her glass against Rosie's.

"Oh! Speaking of, Hazel wanted to know if your books would be open for November? She's home the week of Thanksgiving and wants to get a new piece."

"Do you know what of?"

"Nah, but I can ask."

"Okay cool, that works. Just let me know and we can figure something out. My books are technically filled through the end of the year, but I'm sure I can figure something out."

Callum walked over to their table with another round of drinks and their plate of cheese sticks.

"Mmm, thank God," Noah grabbed the plate of cheese

sticks from Callum's hand before he even had a chance to set them down on the table. "I'm starving."

"Save some for Rosie, Noh," Callum teased her. "And I know you didn't ask, but here's another round of drinks. On the house as promised."

Callum handed Noah another glass of Rosé, this time also leaving her the half-emptied bottle to finish off. As he handed Rosie her Cosmo glass, their fingers brushed. A small, insignificant touch that shouldn't have affected Rosie, but somehow shot straight to her core. Damn, she either really needed to get laid, or needed her brain and her pussy to get on the same page about not sleeping with Callum again. Under any circumstances. Ever. Fair or not, she was resolved to her 'Men Can All Fuck Off' manifesto.

"Let me know if you want another round later," Callum said, glancing at the half-empty wine bottle, "or more cheese sticks."

"Wait! Costello," Rosie stopped him, "question for you."

She put on her best innocent, doe-eyed face as he walked back toward the table.

Callum turned back to their table, "What's up?"

"Do you know if Elena is a fan of strip clubs?"

"Why do you ask?" he looked intrigued.

"If you must know, we're planning her bachelorette party," Rosie smirked up at him.

"That's your big bachelorette party plan? The strip club?" Callum asked sarcastically.

"You say that like it's a bad plan," Rosie's smirk only grew.

She knew exactly what her words were doing to Callum —she just wasn't quite sure why she was doing it beyond the fact that it felt natural. Plus, it was kinda fun.

"You of all people know that there are way better

nightlife options downtown than going to a strip club," Callum murmured, seeming annoyed.

Or maybe he wasn't annoyed—maybe he was jealous. He'd made it abundantly clear how badly he wanted Rosie.

"Jealous that I'm gonna be up close and personal with a bunch of cocks that aren't yours?" she teased him further.

"You can be close and personal with mine anytime you want, Rose," he stared at her with something dark in his eyes.

Lust, she determined.

Rosie had all but forgotten Noah was still sitting across from her until she spit the wine she'd just taken a sip of back into her glass. Before either of them could respond, Callum walked back toward the bar.

"Rose? No one calls you Rose," Noah looked at Rosie with confusion, obviously waiting for an explanation.

"Callum does," she hesitated, "but usually only while he's inside me."

Rosie avoided Noah's eyes, doing a terrible job at hiding the blush that was most definitely spreading across her cheeks.

"Babe, for the love of God, just jump his bones already," Noah pleaded in an exasperated tone.

"Let's just finish planning the rest of Elena's bachelorette party," Rosie groaned, sidestepping Noah's comment and taking a big sip from her glass before Noah could ask anything else.

"By all means, if you want to be stubborn and relocate the Sahara Desert to reside between your legs, be my guest," Noah declared sarcastically.

Rosie cleared her throat, "The party, Noh."

What Rosie would never admit to Noah, would barely admit to herself, was that despite her refusal to hook up with Callum again, being around him was creating the exact opposite of the Sahara Desert between her legs. With his words alone, he was creating the fucking Nile River. Her brain and her pussy were very much *not* on the same page.

"Yeah, yeah. The party," Noah conceded.

"Let's go ahead and book the escape room," Rosie decided. "Six people, yeah?" Rosie asked.

"Yeah, five bridesmaids, plus Elena," Noah confirmed.

"Alright, so we're back to either the strip club or drag show to finish off the night," Noah pointed out.

"Well, we didn't exactly get an answer from Callum about Elena and the strip club—"

"You know," Noah raised her eyebrows in Rosie's direction. "It would've been way more effective to just text Elena and ask."

"Then text her," Rosie gestured to Noah's phone sitting on the table.

While Noah picked her phone up and started typing, Rosie scribbled the itinerary they'd settled on thus far onto a new page in her notebook:

5:30 PM: Picnic on Folly Beach
7 PM: Fish Bowls at Snapper Jacks (leave at 8)
9 PM: Escape Room at The Great Escape

Noah flipped her phone around so that Rosie could read her conversation with Elena.

> Noah: No reason, but what are your thoughts on strip clubs?

> Elena: I'm assuming this has to do with the fact that you're currently at Lafayette's planning my bachelorette party with Rosie?

> Noah: You're no fun.

> Noah: How'd you know?

> Elena: Callum texted me.

> Elena: Specifically, he said he overheard you two talking about getting drunk and looking at dicks.

If they were being technical, Rosie had said cocks, not dicks, but close enough.

"Would you like me to clarify that you were actually asking Callum if he was jealous that you'd be 'up close and personal with a bunch of cocks that weren't hi—'"

Rosie cut Noah off before she could finish that sentence, "No, I would very much not like for you to do that."

Noah typed a response, clicked send, then spun the phone back around, holding it in front of Rosie's face.

> Noah: Isn't that what bachelorette parties are for?

"Look, I was obviously joking about telling Elena," Noah changed the subject back to Rosie and Callum, "but you'd better figure your shit out before the wedding because I could cut the tension between you and Callum with a knife. And if you plan on Elena believing your whole 'not sleeping with Callum' agenda, you're gonna need to be a whole lot more convincing," Noah said matter-of-factly. "That, or you're gonna have to put on your big girl pants and talk to him. Clear the air."

"Tension or not, I'm not sleeping with him."

Rosie crossed her arms. She wasn't sure if she was grateful or resentful of the fact that Noah could clearly see through the front she was putting up. Whether she wanted to be or not, she was attracted to Callum, and that wasn't just going to go away. She just needed to find a way not to act on that attraction.

Around midnight, Rosie mustered up the audacity to ask Callum to drive them home, despite her rather aggressive declaration that she wasn't going to sleep with him again and was refusing to hear him out. Honestly, he had no reason to say yes, but it was worth a shot if it meant not having to pay for the ride back to Noah's.

Rosie walked up to the bar, and sat down on a barstool directly in front of where Callum stood.

"Hi," she said sweetly.

"Hi," Callum responded, mixing a drink in the cocktail shaker.

The movement caused his shirt sleeves to rise, showing off his tattoos and the band of his briefs.

"Can I help you?" Callum raised his eyebrows.

Right. She'd walked up to him to ask him for a ride home, not to stare at his arms, however distractingly enticing they might look.

"Do you think you could be talked into driving Noh and me back to her apartment?"

"And why would I do that when you won't even bother to let me explain myself?"

Well, fuck. She supposed she could agree to hear him out in exchange for a ride. It's not like his explanation would change anything. All men could fuck off. But they *could* give her free rides home while they fucked off.

"Fine. If you drive us home, I'll hear you out. Deal?"

"You have yourself a deal, Rose," Callum smirked.

"Although, I would've agreed to drive you either way if you'd just said please, but it's too late to take it back now."

Ignoring his use of that stupid nickname, she gave Callum an annoyed smirk before turning around to walk back to her table. Infuriating. That was how Rosie would describe Callum Costello if she was only allowed one adjective. At least she'd gotten a ride home out of it.

Sitting down in the booth, Rosie rolled her eyes at Noah.

"You owe me."

"For?"

"Callum said he'd drive us home, so we don't have to pay for a ride."

"I'm still missing the part where *I* somehow owe you for a favor *Callum* is doing us?" Noah raised her eyebrows at Rosie.

"You owe me," Rosie sighed, "because I had to agree to hear him out to get him to agree to drive us home."

"Babe, I didn't ask you to do that. Sure you weren't just curious about what he had to say?"

Across the booth, Noah crossed her arms smugly.

Under the booth, Rosie kicked her leg.

"Ouch!"

"It was warranted."

"Was it? Or are you just annoyed that I am once again fully aware of what's going on in your pretty little head?"

Rosie kicked Noah again, "maybe a bit of both."

As Callum pulled his Jeep into a parking spot back at Noah's apartment, he turned toward Noah in the backseat.

"Noh, would you mind giving me a second alone with Rosie?" Callum asked.

"Not even a little bit," Noah replied, smirking at Rosie as she opened the door of Callum's Jeep.

As Noah started up the stairs to her apartment, Callum turned toward Rosie. She assumed she was about to have to pay up on her end of this whole Callum-driving-them-home deal.

"So, about you giving me a chance to explain."

Callum seemed anxious. This was uncharted territory since any vulnerability between them in the past had always been physical.

"I said I'd give you a chance. I just didn't say tonight," Rosie smirked, glancing up toward Noah waiting in the apartment.

Callum raised his eyebrows as if to ask 'when?'

"Before the wedding," Rosie stated.

"Before the wedding it is," Callum agreed.

As Rosie's hand found the door handle, Callum quietly murmured, "Goodnight, Rosie."

Rosie, not Rose. Interesting.

"Goodnight, Callum."

9

THROW PUNCHES, NOT AXES

Callum:

Since Lilah was a project manager for a local construction company and a damn good one at that, she was always in good shape without having to be conscious about working out. Not in shape in the sense that she was jacked, but in the way that made her strength obvious. Right now, that meant that she was much better at axe throwing than Callum. Callum wasn't in bad shape by any means, but he also didn't spend his days lifting lumber, buckets of cement, and pavers. Like Callum, Lilah also liked to work alongside her crew every so often so that she didn't forget what it was like to be in the trenches of the job. And also maybe because she was a bit of a perfectionist and liked to lend her hand in projects.

"Your crew still working on that restoration project over on Beaufain?" Callum asked in between throws.

"Yeah. It's gonna be a coffee shop once it's finished, and the electrical work has been a nightmare, especially since we're working to maintain the historical significance of the building," Lilah explained.

"Local or chain coffee shop?" Callum inquired.

"Local. It's gonna be a great spot once it's finished—just a lot of front-loaded work."

"I'll have to swing by on the way to the bar sometime once it's done," Callum decided as he stepped up to the throw line.

"Geez Callum, trying to take the target board out?" Lilah snorted as she watched Callum fling his axe a little too aggressively toward the clearly marked circles in front of him.

"I guess I'm just, uh, trying to release some pent-up aggression," Callum muttered.

He hadn't hooked up with anyone since Rosie, and his right arm had been getting quite the workout.

"Isn't that what fucking is for?" Lilah asked, only being half sarcastic as she walked up to the line indicating how far back they were supposed to stand.

"Yeah, well, I uh," Callum hesitated, "I haven't exactly been utilizing that outlet much lately."

The words came out almost as if Callum had just given away a secret, which, in a sense, he had. He quickly took a sip of his beer to hide a wince from slipping out.

The fact that he hadn't slept with anyone since he'd slept with Rosie was out of character for him, and, thus, very telling. Callum was glad Lilah had her attention focused on the marker in front of her because he was sure his face was the shade of a tomato.

Hitting the middle ring of the bullseye, Lilah turned around to face Callum.

"Define 'not much.'"

Looking in every possible direction but Lilah's eyes, Callum sighed and said, "not at all."

"Uh-huh," Lilah eyed Callum suspiciously, eyebrows raised. "This wouldn't have anything to do with a certain redhead, now would it?"

Callum knew that Lilah wouldn't force him into talking about things with Rosie, but she wouldn't go without acknowledging the situation either. That was their deal: they called each other on their shit. No sugar coating.

"I don't know what it is or why it is, but we just get each other when it comes to sex. I haven't found that with anyone else," Callum offered in response as he stepped up to the line.

"What: Rosie is hot as hell. Why: You two have an emotional connection, not just a physical one," Lilah answered Callum's obviously rhetorical question.

"I'm not trying to date her," Callum said defensively.

He threw his axe at the target, missing by at least half a foot.

"Didn't say you were," Lilah smirked, glancing between Callum and his horrible throw. "But you two have known each other, been friends, for what? Over a decade now? Pretty much since I met you?"

"Thirteen years, yeah."

Callum realized before he could stop the words from coming out of his mouth that it sounded very odd for him to offer up the exact amount of time he'd known his sister's best friend without a second's hesitation. It's not like she walked into *his* life all those years ago, she'd walked into Elena's. Callum just happened to be there by proximity.

"Mmhm," Lilah's smirk grew as she lifted her own beer mug to her lips.

"What's that look for?" Callum asked.

"Nothing. You'll figure it out eventually," Lilah said as she took up her stance and threw her axe, hitting the exact middle of the bullseye. Again. "Speaking of Rosie, you ever get her to talk to you? Or are you still planning to wait until the wedding?"

"Sort of? I got her to agree to hear me out before the wedding," Callum shrugged.

"Better than before. What are you going to say?"

"I'm trying to figure out how to explain things to make myself sound the least like an asshole."

"Oh, you mean you didn't wanna lead with 'I broke up with my girlfriend because I'd rather fuck you?'" Lilah teased.

"Yeah, because that would absolutely get me back in her good graces," Callum rolled his eyes. "And it's not like that. Rosie texting me just gave me a push to do what I'd already been thinking about."

"Alright, so lead with that," Lilah suggested.

It didn't make him sound like an asshole, but it didn't *not* make him sound like one either. Callum thought back to his conversation with Hayden that night, how Hayden had basically told him to quit stringing Olivia along. Taking Hayden's advice had been an abrupt decision, sure, but Hayden had been right. Pretending he wanted commitment just because he wanted an easy fuck hadn't been fair to Olivia, so he'd ended things. Callum explained as much to Lilah.

"Everything just kinda happened. I don't regret ending things with Olivia, and I *definitely* don't regret sleeping with Rosie. I didn't mean for it to happen so fast, but it did and I can't change it now."

"Then that's exactly what you should say. Just be honest. Besides, she hooked up with *you* right after ending things with *her* ex, so it's not like she has room to be mad at you. If she can't see the hypocrisy in that, then that's on her."

Callum raised his beer mug as if to say 'fair enough' before taking a long sip.

"Listen though, on the topic of fine as fuck redheads, wanna watch *Black Widow* for movie night next week?" Lilah nudged Callum while giving him exaggerated googly eyes.

Callum wouldn't let himself consider why he felt so defensive at the sound of someone else noticing how attractive Rosie was.

"I always pegged you as a Florence kind of girl," Callum joked, "but yeah, sure."

"Nah, I'm a DC girl—Wonder Woman specifically. I'm a sucker for badass women with long, dark hair."

Callum made a mental note to make sure she and Noah ended up reacquainting with each other at the wedding in a few weeks. As far as Callum was aware, Lilah and Noah hadn't seen each other since before Noah had come out as pansexual a few years back. Since whatever had happened at that house party. As a female tattoo artist, she was the definition of a badass. Plus, she also happened to have extremely long, dark hair. Although, maybe he should wait to get back on Rosie's good side before he attempted to set his best friend up with hers.

Several rounds later, of both beer and axe throwing, Lilah had hit somewhere in the neighborhood of seven bullseyes while Callum had missed the board more than he'd even come close to the outer ring.

Callum hadn't ever played on an official school sports team or anything, but, shit, he was usually more coordinated than this. Ever since things had blown up between him and Rosie, he'd been off his game. He told himself it was because he didn't want his personal life to interfere with Elena's wedding, but that excuse wasn't going to work forever.

Out of the corner of his eye, Callum could have sworn he saw a familiar mop of dark blonde hair attached to a pretentious little five-nine frame otherwise known as Justin, Rosie's dickhead ex. It had been a week since the breakup, and Justin didn't look at all upset over the loss—and losing someone like Rosie *was* a loss. The six beers Callum had consumed were making a very convincing argument for him to waltz over and punch Justin right in his smug little face.

"You okay?" Lilah asked, pulling Callum's thoughts back to a rational sphere.

"That's Rosie's ex," Callum explained, gesturing to the axe-throwing cage a few to the left of their own.

"I mean I was referring to you missing the board *again*," Lilah raised her eyebrows, squaring off for her next throw. "Do you know him or something?"

"Enough to know he's an asshole. What kind of person ends a two-year relationship over the phone, Lih?" Callum responded.

"Okay, sure, he's an ass, but I still don't understand what that has to do with you?"

Callum wasn't sure how to answer that. He honestly couldn't explain why seeing Justin had made him so goddamn angry, but he refused to psychoanalyze that right now. So, he grabbed his axe and stepped up to the throw line.

"She just deserves better," Callum mumbled after missing the target once again. "He clearly doesn't know what he lost."

"And what exactly did he lose, Bolton?" Lilah asked.

Someone worth more than he personally would ever deserve, Callum thought in an answer to Lilah's question. There was no judgment in Lilah's gaze, but rather mere curiosity. A look that said she'd figured something out that Callum was going to have to realize on his own.

Callum swirled the little bit of beer that was left in his mug mindlessly while trying to tamp down the anger that was simmering under his skin. From a few cages over, Callum couldn't help but overhear Justin and his friends talking.

"So, you finally dumped that red-headed bitch, huh?"

Oh, fuck no. Dickbag's friend was *not* going to talk about Rosie like that.

"Fucking *finally*, man. Now that it's just Isa, I don't have anyone up my ass about when I'm going to choose a path for my life."

Now that it's just Isa?

Rosie and Justin had only broken up around a week ago, which meant... Oh, no. Oh, *hell* no. Not only did this asshole break Rosie's heart, but he'd fucking cheated on her too?

Did Rosie know?

Actually, the answer to that question didn't particularly matter right now. Before he realized what he was doing, Callum was storming across the building, blazing a path straight for Justin's cheating ass.

"Costello? What are you do—" Justin started to ask.

But his words were cut off by the impact of Callum's fist.

"The hell man?!" Justin yelled, wiping blood from his face. "I think you broke my fucking nose!"

Before Callum could get another punch in, Lilah's arms were around his waist, pulling him back to try and break things up before it became an all-out fight.

"I hope I did, you cheating piece of shit," Callum retorted. "You didn't seem to give a damn about broken things when you ended a two-year relationship over the phone."

"So that's what this is about? Rosie?" Justin laughed. "You didn't waste any time, did you? I guess I was right not to trust her around you after all."

"Fuck you," Callum spat in his face. "You never deserved her."

"Maybe not, but you never will," Justin crossed his arms in defiance.

"Yeah, well. At least I *know* I don't deserve someone like her. You're just an entitled little bitch who treated her like an object and left her broken, consequences be damned."

"Okay, Bolton, time to go," Lilah urged from behind Callum, still holding him back.

The familiar nickname soothed him. Barely, but enough that he let her pull him backward.

"Drop the self-righteous act. She'd never be with a womanizer like you," Justin taunted as Lilah pulled Callum toward the front entrance.

On the way out, Callum noticed the axe he had released right before storming across the building toward Justin: it was a perfect bullseye, the only one he'd hit all night.

You'll figure it out eventually.

Lilah's earlier comment had been swirling around in Callum's mind for the rest of the night. Callum had already explained that he wasn't after a relationship with Rosie, so that couldn't be what Lilah was insinuating. Yeah, sure, he'd punched Justin in the face. But he would have reacted the same way if he'd overheard someone talking about Elena that way too... right?

Letting his clothes fall in his path, Callum headed for the shower, hoping to clear his mind. As soon as he closed his eyes to scrub his face, flashbacks of Rosie bent over his couch came to the forefront of his mind. He didn't understand what it was about Rosie that always left him wanting more, but at least he was halfway back in now that she'd finally agreed to let him explain himself about the way everything had happened that night. And now that he knew about Justin cheating, he felt even more desperate for a chance to explain himself. He wasn't like Justin. For reasons he didn't yet understand, he *needed* Rosie to know that.

Looking down, Callum realized his mind wasn't the only thing flashbacks of Rosie were affecting. Callum had told himself that he would only jerk off to the memory once, just to get her out of his system, but that excuse had stopped working after the fourth time. Here he was, weeks later, fucking his fist to the same memory, his cock wanting desperately to relive it.

He grabbed his shampoo bottle and squeezed some into his hand. He scrubbed it through his hair as if he could scrub his frustrations away too.

If Callum couldn't even control himself in his own apartment, how the hell was he supposed to keep himself from pitching a tent while occupying the same beach house as Rosie for a whole weekend?

You'll figure it out eventually.

Closing his eyes to rinse the shampoo from his hair, Callum's mind drifted back to a distant memory of a night thirteen years ago...

Callum and Lilah were playing basketball in the driveway of his parent's house when an Expedition pulled in. It must be Rosie's, his sister's new best friend, parents coming to pick her up. Along with almost every other weekend in the last four months, Rosie had spent this one at the Costello's, and Callum hadn't minded. Not one bit.

She was a year older than him, a freshman in high school like Elena, but still paid him attention despite his still being in the eighth grade, which he liked. A little too much.

As the car pulled in, Callum walked up to the driver's side window. He figured he'd introduce himself rather than stand there awkwardly.

"Hey honey," Mrs. Dawson said as she rolled down her window. "You must be one of Elena's siblings."

Callum nodded. "Callum, the one that's going to marry Rosie one day," he crossed his arms as if to show that he meant it.

Mrs. Dawson laughed, not an annoyed laugh, but one of amusement.

Before Callum could say anything else, Rosie was closing the side door next to the garage and walking down the driveway. She smiled at him as she approached the SUV. Callum lingered, waiting to see if Mrs. Dawson was going to say anything about his marriage comment.

She didn't. As Rosie opened the car door to throw her bag in the backseat, Mrs. Dawson turned her attention back to Callum.

"Goodness, your parents must have their hands full with all of you. You be sure to tell your mom that we're happy to have Elena over to our house anytime they want a break from the chaos," she smiled at Callum and put the car in reverse.

Callum's eyes followed Rosie in the passenger seat all the way down the driveway, not looking away until the car turned and disappeared into the cool October night.

"Big declaration to make for a fourteen-year-old, Bolton," Lilah's amused voice emerged from the driveway behind Callum.

"Oh, piss off," Callum gave her the finger across the driveway, *"next basket wins."*

Why Lilah's comment had reminded him of that night, Callum wasn't ready to think about. All Callum knew was that he was well and truly fucked—in more ways than one.

10

BATHTIME

Rosie:

SETTING her keys on the hook by her front door, Rosie headed straight to her bathroom to draw a bath. She'd had a rough Monday back at work given that she'd fucked her sleep schedule with so many late nights over the weekend and was emotionally drained from the call with her mom earlier. As a teenager, Rosie had always assumed that things with her mom would get easier when she was on her own; as it turned out, signing a lease and buying your own groceries didn't stop a person from longing to be accepted. Maybe she was doomed to forever live with that subtle trace of melancholy.

Rosie promptly decided that she needed a nice, warm, stress-relieving bath.

After starting the water, she padded back to the kitchen to pour herself a glass of wine. She was halfway back to the bathroom when she decided just to bring the whole bottle with her—she deserved it after the shitty weekend she'd had.

She set her glass of wine, laptop (open to a potential manuscript she'd been sent), and a lavender bath bomb on her bath caddy and stepped into the tub, careful to avoid splashing water on anything.

She was just about to set her phone on the table beside the bathtub when she noticed a text from Justin of all people. Figuring that he was finally acknowledging the screenshots Noah had sent of Isa's Instagram over the weekend, Rosie's heart sank all over again.

She knew that, ultimately, she wasn't responsible for Justin's actions; even so, she couldn't help feeling like some part of her just wasn't enough for him, that it was somehow her fault that he'd cheated. That if she'd been a better partner, been more patient with him... No, she wasn't letting herself go down that road again. Nothing productive or healthy would come of it. She knew better.

Swiping the screen to unlock her phone, she stared at Justin's text in complete and utter shock.

> Justin: Call off your man.

Huh? She didn't have a man—Justin had personally made sure of that—so what the hell was he talking about? Talking to him was at the very bottom of the list of things she wanted to do right now, but curiosity got the better of her.

> Rosie: The hell are you talking about?

Justin's reply was immediate.

> Justin: Call. Off. Costello.

Words I Should Have Said

Before Rosie could even begin to process, Justin sent another text.

> Justin: The jackass broke my fucking nose tonight. Had to be hauled out by his friend.

The irony in Justin calling Callum a jackass after he'd been the one to cheat on Rosie for a goddamn year was not lost on her. But more importantly: *Callum* had punched Justin and broken his nose? And as if that wasn't enough, Justin had referred to Callum as 'her man,' insinuating that Rosie and Callum were together, which they most definitely were *not*. As far as Rosie knew, Callum didn't even know that Justin had cheated on her, which left her more than a little confused.

Rosie pulled up Callum's contact, her finger hovering over the 'call' button. She could call him, asking what the hell had happened, or... Justin had said that Callum's friend hauled him out. Lilah? She didn't know who else it would be. Calling Lilah would probably give her a lot more insight than asking Callum directly. Before she could change her mind, she pressed 'call.'

"Rosie?" Lilah sounded confused, but not annoyed. "What's, uh, what's up?"

"Uh, hey," Rosie started. "Sorry to call you so late, but, um," she hesitated, not sure how to broach the subject. "Justin texted me a minute ago... he said that Callum broke his nose?"

"Shit, yeah," Lilah sounded flustered. "I'm sure Callum was going to tell you eventually..."

"What the hell happened?" Rosie pressed.

"Justin and some of his friends came into the same axe-throwing place we were at tonight, and I guess he didn't notice us because they were going on about how Justin had 'finally gotten rid of you' and was now only dating some other girl. They were being real dicks about it, and before I knew what was happening Callum was headed straight for Justin..."

Leave it to Lilah not to sugarcoat anything to save anyone's feelings. Rosie had always appreciated her bluntness—you always knew where you stood with her. Lilah reminded her of Noah in that regard.

"So, Callum punched him because he cheated on me?"

"Fuck, did you not know? Oh fuck, Rosie, I'm so sorry," Lilah tripped over her words, a rare occurrence.

"No, it's fine. I mean yes, I knew, but it's okay," Rosie reassured her. "I'm okay."

"Thank fuck," Rosie could hear Lilah's sigh of relief through the phone. "This is why I play for the other team. Women can be particularly cunty at times, but men objectively suck ass. Like *one hundred* percent of the time," Lilah declared.

"Amen to that," Rosie laughed. "Not that I'm particularly upset that Justin's cheating ass got his nose broken, but..." Rosie hesitated. "Why does Callum give a shit?"

"I think you both know the answer to that. Whether or not you're willing to acknowledge it."

"I—"

Silence stretched out between them. Rosie was at a loss for words. Finally, Lilah broke the silence.

"Rosie, listen. I know Callum wasn't upfront about how recently he'd broken things off with Olivia, but that's the thing: Callum *broke things off*, unlike Justin. And he did it because fucking you, even once, was more appealing to him than his entire goddamn relationship with Olivia was. Justin used you *and* that other girl and I know it's not really my place to say anything, but he's my best friend, Rosie. I *know*

Callum isn't perfect, but please don't end up projecting how you feel about Justin onto him. Whether or not he will ever admit it to you, much less himself, comparing him to Justin would really hurt him. You don't have to fuck him again, but he doesn't deserve to be compared to that cheating piece of shit. He's better than that, okay?"

"You're right," Rosie whispered. "I guess being angry at Callum was easier than facing Justin's betrayal. He was someone I could push my pain onto..." Rosie sighed. "That wasn't fair. I see that now."

"Don't tell me that," Lilah stated. "I'm not the one who needs to hear it."

Rosie heard the click of the line going dead. *Shit.* She had some amends to make.

Despite the encroaching feeling of guilt, Rosie couldn't ignore the heat pooling in her core. Callum had *punched* Justin because of what he'd done to Rosie. Suddenly she wasn't so mad at Callum anymore. Suddenly she wanted to express her gratitude in the only way she'd ever known how: on her knees.

Downing what was left of her glass of wine, Rosie set it back on the bath tray and then moved the entire tray carefully to the floor. Reaching into the drawer of the table she kept next to the bath, she pulled out her favorite waterproof vibrator.

She ran it along her collarbone, between her breasts, closing her eyes and imagining instead that it was Callum's cock. She kept imagining as she slowly moved it down the length of her body until she moved against it between her legs.

11

BAD BITCH BACHELORETTE PARTY

Rosie:

"Ugh, I wish we were staring at tits instead," Noah complained.

The strip club was the last stop of the 'Bad Bitch Bachelorette Party' as Rosie and Noah had affectionately named it. Since Elena wasn't queer, they were at a men's strip club. And, though Noah was pansexual, she definitely had a preference for women, which she was making more than apparent at the current moment.

Honestly, Rosie wouldn't mind looking at bouncing tits right now either, but this wasn't her bachelorette party. Damn, she was horny. Or was that the fishbowl she'd downed earlier tonight talking? She hadn't fucked anyone since Callum and had thought about him while touching herself more times than she'd care to admit over the last two weeks... and, yeah, she needed to get laid. ASAP.

"Oh hush, we can go to a women's strip club when *you* get married," Elena rolled her eyes at Noah.

"Here," Rosie extended her hand toward Noah. "Take the money and shove it in the nice man's g-string."

"I think Elena should be the one to do it," Noah passed the twenty across their table, "Bride to be and all. It's probably a rule or something."

Between Rosie, Noah, and Elena, Elena was definitely the most shy in sexual situations. Rosie swore her Cancer sun was to blame.

"Or, Lydia could do it?" Elena eyed her oldest sister across the table in an attempt to get out of having to tip the stripper.

"Nope. I'm pulling the marriage card. Someone single can do it," Lydia deflected with no small level of sarcasm.

"Rosie, you do it! The strip club was your idea," Elena passed the money back to her. "Besides, I'm *practically* married, if that's what we're going off of."

Rosie swore Elena shot Lydia a silent "thank you."

"Great! Rosie will stick the twenty in the man's junk, I'll order us another round of shots, and Elena will look like the most beautiful bride that's ever existed because she is," Noah slurred enthusiastically.

"Uh, hey, Noh!" Rosie called after her, "I'm really not sure we need more shots!"

Either Noah hadn't heard her, or she'd purposefully ignored her, because she kept walking all the way to the bar at the edge of the room.

"Someone is definitely going to have to take that shot for me," Lydia said. "Being woken by a five-year-old who doesn't understand that no one should talk above a whisper before eight AM is bad enough; no way in hell am I going to subject myself to that while also hungover."

"Not me," Rosie lifted her finger to 'nose goes' her way

out of it. "The fishbowl is already threatening to swim its way out if you know what I mean."

As Rosie turned back around to face the stage, she was met with a dick a foot from her face. It wasn't small by any means, but Callum's was definitely bigger. Like, a lot bigger.

Uh-oh. She was definitely not supposed to be thinking about Callum. Or his dick. *Especially* not about how big Callum's dick was. Or the memory of Callum telling her to take it like a good... Nope—Not. Good.

She tucked the twenty in the string tied around the dancer's waist, then turned back around to face her friends triumphantly.

"There," she folded her arms sloppily across her chest, "at least one of us had the balls to pay the very talented man."

Balls. Callum had balls. Ones that she very much enjoyed touching as she took his cock deep into her throat.

NO. Bad Rosie. Bad. Bad. Bad.

"I wouldn't need balls to tuck a twenty into a beautiful woman's g-string," Noah joked as she rejoined them at their table.

"For the love of God, Noah," Elena said in mock annoyance. "You're beautiful, you could pull any woman you wanted. Quit pretending you'd have to go to a strip club to see a woman's—"

"Not any woman..." Noah mumbled.

"What are you talking about?" a look of confusion washed across Elena's face.

"Nothing. It's nothing," Noah muttered, looking down at the table to avoid eye contact.

She was a shit liar, her emotions always blatantly displayed on her face.

"It's obviously something," Elena pressed, "or you

wouldn't be staring at the table like it's the most interesting thing you've ever seen. In a strip club of all places, where there are vastly more interesting things to look at."

"That I just paid twenty to look at up close and personal, mind you," Rosie joked, trying to keep the mood light.

"I... It's nothing," Noah hesitated. "I've just had a super fat fucking crush on Lilah ever since high school, but the only interaction we've had just the two of us happened to be my *actual* fucking gay awakening, but then I *panicked*," she flailed her arms out dramatically. "And I never told her and then I never saw her again because we all graduated and went off to college." She raked her hands down her face in sloppy exasperation, "and then I came out, because *obviously*. I mean, we've established that I'm a tit girl, and wow are Lilah's nice, and I bet she just looks ten times hotter than she did in high school now, and, and..."

Noah ran out of breath.

Rosie had a vague recollection of what Noah was mumbling about. Years ago, during their senior year of high school, a game of Seven Minutes in Heaven had broken out during a house party at the Costello's. It had landed Noah and Lilah in a room together. Rosie had always known that *something* happened between them; she'd actually had to knock on the door after not seven, but *ten* minutes, to let them know their time was up.

When they rejoined the party, Noah made some joke Rosie couldn't fully remember and brushed it off. They'd never talked about it. Rosie had made a point to tell Noah that she didn't give a shit who she wanted to bang and left it at that.

"And you're totally in love with my brother's best friend!" Elena shrieked. "This is perfect, oh my god!"

"Uh, howwww," Noah dragged the word out, "is me being

on the verge of having a panic attack perfect?" She looked offended.

"Because Lilah just so happens to be on the guest list at Elena's wedding," Rosie smirked at Noah across the table. "Oh, we are *so* gonna Cupid this shit," Rosie made devious eye contact with Elena across the table.

"Um, no. No, the fuck we are not," Noah protested, glancing helplessly between Rosie and Elena. "I haven't seen her in years, and we don't even know that she's into me like that, and she's so goddamn pretty that it makes me want to crawl into a hole, and, and I'm drunk and rambling, aren't I?" Noah sighed.

"Babe, I think you hit the rambling threshold five minutes ago," Rosie chuckled.

"What the fuck am I even supposed to say to her? Hi, I'm gay now and would really love to taste your pussy?"

Elena's mouth dropped open. Lydia rolled her eyes and chuckled. Rosie full-on snorted, loudly enough that at least three people stared. Oh well.

Layla, who had chosen that exact moment to return from the restroom, turned a bright shade of red. She looked entirely too sober for this conversation. Being that Layla was only nineteen, they'd pregamed before leaving tonight, but that had been hours ago. Maybe Rosie could casually pawn off the shots Noah had just ordered for her and Lydia onto Layla.

"Whose, um, you know, are you tasting?" Layla asked.

Noah practically slid out of her chair trying to shrink away from this conversation, whisper-yelling, "not a fucking word about this at the wedding, or I'll push you all over like dominos at the ceremony!"

"Yeah, absolutely, lead with that," Rosie could barely contain her laughter long enough to get the words out. "I can't believe that *Lilah* was your gay awakening all this time, and you never told me! You bitch!"

Rosie threw a middle finger in Noah's direction. Rather, she tried to throw a middle finger, but actually threw a peace sign. Uh-oh. Too much alcohol. Too late to do anything about it now.

"You try having a gay awakening in the middle of a crowded house party! I didn't exactly have space to process that shit," Noah defended herself.

"Okay, no. This is so totally fine. We have two weeks until the wedding. That gives us two weeks to enact Plan Cupid," Elena encouraged.

"Yeah, well, let's wait until the floor stops moving first," Noah groaned. "Maybe we can lump Rosie and Callum into this plan too."

"Oh is *that* why he broke up with Olivia?" Lydia asked with more than a little interest.

"No!" Rosie argued, a bit too quickly. "That's not why they broke up but I do have a Callum-related update..."

Rosie still hadn't told anyone about Callum punching Justin in the face, and now seemed like as good a time as any.

"You totally fucked him again, didn't you?!" Noah exclaimed. "Oh, I *so* called that!" She looked more than pleased with herself.

"Ugh, there is not enough alcohol in my body to discuss who my brother is hooking up with," Layla complained.

"Right, sorry, I forgot half this table is related to Callum," Noah apologized.

Lydia, on the other hand, looked at Rosie expectantly.

"No, no, I did not fuck him again. Not yet at least," Rosie tried to contain her smirk, but the copious amount of alcohol she'd valiantly fought against earlier was now biting her in the ass. "But, he might possibly have punched Justin in the face and broken his nose because he found out that Justin cheated on me..."

She phrased it more like a question than a statement because she could still hardly believe it herself.

"No shit!?" Elena and Lydia said in unison.

"Ohh, that's hot as fuck," Noah added. "So now you *want* to fuck him again? Is that it?"

"Does that make me a bad person?" Rosie let her face fall into her hands.

"Babe," Noah said affectionately, "it doesn't make you a bad person for being turned on by a hot-ass man defending your honor." She reached across the table, "stop denying what you want. Like a wise person once told me: no one gives a shit who you want to bang," Noah encouraged, draping her hand across Rosie's and squeezing affectionately.

This was her way of telling Rosie she was okay without having to actually say it.

"Okay, then yeah," Rosie admitted. "I want to sleep with Callum again."

It felt good to say out loud—like a weight off her chest. She didn't have to feel bad for wanting what she wanted. *Who* she wanted. And damn, did she want Callum. God, he was so hot.

"I'm just going to pretend we aren't talking about my brother's sex life, but," Elena paused, "I'm glad you're over your hypocritical bullshit, and I think you should go for it."

Rosie scoffed as if she were offended.

"You know I'll always call you out," Elena reminded her.

"And so will I," Noah added. "And as your best friends, we refuse to let you cock-block yourself just because you're too stubborn to admit that you acted like a total hypocrite. Which you *sooo* did."

"God, I'm so horny," Rosie groaned. "I don't think I've *ever* been this horny. And not just because we're at a strip club. I am the world's horniest hippogriff." Fuck, she was drunk. "Hypocrite. Horniest hypocrite."

Just then, one of the bartenders brought out the tray of lemon drop shots Noah had ordered. He eyed Rosie suspiciously, and she realized he had most definitely heard her declaration about being a horny-ass hypocrite.

"I edit sexy novels for a living," Rosie tried explaining. "I—Romance novels, not sexy novels. Well, I mean they are sexy, but, I—I'm sorry," she buried her head in her hands.

Apparently, this was the night for loudly professing their sex lives in a public place. Oh well, blame whatever the hell was in those fishbowls earlier.

Lydia casually slid her shot glass to Layla who eagerly downed it.

Rosie had the fleeting thought that she probably shouldn't drink anything else. God forbid she did something stupid like actually *text* Callum to tell him that she was a stupid hypocrite and wanted to fuck him. Like really, really wanted to fuck him. So badly.

"To us against the world, even after you get married," Noah held her shot glass up in salute.

If it hadn't already been obvious that Noah was drunk, that would have given it away. She was never this outwardly sentimental.

"Wait, you guys don't have shots!" Noah protested, glancing toward Lydia and Layla. "We need more shots!"

"I gave mine to Layla," Lydia explained. "We're good. Have your bestie moment."

Layla gave a thumbs up in agreement.

"Also, I thought we said no more shots for you, Noh?" Rosie tried to snatch the glass from her hand.

"Oh, fuck off, I'm trying to be sentimental," Noah slapped her hand away.

"I love you guys," Elena smiled. "So fucking much. You know that, right?"

"So fucking much," Rosie confirmed, grabbing Elena's hand from across the table.

With her other, she raised her shot glass to Noah's.

"To the world against us! To us—to the world! Fuck, you get what I'm trying to say," Elena clinked her glass with theirs.

Why was taking shots supposed to be a bad idea? Rosie honestly couldn't think of a single reason as she downed the lemon drop shot. As she felt the liquid slide down her throat, she did, however, think about how badly she wanted Callum's cock there instead. Which was way more than she wanted to hold onto her pride.

Grabbing her phone from her purse, she entered her password.

Callum:

Rather than a strip club, Cole had wanted to do a Brewery Crawl for his bachelor party, which Callum was secretly grateful for. He understood the appeal of a strip club, sure, but they were so loud and made talking nearly impossible. For that reason, he was glad that Cole had chosen something else; it gave the groomsmen the chance to actually talk to one another tonight since most of them hadn't met before that night.

Words I Should Have Said

Having no brothers of his own, Cole had taken an instant liking to Callum after the first family dinner Elena had brought him to. As it was with every significant other of a Costello sibling, you became a part of the family; his parents always said, 'we don't have sons or daughters-in-law, we just have more kids to love.' Cole had been a great friend to Callum ever since, and an even better partner to Elena, and he was incredibly happy for them.

They were currently at their third brewery of the night, a cool place with outdoor seating and cornhole set up. Callum ordered the local IPA the place had on draft, which was pretty good. There were an odd number of groomsmen, so Callum had volunteered to sit the first round of cornhole out. Liam, Callum's younger and only biological brother, was teamed up with Hayden; they were up against Cole and his coworker, Nathan.

Though Callum had only known him for a few hours, Nathan seemed like a super nice guy. He worked with Cole in the IT department of their company. The fifth groomsman, Cole's college roommate, Ben, wasn't able to make it to the bachelor party since he'd moved to North Carolina after graduation; Callum was looking forward to meeting him at the wedding.

Taking another sip of his beer as he watched Liam and Hayden obliterate Cole and Nathan, Callum felt his phone vibrate in his pocket. The last thing he expected was to find a text from Rosie. He entered his password and clicked on the message.

> Rosie: Fine. I wasam a hypocrite.
> Hornypocrite. Ru happy?

Callum knew that Rosie was out with the rest of the bridesmaids for Elena's bachelorette party tonight, and, based on what he'd overheard from Rosie and Noah's planning at Lafayette's, the evening involved *a lot* of drinking. That combined with Rosie's slurred spelling was enough to tell him that she was most definitely shitfaced. And as happy as he was that she was finally admitting that she'd been hypocritical in her reasoning for refusing to sleep with him again, this wasn't a conversation he wanted to have with Rosie while she was drunk. Before he could start typing a response, his phone vibrated with another text, this one from Noah.

> Noah: Look, 'm not trying to get in the middle of anything, but Rosie is with the Fishes Bowl and some shots.

> Noah: Not more than four. I don't think.

> Noah: Definitely more than two.

> Noah: Three?

> Noah: Idkfuck math. 'm drunk.

> Noah: Point is: knowshe texted you. She means it, but she wouldn't have said anything if she was'nt shittyfaced.

> Noah: Trying too say: b careful.

Damn, Callum didn't think anyone had ever sent him that many texts in a row, and that included Lilah. *And* his mother when she was pissed about something. They must all be fucked up. He typed out a response to Noah.

> Callum: Yeah, it didn't take much to figure out that she'd had a lot to drink, but thanks Noh. I appreciate the heads up.

> Noah: What gonna say?

> Noah: PS rooting for you.
>
> Noah: PSS Do NOT tell Rosie I said that.
>
> Noah: She'd kill me, and I verymuch wann be alive.
>
> Noah: If you do I will blame the tequila.
>
> Noah: Nooo, the vodka.

Callum found it endearing that Noah was secretly rooting for things to go back to normal between him and Rosie. He hoped that she was secretly rooting for Rosie to sleep with him again too.

> Callum: That I do still want to talk to her about everything, but not like this.
>
> Noah: Look at that? Chivalry isn'dead after all.

Callum hearted her message, then swiped out of his text thread with Noah, clicking on the one with Rosie instead. He replied to her with the hope that she'd reach out to him in the morning once she'd had a chance to revisit her confession while sober.

> Callum: This conversation is far from over, Rosie, but it's not one I am willing to have with you if you aren't sober.
>
> Rosie: Ur too young to b such a fucky duddy
>
> Rosie: Fuddy daddy
>
> Rosie: I giv up

Liam sat down next to Callum, reminding him of his surroundings. The round of cornhole must have ended.

"Who are you talking to?" Liam asked casually.

"Rosie," Callum answered, offering no context. "Well, Rosie and Noah."

"Figures," Liam smirked.

"Been talking to Hayden, have you?" Callum joked, remembering how Hayden had seen straight through Callum's attempts to conceal his interest in Rosie just a few short weeks ago.

"Nah, just observant," Liam answered. "Why? Does Hayden think you're secretly pining after her too?"

Liam cracked a full-blown smile at that, which Callum promptly elbowed him for.

"Listen, all I'm saying is the two of you are far too comfortable with one another for it not to mean anything," Liam pointed out. "Plus, I love Rosie. She goes through life never apologizing for who she is. She's got this 'take me or leave me, but I won't change who I am for you' aura about her, and I really admire it. You could definitely do worse."

Callum knew Liam was right. He definitely could do worse, but it wasn't as if he could entertain the idea of actually dating Rosie. She might not be off limits physically, but there was no way he could actually entertain the idea of dating his sister's best friend, right?

12

WHAT GOES DOWN, MUST COME UP?

Rosie:

ROSIE'S first semi-conscious thought was concern about what the hell she must have hit her head on last night for it to be hurting like such a bitch right now. Her first fully conscious thought was that she needed to get to a toilet immediately because she was about four seconds from projectile vomiting up the fish bowl and who knew how many shots she'd downed last night.

Ah, that explained the headache.

Flinging the sheets off and practically leaping to the bathroom, Rosie made it to the toilet just in time for neon blue stomach fluid to make its way from her stomach. Rosie hadn't been projectile-vomiting drunk in months, and this was a painful reminder of exactly why she usually didn't let herself drink enough to be.

Attempting to recount last night's events, Rosie remembered walking into the strip club, lemon drop shots, and... texting someone? She'd been out with her two best friends, so who would she have been texting? Unless... Oh fuck, surely she wouldn't have drunk texted Call—

Her train of thought was cut off as more neon blue liquid came up and into the toilet.

Suddenly, Noah was behind her holding her hair up.

"Hey babe, how are you doing?"

Wiping her mouth with toilet paper and flushing, Rosie managed a groan and a "been better."

"So, how much of last night do you remember, exactly?" Noah asked.

"Not a thing after walking into the strip club."

"Oh boy," Noah sighed hesitantly.

"Well, I vaguely remember texting someone, but I don't know who I would have texted. You and Elena were both with me."

"Wager a guess."

"No. Please tell me no," Rosie attempted to stand up to look for her phone.

"Uh-uh. You keep the porcelain pony company. I'll bring you your phone and a glass of water," Noah looked Rosie up and down, "and some aspirin."

After a few minutes of seriously combing through her memories on the tile floor of the bathroom, Rosie concluded that she remembered talking about Callum with Noah, which must have been the reason she texted him. But what had she said?

"Drink," Noah handed her a glass of water. "Good girl, now swallow," Noah prompted Rosie by holding out two aspirin in her hand.

"You sound like the love interests in my smutty romance novels," Rosie smirked up at Noah.

"Ooh a sex joke," Noah laughed. "You must not feel as shitty as you look."

"Ouch," Rosie laughed in return. "Wait, why aren't you on the floor with me? You had just as much to drink as I did."

"True, but last night me did future me a favor by eating some bread and downing a shit ton of water and two aspirin before going to sleep, so."

"Ugh, why didn't you feed me bread?"

"Oh, I tried. You slapped the bread out of my hand and flung it across my kitchen," Noah snorted.

"I'm sorry?" Rosie started to laugh but immediately regretted it when the movement had her leaning over the toilet once again.

Seriously, how was there *anything* left?

"Okay, listen," Noah said as she passed Rosie her phone. "Before you open your messages, allow me to give you some context. We were a fish bowl and who knows how many shots deep. We were talking about the wedding, and Callum came up. You decided it was drunk confession hour, and you informed us about how sexy it was that he defended your honor by decking Justin in the face. You told me, and I quote, 'I am the world's horniest hypocrite.'"

"Oh, God. What did I text him? Not those exact words I hope?" Rosie asked hesitantly.

"Uh, not... exactly. There were a lot of typos," Noah shrugged.

"Great," Rosie muttered sarcastically, reaching out her hand for her phone. "Let me see."

"Finish that glass of water first. Hangover-recovery duty takes precedence over best friend duty."

With a middle finger held in Noah's face, Rosie chugged the rest of the water in the glass. Grabbing her phone from Noah, Rosie entered the password and opened her messages with Callum to see the damage.

> Rosie: Fine. I wasam a hypocrite. Hornypocrite. Areyou happy?

Off to a great start, apparently. At least the conversation didn't appear to be a long one. She scrolled to read Callum's reply.

> Callum: This conversation is far from over, Rosie, but it's not one I am willing to have with you if you aren't sober.

Oh? Callum had done nothing for the past few weeks besides incessantly plead his case with Rosie. Evidently, he genuinely cared about clearing the air and not just potentially getting her back into bed. That was... interesting? And confusing. Especially combined with the whole punching Justin in the face incident that she still hadn't fully processed.

Rosie wasn't quite sure how she felt about everything, but... it wasn't bad.

She scrolled to read the rest of the conversation. She had tried, and failed, to coerce Callum into continuing the conversation, but he hadn't replied beyond that one message. Evidently drunk Rosie realized the rarity in Callum's sincerity, because she hadn't texted him anything else. As far as blackout-drunk texts go, it could have been worse. Much worse.

"So?" Noah raised her eyebrows dramatically, reminding Rosie of her presence.

"Please, like you didn't already go through these while I was passed the hell out," Rosie kicked Noah's leg teasingly.

"Well, obviously," Noah kicked back. "I'm waiting to hear how you feel about Callum's reply."

"Honestly? I don't know. It's way more sincere than I was

expecting. I would have thought he would've taken this as his in to try and hook up again."

"The two of you might not have any intention of dating, but there's more between you than just hooking up. You're friends."

All essence of humor had dissipated from Noah's tone.

"I guess I've just never thought about it that way. We don't talk about things like this. Never have. Never needed to."

"That doesn't mean it would be a bad thing. Especially since we're all gonna be stuck in a beach house together in a week."

"Fair enough. Now, help me off this cold ass tile and feed me something to absorb the literal death swirling around in my stomach right now," Rosie reached up to Noah who peeled her up off of the floor.

Talking about the wedding brought forth another memory from the night before: Noah had told Rosie and Elena that Lilah had been her gay awakening. There had also been something about Cupid?

"Take a shower while I make waffles," Noah instructed while turning on the faucet, "and brush your teeth before *I* start hurling too."

"Hey, wait! Are we not going to talk about *your* drunk confession, too?" Rosie smirked but was careful not to laugh this time.

"I have absolutely no idea what you're talking about," Noah declared.

With a wink, she was out the door and headed to the kitchen.

Rosie wasn't going to let Noah off the hook that easily, but she knew she needed to shower and eat something before she would be in any position to play matchmaker.

While Rosie waited for the water to heat up, she replied to Callum. Then she dragged herself into the shower and focused on not throwing up again.

Callum:

Callum rolled over and stretched his arm out toward his nightstand, feeling around for his phone. After his eyes adjusted to the brightness of the screen, he realized that Rosie had texted him.

If she'd been fucked up enough to text him that she was a horny hypocrite last night, he imagined she probably wasn't feeling too great this morning. Well, technically she'd called herself a 'hornypocrite,' but close enough. Callum snorted to himself while unlocking his phone.

> Rosie: I'm sober. I feel like I got hit by a semi-truck, but I'm ready to talk about things.
>
> Rosie: Lafayette's tonight?

Callum wasn't sure exactly what he was expecting her text to say, but finally giving him space to clear the air between them was honestly the best-case scenario. He decided to keep his response light-hearted.

> Callum: Sure you want to step foot in a bar after last night?

Depending on the state of her hangover, she would either be amused or want to bite his head off. Either worked for Callum. Rosie was somehow even more attractive when she was riled up about something.

> Rosie: Very funny.
>
> Rosie: Sevenish?

Callum decided to stick to the hangover jokes.

> Callum: See you at sevenish. Maybe eat some bread or something first?
>
> Callum: I don't particularly feel like being thrown up on.

Callum couldn't remember the last time a day had passed so slowly. He'd filled the rest of the morning and early afternoon working out, tending to his overflowing pile of laundry, and taking a trip to the grocery store. Finally, evening crawled around.

Callum had put a little more thought than usual into his outfit. He told himself it was to look as irresistible as possible, but really, he found himself wanting to look nice for this conversation with Rosie. He so rarely had these sincere kinds of conversations, so he figured he'd dress the part, which ended up being his nicest pair of jeans, a black henley, and his Doc 1461s. It was July, but with the evening breeze and lack of sun, Callum figured he'd be alright in the henley.

Pulling into the parking deck closest to Lafayette's just before seven, Callum started the walk to the bar. A cool breeze was rolling over the people on the street, carried in from the Cooper River just a few streets over. Nights like this were one of the reasons Callum couldn't see himself living anywhere other than Charleston—when the unforgiving summer sun melted from the sky, shrouding the silhouette of the Arthur Ravenel in the richest shades of orange, red, and pink. Though Callum's favorite view was from the other side of the bridge, looking into downtown from Shem Creek, a Charleston sunset held a magic of its own no matter the vantage point.

As he walked inside, he texted Rosie to let her know that he would be waiting at her usual table. It was a Sunday evening, so hardly anyone was inside.

A few minutes later, Rosie's silhouette came into view.

"Hey," she smiled softly, almost nervously.

"Hey," Callum smiled back. "Feeling better than this morning I hope?"

"Considering I'm not laying on the cold tile floor of Noah's bathroom anymore," Rosie laughed as she sat down, "I'd say so."

"So," Callum muttered nervously.

Why was he nervous? Clearing the air was step one to getting Rosie to sleep with him again and he'd never been nervous about *that* before.

"So," Rosie raised her eyebrows at him across the table, "you wanted to explain, so... um, explain, I guess?"

"Well, uh, obviously we both know that I broke up with Olivia right before you came over," Callum hesitated, waiting to see Rosie's reaction.

"Yep. Sure do."

Her face was the picture of indifference. Not exactly helpful.

"Uh, well basically I just wanted to explain how everything happened," he continued, testing the waters.

All Rosie did was stare back at him with raised eyebrows as if to say, 'Go on.'

"I didn't break up with her just to sleep with you. Things between us weren't exactly serious, we had hardly anything in common, and Hayden kept going on and on about how I was basically leading her on and clearly wasn't happy in the relat—"

"Wait huh? What does Hayden have to do with this?"

"Oh, we were on dish duty at family dinner that night. He called me out for only volunteering to help him to get a few minutes of space from Olivia. Said that I wasn't serious about her and basically insinuated that I was stringing her along."

"Ah," was all Rosie offered in response, but gestured for Callum to continue.

"Walking back into the room with everyone, I realized how all the couples seemed to constantly feel the need to show each other affection, and that I didn't feel that way about Olivia at all. That's when I realized that I *was* stringing her along, which wasn't fair to her. Then you texted me, and, well, we both know what happened from there."

Rosie just stared at him from across the table, but she didn't seem angry. He guessed that was a decent enough sign to keep going.

"You texting me just gave me the push to actually end things with Olivia. And yeah, maybe that makes me an ass, and yeah I'm sure she didn't feel great about it, but at least I didn't string her even farther along and break her heart or some shit later on."

"You made it seem like you'd broken up with her a few days or weeks before that night," was Rosie's only response to everything Callum had said.

"That's not entirely fair, Rosie. You could have asked how recently if you'd really cared that much. Besides, as your blackout drunk self already said, you were being hypocritical."

Callum wasn't exactly sure if his pushback would anger Rosie, but that wasn't going to stop him. If she was allowed to show up at his apartment and fuck him the same night she'd ended a relationship, he was sure as shit allowed to have been the one to open the door.

"I think I actually called myself a *horny* hypocrite, but yeah," Rosie snorted. "Yeah, it was hypocritical of me. And for the record, Noah called me out for that weeks ago. I think she's secretly rooting for us to hook up again."

Callum already knew that, but he had promised Noah he wouldn't say anything about it to Rosie. And he intended to keep that promise.

"And you?" Callum pushed his luck further.

"I know that I'm not mad anymore and I was wrong to ever have been. I was angry with Justin, and I took that out on you. I'm sorry. You didn't deserve that, and I need you to know that *I* know that you aren't him..." Rosie reached her arm across the table to lay her hand across Callum's, "that you aren't Justin."

"Thank you, Rosie," Callum squeezed her hand back.

"As far as hooking up, I... don't know."

"'I don't know' isn't the same as no," Callum stated, more as a question than an observation.

'I don't know' was a far cry from Rosie's former declaration that she would absolutely not be sleeping with him, *ever* again. Still, it wasn't a yes. It wasn't consent. Callum brushed his leg against Rosie's under the table, and she didn't pull away.

"No, it's not," she agreed, the faintest hint of a smirk pulling at the corner of her lips.

"So," Callum smirked back. "Where does that leave us?" His lips flattened into a more genuine smile.

"Nowhere until after the wedding. With less than a week to go, I just want to focus on Elena and my Maid of Honor duties. After that..."

"After that?" Callum encouraged her to finish her sentence by grazing her ankle with his under the table.

"After that, I'm not taking anything off the table."

"Well, in that case, I make no apologies for any shameless flirting that may or may not occur until then," Callum made a gesture that was supposed to say 'smell the roses' and laughed. "It's a wedding, sex is in the air."

"I would expect nothing less from you, Costello."

If she was calling him Costello and sex was neither on nor off the table, then everything was back to normal between the two of them. And Mission Shamelessly Flirt Your Way Back Between Rosie's Legs was a go.

"In the spirit of being upfront about everything from here on out, there's one other thing you should know," Callum hesitated. He wasn't sure if Rosie knew about him punching Justin, but he wasn't going to risk leaving anything else unspoken between them. "I might have, uh, possibly, punched Justin in the face when I found out that he'd cheated on you..."

Rosie laughed harder than Callum had seen her laugh in a while. Though he didn't understand *why* she was laughing, he was glad to be the cause. She deserved to laugh after the shitty past few weeks she'd had. He especially loved that he was the one making her laugh.

"Not exactly the reaction I was expecting," Callum laughed too.

"Justin texted me later that night to inform me that you'd broken his nose. He didn't bother to respond to the earlier messages Noah had sent from my phone with blatant evidence of his cheating, but his bitch ass made time to tell me about his poor, broken nose. As if I'd give a shit," Rosie kept laughing.

"So you're *not* mad?" Callum almost couldn't believe it.

Obviously, the dickhead deserved it, but still. It wasn't exactly his place to have gotten in the middle of their shit.

"Are you kidding?" Rosie looked shocked. "My only regret is that I wasn't there to see it. Too bad you don't have community service hours to fill, or you could log that as an act of public service."

"Well, that went better than expected," Callum relaxed.

"If we're being honest," Rosie's cheeks flushed.

Callum leaned forward, incredibly interested in whatever was about to come out of her mouth.

"I, uh... No one has ever defended my honor like that, and it was..." Rosie hesitated. "I'm just glad I own a lot of, um, toys."

Jesus fucking Christ. That was not what Callum needed to hear in a very public, very crowded place, where he wouldn't be able to adjust the hard-on he'd definitely just gotten from hearing Rosie talk about her vibrators. Callum had never understood why men hated sex toys. If it helped get your girl off, why would you not be for it? Hearing Rosie talk about hers while thinking of him made him feel a little less guilty for jerking off into the lacey thong she'd tucked into his pocket on her way out of his apartment a few weeks ago. None of this, however, helped get rid of the boner he was now sporting.

Yeah, Mission Shamelessly Flirt Your Way Back Between Rosie's Legs was *definitely* a go.

13

BUSH TO BUSH

Rosie:

"Okay, Rosemary, now this is where you'll grab Elena's bouquet, which you'll hold for the duration of the ceremony," Haley, the wedding planner, explained.

Rosie practiced the movement, grabbing the prop from Elena in place of the actual bouquets she'd be holding tomorrow.

"Everyone else, remember: bush to bush! I know it feels unnatural, but I promise you want to hold those flowers low or you'll look like you're hiding from the guests."

To Rosie's right, Noah snickered at the expression.

"Sh!" Rosie elbowed her. "I have way more directions than you! I can't afford to half-ass my way through this."

"Sorry, but you have to admit that it's funny as fuck. C'mon, bush to bush?" Noah laughed but remained quiet for the rest of the time.

"And when you hear, 'you may now kiss the bride,' that's your cue to take your flowers back from Rosie," Haley explained to Elena.

"Got it," Elena acknowledged.

"After the kiss, Elena and Cole will walk back up the aisle together, then each bridesmaid and groomsman pair will follow in the same order you walked down once the pair in front of you has reached the marker."

Haley made sure to make eye contact with each of the bridesmaids and groomsmen to ensure they were paying attention.

"Alright, let's practice the exit and then we'll run the whole thing again from start to finish."

That meant Rosie would be arm-in-arm with Callum another three times this afternoon at *least*. So far, he'd been the picture of cool indifference, but she was waiting for him to fulfill his promise of shameless flirting any time now. The anticipation threatened to kill her.

As Elena and Cole started up the aisle, Haley added, "remember not to walk too fast, to look straight ahead, and to smile."

As Rosie stepped toward the center of the platform, her eyes met Callum's. He extended his arm to her which she looped her own through. Rosie was glad that Elena had chosen for the bridesmaids to forgo shoes; she couldn't imagine trying to hold the bouquet, Callum's arm, *and* trudge through sand in heels all without tripping. She focused on holding the prop that would be a bouquet tomorrow at the right position.

Callum must have sensed her concentration because he didn't taunt or tease her the whole walk back up the aisle. Rosie didn't know what to make of a well-behaved Callum, didn't know how to act around him when he wasn't flirting with her.

Once they reached the end of the aisle, Rosie leaned

closer to Callum and playfully whispered, "What happened to all the shameless flirting I was promised?"

"Vibrator not doing it for you, huh?" Callum murmured back.

There was the Callum she knew and loved. *Woah, loved?* The Callum she knew and loved *bantering with*. That was more like it.

"Not particularly," Rosie sighed.

She'd said nothing would happen between them until after the wedding, but that didn't mean that she couldn't flirt her way to the finish line.

"Shame. If only there were something you could do about that," Callum's eyes swept across the span of her body longingly.

More like some*one* she could do about that.

"If only," she sighed.

Callum:

Several hours after the rehearsal was over, Callum found himself sitting across from Rosie at the restaurant that Elena and Cole had chosen for their rehearsal dinner. It was an elevated seafood restaurant, and Cole's family had rented out the entire place for the evening, complete with complimentary choices of wine and beer. Callum couldn't begin to imagine how much it must be costing them, but he definitely wasn't complaining.

Callum had brought Lilah as his plus one, which put her to his right and directly across from Noah who was sitting to Rosie's left.

Callum wasn't quite sure how he was supposed to act

around Rosie now. He had planned to be nothing but respectful and stay out of Rosie's way until the ceremony ended, which was exactly what he'd done so far. Well, except for his earlier vibrator comment, but Rosie had started that so could he really be held responsible?

When they ran through the ceremony a final two times, Callum had reverted back to respectful and distant, making sure he knew his cue for passing the rings to Cole. Rosie had seemed almost... disappointed by that?

What happened to all the shameless flirting I was promised? she had asked.

That was more than a little interesting, given the solemnity with which she had told him that nothing could happen between them until after the wedding. Had she changed her mind, or did she simply enjoy the banter as much as he did? The easy way they fell into teasing one another?

Before Callum could fall further into his thoughts, a server came by and placed copies of the evening's limited menu on the table. Calamari would be served as an appetizer alongside a crab & spinach dip appetizer. For the main course, they would be choosing between a grilled salmon with a barbeque glaze, crab legs, or shrimp and grits.

"What are you thinking?" Callum asked Lilah, angling the menu so that they could both read it.

"Crab legs on someone else's dime sounds like the logical choice to me," Lilah pointed out.

"Fair enough," Callum laughed.

"I've had the barbeque salmon here before," Rosie chimed in from across the table. "It's fucking incredible."

"I'm with Lilah," Noah said, not quite directed at Lilah. "Crab is delicious, but you won't catch me paying for it myself."

Callum swore there might have been a trace of apprehension in her voice, which was so unlike her. Noah was always forward, always bold. Lilah barely acknowledged Noah's comment, only bothering to offer her a repressed smile.

"You good, Lih?" Callum asked quietly as everyone continued perusing the menu.

"Great," she answered unconvincingly.

"I mean I know you haven't seen most of these people in person in a few years, but you're unusually quiet," Callum pressed.

As if to prove Callum wrong, Lilah turned her attention to Rosie.

"So, Rosie, I'm assuming you took my advice?"

What advice?

"I did, yeah," Rosie answered, eyes briefly meeting Callum's before she turned back to Lilah. "Thanks for not sugarcoating."

"Anytime," Lilah replied.

Had Lilah and Rosie talked about him? If so, why wouldn't Lilah have told him about it? Callum was suddenly very jealous of a woman's ability to 'need an escort' to the bathroom just to have the excuse to talk in private. To Rosie's right, Noah also looked confused. At least Callum wasn't the only person that had been left out of this conversation.

"Can I offer anyone a glass of wine?" a server asked, holding an ice bucket with several bottles.

"What variety of white do you have?" Rosie asked.

"Pinot Grigio, Sauvignon Blanc, or Riesling, ma'am."

"I'll take Pinot Grigio please," Rosie told the server.

Noah predictably asked for Rosé. Callum and Lilah elected to wait for the beer options.

After the server left the table, Rosie said, "If you *ever* see me drinking a riesling, something has gone severely wrong."

"God, I swear, never again," Elena chimed in from further down the table.

"Top three worst nights of my life," Noah agreed.

"Wait, what am I missing?" Cole asked.

"Back in high school, these three drank an entire bottle of riesling in under two hours *each* and spent the rest of the night taking turns with their head in the toilet," Callum laughed at the memory.

"I'm just glad we weren't at my house or Rosie's," Noah snorted. "There would not have been enough bathrooms."

"The perks of having a fuck ton of siblings," Elena laughed.

Callum thought back to that night. Even in their near-blackout state, the three of them had been so desperate to avoid waking up his parents that they'd pleaded with Callum to let someone use his bathroom in the basement. He'd spent his night holding back Rosie's hair as the bottle of wine she'd drank found its way back out of her stomach.

Eventually, when he was sure there was absolutely nothing left to throw up, Callum had brought her a bottle of water, two ibuprofen, and some toast before insisting that she take his bed for the night. He definitely hadn't been as helpful to Noah, let alone his own sister. And as far as he knew, Rosie had never said anything about it to them. As if they had a mutual understanding that his taking care of her had to remain a secret.

Even at fifteen, Callum understood that Rosie was off limits as anything more than a secret friend with benefits. Should his parents find out that something was going on between the two of them, she wouldn't be welcome to have sleepovers with Elena anymore. Sure, he might have kept things secret out of his own self-interest, but he'd kept the secret nonetheless.

"Why was riesling even an option for tonight?" Noah asked Elena, still laughing hysterically. "Just feels like tempting fate."

"In my defense, it's a popular white, and we needed something sweeter than Pinot Grigio."

"Any other triggering drinks I should be aware of?" Cole teased.

"Don't give her tequila," Rosie warned.

"Unless you're in the mooood," Noah teased, raising her eyebrows dramatically.

"Both of you, shut up!" Elena jokingly scolded.

As the meal was wrapping up, Rosie kicked Callum's ankle under the table to get his attention.

"We need to give our speeches, but I don't know how to get everyone's attention without yelling."

Before Callum had the chance to respond, Noah began clinking her knife against her water glass like a chime. Evidently, that only worked in movies because on the third clink, a piece of the glass fractured, falling in on itself. Everyone was now staring at Noah, whose cheeks turned bright red.

"Well, that's one way to do it," Rosie whispered, clearly trying to contain a laugh.

"For the love of God, one of you start giving your speech so people will stop staring at me," Noah whispered-yelled at the both of them.

"I'll go first," Rosie offered in Callum's direction.

Callum made the mistake of allowing his eyes to roam

over the length of her body as she walked toward the front of the room where everyone would be able to hear her. She wore a sage green floral print dress that cut low in the front and laid perfectly over her curves as it flowed down to her mid-calf. Having four sisters, Callum knew that women often used some kind of magical boob adhesive to keep them in place in dresses with non-traditional necklines, but there was absolutely no way Rosie was wearing anything under this dress—a fact that Callum found entirely too distracting.

Callum needed to muster up the willpower to look somewhere other than her tits because, in just a few minutes, he would be the one standing at the front of the room. And a hard-on didn't exactly say 'happy wedding big sis!'

To his right, Lilah leaned into his ear and sighed, "I'm no better than a man."

"Oh, fuck off," Callum said as he elbowed her. "We both know she's not your type," he teased as he looked from Lilah to an oblivious Noah across the table.

Callum still hadn't broached the idea of setting the two of them up, but he'd paid enough attention to notice how many times Lilah had glanced longingly across the table tonight.

"Yeah? And who is?" Lilah responded defensively.

Before Callum could answer, Rosie began addressing the guests, immediately captivating.

"So, I didn't write this out beforehand because the whole scripted thing is just not my style, so please forgive the potential rambling I might be subjecting you to as a result," Rosie joked as she stood up from her chair to address the room. "But, uh, here goes nothing."

"When I was sixteen years old, I met a girl named Elena

Costello who made me whole in a way I had never thought I would experience."

Rosie smiled in Elena's direction, and Callum swore he could see her eyes watering.

"It took all of two conversations in English class for Elena to insist that we hang out at her house after school. She opened not only her heart to me but her home as well. From the first moment that I walked through the Costello's front door, I was treated as one of their own. Elena showed me what a family could be; she taught me that, just because the family you were born with doesn't know how to love you, doesn't mean you can't find one that will."

Rosie was now crying softly. She let out a small sniffle before continuing.

"I will never be able to express how grateful I am for you, Elena Costello. You gave me the greatest gift I could have ever asked for, the thing I always longed for: a family that loves me without reservation, for exactly who I am."

As Callum's gaze shifted from Rosie to Elena, he noticed that his mom was wiping a tear from her cheek too. His whole family truly did love her as their own.

"Elena, you are endearment personified. You touch the lives of everyone around you, making sure they know that they matter. Getting to watch as you opened your heart to Cole, as your lives grew further and further intertwined, as he became your family has brought me an insurmountable amount of joy. And I know that one day when the two of you start your own family, your children will know without a trace of certainty just how loved they are. Oh, and Cole, I know she's technically yours now, but Noah and I still fully intend to steal her for girls' night once a week," Rosie laughed.

"I would expect nothing less," Cole acknowledged, smiling.

"I could not be happier for the two of you. Here's to your love; may it always remain abundant," Rosie raised her glass. "Cheers to the Scotts!"

For someone who claimed to be winging it, that was one hell of a speech. It wasn't like Callum was unaware that Rosie worked in publishing, but damn was he impressed. And also a bit nervous to follow.

Before he had time to dwell on the feeling, he was being nudged to stand.

"Damn, I really should have gone first, huh?" Callum started, trying to calm his nerves. "That's nearly impossible to follow, but I'll try."

Self-deprecating humor was easy to fall into. It was familiar. Comfortable.

"I want to start with an observation, and I promise there's a point to it, so stick with me here. Cole, man, in case you hadn't noticed: this family is full of women. The Costello men are severely outnumbered."

Cole laughed, along with most of the guests in the room. That was good. Making people laugh was something Callum knew he was good at. Eliciting genuine emotion from them, not so much. Even if the second part of his speech flopped, at least people would remember that he had been funny.

"I really thought things were looking up for us when Hayden and Lydia got married, but then they went and had a daughter."

Callum jokingly shook his head at the couple across the table as if to say 'shame on you.'

"Don't get me wrong, Willow is the cutest kid to ever grace the Earth, but she's not exactly helping our numbers now is she?" Callum continued. "With the addition of Cole to the family, however, the women only have us beat five to *four*. So thank you for marrying my sister and inadvertently making us a little less outnumbered."

Callum feigned returning to his seat just for a second before moving into what he actually wanted to say.

"All jokes aside, one of the best things to ever happen to me was growing up surrounded by women who knew their worth, and men who made sure they never forgot it. The fact that Elena chose you, Cole, told me everything I needed to know about the kind of man you are before I had the chance to get to know you and see it for myself. I couldn't imagine a better partner for Elena."

Callum raised his glass in Cole's direction—a wordless exchange that conveyed all the emotion Callum didn't know how to properly express.

"To you and Elena. My brother and my sister. I'm a better person for knowing you both."

14

PLAN CUPID

Rosie:

EVERYONE HAD DROPPED their bags off at the beach house this morning before heading down the street to the venue for the rehearsal but hadn't had any time to unpack. It was a massive, two-story house complete with twelve bedrooms, four and a half bathrooms, and a full bar. The bridesmaids would take the top floor with the kitchen, the groomsmen the bottom with the bar.

Because there were just enough bedrooms for each member of the bridal party to have their own, plus ones would be sharing rooms with their partners; the only exception would be Hayden and Lydia since they were each part of the bridal party. Rosie refused to allow herself to consider how much relief she felt at the fact that Callum had chosen to bring Lilah as his plus one rather than a date he could have easily managed to get. She definitely refused to let herself wonder whether Callum felt the same sense of relief at the fact that she'd shown up without a plus one at all.

Tomorrow night, after the wedding, Elena and Cole

would be staying in a cozy, one-bedroom beachfront cottage before leaving for their honeymoon the next morning. But for tonight, it would be Rosie and Callum's job to keep Elena and Cole on their respective floors.

"So, what do we do when we want a drink? Why did we give the floor with the bar to the boys?" Lydia asked.

"We place orders with the bartender," Rosie joked.

"Plus, we have the more important part of the house: the kitchen," Elena pointed out. "The boys might have the alcohol, but we have the oven and, with it, the ability to make midnight bagel bites."

"Oh, *now* you want to drink, Lydia?" Noah crossed her arms in defiance as she bounded into the kitchen from the hallway. "You wouldn't even take shots with us at the bachelorette party."

"Willow is with her grandparents until after the ceremony tomorrow, which means I won't be woken up at the ass crack of dawn to a squealing toddler," Lydia defended herself. "I'm sure Callum will have Hayden drunk in less than an hour. The two of us never get a night to let loose anymore."

"In that case, let's take shots!" Noah cheered.

"I'll go tell the bartender," Rosie smirked and headed for the stairs to the bottom floor of the house.

Halfway down the stairs, she could already feel the bass vibrating through the floor. It figured that the groomsmen would think to drink first, unpack later.

She headed down the hallway at the bottom of the stairs to the left where Callum was currently mixing a drink. He'd changed into sweatpants and a t-shirt that was currently riding up just enough that she could see those deep v-lines of his disappearing into the waistband of his pants. Did he have to be so distractingly attractive?

As she approached the countertop, Callum smirked at her as if he knew she'd been looking. That was fine. Lucky for her, she hadn't had time to change out of her dress from the rehearsal dinner, and she knew just how much Callum loved her tits.

"I'm here to place an order," Rosie said sweetly, making sure to lean forward on the countertop to accentuate her chest.

Callum's eyes dipped down to her chest for a fleeting moment, but long enough for Rosie to know her plan was working.

"What can I make for you, sweetheart?" he asked sensuously.

Fuck, this was going to be a long night. She supposed she'd asked for it earlier.

What happened to all the shameless flirting I was promised?

"The bridesmaids have requested shots."

"Of?"

"Mmmm," she drew out the sound, "surprise me, Mr. Bartender."

While Callum busied himself mixing the shots, Lilah sidled up next to Rosie. She quickly adjusted her posture like a child who had almost been caught with their hand in the cookie jar.

The last time Rosie had spoken to Lilah, she'd been called out for her blatant hypocrisy. Now, she was very obviously flirting with the same man she had said was off-limits until the wedding was over right in front of Lilah. What the hell was she doing?

"How are things going upstairs?" Lilah asked Rosie.

"Pretty tame right now, though I don't think that'll last very long with Costello as bartender."

"He does tend to pour with a heavy hand," Lilah laughed.

"Most people find that to be a good thing," Callum interjected. "You can't honestly say you prefer a skimpy bartender."

Lilah rolled her eyes, ignoring him.

"So, how are things?" Rosie asked, returning her attention to Lilah.

She had every intention to play matchmaker with her and Noah, but she needed an in that wasn't so overt.

"Good. Busy," Lilah answered. "I'm currently managing a restoration project downtown that's been a real pain in the ass," she sighed. "Don't get me wrong though, it's a real labor of love—just, heavy emphasis on the labor part right now."

"What's it going to be when it's finished?"

"A local coffee spot. You should come check it out when it's finished—Callum mentioned that he's hardly ever seen you without a cup of coffee."

Callum noticed she was never without coffee, did he? How *very* interesting of him.

"Tequila sunrise shots," Callum placed five glasses down in front of Rosie on the counter. "You should help Rosie carry them up, Lih."

Lilah flashed Callum a look Rosie couldn't quite interpret, but scooped up three of the shot glasses and headed for the hallway anyway.

"I know it's been a few years since we've all hung out together," Rosie started to say as they started up the stairs.

"More like just shy of a decade."

Damn, had it really been that long?

"I could have sworn we were all at Harper's eleventh birthday party a few years back?" Rosie clarified.

"Not everyone," Lilah took a deep breath. "Noah wasn't there."

Everything started to click into place: Callum's suggestion that Lilah help Rosie carry the shots up, Lilah's exasperated but not quite angry expression in response, and her very quick observation that she hadn't seen Noah in a decade...

Was Lilah just as interested in Noah? Rosie could *definitely* work with that.

As the two of them crested the top of the stairs, they heard quite the commotion coming from the living room. Passing through the kitchen and making their way toward everyone, Rosie saw that they'd been busy while she'd been grabbing the shots. For The Girls, a cheeky girl's night card game, was set up on the coffee table. On the couch, loveseat, and two end chairs sat Lydia, Layla, Noah, and Elena.

"Those are *by far* the prettiest shots I've ever seen!" Layla exclaimed.

"Says the nineteen-year-old college student whose liquor of choice is fireball," Lydia teased.

"What are they?" Elena asked.

"Tequila sunrise shots," Rosie explained, setting one down in front of each bridesmaid.

"Wait! Lilah doesn't have one," Noah pointed out.

"I don't need—"

"Don't be silly," Rosie gently passed her shot to Lilah. "Take mine, and I'll go grab another from Callum. Honestly, I'll just go ahead and have him make another round."

"Okay, Rosie, I know you barely passed math in high school, but we both know you're not 'two plus two equals five' bad at math. Just say you want to go flirt with Callum," Elena smirked.

"Though I'm sure she does want to go flirt with him—"

"Hey!" Rosie scoffed.

"Am I wrong?" Lilah asked.

"That's beside the point."

"Mm*hm*. As I was saying," Lilah shot her a look of incredulity, "though I'm sure she does want to flirt with him, Rosie's not lying actually. Callum just told me I should help her carry these up. None of them were meant for me."

"Well, one is now. Rosie, go grab another round—enough for Lilah too this time," Elena declared. "That is if she wants to stay and play with us?"

Elena gestured to the card game and the open half of the loveseat next to Noah. Elena flashed Rosie a look that said 'Plan Cupid is working!'

"Yeah, sure," Lilah answered, taking the empty seat. "I guess this does look more enjoyable than sitting on the couch with drunk groomsmen and talking about sports," she laughed.

"Be right back!" Rosie announced cheerfully, heading for the stairs.

She descended the stairs with a bounce in her step, excited that she and Elena's plan was working.

"I need another round of those shots, plus an extra for Lilah," she told Callum as she reached the bar.

"Oh? She decided to stay upstairs?" he asked with a trace of amusement.

"Yeah, and speaking of—what's with your weird 'help Rosie carry those' suggestion? What are you up to?" Rosie eyed him suspiciously.

If they were up to the same thing, they could work together.

"I have absolutely no idea what you're talking about," he smirked.

"Shame," Rosie sighed. "I just thought that if we

happened to be on the same page, we might be able to help each other."

Callum abruptly paused what he was doing—cocktail shaker in mid-air.

"And what are we on the same page about?"

"*You* have a best friend, *I* have a best friend..."

"Ahh," Callum replied. "Both of whom are single."

"Exactly," Rosie folded her hands together and propped them on the bar counter. "So, what are we gonna do about it?"

"*I've* already done something about it," Callum pointed out. "I sent her upstairs, where she has apparently decided to stay. Your move."

Turning toward the rest of the groomsmen in the living room area downstairs, Callum yelled, "Cole, here's your Jack and Coke, man."

"Thanks!" Cole said as he came to grab the drink. "Oh, hey Rosie. How's my future wife?" he asked.

"Lovely as always," Rosie answered.

Taking a sip of his drink, Cole mused, "Would it really be so bad if I just went to give her a quick goodnight kiss?"

"Yes!" Callum and Rosie asserted in unison.

"I'm the troll under the bridge that decides who's allowed to pass. And you, Mr. Scott, shall not pass," Rosie said definitively.

"You're both mean," Cole feigned annoyance and walked back to sit with the rest of the groomsmen again.

Callum lined up six shot glasses on the bartop and began pouring tequila into each, "Who didn't get one the first time?"

"I gave mine to Lilah."

"Open up," he murmured.

"Excuse me?" Rosie scoffed, though she could feel her cheeks heat at the words.

"Your mouth," he laughed, gesturing with the bottle of tequila.

Rosie tipped her head back and opened her mouth, feeling the spice of the liquid as she swallowed. And swallowed. *And swallowed.*

"You can take it," Callum smirked down at her before setting the bottle upright again.

Rosie could do nothing to stop herself from imagining those words passing through Callum's lips under entirely different circumstances.

"That was *way* more than a shot," Rosie argued, wiping the drop that had darted down her chin.

"Oops," Callum whispered, sounding the exact opposite of apologetic.

Callum topped each shot glass with a splash of grenadine, then reached under the counter to grab a tray. As he moved the glasses carefully onto it, Rosie laughed.

"Lilah is going to figure out exactly what you're doing the second I walk back up there holding a tray."

"Tell her I didn't see it," Callum shrugged.

Rosie was definitely feeling the 'extra shot' of tequila Callum had poured down her throat, which, in reality, was probably closer to three. Evidently, Elena was also feeling the effects of her shots because when she 'rolled' the dice, it ended up halfway across the room. Layla leaned over the arm of the couch to reach.

"Blue! Most likely to..." she said, passing the card to Elena to read.

Immediately, Elena began cackling.

"Are you gonna tell us what the card says?" Noah complained. "We would also like to laugh."

"Most likely to—" she could barely get the words out through her raucous laughter, "to hook up with their best friend's sibling."

"Rosie!" Everyone screamed at the same time, clearly amused.

Across from Rosie, Noah snorted. Even Lilah was laughing hysterically.

"No fucking way that's actually what the card says," Rosie groaned, letting her face fall into her hands.

Elena waved the card at her from across the coffee table.

"Read it and weep, bitch," she sing-songed.

"You've more than earned it," Lilah smirked next to Noah on the loveseat.

"Hey!" Rosie scoffed. She could feel her cheeks heating. "Just give me the damn card," she muttered as she snatched it from Elena who was still waving it in amusement.

"Your turn, Noah," Elena said, handing her the die.

Rosie took a quick picture of the card, texting it to Callum.

> Rosie: It's going really well up here, in case you were wondering.

Noah rolled, the die landing on purple.

"Pass me a card please," she asked, reaching toward the stack of purple cards on Rosie's end of the table.

"Never have I ever..." she trailed off, cheeks flaming. "Never have I ever, um, had a sex dream about another player," she finished.

She set the card down in front of herself in silent admission. Rosie made eye contact with Elena, trying to maintain a neutral facial expression. She spared a quick glance to Lilah, who was also blushing.

"Your turn," Noah said, passing the die to Lilah.

As she did, Rosie noticed that their hands lingered together over the die for just a moment.

"Um, yellow," Lilah announced. "Which one is that again?"

"Categories. Whoever can't think of another answer or repeats is out. Last player standing wins the card," Layla explained, passing her a yellow card.

"What's the category?" Lydia asked.

"Ways to say sex."

"God, I fucking love this game," Elena laughed.

"Okay, uh, fucking," Lilah started.

"Smashing," Layla offered.

"Shagging," Rosie threw out.

"Making love," Elena said.

"Oh, you would say that, wouldn't you?" Noah laughed at her.

"Pardon me for thinking of my husband-to-be," Elena defended. "Ugh, I miss him. Downstairs is too far away," she complained.

"Don't get any ideas. Like I told him earlier: I'm the bridge troll, and you shall not pass," Rosie folded her arms in defiance.

"Aww, you talked to him? I want to talk to him."

"You can in, approximately," Rosie tapped her phone screen to check the time—twelve o'six in the morning—"eighteen hours."

Rosie saw that Callum had replied to her text. Maybe now would be a good time to stop drinking because she couldn't remember what she'd sent him. That was, until she read his response.

> Callum: What are the odds that card comes true tonight?

Well, shit. She wasn't exactly sure what she'd intended to achieve by sending him a picture of the card.

> Rosie: Ask me after I've successfully gotten the bride into bed.

"That's so *long* from now," Elena groaned.

"Oh hush," Noah teased her. "You'll survive. Whose turn is it?"

"Mine," Lydia said. "Getting railed."

"Boning."

"Doing the horizontal tango."

"Jumping someone's bones."

"Getting balls deep."

Damn, there were a lot of ways to describe having sex. They went on like that for several rounds until, finally, Layla was the only one left standing.

"What?" she said innocently. "I'm in college."

"Whose card was that originally?" Lydia asked.

"Mine," Lilah answered. "Layla's turn."

15

TEQUILA MAKES HER CLOTHES FALL OFF

Callum:

There was a very good reason that so many songs had been written about tequila. It had landed him and Rosie at opposite ends of the beach house's staircase, blocking the bride and groom's access to one another.

"I just want you to know that I hold you responsible for this," Rosie yelled down to Callum from the top of the staircase.

"Me! I'm not the one who kept flouncing down here demanding more shots," Callum chided from where he sat on the bottom step.

"Maybe not, but you *were* at the same dinner table as I was earlier when Noah warned Cole not to give your sister tequila unless he wanted her in the mood," Rosie had the audacity to sound offended.

"You'll have to excuse my tuning out at the types of liquor that make my sister horny," Callum replied, unamused.

"And I was not," she added.

"What?" he asked.

"*Flouncing*."

"Oh? Is that not what you call it when a girl bounces up to the counter and constantly adjusts her posture to give the bartender the clearest possible view of her tits?"

"Says the man who poured three shots worth of tequila straight down my throat while telling me that I 'could take it.'"

Callum laughed. He didn't know what had possessed him to do that earlier, but the blush that had spread across Rosie's cheeks in response had made it more than worthwhile.

"Let's not pretend I don't know how much you enjoy being praised," Callum threw back.

Something about the fourteen steps standing between them gave him a sense of security in talking to her this way despite her declaration that sex was off the table until after the wedding.

"God, you suck," Rosie sighed, defeated.

"So do you. Incredibly fucking well, if you ask me," Callum teased.

"Ugh!" she groaned. "This is going to be a painfully long night, isn't it?"

"Doesn't have to be."

"Callum…"

"I know, I know," he sighed. "Off the table until after the wedding. But then why did you complain about my 'lack of shameless flirting'? Why text me a picture of that card earlier?" He paused, not sure how far he could press things. "Tell me, Rosie, what exactly is it that you want?"

"I—"

Her answer was cut short by the sound of banging from the other side of the door at Rosie's back.

"Rosemary June Dawsonnnnn," Elena whined. "I want to see my husband."

"He's not your husband yet, babe," Rosie patiently answered, cracking the door just so. "That's why you aren't allowed to see him right now, remember?"

"That's stupid."

"Noh!" Rosie yelled through the inch of space between the door and the frame.

"On it!" Noah called back from somewhere on the first floor.

"Give her some ibuprofen and more of those bagel bites and try to get her into bed," Rosie pleaded.

Hearing footsteps heading in the opposite direction of the door, Callum turned his attention back to their conversation.

"Look, I'll go back to distant and respectful if that's what you want, but—"

"It's not," she hesitated, "what I want, I mean. It's just... harder than I expected to flirt with you and not actually do anything about it."

It pleased him an indecent amount to know that she was so affected by his teasing.

"Good thing you have your," he added an extra flourish to his next word, "toys then, huh?"

"I really shouldn't have told you that," she laughed.

"Oh, no, I'm glad you did. The thought is alarmingly attractive."

"Really?" Rosie sounded surprised. "Most men hate sex toys. Or, at the very least, they tolerate them."

"Not that you weren't already aware, but your ex is a shitty excuse for a man," Callum stated the obvious. "And I'm not sure what other men you're referring to, but I am definitely not one of them. Why the fuck would I be against anything that helps make you come?"

"I—"

"And," he said, cutting her off, "just for the record, I'd do just about anything to watch you fuck yourself with one."

"Fuck," she whispered.

Callum didn't miss the way she crossed her legs as the word left her mouth. Didn't dare look away from her as his words washed over her.

"Well, it seems like Noah has Elena under control so..." Callum sighed. "Goodnight Rose."

Without giving her a chance to reply, he turned and walked down the hallway toward his room.

16

MOST DEFINITELY NOT JEALOUS

Rosie:

It was her best friend's wedding day—Rosie *should* be thinking about all things Elena, yet she couldn't keep her thoughts from drifting to the fact that in a few hours, she'd be arm-in-arm with Callum. They'd practiced walking down the aisle together a good six times at the rehearsal, but Rosie had been so preoccupied with ensuring she learned all of her cues that she hadn't had time to dwell on the feeling of her body pressed against his... Combine that with everything he'd said to her last night on the stairs... She was more than a little preoccupied.

Mimosas—that's what she was supposed to be focused on right now. As the Maid of Honor, she was in charge of making sure Elena's day was everything she'd dreamed of, and Elena's dream included a mimosa bar that all the bridesmaids could sip on while they got their hair and makeup done. Well, all of the bridesmaids except Harper who would be drinking sparkling orange juice since she was only thirteen.

Rosie was really proud of the setup: she'd gotten peach, strawberry, and mango juice in addition to orange juice so that everyone could customize their flutes. She'd even made sure to get an assortment of flavored, sparkling waters so that Harper was still included in the fun of mixing her own drink.

"Okay ladies, the mimosa bar is officially open for business! Come and get 'em! Except for Elena—you aren't allowed to do anything but let people take care of you today," Rosie happily declared.

Elena laughed as the rest of the bridal party ran toward the bar at the end of the bridal suite where the kitchenette was. Rosie made her way through the rush of women toward Elena.

"So, my beautiful best friend and bride-to-be, what flavor do you want?" she asked Elena.

"Hm, surprise me."

"Strawberry mimosa, coming right up!" Rosie joked, knowing how much Elena hated strawberries.

She hated all fruits with little seeds like that, but somehow she was fine with pulp. It made absolutely zero sense to Rosie.

"Isn't my best friend supposed to be extra nice to me on my wedding day?" Elena playfully shoved Rosie in the arm.

"You said to surprise you," Rosie playfully shoved back. "*Peach* mimosa, coming right up."

"Thank you," Elena called after Rosie sarcastically as she went to make her peach mimosa.

Rosie nearly dropped the flute she was pouring champagne into when Noah came up behind her, putting an arm around her waist.

"Noh!" Rosie shouted using her nickname to let her know she wasn't actually mad.

"You almost made me spill champagne on everything!"

"You didn't spill it though, did you? Exactly," Noah answered her own question before Rosie had even had the chance. "So, how drunk do you think the groomsmen are by now?"

"Considering the Best Man was treating the beach house like his own bar last night, I'd put my money on *very*."

"Speaking of the Best Man," Noah raised her eyebrows at Rosie dramatically. "How are you feeling about being all cuddled up to him when you two have to walk down the aisle together in a few hours?"

"Why would I be feeling any particular way about it?" Rosie tried to deflect Noah's question.

"Uh, because you told him that sex was back on the table? And because you looked extremely flushed when you came up the stairs to go to bed last night," Noah stated more so than asked.

"Not until *after* the wedding, Noh," Rosie rolled her eyes.

"Well technically, it will be '*after* the wedding' in a few hours when the ceremony ends," Noah smirked.

"Hey speaking of things happening or not happening after the ceremony ends, have you decided what you're going to say to Lilah? Things seemed to be going really well last night," Rosie raised her eyebrows dramatically.

Rosie knew that bringing up Lilah would halt any further questioning about Callum from Noah. Rosie had always suspected that there was something between them ever since that night during their senior year of high school, but she hadn't known the extent of it. Not until a few weeks ago when Noah had drunkenly admitted that Lilah had been her gay awakening.

Lilah had confirmed last night that the two hadn't seen each other since before Rosie, Noah, and Elena had left for college, and wasn't even one hundred percent sure that Lilah knew Noah was out. Rosie had always been the bridge between Elena's family and Noah; so, after everyone left for college, there wasn't much overlap.

"Don't you have to take that mimosa to Elena? Maid of Honor duties and all?" Noah deflected.

Rosie just smirked at her as she garnished the champagne flute with an orange slice and walked away.

Somewhere around Rosie's third mimosa, the hair and makeup team had gotten set up and started getting the bridal party wedding ready.

"So," Rosie turned to overhear Audrey, the makeup artist, ask Lydia, "*who* is the tall, drool-worthy, tattooed groomsman?" Audrey smirked. "And is he single?"

Rosie balled her fists. Who did this bitch think she was? She was here to do a job, not to suck the Best Man's dick. Besides, if anyone was doing that, it was going to be Rosie.

"That would be my brother, Callum," Lydia laughed. "And yes, he's single. But let me save you the trouble: he's not the dating type."

"Oh, that's what I'm counting on," Audrey smirked. "Oh sorry," Audrey laughed nervously, "you probably don't want to hear that about your brother."

"Eh, it's okay," Lydia reassured her. "I'm used to that with him. If Playboy gave out an award for 'Fuckboy of the Year,' he would win it," Lydia snorted.

Across the room, Noah's eyes locked on Rosie's as if to say 'whatever you're thinking, don't do it.'

Too late.

Before Rosie had a chance to think it through, she was

grabbing her mimosa and heading in the direction of Audrey and her big mouth. Careful to avoid Lydia, Rosie 'tripped' and spilled what was left of her mimosa all over Audrey's pants. It looked a bit like she had peed herself. Good.

"Oh my god, oh my god!" Rosie feigned doe-eyed and apologetic. "I'm *so* sorry!" She looked up at Audrey from the floor as she held up the glass, doing her best to seem embarrassed, "I guess that third mimosa wasn't such a good idea. God, I'm so fucking sorry."

It wasn't like Audrey would ever see Callum after today, so this was her only chance to make a move. Rosie would like to see her try to get his attention, let alone his number, looking like that.

"No, no, it's okay," Audrey insisted, brushing Rosie's shoulder sincerely. "Seriously, no big deal. I have a change of clothes in my bag—I have a tendency to end up wearing everyone's makeup by the end of these things," she smiled, walking in the direction of her bag.

Damn it, why did Audrey have to go and be so nice about Rosie spilling sticky-ass orange juice all over her crotch? It was a hell of a lot easier to be mean to her when Rosie thought she was just the bitch trying to sleep with Callum. *And* she had a change of clothes? Rosie's plan was unraveling rapidly.

"I'm gonna go find a towel to clean this up," Rosie muttered as she stood.

Before she even made it a step, Lydia grabbed her arm and spun her around.

"Little jealous, are we?" Lydia glanced up from the now-empty glass in Rosie's hand to meet her eyes.

"I have absolutely no idea what you're talking about," Rosie deflected, trying to hide her smirk.

"Oh, yeah," Lydia snorted, "because you just so happened to become a clutz the second someone expressed interest in Callum? Save that for someone that hasn't known you for over a decade," she deadpanned.

"Shit, Lyds. You're worse than Noah," Rosie sighed dramatically. "I'm not *jealous*, okay? But she's here to do a *job*, not to suck Callum's dick. It was," Rosie paused, racking her brain for anything that sounded half-logical, "unprofessional."

"Correct me if I'm wrong, but *you're* the one who turned *Callum* down. So unless you're ready to admit that you're jealous—and I'm going to pretend this isn't my baby brother we're talking about—" Lydia fake-gagged, "there's no reason he shouldn't be allowed to hook up with her later if he wants to."

Rosie huffed rather unconvincingly, "not jealous."

"Great. Then I'll tell Audrey that I'm happy to pass along her message to Callum?" Lydia raised her eyebrows in a silent challenge.

"Sounds great!" Rosie replied far too enthusiastically, rolling her eyes as she walked away.

Rosie entered the kitchenette area of the bridal suite in search of a towel to dry the bit of her mimosa that Audrey's pants hadn't absorbed. Rummaging through the drawers, all she could find were white hand towels. This *was* a bridal suite, but, damn, would it have killed them to buy a single towel in a darker color that the orange juice wouldn't stain? Rosie opted for the roll of paper towels on the counter and walked back over to clean the floor.

17

MISSION SFYWBBRL

Callum:

CALLUM WASN'T sure if it was the two shots of whiskey he'd downed twenty minutes ago or the anticipation of being so close to Rosie after their conversation last night, but he felt warm. He hadn't hooked up with anyone since the night Rosie had left him standing in his kitchen with her thong in his pocket, but he'd fucked his fist to the memory more times than he'd care to admit.

The dynamic between them had gone back to normal—undeniable tension alleviated by mindless flirting—ever since their conversation at Lafayette's when Rosie had said that, after the wedding, sex wasn't off the table anymore. And Callum had never craved the taste of someone as badly as he craved the taste of Rosie; he wasn't sure what to do with that—well, besides officially enacting Mission Shamelessly Flirt Your Way Back Between Rosie's Legs.

Callum intended to use their status as Best Man and Maid of Honor to his advantage. As they walked down the aisle, he planned to press his body as closely to Rosie's as possible so that she would be forced to remember what his touch felt like.

Everyone was lined up on the boardwalk waiting to be directed down the aisle by the wedding planner. Everyone except for Elena who would be escorted by their dad after everyone else had taken their places at the altar. Cole walked up next to Callum, drawing him from his thoughts.

"How are you feeling man?" Callum asked him.

"Honestly? Just hoping I don't fuck up my vows," he laughed nervously.

"Just speak from your heart—what could go wrong?" Callum clapped Cole on the back.

"I didn't know people who dodged commitment like the plague were qualified to give relationship advice," Cole joked.

He knew Cole was probably just nervous and hadn't meant anything by the joke. Historically, Callum had run from any form of commitment faster than an Olympic sprinter. Even so, he always tried to act with reason. He'd ended things with Olivia because Hayden had rightfully called him out for unfairly stringing her along, not because he didn't give a shit about her feelings. Despite this, all people ever seemed to see in him was a fuckboy who didn't give a shit about anyone else, which stung. Not wanting commitment didn't make him an insensitive asshole.

Luckily for him, everyone was starting to line up, so he was back to thinking about Rosie and her soft skin pressed against his the whole way down the aisle. He just wished that there would be less clothes between them.

As he followed the wedding planner's directions, his eyes met a familiar pair of green ones. Damn, she looked stunning. She was beautiful without even a trace of makeup, but Callum gave mental applause to the makeup artist because today, Rosie was art.

The sage green bridesmaid dress complemented her long, copper hair that was blowing gently in the wind, and the brown eye makeup she wore made her eyes look even softer than usual. Never mind that the dress perfectly accentuated the curve of Rosie's ass and was just low enough in the front for Callum to see the curve of her tits. Not quite as low as the dress she'd worn to the rehearsal dinner, but still enough to be enticing.

Callum felt his own pants tightening, which was definitely not good considering he was two minutes from walking her down the aisle, where everyone would be able to see the precise reason that his pants were now a little snug. He needed to focus his attention elsewhere, back on Mission SFYWBBRL. He could tease her all he wanted—it's not like everyone would be able to see if *she* was aroused.

"You look lovely, Rose," Callum smirked.

"Hey Costello, you look… handsome," she smirked back.

"I don't think you've ever called me handsome before."

"Well, 'damn, you look hot' didn't really seem fitting, considering you just told me that I look 'lovely.'"

"So I'm hot, huh?" Callum's smirk grew.

"I blame the suit," Rosie shoved him playfully.

"Blame whatever you want, Rose. As long as you're thinking about what's underneath," Callum held out his arm to her, knowing she couldn't deny him given that the ceremony was starting.

"You're so full of yourself," Rosie rolled her eyes and looped her arm with Callum's.

Leaning down so that only she would hear him, Callum whispered, "I'd rather *you* be full of me."

Before Rosie had time to react, they were directed

toward the boardwalk to make their way down the aisle. He felt Rosie tense at his side, but the deep blush of her cheeks was sending an entirely different signal, one that said she was most definitely thinking about what was underneath his suit.

"Relax, Rosie, you look like you hate me or something," he whispered in her ear.

"Let's go with 'or something,'" she shot back.

Oh yeah, the plan was in full swing. Callum lowered his arm from where it was looped with Rosie's to around her waist so that his hand just barely grazed the top of her ass.

"Callum," she whisper-hissed at him.

"Yes, Rose?" he asked innocently, intentionally using *that* nickname.

He deserved an award for somehow not blue balling himself in the process.

"What in hell do you think you're doing?" she asked.

"What I do best," he responded confidently.

"And what's that?"

"Turning you on."

"Whatever you say," Rosie seemed like she was trying to come off as indifferent, but instead, it came out as breathy.

Uh-oh. Maybe not blue balling himself wasn't going as well as Callum thought.

"Are you really trying to tell me," his hand reached slightly lower, "that if I slid my hand up your dress right now," his hand slid back up to graze the underside of her breast, "I wouldn't find you wet for me?"

Callum had thought she'd been blushing before. Her cheeks grew an impossibly deeper shade of red. He looped his arm with Rosie's again just as they approached the edge of the aisle, now visible to all of the wedding guests.

"You might want to look less like you're ready to spread your legs for me," he whispered against the shell of her ear, "unless that's just the look you're going for in your best friend's wedding photos."

"Fuck you, Costello," she mumbled.

"As you wish, Rose," he murmured back.

Arm in arm, they walked under the lush, leafy, floral archway marking the official start of the aisle. The rest of their walk toward the altar was silent, but the tension between them was so palpable that Callum could have reached out and grabbed it. As they took their places on each side of the altar, Callum didn't look away from Rosie once. She attempted to look everywhere but at him, however unsuccessfully.

Rosie:

Fuck Callum and his ability to make Rosie absurdly wet as she walked down the aisle as Maid of Honor at her best friend's wedding. She'd tried desperately to avoid any additional eye contact with Callum after they each took up their positions on either side of the altar, but his eyes were piercing and filled with hunger. Only when Elena began her walk down the aisle, escorted by her and Callum's dad, did Callum's eyes soften and turn away from Rosie. Elena looked absolutely breathtaking. Rosie glanced toward Cole to see that he had tears in his eyes as he watched his bride walk to him, ready to start their life together.

Rosie was immensely happy for Elena, but she couldn't shake the thought in the back of her mind that she once thought she'd see Justin at the end of the aisle, waiting for her with tears in his eyes. Rather than feel bad for herself, she decided to feel bad for the version of herself that would've ended up marrying Justin, only for him to inevitably divorce her when his affair came out. Had Justin hurt her? Yes, but more than anything she'd simply felt betrayed. At least betrayal was easier to mourn.

Pushing her feelings aside, Rosie's heart swelled for Elena as she and Cole exchanged their vows against the backdrop of the setting sun. The peachy shades of the gerbera daisies, calla lilies, and amaryllis, blended with the green undertone of eucalyptus draped across the driftwood arch at the head of the altar was a mirror image of the sunset and contrasted perfectly with the sage green bridesmaids dresses Elena had picked.

"I promise, Elena, not just to love you as you are today, but to love every possible version of yourself that you might become."

"Cole, I promise to love you today, tomorrow, and always. I promise to view every potential fight as a chance to grow my love for you."

Everything was perfect, except for the Best Man who wouldn't stop smirking at her from across the aisle. At least she didn't have to walk back up the aisle with him. What Elena had planned for the end of the ceremony was much more enjoyable than that.

As the officiant said the familiar words, "you may now kiss the bride," and Rosie watched her best friend kiss the love of her life, she beamed.

As Elena and Cole broke apart from their kiss, Rosie passed her bouquet back.

Now, the real fun could begin. The sky was filled with shades of orange as the flower bouquets were tossed into the sea of wedding guests and sand sprinkled the air as the wedding party ran down the beach straight toward the ocean. *Thank God* Elena wasn't one of those boring brides who cared about what happened to her wedding dress after the ceremony.

At the edge of the surf, Cole twirled Elena into his waiting arms, then immediately lifted her by the waist and spun them both in circles. Rosie had never seen Elena so happy and was beyond thankful to be a part of what she knew was the best day of Elena's life. As Cole gently set Elena's feet back on the sand to kiss her, the rest of the wedding party ran past them into the ocean, splashing water around like confetti.

The wedding photographer had taken all of the formal, posed pictures before the ceremony so that the bridal party didn't have to worry about anything else in the moments after the bride and groom said 'I do.' There was an open bar set up under the pavilion area for the guests who didn't want to join the bridal party for a dip in the ocean.

Noah caught Rosie's hand as she ran past, pulling her into waist-deep water. The two of them splashed each other, giggling like they had under that tattered camp comforter all those years ago when they'd first met. Rosie couldn't help the overwhelming wave of emotions that propelled through her. More than anything else in that moment, she was grateful for her life, grateful for the people in it, and grateful that she had the freedom to find the Cole to her Elena one day even though it wasn't Justin. Especially because it wasn't Justin.

Taking advantage of the fact that she was distracted by her thoughts, Callum grabbed Rosie by the waist, spinning her around and then pulling her under the water. Once her head was above the surface again, she sent the biggest wave of water she could muster straight for Noah.

"Hey! What was that for?" Noah laughed, sending a wave straight back for Rosie.

"For not warning me that Callum was behind me. Which reminds me," Rosie spun around, jumping up in an attempt to shove Callum down by the shoulders with all of her weight and pull him under the water as he'd done to her.

Callum, unfortunately, did not budge. Apparently, being six-three with killer abs meant you couldn't be easily knocked over. Callum stood, unmoving and failing to hold in a laugh.

"Fuck, you're too big. It wasn't a fair fight," Rosie splashed water into Callum's open mouth as he laughed at her.

The salty water clearly didn't phase him because he just kept laughing.

"Damn right, I'm too big," he smirked, looking more than pleased with himself.

Caught up in the euphoria of the moment, Rosie had completely forgotten that she hadn't worn a bra underneath her bridesmaid dress. Conveniently, the water was a little chilly, and her nipples were definitely hard enough to show through, hard enough for Callum to notice. Good.

She'd tease him back for his little act down the aisle earlier, and for pulling her under the water just now. She only prayed that Callum didn't know just how spot-on he'd been about the fact that she'd been dripping for him. He'd barely laid a hand on her, and she'd been so turned on that she could barely focus on the ceremony. It had taken every ounce of her willpower to avoid staring at him the entire time. To remember her cues. Callum was hot, but Callum in a suit? Panty-dropping.

Slowly, Rosie reached both hands behind her head to squeeze the water out of her hair, giving Callum an unobstructed view of her hardened nipples. His eyes darkened and she was met with the same hungry stare he'd worn earlier.

"Rosie?" Noah said her name, pulling her from the moment.

"Yeah?" Rosie replied without breaking eye contact with Callum.

"Come with me to help Elena change into her reception dress?"

"She's not even out of the water ye—"

"Now. *Right now*," Noah repeated sternly.

After they'd walked far enough from the water that no one was within earshot, Noah lept on her.

"Uh, what exactly do you think you're doing?" she asked as she pulled Rosie up the beach toward the venue's building that housed the bridal suite and groom's suite.

"Going to help Elena change into her reception dress with you? Or did you just want to talk about Lih—"

Rosie was cut off before she could finish her question.

"No, I mean what are you doing with Callum? I thought you said you didn't want anything to happen between the two of you until after this weekend was over?" Noah pushed.

She had said that, and she'd meant it. But that was before Callum had teased her all the way down the aisle looking more attractive than any man had a right to in that goddamned suit. Fuck, it should be illegal to wear a suit that well.

"Well, I mean, *technically* the wedding *is* over..." Rosie murmured without looking Noah in the eye.

Noah just laughed, "I totally called that by the way. The two of you have never been able to stay away from each other."

"I didn't say I was gonna do anything for sure, okay? I just said the wedding is *technically* over."

"Mmhm," Noah smirked. "Whatever you need to tell yourself, babe."

18

TWO CAN PLAY AT THAT GAME

Rosie:

Rosie and Noah had successfully gotten Elena out of her wedding dress and into her dress for the reception; though still elegant, it was shorter, dry, and allowed her much more freedom around the reception area than her ceremony gown would have.

The bridesmaids didn't have secondary dresses, but Rosie and Noah had taken a minute to dry off and touch up their makeup before heading back down to the pavilion to join the guests at the reception. The fairy lights Rosie had helped string earlier looked beautiful now that the sun had set, casting a warm glow over the wedding guests enjoying the cocktail hour.

"I'm thirsty," Rosie turned to walk toward the bar as a way of cutting off any other potential conversation about her and Callum.

She didn't have a plan—didn't want one. If she started to think about things for too long, she'd likely overthink herself out of letting anything happen between them: it was too soon, she should just take time for herself, blah blah. Thus, she was going to allow herself the freedom to act on whatever impulse she desired.

"What can I get you two lovely ladies?" the bartender asked Rosie and Noah, who had followed right behind her.

Conversation not over, apparently.

"Rosé, please," Noah smiled.

The bartender's glance moved to Rosie.

"Pinot Grigio, please."

The bartender nodded and began to fill their glasses.

"*Someone* is looking right at you," Noah elbowed Rosie dramatically. "Honestly, I don't blame him. Your ass looks fantastic in that dress, especially since it's still a little wet and practically glued to you," Noah ran her eyes over Rosie's ass in emphasis.

"It does, doesn't it? Although you might want to stop checking me out in front of the girl you actually want to go home with," Rosie's eyes moved in the direction of Lilah, who had taken her seat at a table across the pavilion. "I guess it doesn't count as going home since she's already staying in the beach house, but going back to the room with? Ugh, you get what I'm trying to say."

She'd give it to Noah, Lilah was attractive, especially in the jade green suit she was currently wearing, her button-up undone just enough to be flirty.

"Oh my god, oh fuck," Noah rambled. "Holy hell, she looks so hot in a suit. The fuck do I do?"

"Go talk to her?"

"Yeah because that's so easy," Noah groaned. "I'm on the verge of a panic attack."

"Noh," calling Noah by her nickname usually calmed her a bit, "She's just a woman."

"She's not just a woman. She's the gay awakening I've seen once in the past decade, but have thought about ceaselessly," Noah protested.

"Okay, okay. Maybe go ask how she slept?" Rosie squeezed Noah's arm. "Go get the girl. I have a Best Man to tease."

As she watched Noah walk over toward their table, Rosie had an idea. As the bartender picked up her glass of pinot, she flipped her still-damp hair over her shoulder, drawing the bartender's eyes downward, to the outline of her hardened nipples beneath her bridesmaid dress. As she reached to accept the wine glass, she brushed her fingers across the inside of his wrist and looked up at him through her lashes. She offered a soft smile.

"I'm Rosie by the way," then, dropping her voice to a low enough volume that it drew him even closer to her, said, "I figured I should introduce myself—I have a feeling I'll be seeing a lot more of you before the night is over."

"Um," he offered her a shy smile, "I'm Max."

"Max," Rosie parroted back to him. "Cute, just like you."

She walked away before he could respond. She'd said just enough to keep him interested.

She met Callum's eyes across the room, and he did not look pleased. But he was the one who'd started this game, and Rosie was more than willing to play.

The groomsmen and the rest of the bridesmaids had all gone back up to the suites to freshen up while everyone else had busied themselves with cocktails. Because Elena and Cole wanted a sunset ceremony, they had decided on just serving desserts and hour d'oeuvres at the reception since it would be too late in the evening to warrant a full-course dinner.

People began to shuffle toward their tables as the officiant approached the podium area that had been set up with a schedule of the night's events. Rosie, along with the rest of the wedding party and immediate family, was seated at a long table toward the front of the pavilion. Their table had a prime view of Elena and Cole's table, though Rosie doubted they would actually sit for longer than ten minutes all night. Noah took the seat immediately to Rosie's right, Lydia to her left. Callum sat directly across from her, his angry expression from earlier replaced by a smirk of amusement.

"You *do* know that you don't have to flirt with the bartender to get free drinks, right? That's why they call it an open bar..." Callum grinned at her smugly.

"You *do* know that I'm single, right? Or is it that you're not bothered by my flirting, but jealous that it's directed toward Max instead of you?" Rosie retorted.

Callum: one. Rosie: one. Not that she'd been counting.

"Please," Callum rolled his eyes. "We both know he's not your type."

"Oh?" Rosie scoffed incredulously. "And what *is* my type? Since you seem to consider yourself an expert on the subject?" Rosie raised her eyebrows in silent challenge.

"Well for starters," Callum glanced over his shoulder at the bartender, Max, "he has no tattoos from what I can see. And I happen to know just how much you like mine."

"I don't think I've ever actually complimented your tattoos."

"Maybe not with your words," Callum's smirk only grew, "but *definitely* with your mouth."

Rosie's cheeks heated. Underneath the table, Lydia kicked Callum in the shin.

"Uh, hello? I do *not* need the details of your sex life,"

Lydia barely concealed her amused smile as she turned toward Rosie. "No offense, Rosie."

Rosie muttered, "None taken, Lyds."

Though she said nothing else on the subject, Lydia's eyes seemed to convey an unspoken question: *ready to admit to being jealous, yet?*

Before Rosie had time to think of what the hell to say to Callum, the MC quieted the guests to introduce the bride and groom. It was just as well with Rosie; she had absolutely nothing to say in defense of herself. Callum had been attractive before he'd gotten the tattoos, but they certainly didn't hurt his appearance. God, she loved those tattoos. Had kissed her way down the ones covering his chest more times than she'd care to admit.

"It is my honor to present to you, for the first time ever, Mr. and Mrs. Cole Scott!"

They entered the pavilion hand-in-hand, Elena smiling more broadly than Rosie had ever seen. Again, she felt that small twinge of pain for the life she thought she'd have with Justin. She knew it was for the best, but the idea of starting all over with someone new overwhelmed her. She wanted what Elena and Cole had. She was immensely happy for them, but she was finding it more and more difficult to feel that joy without acknowledging the pain.

Cole spun her into his arms just in time for the officiant to announce their first dance. They swayed together, Elena staring adoringly into Cole's eyes as Etta James' voice rang through the pavilion.

The father-daughter and mother-son dances were next. Rather than slow dance to something cheesy, Elena and Mr. Mark feigned air guitar to Sweet Child O' Mine. He and Mrs. Pammy had always been huge classic rock people and had made it their life mission to ensure that their kids ended up as fans of the genre too. In addition to Guns N' Roses, the Costello kids' childhood had been set to the soundtrack of Aerosmith, Fleetwood Mac, Queen, CCR, Eagles, Bon Jovi, Foreigner... If there was a classic rock band from the '70s and '80s, the Costellos had every album.

As Cole danced with his mom for their mother-son dance, Rosie realized how easily a person could gauge the integrity of a man based on the way he treated his mother. Cole and his mom opted for a traditional slow dance, which was really more swaying while hugging. Anyone could see the duality of emotion that shone in Cole's mother's eyes: a twinge of sadness that her baby boy was now starting his own family, but immense pride for the man he had become.

Rosie didn't have a single memory of Justin and his mother like that. Of course, Rosie had been around Justin's mom plenty of times over the two years that they'd dated, but she didn't ever really feel like she knew anything about the woman. Of the times Justin spoke of her, which were few and far between, annoyance or regret had always laced his tone. He seemed to think of her as a leash holding him back rather than as his mother. That wasn't to say that Justin held the sole responsibility for their strained relationship; Justin's mother had always set unrealistically high expectations for him, setting him up to never be good enough for her. Even so, he had never been willing to stand up to her, instead letting his resentment fester into the barely tolerable, always waiting for the other shoe to drop kind of relationship it was to this day. A direct contrast to the warm, loving relationship emanating from Cole and his mom.

After all of the dances were over, the officiant announced that it was time for the bride and groom to cut the cake. Even with her hair still a tad damp from their dip in the water, Elena was the most beautiful bride Rosie had ever seen. Everyone focused their attention on the table with the three-tier wedding cake garnished with flowers in shades of peach to match the bouquets and centerpieces.

Hands together on the cake knife, Elena and Cole cut through the second tier of the wedding cake. Cole gently maneuvered the slice onto the plate in Elena's hand, swiping the excess icing off onto Elena's nose. She scooped up icing into her own fingers and swiped it across Cole's lips, leaning in to lick it off before kissing him deeply. Everyone cheered.

Mrs. Pammy helped remove the top tier of the cake and put it into a box to be frozen and saved for Cole and Elena's first anniversary as wedding guests began moving about the pavilion area to get a slice or to refresh their drinks. Rosie was starving since the last meal she'd eaten was a mimosa with a side of granola bar. She walked over to the table with Elena and Cole's wedding cake to help herself to a sizable piece. As she was cutting a slice, a familiar shoulder brushed hers. Turning, she was again met with Callum's eyes. The hunger she'd seen there earlier had returned.

Taking the knife from Rosie's hand, he cut himself a slice of cake. Callum groaned in delight as he tasted it, seemingly on purpose because he followed it with a wink and, "oh, I'm sorry. I didn't mean for that to slip out."

Rosie found the words, "I mean, it's not like I haven't heard it plenty of times before," slipping out of her mouth and was rewarded with the sight of Callum choking on his bite of cake in surprise.

Clearly, he'd fully expected her to keep up their game of cat and mouse: Rosie flirting with the bartender, Callum trying to win her attention back.

Honestly, Rosie had surprised herself too. She *had* intended to flirt with Max, at least until the end of the night.

Taunting Callum by flirting with someone else was fun, so why had she given up the game so quickly? She refused to contemplate how natural it felt to flirt with Callum like this, how easily they seemed to fall into this dynamic with each other.

Fuck it.

Taking advantage of his surprise, Rosie swiped her finger across the top of Callum's slice of cake, scooping a bit of icing onto her finger. She slowly sucked her finger into her mouth, letting out a delighted groan as Callum had at the sugary-sweet taste. She did this all without once breaking eye contact with Callum. His lips parted slightly in reaction and his eyes seemed to glaze over as they bounced between her still-hard nipples and her lips.

Before Callum had the chance to say anything, she said, "Thanks for the taste, Costello," winking at him as she walked across the room to rejoin Noah.

Callum:

Rosie's teasing was going to drive him mad. He supposed it was his fault since he'd teased her down the aisle earlier. Rosie always took what he gave her and gave it back to him tenfold. It was one of the things he loved the most about her.

Woah, *loved?*

Callum needed to slow down on the Old Fashioneds. Needed to get back to his mission to shamelessly flirt his way back into bed with Rosie. Luckily, now people had begun to move onto the dance floor, which would hopefully allow him the excuse to press his body close to Rosie's for the second time tonight.

He'd also been practicing his slow dancing in preparation for the wedding, not wanting to look like an idiot when all the couples paired off around him to hold each other close as Elvis serenaded them. Not so that he could impress Rosie. *Definitely* not so that he could impress Rosie.

Dragging Lilah with him, Callum waded through the sea of wedding guests to the middle of the dance floor where most of the bridal party had wound up. Elena swayed to the beat, her hands laced together behind Cole's neck as if it were a slow song instead of No Hands by Waka Flocka. As if she couldn't bear to break from their embrace, couldn't bear to avert her gaze from her husband's eyes even for a second. Callum had never felt that way about anyone. Never felt that inherent, burning need to touch, to claim.

Except, hadn't he?

If the last few weeks had proven anything, it's that Callum had exactly zero self-control when it came to Rosie. He'd punched Justin in the face. Not that Justin hadn't deserved it, but still. Callum had broken the guy's nose. And, as little as he wanted to admit it, he'd been jealous out of his mind when he'd seen Rosie flirting with that bartender earlier: Max, she'd called him. He resented that she'd even gotten to a first-name basis with him. He'd taken full advantage of their proximity down the aisle, letting his hands roam across her body simply because he *wanted to*. Had waded onto the dance floor just now for the small chance that she'd allow him to be near her without trying to push or tease him away. Callum couldn't help but remember Lilah's comment from a few weeks ago.

You'll figure it out eventually.

Callum decided that further reflecting on Lilah's

comment would have to wait as his gaze traveled from the newlyweds to Noah and Rosie. Noah's back was pinned to Rosie's chest as they danced together. Callum had to fight not to grab Rosie from Noah as he watched her hands resting on Noah's hips. Just weeks ago, those hands had touched *his* hips, had touched every inch of his body...

Lilah swayed next to Callum, their dancing friendly, comfortable, but nothing more than platonic. She still hadn't commented on seeing Noah again, but watching her watch Noah and Rosie told Callum enough: she was still attracted to Noah, but was, for some reason, resentful about the fact.

Leaning down to mutter to Lilah without anyone else hearing, Callum tested his luck. "Are we gonna talk about it? About her?" His eyes traveled to Noah.

"What's to talk about?"

"Well, for starters, you're looking at her like you're not sure if you want to fuck her or fight her," Callum raised his eyebrows.

"I am *not*," Lilah defended rather unconvincingly.

"Lih, I've been your best friend for over a decade. You can't lie to me. I know all of your tells."

Lilah scoffed but didn't try to say that Callum had been wrong or off base.

"You're simultaneously blushing and gritting your teeth hard enough to concern a dentist," Callum offered as evidence.

"Fine, Noah looks incredibly sexy, and I would love nothing more than for her to use my face as a chair. Happy, Bolton?"

"Only if you make a move," Callum teasingly shoved Lilah in the shoulder while making googly eyes at her. "Why do you think I sent you upstairs last night?"

"Yeah, well. Unfortunately, attraction doesn't negate resentment."

"Why are you resentful?"

"Because. Years ago, at that stupid fucking party, we kissed and it was the best fucking kiss of my entire life, and I thought I finally had a chance with her, then she brushed it off like it meant nothing," Lilah explained.

Ah, well that made things make a little more sense.

"Like *you* meant nothing," Callum voiced what Lilah wouldn't.

What she couldn't.

"Yes," Lilah's eyes moved to the floor as if she could hide from the emotions she was feeling.

"Maybe things would be different this time, now that Noah is out," Callum encouraged.

He made a mental note to talk to Lilah more about this later, about how long she'd felt that way for Noah before everything had gone to shit.

"Even so, I don't know how to let go of my resentment. Hearing her joke like it was nothing to her when it was so *obviously not* nothing to me... It was one of the most humiliating moments of my life," Lilah admitted.

"You don't have to do anything you don't want to do, Lih. And your feelings are valid. But, for what it's worth, I think she might have just been scared."

"Yeah, well... so was I. But I wasn't the one who ran away from my feelings. Moving on, what's up with you and Rosie?" Lilah changed the subject.

"She said she just wanted to get through this weekend focused on Elena, but that nothing was off the table after the wedding. So, naturally, we're back to merciless teasing," Callum glanced back at Rosie again, still moving to the music with Noah.

"After the *weekend*, or after the *wedding*? Because those aren't the same," Lilah inquired.

"Not a damn clue," Callum sighed.

"So why are you dancing with me, when you could be finding out the answer to that question?"

"Because I'm the world's greatest best friend?"

"Fuck off and go get your girl," Lilah laughed, shoving him in Rosie's direction.

"She's not *my* girl," Callum defended.

Even so, he allowed himself to move closer to Rosie. Between them, Noah caught his eyes, mischief written across her face. Noah turned around so that she was facing Rosie, casually moving Rosie's arms so that they draped across her shoulders instead of resting at her hips.

Callum wasn't sure what he'd expected Noah to do next, but it sure as shit wasn't to back into him so that Rosie's arms were now touching Callum too, then to duck out of the way, leaving Callum and Rosie face to face with each other. As if he wasn't surprised enough, Rosie closed the small distance left between them, draping her arms over his shoulders.

Rosie looked up at him as she pressed her body to his, "don't make it a thing."

"Definitely not a thing," was all Callum could manage back.

She was touching *him*. And not just touching him, but moving her hips with his. Callum wasn't sure what had caused the ceasefire in their tease-each-other-into-oblivion game, but he'd never been happier not to win something in his entire life.

Behind Rosie, Noah mouthed, "You're welcome."

Luckily, Rosie was nearly a foot shorter than him, which

allowed him to mouth a "thank you," back to Noah without Rosie seeing.

Callum's hands found Rosie's hips. When she didn't make any effort to remove them, he tightened his hold, pulling her even closer to him. Her hands laced in the long strands of his hair in response. *Oh fuck.*

An inch. That's all that was between their lips. Callum nearly trembled with anticipation as he fought the urge to kiss her, to claim her, with everything in him. *What the fuck was going on?* He needed to get back to familiar ground where he didn't get nervous, where he teased Rosie like it was his sole purpose in life.

He smiled down at Rosie, letting her see the hunger in his eyes, then leaned down to whisper, "you have that look again," in her ear.

"What look?" Rosie glanced innocently up at him.

"Like you're ready to spread your legs for me," he purred, sliding his hands around to her lower back.

He rested them just above her ass, just enough to put them back in that comfortable territory of merciless teasing.

"I'm not the only one with a look," Rosie purred back.

So she wasn't denying that she wanted this too? Callum could definitely work with that.

"Oh?" Callum breathed. "And what look do I have? Do tell."

Rosie stretched up on her tiptoes to whisper sensually into Callum's ear, "Like you're ready to drop to your knees and *beg* me to spread my legs for you."

He was. Fucking hell, he was.

"Alright, alright. It's time for a slow one," the DJ called over the speakers. "So grab your partners and hold them tight because you definitely don't want to miss a *thing* about this dance."

Steven Tyler's voice filled the pavilion and trailed across the beach and into the night.

Rosie made to turn away from him and leave the dance floor, but Callum pulled her back with a gentle tug of her arm.

"What are you—"

"Dance with me?" he asked gently.

Something in her gaze softened at that.

"I—" she started.

"Please?" Callum cut her off before she could utter an excuse that would result in him having to let her go, which he really, *really* didn't want to do.

"I wasn't going to say no," she smiled softly up at him.

"Well, then what were you going to say?" He took a step toward her.

"I was just going to say that I was surprised you wanted to dance..." Rosie glanced down, almost nervously, "with me."

"In a bad way?"

"No," Rosie grabbed his hands and moved them back to rest on her hips. "No, not in a bad way."

She gently laced her hands together behind his neck.

Callum breathed a sigh of relief at that. He still wasn't entirely sure what he was doing, but he felt content here with her, the two of them swaying together under the warm glow of the fairy lights that had been strung up across the pavilion. Everything about the moment was beautiful.

Neither one of them spoke another word, content to simply enjoy the stillness of the moment. Callum and Rosie were surrounded by so many real couples: his parents, Hayden and Lydia (who raised her eyebrows at him as if to say, 'what's that about?'), Cole and Elena. He'd almost forgotten that Rosie wasn't his—at least not in any way that mattered.

But that wasn't what he wanted. Rosie was still very much off-limits as anything more than a friend with benefits, and that was just fine by him. He just wanted to be sure that if Rosie went home with *anyone* tonight, it was him.

Right?

19

FUCK THE RULES

Rosie:

At some point between the end of the reception and arriving back at the beach house, Callum had undone the top two buttons of his shirt. She could just barely see the snake tattoo she had kissed her way across so many times before, and her body evidently cared more about making that happen again than it did about thinking logically enough to remember that she'd said this weekend was about Elena, not her and Callum. But after dancing with him at the reception...

The vulnerability he'd shown when he'd asked her to slow dance with him had only heightened the desire she felt for him. It was a side of Callum she seldom ever saw; having that attention directed toward her had cracked a little piece of her heart. Lilah had been right that she'd fucked up by mentally comparing him to Justin. Callum wasn't Justin—would never be Justin—and it felt like asking her to dance with him had been his attempt at proving that to her. She hated herself for putting him in that position, for making him feel as if he *had* to prove himself to her.

Whatever his motivation had been, Rosie had walked away from that dance wanting Callum more than she'd ever wanted anyone. Maybe flirting hadn't been such a harmless idea after all... She was fucked. No, she *needed* to be fucked, and that was exactly why she absolutely could *not* continue to flirt with Callum, at least not until this weekend was over. Now sounded like a great time to go wash her makeup off and splash some cold water on her heated face.

Emerging from the bathroom after scrubbing her face, and her mind of all thoughts that revolved around Callum naked, Rosie ran straight into what was hard enough to be a wall but was definitely not a wall—Callum's perfectly carved body. Great, just the person she was hoping to avoid.

He didn't dare to move, yet he didn't dare to *make* a move either. Callum's gaze focused intently on her cheekbone, and then, ever so slowly, he lifted his hand toward her face as if he planned to tilt her chin up just enough for their lips to meet. The weekend wasn't technically over, but the *wedding* was, and Elena was happily married and on her way to her honeymoon with Cole... Callum's face was an inch from hers—could she really be blamed if she were to accidentally lean forward, to accidentally brush her lips against his?

Just as Rosie began to close her eyes in anticipation, she felt Callum chuckle against her, whispering, "you had an eyelash."

His palm lingered against the side of her face just long enough for her to note it.

"Oh, um, thanks," she whispered back.

"Anytime," he made no move to step out of her way.

"I, uh... we should... get back to everyone else."

"Should we?"

Rosie knew exactly what would happen if they didn't. Her resolve to wait until the weekend was over would deteriorate, she'd pull him back into the bathroom with her, and let him fuck her against the sink.

She was definitely blushing. Had he noticed? Her face was hot to the touch, and his hand had just brushed her cheek. Of course, he had noticed. *Shit*. She shoved against his chest in an attempt to move past him, but that proved to be an even worse idea than standing still in front of him because she felt his abs contract beneath her hand.

Willpower. Slowly. Dissolving.

"Rose, we could talk about—"

Oh no. Oh *hell* no. He was using *the* nickname—the one he only ever used while they were hooking up. Any other time it was Rosie or Rosemary, which meant that he knew exactly how badly she wanted him right now.

"Callum, don't..." she cut him off.

"You're right. The weekend isn't over. I'm sorry."

Somehow, Callum not pushing her boundaries was worse. It was reminiscent of the vulnerability he'd shown her earlier when they'd danced. Yes, she'd been the one to say nothing could happen between them this weekend, but the realization that *he* was taking sex off the table hit harder than she expected it to. And she didn't like it.

Before she realized what she was doing, her hand was on his waist. He leaned into her touch, his lips less than an inch from hers. Rosie could feel that he was hard, and she had barely even touched him.

"What are you—"

Hearing that name on his lips broke what was left of her restraint. Rosie closed the distance between them, pressing her lips to his. Callum kissed back for all of two seconds before his hands found her hips and pushed her back from him.

"But you said—"

"I know what I said. But... I mean, the wedding *is* over..." Rosie hesitated.

"I'm trying so fucking hard to be respectful of your boundaries, Rosie," Callum breathed heavily against her, "but you're making it incredibly difficult not to fall to my knees for you."

Rosie grabbed his hand with hers, slowly guiding it under her shirt to lightly trace the underside of her breasts as she leaned up to graze his lips again.

"Tell me what you want, Rose. I need you to use your words," Callum breathed onto her lips.

"I want—"

"Rosie! Are you almost done in there?" Noah called down the hallway from the living room, cutting her off before she could tell Callum that what she wanted was to drag him back into that bathroom with her and finish what they'd started.

Before she could tell him that the wedding was over and sex was *very much* back on the table, that sex *on* a table sounded especially great.

Callum followed her back out into the living room, earning suspicious glances from several people in the wedding party, and a smirk from Noah who waltzed over to Rosie with two shot glasses in her hand. Rosie had never loved her more.

Several shots later, Noah pulled Rosie onto the couch with purpose.

"Spill," was all she said.

"Spill what?" Rosie asked, innocently.

"Bitch, don't even. Spill whatever the fuck happened

between you and Callum in the hallway that had you walking back in here like that."

"*Technically* nothing" Rosie deflected.

"Spare me the technicalities, babe," Noah glanced over her shoulder. "I *could* just go ask Callum myself?"

"You would not," Rosie lifted her eyebrows in silent challenge.

She had quite literally, never in her life, been more horny than she was in that moment. If Noah called Callum over, she might just pass away right there on the couch. She'd already exerted every ounce of her willpower by walking away from him in that hallway.

"Please. Hey, Call—"

"Shut the fuck up, Noh!" Rosie whisper-yelled, softening her words. "Great, now he's walking over here."

"Need something?" Callum asked Noah, winking in Rosie's direction.

Yeah, she did actually—she needed him inside her. Immediately. Fuck her rules. The wedding was over.

"I was just wondering if you'd use your fancy bartending skills to make me and Rosie another drink," Noah said sweetly.

"Anything for Elena's best friends," he replied with a smirk on his face.

Did he seriously just refer to her as 'Elena's best friend' like they hadn't just been about to fuck in that bathroom? Like he hadn't *actually* fucked her not even a month ago? 'Elena's best friend' didn't even begin to cover their relationship. She supposed she didn't have the right to be angry with him for referring to her that way—it's not like they were more than friends, not technically anyway. Still, she and Callum were *something* to one another, she just didn't know exactly how to define it.

Watching Callum cross the threshold behind the bar out of the corner of her eye, Rosie focused her attention back on Noah.

"Alright, long story short: I walked out of the bathroom, smacked into Callum, thought he was going to kiss me: he didn't. But he also wouldn't move out of my way. Then the next thing I know he's respecting the fact that I wanted to wait until we got home for anything to happen which effectively made me want him even more. I was two seconds from dragging him back into the bathroom with me when you called down the hall."

"Good thing or bad thing that I interrupted?" Noah asked.

"Good. Bad? I don't know?" Rosie flailed her arms as if trying to convey just how ambivalent she was. "I know I said nothing this weekend, but then I saw him in that stupid fucking suit and the wedding is over and the only thing I know for sure is that I have quite literally never been more desperate in my life," Rosie babbled.

"You know, the only one holding you to this whole 'no sex until after wedding weekend' thing is you, right?" Noah pointed out.

"I know," Rosie sighed.

"So? What's your hesitation?"

"I guess I just don't want the entire wedding party, half of which are Callum's family members, to be privy to whatever the fuck is going on between us? I mean, it's not like they don't know about everything between us up to this point, but I just don't want to make this weekend about things between us. I want this weekend to just be about Elena."

"Okay, fair," Noah agreed.

"Can you die from being too horny? Because I think I

might," Rosie groaned, falling back into Noah's lap on the couch.

"Mm, no," Noah laughed. Leaning down to whisper into Rosie's ear, Noah asked the obvious: "You did bring the Red Devil, didn't you?"

The Red Devil was Rosie's most trusty, travel-size vibrator. It fit in a small, inconspicuous red clamshell case, was powerful but quiet, and Rosie absolutely refused to go on a trip without it. Of course, she'd brought it.

"Obviously."

"Brought what?" Callum asked, lifting Rosie's legs into his lap to sit between Noah and Rosie, whose head was still in Noah's lap, on the couch.

Rosie could feel that Callum, although he'd repositioned, was still hard and was doing absolutely nothing to hide it from Rosie. She would even venture to guess that he'd placed her legs in his lap just so that she would be forced to acknowledge how desperately he wanted her too.

"Nothing!" Rosie said at the same time that Noah said "oh, just girl stuff. Not for your ears."

Damn it, Noh. Way to not make it obvious.

"You'd be better off just telling me. Now I have all kinds of ideas floating around my head," Callum winked at Rosie.

You aren't the only one, Rosie thought.

Luckily, before Callum could vocalize any of those ideas, they were interrupted.

"Hey, Rosie," Liam walked over and sat on the arm of the couch. "Could I, um, talk to you for a minute?"

"Of course," Rosie answered, maneuvering her body to an upright position. "You okay?" she asked Noah before standing.

"Yeah," Noah answered. "I'm actually gonna try to go

talk to..." she trailed off, not wanting to say Lilah's name with so many people within earshot.

"So, what's up?" Rosie asked Liam as they walked down the hall toward what she figured was his bedroom.

"I hope this isn't weird for me to ask... It's just that you're the only person I know who would understand how I'm feeling and that I would feel comfortable talking to about something like this. And I'm sorry for interrupting your night..."

Liam was the quieter of the two Costello brothers, but, when he did speak, he was usually much more self-assured. This rambling version of Liam was extremely out of character, and Rosie couldn't imagine what he wanted to talk to her about.

He turned the doorknob of the last door on the left, and Rosie followed him inside the room.

Sitting on the edge of the bed, he quietly asked, "How, um, how did you know that you were bisexual?"

Oh. That explained the nervous rambling. And why he'd wanted to talk to her specifically.

"It wasn't one thing, really. It was more realizing that a lot of my experiences weren't ones that the other girls at school had," Rosie explained.

"Like?"

"Well, for one, I found myself staring at women's bodies a lot. Like, all the time. When I talked to other girls my age, they only talked about other girls' bodies in comparison to their own, never appreciatively. I, on the other hand, would think about how soft a girl's skin looked, how the curve of her ass looked in her jeans, how her tongue drifted across her lips to moisten them, the way it would feel to run my fingers across her ribs, how it would feel to squeeze her boobs..."

"Oh," was all Liam said.

Rosie was quiet, giving him the space to think.

"And what kinds of thoughts do you have about men?" he asked after a few minutes.

"I think about," Rosie began, concentrating all of her efforts on ensuring that she didn't slip up and replace any 'he's' with Callum's name, "his arms. I think about how they would feel around me, pulling my body to his. I think about his fingers, how dextrous they are, and what else they could do. I think about the muscles of his thighs. I think about how his teeth would feel scraping against my lower lip..." she trailed off, not sure how specific she could be without making it weird.

She figured that Liam was comparing her thoughts to his own in an effort to make sense of what he was feeling. When he didn't say anything for a while, Rosie decided to try something else.

"Hey Liam?" she asked.

"Yeah?"

"Did anyone in particular come to mind while I was talking?"

"Um, yeah..." he answered, not looking at her.

"You don't have to tell me anything you aren't comfortable with, but I promise I understand how you're feeling," Rosie rested her hand on his thigh, squeezing gently in encouragement. "I've been exactly where you are. And it's okay to be scared, or unsure, or whatever else you might be feeling."

"There is someone... he," Liam turned to face her then, "he went to college with me, and we still hang out a lot. I really enjoy being around him, being close to him."

"Okay," Rosie smiled. "I think that's great."

"Yeah?"

"Absolutely," she answered with confidence.

"I don't even know if he's, yanno," Liam gestured to Rosie. "Bisexual? Gay? Fuck, I don't even know for sure if I am, but... we were hanging out at his place a few weeks ago, just watching a movie, and all I could think about the whole time was how close he was sitting to me. How it felt when his thigh brushed against mine, and I—"

"Were you uncomfortable with the close proximity?" Rosie questioned gently.

"No. I mean, I don't think so. I was nervous, but I didn't want him to move away," Liam explained.

"Do you remember what you felt like the first time you ever did more than make out with a girl?" Rosie asked.

Liam nodded, "I was scared shitless that she would know I had no clue what I was doing."

"But it got easier, right? Better, more enjoyable the more experiences you had?"

He nodded again.

"I think that a lot of times, people mistake first-experience nerves for disinterest," Rosie explained.

"That actually makes a lot of sense," Liam sighed in what appeared to be relief. "Thanks, Rosie."

"Of course, Liam," Rosie reached out to pull him into a hug. "In case no one else has had the chance to tell you, I'm proud of you. It takes a lot of courage to be yourself sometimes."

Liam squeezed her tighter. Rosie could hear him sniffle.

"Hey," she said, tilting his face to look her in the eyes. "You're going to be okay. Promise."

"Thank you. Seriously. You're the first person I've said anything to, and I just really appreciate you being here," Liam admitted.

"I'm honored. I am also going to insist that you fill me in

on what happens the next time you see him," Rosie shoved his shoulder playfully. "I'm unapologetically nosy."

"You got it," Liam laughed.

Standing and walking in the direction of the door, Rosie asked, "Shall we?"

Callum spent the rest of the night finding reasons to be near Rosie. She went to the kitchen for another drink, and he followed, offering to mix it for her. She sat on the couch, he sat next to her despite there being a perfectly empty end chair two feet away. She was cold, he was oh so happy to share his blanket with her. Slowly, painfully so, the rest of the wedding party made their way to their rooms for the night, Noah included, leaving her alone with Callum.

Rosie decided it was time for her to make her exit too, knowing that without someone else as a buffer, she wouldn't have the willpower to prevent the night from ending with Callum inside her.

"I think I'm gonna head to bed, too," Rosie stood from the couch, Callum following suit. She playfully ran her hand down his biceps, whispering, "goodnight Callum."

Before she had the chance to react, Callum grabbed her by the waist and hauled his lips to hers for a gentle kiss that left entirely too much to be desired.

"Goodnight, Rosemary June," Callum whispered against her lips.

Rosie stood, stunned, as Callum turned from her and walked straight into his room without so much as glancing back in her direction.

The desire to follow him into his room was almost compelling enough to make her feet move; but, as much as she wanted Callum, it would be smarter to just wait until they were back home. She didn't exactly want the entirety of the wedding party as an audience. So, instead, Rosie settled for the Red Devil she'd packed and closed her eyes, pretending instead that it was Callum's face she was riding.

20

DON'T BE FOOLED BY THE CARTOON COVER

Callum:

Callum had no one to thank besides his own heavy-handed pouring for the liquid courage that had compelled him to kiss Rosie goodnight. He hadn't given himself time to think about it before he had grabbed her. He knew tonight wasn't going to be the night for hooking up with Rosie again; she'd set clear boundaries and damn if he was going to adhere to them even if it killed him. He'd nearly given into crossing them when she'd kissed him as though she needed his lips like she needed oxygen in the hallway earlier. Almost. Still, he couldn't go to sleep without initiating a kiss of his own. Without her knowing he craved her just as deeply.

Already starting to feel the beginnings of a hangover, Callum decided to head up to the kitchen to get some water and a snack before going to bed. Though he'd spaced his drinks out, needing to stay relatively sober on the chance that Rosie decided she wanted to talk about things between them, he'd still ended up with enough alcohol in his system to give him a headache in the morning if he didn't do future Callum a favor and drink a shit load of water before bed.

As he reached the kitchen, Callum heard a faint humming sound coming from Rosie's room—the closest to the kitchen—and figured she must be brushing her teeth. He grabbed a glass from the cabinet and went to the sink to fill it up. He quickly emptied the glass and began to refill it. Callum guessed that he'd need to drink at least three glasses if he wanted to wake up headache-free.

As he gulped down his second glass of water, Callum glanced around for bread or crackers, anything that would help soak up the alcohol in his system. On the far end of the kitchen island was a bag of pita bread that Callum remembered being set out earlier with—he pulled the handle on the fridge door—hummus. *Jackpot.* Grabbing the hummus container from the fridge, Callum opened the bag of pita bread and ripped off a piece small enough that he wouldn't have to double dip in the container.

A few minutes later, satisfied with the two slices of pita bread and hummus he'd consumed, Callum walked back over to the sink to refill his water glass one more time before heading back down to bed. When he turned the faucet off, he realized he could still hear that faint humming sound coming from Rosie's room. Callum wasn't sure exactly how long he'd been in the kitchen but it was definitely way longer than necessary for someone to brush their teeth, which meant that humming sound wasn't coming from a toothbrush. Was Rosie... Could that humming have been coming from one of her vibrators? He thought back to their conversation at Lafayette's when she'd admitted to touching herself in response to finding out that Callum had punched Justin...

I'm glad I own a lot of toys.

Callum walked closer to her door in an attempt to discern exactly what he was hearing. As he did, the humming sound blended with a breathy moan. Callum had elicited those beautiful sounds from Rosie enough times to know with a hundred percent certainty what was happening behind her door. Fuck, what he wouldn't give for it to be his cock inside of her and not that damn vibrator.

Callum hadn't exactly been quiet in his quest for water and bread, so she had to know that someone was out here. And if she did, why wasn't she trying to be more discreet? Unless she knew it was Callum... Unless she'd wanted him to hear her...

He contemplated knocking on the door but decided against it. She'd had a lot to drink tonight, and he wouldn't take a chance on her waking up tomorrow regretting anything as a result. He may not have been good at commitment, but he understood the importance of consent.

With nothing better to do besides torture himself with the sounds of Rosie fucking herself, Callum decided now was as good a time as any to walk back downstairs to his room. Immediately, he noticed that Lilah was nowhere to be seen; he secretly hoped she was busy with Noah. Speaking of Noah... Earlier this weekend, he'd seen Rosie and Noah blushing at various pages of the book she'd brought on the trip to Edisto. He wanted to know why.

He tried to recall the title. Something about a roommate? He remembered that the cover was pink. Hoping for the best, Callum typed 'Roommate romance book pink cover' into Google. In a matter of seconds, he found what he was looking for. Clicking on the listing for the book on a website called Goodreads, he scrolled to the synopsis; he gleaned that the book was about a girl who moved across the country with the intent of living with her best friend, only to be ditched and ended up living with a stranger that turned out to be a mega-famous porn star. Interesting...

A few clicks later, Callum discovered that he could buy the novel as an ebook through his Amazon account for only ten dollars. Really, he reasoned, why the fuck not? It wasn't like he'd be falling asleep anytime soon. If nothing else, he would learn something about Rosie from all of this. After purchasing the book, Amazon prompted him to download the Kindle app to begin reading, which he did.

Before he realized how much time had passed, he was several chapters deep into the book. The porn star had come back to the apartment he shared with the female main character to the familiar sound of his own moaning. She was watching one of his films. Callum had read the words cock, pussy, fuck, and moan more times than he could count, and he was still less than a hundred pages into the story.

The book was nothing like Callum had expected from an innocent-looking cartoon cover. Sure there was a plot, but there was no denying that this book was written porn. Now that he thought about it, he'd seen countless women, Rosie included, carry these cartoon cover books around everywhere. Were they *all* like this? Were women reading straight-up porn... in public? Surely not...

Clicking back to the website where he'd found the original listing for the book, Goodreads, he thought it looked vaguely familiar. He knew Rosie posted book reviews somewhere since she announced new reviews on her Instagram all the time. Navigating to her profile, Callum saw a link to her Goodreads account in her bio. Curious, he clicked.

Sure enough, there was a review for all of the books he'd ever seen her carry around or post about. He clicked on the one for the book he'd just downloaded:

House rule #1: DO look up your roommate online. Then let him catch you watching his porn videos.

Well, well, well... sweet little Rosemary was reading *porn*. Callum planned to tease her about this later. Did Rosie touch herself after reading these books, too? The next line of Rosie's review caught his attention:

Highly suggest reading this one on your Kindle—a one-hand read for sure.

One-hand? As in one for reading, and one for... *Jesus. Fucking...* How many other men were entirely oblivious to the fact that women were consuming their porn in the form of these little cartoon-cover romance novels? Yeah, Callum would definitely be teasing Rosie about this the next time he saw her carrying one around.

Right now, however, he needed to deal with the massive erection he now had thanks to the chapter he'd left off on. He figured he'd save himself the clean-up and headed straight for the shower, especially since Lilah could come back at any minute. They were close, but she wouldn't invade the privacy of a closed bathroom door.

Though the book had been the cause of his arousal, it was Rosie's face, Rosie's body, that Callum thought about as he stood underneath the spray of the water, gripping his cock. He thought about the sweet little noises that escaped her as he'd buried his face between her thighs, how it felt as she came on his face, around his cock, how she'd given him her panties before she left, how he'd fucked his fist into the black lacy fabric later.

He came, hard, yet even then he felt unfulfilled. He thought that he'd likely feel that way until the next time that he came inside Rosie's perfect cunt.

21

ROSIEMARY

Callum:

After getting Lilah safely into the ride he'd called for her, Callum was left to figure out how he was going to get home. It had been nearly two weeks since the wedding, and, still, neither one of them wanted to talk about things. So, he and Lilah had made a fool's bargain with each other while they were hanging out tonight. Any time Lilah didn't want to answer his questions about Noah, she had to take a shot; anytime Callum didn't want to answer a question about Rosie, *he* had to take a shot. Namely, Callum wanted to know what had happened in the hours between when he'd gone to bed, Lilah nowhere to be seen, and when he'd woken up to her on the other side of the bed. Lilah wanted to know what Callum was doing with Rosie. Naturally, they'd both ended up incredibly drunk.

Callum's contact list was blurry as he stared at his phone, trying to find her name. There it was: Rosie. He pressed the call button before he could lose her name again.

"Hey, Costello, what's up?"

He loved it when she called him that.

"What did you say? It's hard to hear you with all that background noise."

Fuck, had he said that out loud? Maybe drunk calling Rosie wasn't his best idea. But he needed a ride home, and the only person he wanted to see right now was Rosie. He could call himself a ride like he'd done for Lilah, but then he wouldn't get to see her.

"Will you be a rose and come pick me up from Lafayette's?"

A rose? He needed to get it the fuck together, but that was proving rather difficult at this moment.

"Callum, are you drunk?" she guessed correctly, sounding incredibly amused.

"Nooooo, ofcourse not," he slurred his response rather unconvincingly.

"Okay, Costello," she laughed.

He loved her laugh.

"I'll come get you, but I need you to drink some water in the meantime. I'd rather not have to clean puke out of my car," Rosie joked.

Rosie was so funny, and Rosie always made him laugh.

"You're just drunk," she laughed again.

Uh-oh. Had he said something else out loud too?

"I'll be there soon," she told him.

Where was this coming from? Callum didn't think about sappy shit like this? But Rosie was coming to pick him up and she would probably smell so good, like lavender and vanilla. She always smelled so good like lavender and vanilla.

"Thank you Rosie Posie, I'll see you sosooon," he said before hanging up the phone.

Jesus Christ, he was drunk off his ass if he was calling her 'Rosie Posie.'

He needed to drink his weight in water before she got here. And eat some bread. Bread would help soak up the alcohol, or at least give his mouth something to do that didn't involve talking out of his ass about lavender and vanilla and Rosie's laugh that was so nice to hear.

About thirty minutes later, Rosie texted Callum to let him know that she was parked out front, waiting for him. Callum managed to walk out the front door of Lafayette's without falling on his ass, which was an improvement from earlier when he actually *did* fall on his ass on the way to the bathroom. He really hoped Lilah was as drunk as he was and that she wouldn't remember that tomorrow.

Rosie started laughing the second they made eye contact, and Callum couldn't help but laugh too as she helped him into the passenger side of her car.

"So," she looked him up and down, "how much did you have to drink tonight?" she asked him as she put her seatbelt on.

Callum was too busy trying to make his own stupid seatbelt make the "click" sound to give her an answer. Noticing his inability to do something most toddlers could manage without help, she leaned over to help him. When she did, her long, copper-toned hair fell over her shoulder and into Callum's face. Rosie's hair smelled so good, like vanilla. He wanted to bottle it so he could smell it forever.

"Did you just smell my hair?" she raised her eyebrows in question.

"No," he replied a little too quickly to be convincing.

"Nope," he tried again, attempting to sound a bit more sure of himself.

"I'm going to go with you had a lot to drink tonight," she surmised.

"Only like one or three beers," he declared. "Aaand maybe some shots," he added, exposing himself.

"Alright, well how about some food on the way home?" she asked.

"Food is so good. You're so good to me, Rosiemary."

You're so good to me, Rosiemary? What the hell was he even saying? His mouth needed to find something else to do right now. Kissing Rosie would be a good thing for Callum's mouth to do right now, he thought. Kissing her on her pretty, rose-colored lips that were always glossy, on her perfect tits—man, he loved those tits, on the inside of her thighs, between her thighs... but Rosie was driving, so he couldn't do any of that.

Why did his pants suddenly feel like they were too small? Uh-oh. Not too small—too *tight*. His cock apparently did not get the memo that now was not an appropriate time to touch Rosie or to think about touching Rosie. Had Rosie noticed? He hoped not.

"Hey, Callum?" Rosie laughed.

"Yeah?"

"You're thinking with the wrong head," she snorted. "How about you tell me what you want to eat?"

You.

"You're too drunk to do that," Rosie smirked.

Shit.

"I said that out loud?"

"Yep. And a lot of other things I assume were meant to stay in your head," Rosie laughed.

Not good, Callum thought to himself. At least Rosie was

amused and not mad. And since he was already saying things that really should stay in his head, he figured it couldn't hurt to add one more.

"Why Justin?" he asked Rosie abruptly.

"What?" Rosie responded, looking caught off guard.

"Why did you date him?" Callum clarified.

"What do you mean?"

"You're too good for him, Rosie. You're so bold, and you're so sure of yourself, and you work so hard all the time, but not Justin. Nooo, never Justin. But always you."

"You know, it's funny, I actually said the same thing to him when we broke up. He said that he needed to 'find himself' and that I 'deserved better than him.' I think saying those things was just a cop-out so that he didn't have to admit that I made him feel inferior. But that's the thing—I shouldn't have to make myself smaller, to take up less space to make him feel comfortable. If I was too much for him, then he can go find less."

Maybe it was the alcohol, but Callum couldn't seem to understand how Justin had become the person Rosie gave so much of herself to. Justin was undeserving of her in every way, but she had still loved him. Callum didn't understand.

"But you loved him. Why did you love him?" Callum wondered aloud.

"I thought I did. Looking back on everything, I realize now that I loved the version of him I thought I could help him become. And those aren't the same," she admitted.

The light in Rosie's eyes seemed to dim, and Callum didn't like that. He wanted the silly Rosie back from a minute ago.

"You know what I think?" he asked her.

"That you're too drunk to remember this conversation in the morning?" Rosie answered.

"Shh," he leaned over and pressed a finger to her lips to shush her. The light returned to her eyes, not fully, but enough to encourage Callum to keep talking. "I think that Justin didn't deserve your love. And I think that you can't change people. They have to do it all on their own. But I wouldn't change you, Rosie Posie. No, I wouldn't change anything about you—not your big brain that makes you say things that are too smart for me to understand sometimes, not your pretty red hair that smells sooo good like vanilla. Did you know that? It smells like vanilla."

"Okay, Callum." Rosie laughed. "Whatever you say."

"Excuse me," he said, again pressing a finger to her lips. "I wasn't finished. I wouldn't change your pretty lips that I love kissing, and I wouldn't change your perfect tits. They're so nice, Rosie. I love them so much."

He couldn't help but look at them then. Was she even wearing a bra underneath her tank top?

"Callum?"

"Rosie?"

"You're making it really hard to concentrate on driving."

"Well, *you're* making it really hard not to be hard," Callum retorted.

For the love of God, he needed to stop talking.

"Yeah, I can see that," Rosie snorted.

"Oh. Oops. I'm sorry," he muttered.

"It's okay, but nothing can happen between us tonight. You're too drunk to know what you want," she decided.

Tonight. She didn't say nothing could happen between them at all. He really hoped he remembered that tomorrow.

"You said 'not tonight.' Does that mean something can happen when it's not tonight anymore?" he asked.

"I told you my answer to that already," she hesitated. "At the beach house in Edisto."

"Nuh-uh," Callum argued.

Really, he just wanted to hear her say it.

"Yes, I did. In the hallway..." she admitted.

When he'd backed her into the bathroom door, trailed his hands up her waist to graze the underside of her breasts, and begged her to let him get on his knees... He really, *really* hoped he remembered this conversation tomorrow.

"So, food. How does Cook Out sound?" Rosie asked him, changing the subject.

Callum was so hungry that he didn't care where she took him.

"Can we get a milkshake?"

"Yes, Callum, we can get a milkshake," Rosie laughed again.

He wanted to hear her laugh forever.

Rosie:

Rosie hadn't laughed this much since... Honestly, she couldn't remember the last time she'd laughed this much. This goofy side of Callum was one she rarely ever saw, and she was beginning to grow very fond of it. That wasn't to say that she didn't also love the cocky side of Callum whose face seemed to be permanently arranged into a smirk, but this was nice, comfortable even.

Rosie had probably been too honest, too vulnerable with Callum tonight, but she figured it didn't really matter—it's not like he was going to remember any of it in the morning. He was absolutely drunk off his ass.

Still, she couldn't help but wonder where all of his compliments had come from, all those things about how

Justin was undeserving of her, or why he'd even decided to call *her* in the first place. Callum could have called Elena, Lilah, Cole—hell, he could probably have even gotten a ride home with one of the bartenders when they got off. Or just called a ride. But he'd called Rosie, and she wanted to know why.

"Callum, why did you call me to pick you up tonight?"

"Did you forget that I'm drunk?" he looked confused by the question.

"No, I mean why did you call *me* to pick you up? Why not Lilah or Elena or someone else at the bar?" Rosie clarified.

"Well, Lilah is also very drunk. But... because I couldn't stop thinking about you," he admitted. "And I wanted to see you."

No shit, Rosie thought. She hadn't been able to stop thinking about Callum either since she basically said, 'yes, Callum, please get on your knees for me,' in the hallway at the beach house. If she was being honest with herself, she probably would have let something happen between them tonight if Callum wasn't shit-faced.

Callum fell asleep before they even made it to Cook Out, so Rosie ended up just taking him straight to his apartment. She woke him up, walked him up the stairs to his door, and then down the hall to lay him on his bed. She made sure he had a trash can and water close to his bed.

As she walked toward the door to leave, she could have sworn she heard him whisper one small, nervous word.

"Stay."

22

CALLUM JAMES COSTELLO KNEW FOUR THINGS

Callum:

MOTHER*FUCKER*, Callum's head hurt. That was his first thought as he woke up the next morning. His second thought was that he remembered calling Rosie to pick him up from the bar last night, but couldn't remember which of his thoughts had stayed in his head and which had made it out. He did remember Rosie laughing more than he'd seen her laugh since she and Justin had broken up. If anything, that was probably an indication that he'd said a decent amount of things out loud that he hadn't meant to. He hoped his memories would come back to him as the day progressed.

He reached blindly toward his nightstand to check his phone—eleven AM. He unlocked his phone to find a text thread with himself. That couldn't be good.

> Callum: Dear tomorrow morning Callum:

> Callum: Rosie is so nice to come get you. Beso nice to Rosie Posey.

> Callum: Rosie's hair smells good like vanilla. I think you told her that?
>
> Callum: You definitelydid. Oops.
>
> Callum: Hey I hope you don't throw up later
>
> Callum: DONOTFORGET Rosie said nothing can happen tonight because you are stupid and drunk.
>
> Callum: She didn't call you stupid. You are stupid because youare drunk and cannot have your Rosiemary.
>
> Callum: Rosie Posey said something can happen when it's not tonight nymore.
>
> Callum: Don't forget that dumb
>
> Callum: Ass
>
> Callum: Rosie's laugh is the bessound in the world. Please make her laugh for forever so can always hear herlaugh.
>
> Callum: Rosie is buying you a milkshake. She's sonice.

Callum knew he'd been absolutely off his ass, but he didn't anticipate it being *this* bad. He wondered how much of that he'd voiced out loud to Rosie. *Fuck*. At least there wasn't anything about Rosie being mad or annoyed in his diary of texts to himself.

Along with everyone else in the world, Callum had heard the adage 'a drunk mind speaks a sober heart,' which left him with a raging headache and the inability to avoid facing the implications of those texts. He would go for a run. Running would clear his mind *and* revive his body from the hangover, he decided.

Though his favorite place to run was by The Battery

downtown, he decided to just run on the treadmill at his apartment complex's gym so he wouldn't have to come all the way back here to shower just to turn around and head back downtown for work later. Callum slipped on a pair of gym shorts and his favorite vintage Eagles '77 tour t-shirt, then headed to the kitchen to fill up a water bottle on the way out the door. He would eat after he ran—it was nearly lunchtime anyway. As for contemplating the undeniable meaning of the texts from his drunk alter ego, he really, *really* hoped his run would help him make sense of things.

Kicking the speed on the treadmill up to eight MPH, Callum put his AirPods in and turned on his favorite running playlist. Usually, he focused on the beat of each song as he pushed through a three-mile run. Today, his thoughts kept drifting incessantly back to Rosie. Back to everything that his drunk thoughts implied.

As he ran, memories of the night started coming back to him in bits and pieces. He remembered asking about Justin, remembered Rosie saying she'd been in love with who she thought he might become and not who he actually was.

You're too good for him, Rosie. You're so bold, and you're so sure of yourself, and you work so hard all the time. Never Justin, but always you.

He'd always believed that of Rosie, Callum realized. Even though he'd never voiced it aloud until last night, he'd always admired Rosie deeply. She was so sure of herself—something Callum had never been.

I think that Justin didn't deserve your love. And I think that you can't change people. They have to do it on their own. But I wouldn't change you, Rosie Posie. I wouldn't change anything about you—not your big brain that makes you say things that are too smart for me to understand sometimes," and... and something about her hair smelling like vanilla?

He remembered Rosie laughing. A lot. He remembered her asking why he'd called her to pick him up. He remembered, though it scared the absolute fucking shit out of him, what he'd told her when she'd asked.

Because I couldn't stop thinking about you. And I wanted to see you.

And he had. He'd wanted nothing more in that moment than to see her. Callum had never, not even once in his life, genuinely committed to anyone. Had avoided it at all costs. He had thought he liked the freedom of being able to do whatever he wanted, but he couldn't help but wonder if, maybe, the freedom to be a hundred percent yourself with someone else was better somehow. He'd never cared enough to find out, but, after last night with Rosie... For the first and only time in his life, Callum realized that he'd begun craving the easy, comfortable presence of another person. Of Rosie.

He was again brought back to that night, all those years ago, when he'd proudly declared to Mrs. Dawson that he was going to one day marry Rosie. He'd always written it off as adolescent hubris; the fact that, as an eighth grader, he'd garnered the attention of a *high school girl* had made him feel important. Turning the memory over in his mind now, he realized that it had nothing to do with her age and everything to do with the fact that it was Rosie's attention that he'd captured.

He wondered if, maybe, the reason he'd always found something wrong with the women he dated, always found some reason to abandon ship was because none of them were *her*. That no one's attention would ever compare to hers. He wondered if the years of Rosie being off limits had molded Callum into the non-committal person he was today. And just what the fuck was he supposed to do with that?

At that moment, Callum James Costello knew four things with absolute certainty:

1. He had been secretly harboring feelings for Rosemary Dawson for the better part of the last decade. For him, it was Rosie or no one.
2. Proving that he was capable of committing to her would be an uphill battle.
3. He was willing to do whatever it would take for the chance to be with her.
4. He had absolutely no idea where to go from here.

Telling Rosie how he felt was far beyond his comfort zone. Really, any kind of emotional vulnerability was. Physical vulnerability? No problem. Callum knew he was attractive and knew how to please a woman. He had a natural confidence when it came to the physical aspects of a relationship. But how to talk about his *feelings*? Not a goddamn clue.

Maybe Callum didn't have to *tell* Rosie anything. Maybe he could show her how he felt around her—physical gestures were his thing. He could figure that out, right? He totally could. He hoped...

23

TEAM SLEEP WITH CALLUM INSTEAD OF FINISHING THIS DATE

Rosie:

Stay.

That one word had haunted her all day at work on Thursday.

"I think that Justin didn't deserve your love. And I think that you can't change people. But I wouldn't change you, Rosie Posie. No, I wouldn't change anything about you—"

Rosie had no idea how much Callum remembered of what he'd told her last night, but she remembered everything. And she had absolutely no idea what the hell to make of it. Every exchange between the two of them had always been shrouded in flirtation. Last night was no different, especially given the boner Callum had been sporting; yet, somehow, his drunk confessions felt different, not wholly playful.

When Rosie got done with work, she headed straight home to get ready for the date she'd been dreading for the past week. After last night, she had been dreading it even more. Elena and Cole were back from their honeymoon in

Greece and all settled into married life, which meant that Elena was back to spending her free time trying to set Rosie up with people. Rosie had grown tired of constantly turning down Elena's date propositions, but she figured that if she said yes to one, Elena might leave her alone about them for a while.

Elena was more than aware that Rosie and Callum were —sort of—friends with benefits right now, and had even encouraged Rosie to go for it herself. Still, that hadn't stopped her from trying to play matchmaker in Rosie's life. It was as if the idea of Rosie and Callum as anything more was so preposterous that it didn't even deserve a passing consideration; Rosie would have agreed... that is, until last night.

She'd originally agreed to the date on the condition that it take place at Lafayette's; Rosie wanted the reassurance of knowing someone would be there to intervene if the date went sideways—the joys of being a woman in today's world. Now, she felt almost guilty for flaunting a date at Callum's place of work, given whatever shift had happened between the two of them in the last twenty-four hours.

She needed to be at Lafayette's at seven, which gave her an hour to get ready—plenty of time, maybe even enough that she could read a chapter or two of the manuscript she was currently evaluating. If she was being honest with herself, she'd rather skip the date altogether and stay home to read, but then Elena would be back to pestering her about the newest person she thought would really hit it off with Rosie. And avoiding Elena's pestering was the sole reason she'd agreed to this date in the first place.

Rosie did the bare minimum on her makeup and pulled her copper-toned hair into a low ponytail, leaving a few face-framing pieces out in the front. She could have done a lot more, especially for a first date, but she looked good, and, more importantly, she had time to read the manuscript before she left.

After reading two chapters, she pulled on her favorite black heels, grabbed her purse, and walked down the three flights of stairs from her apartment to the parking lot. Driving into downtown, there was hardly any traffic. Rosie easily found a spot in the parking deck closest to Lafayette's and began the short walk there.

Cole's coworker, Tyler, was waiting for her outside the bar, wearing loose-fitting jeans, a graphic tee, and Converse. Rosie instantly felt overdressed next to him in her sundress and cardigan as they walked in together.

After checking in at the hostess stand, they were seated at a table toward the back of the downstairs level. After the usual first-date small talk, Callum made his way to their table to get their drink orders. This wasn't his usual section, and Rosie couldn't help but wonder if he'd traded sections with someone to wait on their table.

Was he upset that she was on a date? It's not like he remembered what she'd told him the other night when she'd given him a ride—he was too drunk. *Right?* Even if he did, it's not like her agreeing to sleep with him again meant she'd agreed to anything exclusive. Even so, Rosie couldn't manage to shake the growing feeling of guilt...

"You aren't one of those girls who only drinks fruity little cocktails are you?" Tyler asked her.

Rosie was in disbelief; from the look on his face, so was Callum.

"Your usual Cosmo, Rose?" Callum asked her, ignoring Tyler altogether.

It hadn't evaded her that he'd used that damn nickname. Tyler wouldn't think a thing of it, while it would direct

Rosie's own thoughts in a very specific direction that was definitely not appropriate while on a first date with someone who was *not* Callum.

"You know this kid?" Tyler raised his eyebrows at her.

"I've known her since we *were* kids," Callum answered for her.

"He's Elena's brother," Rosie offered, trying to quell the need for either of them to assert their dominance. "So yes, I know him. We grew up together."

"Assuming you won't be ordering one of those fruity little cocktails," Callum emphasized with air quotes, "what can I grab for you?"

"Beer is fine, and whatever she wants," Tyler responded.

Evidently, he either chose to ignore Callum's earlier note about her usual, or he genuinely hadn't cared enough to pay attention.

Before she could answer, Callum said casually, "I've got your Cosmo, Rose," smirking at her before walking back to the bar to grab their drinks.

Fuck, that damn nickname combined with the insufferable way her date was behaving was swaying her very quickly in favor of Team Sleep With Callum Instead of Finishing This Date.

Callum:

What the fuck?

She was on a date? At *his* bar? The only woman he'd ever even *considered* genuinely committing to was on a *date* at *his* bar. So much for trying to show Rosie how he felt with some grand gesture.

Jealousy surged through Callum as he walked back behind the bar to get Rosie and that asshat's drinks. Of all the people Rosie could have gone on a date with, it just *had* to be someone like that. Callum knew he wasn't exactly boyfriend material himself; but, shit, he was a better choice than that misogynistic prick. How did Rosie not see that? He nearly broke the lid off the garnish tray sliding it open to get the orange twist for her Cosmo.

Callum hadn't meant to go all 'dog pissing on his territory,' but when Tyler had asked if Rosie knew "this kid" referring to Callum, it triggered something possessive in him. He may not be Rosie's boyfriend, but he sure as hell knew her. Way better than Tyler ever would if Callum had anything to say about it. Pouring the draft beer Tyler had ordered, Callum gripped the glass he was holding so tightly that it shattered in his hand. And now he was bleeding. Fuck him—this night just kept getting worse and worse.

Callum yelled across the bar to Carter, the main bartender on shift.

"Broken glass, man, watch out! Gonna run to the office to take care of this," Callum held up his bleeding hand. "Be back to clean that up in a sec!"

Carter nodded his acknowledgment as Callum headed for the office to see how deeply his hand was cut. Hopefully not deep enough to need stitches, because there was no way in hell he was leaving work early tonight. Jealous and pissed off or not, he wasn't about to leave Rosie alone with Tyler.

"Shit," Callum muttered to himself as he dabbed at the cut with a towel, attempting to dry the blood enough to see what the cut looked like.

Once he got it dry, he realized that he didn't need stitches, but that he was definitely going to need more than a bandaid because the cut likely wasn't going to stop bleeding for a while.

Gauze, there was gauze in the office somewhere…

As he searched the office, Callum's thoughts floated back to Rosie. Clearly, she hadn't taken anything he'd said while drunk seriously. And, really, why would she? It's not like Callum had ever shown Rosie any version of himself beyond the fuckboy persona everyone knew him for. How could he expect her to think he was suddenly being sincere? And, clearly, Rosie didn't feel the same way about him if she'd come to Lafayette's on a date with someone else.

Callum had fucked things up before he'd even gotten the chance to show Rosie the person he wanted to be for her, which felt like as good a sign as any that he was better off continuing to avoid commitment for the rest of his life. If this was how it felt to lose the *possibility* of being with someone, he wanted no part in the possibility of *actually* losing Rosie.

After rummaging around the cabinets, he finally found Lafayette's first aid kit and took out enough gauze to wrap his hand thoroughly. With medical tape to secure the gauze in place, Callum opened and closed his hand to make sure everything would hold.

Satisfied that the gauze wouldn't slip off, Callum pulled his phone from his back pocket and texted Lilah.

> Callum: She's on a fucking date.

> Lilah: Ooh, you sound jealous. We're talking about Rosie, I assume?

> Callum: The guy is a grade-A jackass. He doesn't deserve her.

> Lilah: And you do?

Callum knew she was teasing him—he hadn't told her yet about his new-found feelings for Rosie. In all honesty, he'd been too scared. Like saying it aloud to someone made it real. But after the jealousy he'd felt tonight, he knew he couldn't ignore the way he felt any longer. Here went nothing...

> Callum: I'd like to try to be someone who does.

Immediately, Callum's phone lit up with an incoming call from Lilah.

"Hey, Lih," Callum answered.

"What the fuck do you mean you'd like to try?" Lilah asked so loudly that Callum had to pull the phone away from his ear.

"I fucking like her, okay? And let's skip the part where you tell me you were right all along and that you told me so. Just tell me what the fuck to do before I break another glass," Callum rambled exasperatedly.

"Back up. You broke a glass?"

That's what Lilah was stuck on? Not the part about him having feelings for Rosie?

"I went to pour the dickhead's beer, and I just squeezed the glass a little hard. It's not a big deal," Callum tried to explain in a way that made his actions sound rational.

"So, to recap: you're willingly admitting to having feelings for Rosie, you're jealous because she's on a date with someone else, and you got so mad at the guy that you broke a glass?"

"Yes, yes, and yes. Now tell me what to do, Lih," Callum pleaded.

"Ruin her for anyone else," Lilah answered without hesitation.

"Huh?" Callum wasn't following.

As far as this date suggested, Rosie saw Callum as nothing more than a convenient fuck. How was he supposed to ruin her interest in other people?

"You might not be good with expressing, or, let's be honest, *recognizing* your own feelings. But you *are* good with physical gestures," Lilah went on. "So, use that. Ruin her. Make her realize that no one else could ever come close to fucking her as well as you do."

"And how exactly does that help me tell her how I feel?"

"Once she realizes that you're the best she'll ever have, she'll have nothing to do but confront why that is," Lilah stated like it was obvious.

"And why is that?" Callum asked.

"Because you have both been pining after each other for the past decade, even though you're both too dense to realize it."

Rosie:

Not acknowledging, let alone apologizing for, his rude comment earlier, Tyler continued the conversation.

"So, tell me about yourself. What do you do for work?"

"I'm an acquisition editor. Essentially, I evaluate manuscripts to decide if they're marketable, then I work with the author on their contract and help walk them through strategies for publication."

"What kind of manuscripts do you read?"

"A lot of the manuscripts I receive are in the romance genre, but I do evaluate a lot of fiction manuscripts as well."

"Romance is such an oversaturated genre. I've never understood why. Romance novels have no substance."

Was he serious? First, he invalidated her drink choice, and now her literal *job*? In what world did he think this was the way to treat a person on a date? In what world was this the way to treat a person in general? The world where he didn't get laid at the end of the date, that was for sure.

Before Rosie could think of a way to respond that didn't involve punching Tyler in his pretentious little face, Callum came back with their drinks. As he set her Cosmo down, she noticed that his left hand was wrapped in gauze that had definitely not been there when he'd been by their table earlier.

Rosie grabbed his hand, pulling it in her direction to look more closely, "What happened? You okay?"

"Yeah, nothing," Callum pulled his hand away before she could get a good look. "I'm fine."

"Clearly not, considering your hand is wrapped in gauze," Rosie pressed.

Why wouldn't he tell her what had happened? She raised her eyebrows at him, prompting him to elaborate.

"Look, I'm fine, okay?" Callum sighed. "I just grabbed a glass a little too tight and a piece of it cut my hand, but I'm fine," he explained.

It seemed like he wanted to avoid talking about it right now, so she decided to drop it until she could talk to him alone. She could ask him about it again later when this nightmare of a date was over.

And, honestly, thank God for Callum's timing because Rosie was going to need alcohol, and a lot of it, to get through the rest of this date. She chugged at least four sips worth of her Cosmo in one gulp.

Callum noticed, but it was obvious that Tyler didn't

when he decided to expand on his earlier thoughts about Rosie's job.

"It must be incredibly unfulfilling to have a job that requires you to read such vapid manuscripts all the time."

Callum's gaze shot straight to Rosie, and her face turned bright red. She did *not* need him to witness this failed attempt at a first date. It would give him further basis for his argument that he was the better option for a hookup. *Why suffer through horrible first dates like this to get someone into bed when you could just call me?* she could already hear him saying to her later.

"Rose has actually dreamed of being an editor ever since I met her. I can't imagine a better job for her; she always has a book with her, and she's the only person I know who actually liked the assigned readings when we were in high school. She read *The Great Gatsby* at least four times before graduation," Callum inserted himself into the conversation yet again.

Uh, where was this coming from? Why was Callum being so defensive of her? It almost seemed like Callum was... *jealous*? Of Tyler? It wasn't off base for him to remember her talking about becoming an editor, she'd been incessant about it as a teenager, but he'd paid attention to how many times she'd read *Gatsby*? That was new information. New and confusing information that was currently affecting her no longer dry underwear.

"What's the deal with you two?" Tyler asked, head motioning between Rosie and Callum.

"Nothing," Callum said at the same time as Rosie.

"Tell that to his hand," Tyler deadpanned.

Oh, no. Oh, *hell* no. Rosie was done. Done with Tyler, and done with this date.

"Okay no. You're not going to invalidate my drink choice,

my job choice, and then try to gaslight me into saying that my friendships are anything more than just that: a friendship," Rosie scoffed.

"That's a little dramatic. All I did was disagree with you," Tyler tried defending himself.

"All you did was make an ass of yourself," Rosie retorted. "You should go."

"Seriously? Remind me not to let Cole's wife set me up with any more of her friends."

"Her *name* is Elena, and besides, none of them would go out with you after I tell her about this disaster of a date."

"Well, I'm not paying for your drink," Tyler offered as a final fuck you.

"You're right. You're not. *I* am," Callum stated bluntly in Tyler's direction.

"Still trying to convince yourself that nothing is going on between the two of you?" Tyler asked her as he stood up to leave.

She watched him walk out of Lafayette's, happy that this nightmare of a date was over.

Callum looked at her not with pity, but with something dark in his eyes that looked distinctly like desire, "Hang around another hour, and I'll give you a ride home."

"And another Cosmo while I wait?" she replied sweetly.

"One, four... whatever you want, Rose."

He hadn't called her Rosie, or even Rosemary, once tonight.

24

PERHAPS THE ROMANCE GODS ARE REAL, AFTER ALL

Rosie:

After watching as Callum waited on different tables for thirty minutes or so, Rosie ventured up to the speakeasy side of the bar's rooftop with yet another Cosmo. She decided to call Noah while she waited to pass the time.

"Hey, babes! How's the date going?" Noah questioned. "I'm assuming not that well if you're calling me instead of talking to him."

"Remind me to call Elena tomorrow and bar her and Cole from setting me up with anyone. *Ever* again," Rosie retorted.

"Uh, oh. What happened?"

"He was a misogynistic ass."

"Aren't they all?" Noah sighed. "Need a ride home?"

"Actually no, um, Callum said he'd give me a ride after he closed up for the night," Rosie told her, arms braced on the roof's ledge as she gazed toward the Arthur Ravenel Jr. Bridge.

"Give you a ride home, or give you a ride to his apartment?" Noah questioned smugly.

Rosie could tell Noah was smirking without even needing to see her face.

"Uh, home?" Rosie answered, uncertainty painting a big question mark at the end of her words.

"Home?" Noah sounded more excited than surprised at Rosie's hesitation.

Rosie looked down from the rooftop at all the people moseying around on Market Street below: people in various states of intoxication, couples walking with fingers intertwined, leaning on one another as if their worlds would fall apart if they stopped touching, restaurant employees walking back to their cars after their shifts had ended...

It filled Rosie with a strange, but not unwelcome, sense of peace. She didn't know these people, and they didn't know her. She was ultimately insignificant on this pale blue dot. Who gave a shit if she hooked up with Callum tonight? The universe certainly didn't. And that realization was freeing.

"I think," Rosie let the night breeze wash over her. "I just—tonight he was acting really defensive of me with Tyler, and I don't know, it got to me... certain parts of me," Rosie admitted.

"No shit it got to you. He's been under your skin ever since the hallway incident at Edisto."

"And..." Rosie hesitated.

"Yeah?"

"He cut his hand while working tonight. He says he just grabbed a glass too hard, but that's not like him. I've been to Lafayette's while Callum was bartending more times than I can even begin to count, and I've never *once* seen him break anything," Rosie looked over her shoulder, not wanting anyone but Noah to hear her next thought. "You don't think he was..."

Rosie wasn't sure she wanted to let herself go there.

"Was what?" Noah prompted her to voice her thoughts.

"Jealous," Rosie admitted in a murmur, afraid that if she said the words too loud it might somehow make them true, "of the fact that I was on a date with someone else?"

"Babe, I love you, but you are so fucking dense sometimes," Noah snorted.

Rosie had no idea if she actually wanted Callum to be jealous or not, but she was not about to start unpacking that right now. Not when she was about to be alone with Callum in his Jeep for the thirty minutes it took to get from downtown back to her apartment.

"Ugh. Okay, well, I'll text you later."

"I'll be waiting in anticipation. Love you, babe," Noah replied.

"Love you most."

As she hung up with Noah, Rosie turned to the giant mirror wall of the rooftop, hoping to see something of clarity in her reflection. Instead, she saw Callum walking up the stairs to the rooftop she was currently occupying alone.

"Why'd you come all the way up here?" he asked her, stopping to stand right behind her.

"You can see the bridge from here. It's my favorite part of downtown at night," Rosie replied.

Slowly, she turned to face him, moving to stand closer to the ledge of the rooftop opposite the mirror wall.

"You know, I Googled some of the books I've seen you reading. Tyler is an idiot for calling them vapid; maybe you should send him one. He could probably learn a lot," Callum smirked at her.

Googled the books he'd seen her reading? The books she'd

been reading recently had all been smutty romances... maybe all Callum's Google search had yielded was a loose plot summary, sans highly explicit sex scenes. She decided to test the waters before admitting to anything that Callum would absolutely have a field day with.

"Learn a lot, huh?" Rosie prodded. "Like?"

"Like," Callum braced his hands on the ledge behind her, boxing her in. At six-three compared to her five-six, he was the perfect height to whisper in her ear, "that the girls who read them aren't nearly as innocent as they seem," he smirked at her, his lips mere inches from her own, "though, I already knew that about you."

So, he'd done more than look at a vague plot synopsis. Interesting.

"Well, since you've apparently done so much research on what I like to read, why don't you tell me how this moment would end if it were a scene in one of my romance books."

"We'd fuck on this rooftop," Callum closed the distance between them.

Oh.

Fuck.

The romance gods would be impressed.

"I'd kiss you," he whispered against her lips, "tease you," he tugged on her lower lip with his teeth, "I'd pull this flirty little dress up," he moved his hands to her upper thighs, "then I'd drop to my knees," he moved to kiss her neck, "I'd pull that lacy thong of yours down your hips, and I'd bury my face between your thighs," he whispered straight into her ear.

"Your plan has one flaw," Rosie's breathing was ragged. "I'm not wearing anything under this skirt."

"Fuck, Rose," he trembled with restraint against her.

His hands slowly slid the rest of the way up her thighs, his breathing growing heavier as he found nothing but skin, confirming that she was in fact not wearing anything under her dress.

"Tell me you don't want this, and I'll stop," he growled.

Rosie said nothing.

"Rose. Tell me to stop," he repeated.

"I don't want to," she breathed.

And that was true. At this moment, the only thing she could think about was the feeling of Callum's skin on hers, the freedom she'd felt as she'd looked down at the people on the street below. If letting Callum touch her felt wrong, then letting him touch her on this rooftop for anyone to see felt forbidden. But the excitement of letting him do so anyway shot straight to her throbbing core—she didn't want to be right, she wanted to give in to the electricity between them.

"Rose—Tell. Me. To. Stop," was Callum's final attempt at self-control.

Moving his hand closer to her throbbing core, she surrendered herself to the feel of him, whispering a single word onto his eager lips: "Don't."

"Fuck," Callum groaned and hauled his mouth to hers, kissing her like nothing else mattered to him right now.

Sloppy, desperate kisses that threatened to send her over the edge before he was even inside of her. His lips found her neck as her hands tangled in his long, curly hair.

He kissed his way down her neck, pulling the straps of her sundress down and exposing her chest to him. She didn't give a fuck that they were on a public rooftop and that anyone could walk up the stairs. All she cared about was that he didn't stop touching her.

He sucked her nipple into his mouth and stared straight up at her as a moan escaped her lips.

"Quiet, baby," he purred, satisfaction flaring in his eyes.

Callum dropped the rest of the way to his knees and hooked her left leg around his shoulder. He kissed the inside of her thigh at a torturously slow pace that threatened to kill her. Her hands found his hair and pulled.

"Let me savor you, Rose."

"I don't want to be savored, I want to come," she begged.

That seemed to strip him of any lingering self-restraint as he buried his face between her legs, tasting, circling. He moaned as he sucked her clit into his mouth. Just as she was about to beg for the second time, his fingers found their way inside her, two of them at once as if he anticipated how badly she needed to be filled by him.

He pumped his fingers into her, continuing to suck at her clit as he did. She rode his face, not caring at all that they were on this rooftop, that her breasts were still exposed, or that she had conceded any and all allure of her self-control to this man. He pulled his lips from her briefly. They glistened with evidence of the fact that they'd just been buried in her pussy.

"Don't look at me, look at yourself in the mirror. I want you to see what you look like when you come, when *I* make you come," he ordered.

Rosie did as she was told. The sight of herself in the mirror, Callum on his knees before her, would be etched into her memory forever. Her face was a deep shade of pink. She looked as undone as Callum made her feel.

Clearly satisfied, Callum's fingers began to curl inside of her, finding the spot that would send her over the edge. Her eyes fluttered closed as she felt her release building. Callum's tongue and fingers stilled.

She pulled Callum's hair by the fingers she had wrapped there, urging him to move against her again. She gave a moan of protest when he remained still.

"Eyes open, Rose, or I stop," he breathed beneath her legs. It was torture. "Be a good girl and watch yourself fall apart with my face between your legs."

She looked to the mirror again, and Callum immediately resumed where he'd left off. He tasted her greedily as if it had tortured him to stop just as much as it had tortured Rosie.

"Fuck, Callum, I'm about to..."

Her orgasm rolled through her, preventing her from finishing the thought. He worked her through every wave until her legs were shaking and he had to stand, holding her by the waist, to keep her from falling over. He gripped her tightly; the pain he must have been feeling from the cut on his left hand seemed of no consequence to him. He brought his fingers to her lips, in invitation she realized. She took them into her mouth, sucking slowly, tasting herself on him and loving that she did.

"That was..." Rosie whispered.

"I know," Callum whispered back.

He's just given her one of the most intense orgasms of her life, and she desperately wanted to return the favor, desperately wanted to feel more of his skin on hers. She started to undo the buckle on his belt, but he grabbed her hand, pulling it away.

"Why—" she tried to say, but he kissed her, cutting her words short.

"Because I have fucked my fist to the memory of you since the night you put your panties in my pocket and walked out of my apartment. Because I have never needed the taste of someone on my tongue as much as yours.

Because the next time I fuck you, I want you begging on your knees for me to be inside of you so that you know how desperate I've felt for the past month," he whispered onto her lips.

Before Rosie could wrap her mind around the meaning of his words, he pulled the strap of her dress back onto her shoulder, laced his fingers with hers, and pulled her toward the stairs that led back downstairs, muttering, "Come on, let me take you home."

Rosie knew what they looked like walking through the bar, his hair was out of place from how hard she'd been pulling it, and both of their lips were swollen—Rosie's from tasting Callum's, Callum's from tasting her. If anyone guessed what had happened between them on the rooftop, they didn't show it.

Taking a right as they walked out of Lafayette's, they passed the empty market that would be bustling with people by morning and walked the quarter mile to the parking deck. Callum hadn't said a word since they left the rooftop, but he hadn't let go of her hand either. Rosie wasn't quite sure why, but she knew she didn't want him to.

Callum's red Jeep now in sight, Rosie veered to the passenger side expecting Callum to drop her hand and walk to the driver's side. Instead, he changed direction with her, opening his passenger side door for her before finally dropping her hand and climbing in the driver's side. If she could separate herself from who she was, who Callum was to her, it almost felt like the end of a date.

In the still darkness of Callum's Jeep, the weight of Callum's earlier declarations started to sink in. Suddenly, she couldn't keep herself from voicing the question she'd wanted the answer to since the moment Noah put the thought in her mind.

"Have you been with anyone since that night?"

"Why does it matter to you?" Callum didn't sound defensive, just matter-of-fact.

Intrigued.

Rosie opened and then closed her mouth, realizing she didn't have an answer to give him. She chose silence. Evidently so did Callum, because he didn't offer a single other thought for the rest of the drive.

When Callum finally parked at her apartment complex thirty minutes later, Rosie hesitated to get out, hoping Calum would say something, anything that would explain what had happened between them tonight. When he said nothing, she decided to let things be, unsure of what to say herself.

"Goodnight, Callum," she whispered.

"Goodnight, Rosemary," he whispered back.

She walked up to her apartment door without looking back. As she walked inside, her phone buzzed in her hand. She looked at the screen to see a message from Callum.

> Callum: No, no one since you.

25

NOT UNTIL YOU BEG

Rosie:

At ten until six, Rosie found herself walking through the Costello's front door for Harper's birthday party. The youngest of the Costello children, Harper was the baby of the family and was loved by everyone. She was turning fourteen today. Rosie was the only non-family member there, making it even more evident that the Costellos genuinely viewed her as their own.

Rosie had always loved the atmosphere at the Costello's house. Including Elena and Callum, there were a total of six Costello children. Half of them were grown, several had partners, and Lydia had Willow, which meant that there was always a horde of Costellos running around at these family events. Rosie never got to experience that kind of joyful chaos with her own family, given that she and Hazel—her only sibling—were six years apart.

Since the Costello's had moved to South Carolina, Rosie had been to every one of Harper's birthday parties over the years and was just as happy to be at this one. However, she may have had a secondary motive for being in attendance tonight: she needed to get Callum alone to talk to him about whatever the fuck was going on between them. Or maybe to get him between her legs again. Or maybe both... She was just hoping she could do so without attracting the attention of the small village that was his family.

Rosie went to the living room to set down the gift she'd brought for Harper and was immediately greeted by Elena's parents.

"Rosie, honey, how are you doing? We haven't seen you in forever!" Mrs. Pammy, Elena's mom, wrapped Rosie in a warm embrace.

Rosie loved Elena's parents. They were kind, accepting, and always kept up with what was going on in her life.

"It's only been a few weeks, Mrs. Pammy!" Rosie laughed.

Despite her constant insisting that Rosie was now an adult and could call her Pammy, sans 'Mrs.,' Rosie refused to call Elena's mother anything but Mrs. Pammy. That was how Elena's mom had introduced herself to Rosie all those years ago, and she'd grown attached to the sound of it.

"A few weeks too long if you ask me," she planted a kiss on Rosie's cheek.

Rosie loved Pamela Costello. The woman was an angel.

"Where should I put Harper's gift?" Rosie asked.

"There's a stack of presents to the left of the hearth, you can add yours to it," Elena's dad answered, now coming to give her a hug as well.

"Thank you, Mr. Mark," she returned his hug.

"You can stop calling us Mrs. and Mr. you know? We don't care about the formalities," he insisted.

She knew, but she'd continue to do so anyway.

"I know, Mr. Mark," she smiled jokingly and turned to

put her present in the stack when she was stopped by a frustratingly good-looking Callum.

"I can take that for you," Callum reached for the present in her hand.

Instinctively, Rosie pulled it away from his reach, which was a terrible idea because Callum only stepped into her to try to grab it from behind her back, sending her thoughts in the direction of the last time Callum had been this close: when he'd made her come on a very public rooftop.

"I think I can handle carrying this five feet to the hearth, thank you very much."

Rosie tried to side-step around Callum, but he managed to grab Harper's present in the process, smirking at her as he carried it toward the stack for her. So, he was back to the cocky, mouth-permanently-fixed-in-a-smirk version of himself. Interesting.

He'd said that the next time they fucked, he wanted Rosie begging for him, but begging wasn't her style. Mercilessly teasing until Callum caved was more her speed.

She walked over toward Callum and the stack of presents, and, facing away from him, bent down to pick up her present.

"Oops, I actually forgot to put Harper's card in here," she said over her shoulder. "Silly me."

The floral dress she was wearing was dangerously short, but bending over in it was worth the risk as it had been effective in getting Callum's attention. Rosie winked at him, then walked into the kitchen to find Elena and say hi to the rest of the Costellos.

Lydia was setting out plates and silverware when Rosie walked in. The kitchen was massive, yet every inch of counter space was covered in various snacks, desserts, and drinks. If there was one thing the Costello's knew how to do, it was hosting a party.

"Rosie! How are you? How was your blind date Elena set up?" Lydia asked enthusiastically.

"Considering he was a misogynistic ass, not well."

Lydia faked a gagging sound to demonstrate her repulsion, "Yikes."

"Why does everyone get to say ass but me?" Harper complained from where she stood in the kitchen.

"Because you're only thirteen," Lydia teased.

"First of all, I go to public school. I hear way worse on the bus. And second, it's my *fourteenth* birthday," Harper crossed her arms defiantly.

"Maybe, but you're not officially fourteen until eleven fifty-six PM."

"Oh, and we forgot to tell you," Rosie teased Harper, "you have to wait to open your presents until then, too."

"Don't be an *ass*," Harper retorted, looking absolutely smug.

"Touché," Rosie laughed. "Happy birthday, Harps."

Turning back to Lydia, Rosie continued their earlier conversation, "at least it'll get Elena off my back about dating for a whi—"

"Rosie!!!!!!" Little arms and legs wrapped around Rosie.

Reaching down to scoop up Willow, Lydia's five-year-old daughter, Rosie beamed, "how's my favorite little girl?"

Willow's little arms wrapped around Rosie's neck as she asked, "Rosie, why are you at my nonna's house?"

"I'm here to celebrate Harper's birthday," Rosie answered. "Just like you."

She kissed Willow's adorable little nose.

"Uncle Callum! You're here too!" Willow shouted as Callum entered the kitchen.

He walked over and kissed Willow on the cheek while Rosie was still holding her. Willow's arms reached for Callum, and he scooped her up willingly from Rosie's arms. Uh-oh. Attractive man with a cute kid staring at him in adoration? This did not bode well for Rosie's self-control.

"Uncle Callum is so big," Willow declared, glancing down to see how much farther from the floor she was compared to when she'd been in Rosie's arms.

Yeah, Uncle Callum *is* so big, Rosie thought.

"Are we still waiting for anyone?" Layla yelled through the kitchen toward Mrs. Pammy who was still organizing presents in the living room.

"Has Liam gotten here yet?" Mrs. Pammy yelled back across the house.

As if they had summoned him, Liam walked in through the kitchen door carrying a huge gift bag.

And another man's hand. The man was slightly taller than Liam, with dark brown curly hair and the brightest blue eyes Rosie had ever seen.

Good for you, Liam, she thought.

This had to be the guy Liam had asked to talk to her about after the wedding. Rosie was so excited—both that everything had worked out and to finally meet him.

Practically leaping from Callum's arms, Willow screamed, "Uncle Liam!!!!!!!"

Both attempting to catch her, Rosie and Callum ended up tangled together. After getting Willow safely on the ground, neither of them made a move to regain the space that had been between them a few moments before. Instead, they stayed, Rosie's left shoulder casually resting against Callum's chest behind the kitchen counter.

"Um, everyone, this is Charlie," Liam raised their interlaced hands. "Charlie, this is my family."

Liam's look of nervousness instantly morphed into a smile the second his eyes found Rosie's. He mouthed a shy 'thank you' in her direction. She winked at him—a reminder of just how proud of him she was.

"Why don't you look surprised?" Callum leaned down to whisper in Rosie's ear.

"Remember when he wanted to talk to me at the beach house? After the wedding?" Rosie asked, turning to face him.

"Yeah," Callum replied.

"He—Charlie—is what Liam wanted to talk to me about. He asked how I knew I was bi," Rosie explained.

"Though I am slightly jealous that he told you before me," Callum teased, "I'm really glad he had you. I wouldn't have known how to help."

"I'm glad too. And I'm really happy for him."

"Well, hello, Charlie," Mrs. Pammy bounded across the kitchen to wrap him in a hug. "Aren't you just a pleasant surprise?"

Charlie beamed at the warm welcome from his partner's mother, "It's very nice to meet you, Mrs. Costello."

"Why does everyone always insist on calling me that? At least let me pretend I'm not so old," Mrs. Pammy laughed.

At this, Charlie looked a bit nervous, perhaps wondering if he'd accidentally offended her.

"Don't worry Charlie," Rosie piped up. "She yells at me for the same thing."

"If only there were something you could do to stop my yelling, Rosemary June," Mrs. Pammy called sarcastically across the kitchen.

"Still not calling you Pammy," Rosie argued.

At the playful banter, Charlie seemed to relax.

"Will someone take this present so I can hold my favorite niece?" Liam smiled in the doorway.

"It's nice to meet you, Charlie," Lydia said, nodding her approval in Liam's direction. "And she's your only niece," Lydia laughed, grabbing the present from the youngest Costello brother.

"Still my favorite," he chuckled as he scooped Willow up into his arms.

"Alright, alright! Now that everyone's here, let's light the candles so we can eat this cake!" Mrs. Pammy sang as she walked back across the kitchen.

Cole held up the pink-swirl candlesticks, "got all fourteen candles right here, Mrs. Costello."

"Oh, you're just as bad as the rest of them," Mrs. Pammy said to Cole. "There's no need for all that Mrs. Costello mess. Just call me Pammy," she insisted for the third time tonight.

"I've got all fourteen candles right here, Pammy," Cole amended.

"*Much* better."

Gesturing toward the counter where the cake was sitting, Cole enlisted Elena's expertise: "Babe, help me arrange them?"

The kitchen lights were turned off as Elena lit the candles and carefully placed the cake in front of where Harper was seated at the kitchen table. As everyone gathered around the table to sing Happy Birthday to Harper, Rosie casually stopped in front of Callum. She told herself it was so that she'd be able to see Harper blow out the candles; though Callum *was* extremely tall, the excuse didn't justify Rosie taking a slow step back into Callum, unnoticeable to anyone but the two of them. He leaned into her, barely perceptible, but enough.

Rosie felt content. Not just to be close to Callum, but to be in the proximity of so many people who loved her like she was theirs. It was honestly a bit overwhelming but in a good way. A really good way. She wasn't sure what she'd done in a past life to deserve such happiness, but she was glad for it. Would never take it for granted.

As slices of cake began to be distributed, she noticed Callum walk in the direction of the bathroom. She followed, intent on getting him alone. To kiss him or question him, she still wasn't quite sure.

Callum had barely managed one foot across the threshold before Rosie shoved him back into the bathroom, locking the door behind them.

"Rosie, what are you—"

She shoved him back into the wall and kissed him greedily, cutting off his question. His hands tangled in her hair as he kissed her back with just as much passion. He groaned as she took his bottom lip between her teeth and tugged lightly.

Knowing they didn't have long before people would start to put two and two together about why they were both missing from the party, Rosie slid her hand to the waistband of Callum's jeans.

He immediately grabbed her wrist, not pulling her hand away but not letting her move it any farther, and whispered against her lips, "not until you beg, Rose."

"Shut the fuck up and let me suck your cock, Costello."

"As much as I'd like to see your pretty little lips around my cock, it's not happening until you beg for it," he lowered her hand to her side.

She was *not* going to beg. But she *was* going to make things even between the two of them. Rosie rocked into him, grinding her hips against his in protest. Callum grabbed her by the thighs, lifting them up to wrap them around his waist. He flipped them around so that Rosie was now the one pressed against the wall and rolled his hips into her.

She couldn't help the moan that slipped past her lips. His hand slid up the inside of her thigh to meet the thong she had on under her dress. His fingers grazed along the inside of the band, dancing torturously around where she really needed them.

"If I slide my fingers underneath your panties, how wet would I find you for me?" he teased.

'Very' was the answer to his question, but she wasn't about to tell him that.

"Why don't you touch me and find out?"

He moved her underwear to the side and slid his fingers up her center.

"I love that you're so wet for me," Callum drew his fingers up to his mouth, tasting her. "You taste... fucking incredible, Rosie," he breathed.

He reached between her legs again, but, rather than touching her, he just slid her underwear back in place, and lowered Rosie back to the floor.

"I told you, Rosie. Not until you're begging."

With that parting comment, Callum walked out of the bathroom to rejoin the rest of the party.

I want you begging on your knees for me to be inside of you so that you know how desperate I've felt for the past month.

Rosie was damn near ready to do just that.

"Hey, I think we're gonna head out," Elena said, hugging Rosie.

"I'll walk out with you guys, I was just about to leave too. Just let me grab my keys from the kitchen!"

"Would you mind giving Callum a ride home? He rode here with us, but his apartment is in the opposite direction and it's already late."

Actually, Rosie wouldn't mind giving Callum a ride home in the slightest.

"Yeah, sure. His place is on the way to mine anyway," she told Elena casually.

"Thanks—we owe you one," Elena squeezed Rosie again.

"No big deal. I'll be right back," Rosie dismissed herself to the kitchen to retrieve both her keys and Callum.

On her way, Liam blocked her path, pulling her into a hug.

"I just wanted to thank you again," he said into her shoulder. "I was scared shitless, and you made everything seem so simple."

"I'm really fucking happy for you," Rosie squeezed Liam before letting go.

"I am too," Liam smiled sheepishly, "really fucking happy. With him."

"Good," Rosie returned the smile. "You know I'm always here, right?"

"You know *I'm* always here too, right?" he asked, his eyes moving toward Callum's frame in the kitchen.

"Ugh, not you too," Rosie rolled her eyes. "Lydia's already on my case about him."

"Maybe that should tell you something," he stated with a smug expression. "Love you, Rosie," Liam pulled her in for another quick hug.

"Love you too, you goof," she said. "And I'm still going to

insist that you tell me all about how things happened with you two," Rosie teased, heading into the kitchen.

Rosie grabbed Callum's sweatshirt off the counter and started heading back toward the front door.

"You're taking my sweatshirt, because?" Callum called after her.

"I'm cold?" she said innocently.

Callum raised his eyebrows.

"Nah, I'm kidding," she shoved his arm playfully. "Elena doesn't want to drive you home, so you're riding with me."

Rosie couldn't quite read Callum's expression. He looked somewhere in between nervous and wanting to rip her clothes off the second they got into her car. Interesting.

"Come on, I'm ready to go," she pulled him toward the front door.

Together, they walked to Rosie's car which was parked at the end of the driveway.

"Thanks again, Rosie!" Elena called after her.

"You owe me a drink next girl's night!" Rosie yelled back.

"My company is really so bad that you feel like you deserve compensation? I'm wounded," Callum teased, dramatically pressing a hand to his heart.

"Yeah, I'm only driving you for the free drink," Rosie joked back.

"Funny, that's not what you said earlier," there was a smirk plastered on Callum's face. "You know, in the bathroom when you told me to shut up so that you could suck my co—"

"Temporary lapse of judgment," Rosie deflected.

"Oh, yeah?"

"Yeah."

"Then what do you call me going down on you until you came on the rooftop of Lafayette's?"

Rosie had absolutely no answer to Callum's question that didn't make her sound desperate, so she decided to change the subject entirely.

"I'm hungry. How do you feel about stopping somewhere for food?" Rosie asked once they were both in the car.

"Sure, where did you have in mind?" Callum asked.

She was relieved that Callum had agreed without any further explanation, and without any joking about her being hungry for his cock. Rosie still wasn't quite sure how she planned to initiate the conversation she wanted to have with him, but she knew it would be easier over food, the scraping of forks on their plates would help to fill any potential uncomfortable silence.

"Waffle House?"

"Waffle House is dine-in only," Callum raised his eyebrows.

"I know."

Callum was quiet the rest of the way to Waffle House. In the silence, her mind drifted back to some of the things Callum had said a few days ago when she was too high on his touch to really process the gravity of his words.

Because I have never needed the taste of someone on my tongue as much as yours.

At that moment, Rosie had written those words off as dirty talk. Now, she considered them under the weight of his earlier declarations about her liking the required readings and the number of times she'd read *Gatsby* before graduation, neither of which were things she'd ever told him. The only way he could've known was if he'd paid attention, if he'd cared to learn more about her than what she was like in bed.

26

IT'S NOT A WAFFLE HOUSE, IT'S A WAFFLE HOME

Rosie:

As they walked toward the entrance to the Waffle House, his hand slid to the small of her back. Strangely, it didn't feel wrong to her. It felt safe. *She* felt safe.

"Hey y'all, find a seat anywhere you like," the server, 'Loretta' her tag read, yelled over her shoulder as they walked inside.

Rosie walked toward the booth furthest from the front of the restaurant, intending to give them a little privacy for the conversation she was about to initiate.

Wasting no time after they sat down, Rosie asked, "so, wanna tell me why you kept butting in on my date?" prompting him to say something, anything about the way he'd acted.

"The guy was an ass, and you didn't deserve that," was all he said.

"I can handle myself," she argued.

"I know you *can*, but you shouldn't have to," he said without making eye contact with her.

Shouldn't have to? That sounded almost thoughtful, which was not usually an adjective she would use to describe Callum. But then again, none of Callum's recent behaviors fit with the usual adjectives.

"How did you know I read Gatsby so many times?" she asked.

"I paid attention."

"Why?"

Before he could answer, Loretta came over to get their drink order.

"I'll have water, and whatever she'd like," Callum told Loretta while nodding in Rosie's direction.

"Water, please," Rosie answered.

"And will this be one check, or two?" Loretta asked.

"One," Callum said at the same time that Rosie said, "two."

"One," he repeated, not taking his eyes off Rosie.

"Alright. I'll be right back with those waters, and I'll grab your food order then," Loretta said as she walked behind the counter to fill their cups.

As soon as Loretta was out of earshot, Rosie pressed, "alright, that's the second time this week that you've offered to pay for me, and notice I said 'offered' because I'm not letting you—what's the deal?"

"Am I not allowed to be polite?" he asked, evading her question.

"You and I don't do polite, Callum. We do each other, and then we go our separate ways."

Rosie wasn't going to let him get out of answering her question that easily.

"You had to suffer through a date with that pretentious ass. I'm just trying to be nice."

"Well, nice is confusing," she commented defensively.

"But not bad?" his brows furrowed as he asked.

It almost seemed like he was anxious. Rosie hesitated but decided that maybe if she admitted something, then he would too, and she so desperately wanted to know what was going on inside his head.

"No, not bad," she admitted. "Just—unfamiliar."

Callum relaxed a little at her answer, but it looked like there was something else he wanted to say.

Rosie prompted him by returning to her question from earlier, "tell me why you paid attention to how many times I read *Gatsby*."

"I... I'm worried that the answer will fuck everything up between us," he hesitated.

"What if I answer something you want to know first? Truth for a truth?"

"Why did you hook up with me the night you and Justin broke up?" he asked, agreeing to her proposition.

Well, shit. She hadn't expected him to ask that. She hadn't let herself think about the answer. Truthfully, she should have been hurt and upset about things ending with Justin; but instead, she'd been excited that sleeping with Callum was back on the table. She wasn't sure how to tell Callum that. Thankfully, Loretta chose that moment to come back with their waters and take their food orders.

"I'll do the All-Star special. Eggs scrambled, white toast, and hashbrowns scattered well please," Callum ordered, passing his menu to Rosie to stack with hers.

"Could I please have the omelet plate? I want to add bacon to the omelet, and hashbrowns scattered well instead of grits," Rosie told Loretta, handing the stacked menus back to her.

"I'll have that out for you two soon," Loretta smiled, leaving them alone again.

"Well?" Callum urged her to continue.

"You promise to answer my question honestly if I answer yours?" Rosie hesitated.

"I promise, Rose," this time his use of the nickname felt endearing rather than taunting.

"Alright, well... When Justin broke up with me I was so infuriated at the fact that he'd tried to manipulate me into thinking it was my idea just so he could assuage his own guilt. The breakup came out of nowhere, and, honestly, I wanted him to feel betrayed in the same way that I did. He was always worried about me being around your family, being around you, and so I thought that fucking you the night he broke up with me would be the perfect way to get even. Obviously, getting even was satisfying for more than one reason, considering you made me come. Twice. But... yeah, it was about getting even. At least at first," she admitted.

"And the rooftop? What was the rooftop about?" he asked.

Rosie could have sworn it looked like Callum was holding his breath in anticipation of her answer.

"The rooftop was..." she hesitated, "the rooftop was pure desire. I *wanted* you, Callum."

"I wanted you too, Rosie. And not because I cared about showing off in front of Tyler. I just—*wanted*."

"Tell me why you paid attention."

"Because I am absolutely fucking enamored by you, Rosemary June."

Rosie stared at him in disbelief.

"I don't know when it happened, or if it was always there and I just didn't want to see it, but... there it is."

"There it is..." she repeated his words back to him, in absolute disbelief about the way this night had gone.

"Say something," he pleaded.

"I don't know how to do this," she admitted, motioning between the two of them.

"But you're saying this... us... there's *something*?"

Callum's expression held more vulnerability than she'd ever realized he was capable of. Rosie wondered if this was one of those life-altering moments people always talked about, that if the way she answered his question would change everything. She saw the hope, the longing written in his eyes, and realized that she didn't want to shatter it.

Rosie hesitated, "I don't know if I want there to be, but... yes, there's *something*."

"Would it really be so bad? Things between us being more than just a convenient hookup?" He looked discouraged.

"You mislead me about when you broke up with Olivia just so that you could fuck me that night, Callum. I don't know how to trust you," she admitted.

"I broke up with Olivia because I wanted *you* Rose, not because I wanted a quick fuck. I just didn't know how to say it. Why do you think I insisted on making that night all about you? I didn't know how else to show you that I cared. I've never been good with words, so I tried to convey the way I felt through my actions. I don't know how to do this either, but I know that I want to try. For you. For us," Callum's eyes dropped to the table, "for what we could be."

Rosie thought back to that night, how he'd stopped her every time she tried to get on her knees for him, even after he'd been on his for her. She thought back to everything he'd said when she picked him up from Lafayette's about Justin not deserving her, and how he wouldn't change a thing about her. That he'd called her *'because I couldn't stop thinking about you.'* His quiet plea for her to stay when she'd dropped him off. She thought back to what he'd said on that damn rooftop.

Because the next time we fuck, I want you begging on your knees for me to be inside of you so that you know how desperate I've felt for the past month.

Maybe Noah had been right all along. He wasn't just an insensitive fuckboy; he just didn't know how to express his feelings in any way that wasn't physical touch. Still, she didn't want to end up like Olivia: with Callum dumping her to get with the next person he wanted.

"I want to believe you... I just..." she hesitated.

"Then let me prove to you that I'm not just fucking around," Callum reached a hand out across the table toward hers, his larger hand delicately surrounding her petite one. *"Please,"* he pleaded, squeezing her hand in his.

"How?" Rosie didn't draw her hands away.

"Go out with me? On a real date. Let's start from the beginning."

"We've known each other for over a decade—how can we start from the beginning?"

"I've known *pieces* of you for over a decade. I've known what you've shown me as Elena's brother. I want to know *you*, Rosemary. I want to be someone you know about by choice, not someone you have to know about because of forced proximity."

"Okay," Rosie found herself agreeing.

"Okay? Really?" The hope written in Callum's eyes was nearly enough to make her eyes water.

"Okay. Really," she laced her fingers with his. "But can we maybe..." Rosie fumbled for the best way to convey her reservations, "wait on telling your family? Not forever," she rushed to add. "I just don't want the pressure of their questions when we don't even have answers to them yet ourselves."

"Whatever you need, Rosemary. I just want this chance with you."

They ate their food in comfortable silence, each adjusting to the truth now sitting between them.

As Rosie put her car in park outside of Callum's apartment complex, he turned toward her and smiled. At that moment, Rosie realized that she'd never seen Callum genuinely smile. That stupid little smirk of his was etched into her memory forever; but this, his genuine smile, was new to her.

"I could come inside if you want?" Rosie asked him, not really sure how to end this night.

"I want nothing more," he said but made no move to get out of the car.

Rosie moved to open her door, but Callum clicked the lock button from the passenger side before she could.

"You do realize that you have to let me out of the car for me to come inside, right?" she laughed.

"I said I want you to, not that I'm going to let you," he smirked at her.

"And why not?"

"Because you're more than a quick fuck to me Rosie, and I'm going to prove that to you. Starting now. By not allowing you to come inside my apartment."

Callum gave her an irresistible mix of a genuine smile and that teasing smirk, and it was just about the best damn thing she'd ever seen.

"No matter how badly I want to," he sighed longingly.

Somehow, that declaration made her want Callum more

than she ever had. Before she could stop herself, she leaned over the console, grabbed the front of his shirt, and kissed him. It was different from any kiss they'd ever shared. It was a kiss without expectation. A kiss solely because she wanted the feeling of Callum's lips pressed to hers.

Pulling away just enough that their foreheads were still pressed together, Callum whispered against her lips, "Goodnight, Rosemary June Dawson."

It was eerily reminiscent of the last time he'd called her Rosemary June when he'd kissed her goodnight at the beach house.

"Goodnight, Callum James Costello," she whispered back.

Trying to hide her smile as Callum exited her car, she watched to be sure he made it safely inside before driving away. As she put her car in reverse, her phone vibrated in her purse. She tapped the screen to see that it was a text from Callum.

> Callum: Saturday morning. I'll pick you up at ten AM. Wear something comfortable.

> Rosie: With or without underwear?

> Callum: Tease.

> Rosie: This wouldn't be half as fun if I weren't.

> Rosie: See you at ten. <3

27

A BOOKSTORE, THE KEY TO A WOMAN'S HEART

Callum:

CALLUM HADN'T EVER PUT this much effort into planning a date in his life; Callum had also never wanted to know someone as deeply as he wanted to know Rosie. He had everything perfectly arranged:

1. Callum would pick Rosie up and take her to a local bookstore.
2. They would walk from the bookstore to his favorite local coffee shop in downtown.
3. At the coffee shop, they would read the books they bought from the bookstore, and he would also memorize her coffee order so that he could surprise her with coffee at work next week.
4. After coffee, they would walk down to the Battery. Callum was sure he and Rosie had both been to the Battery more times than they could count, but he remembered her saying how much she loved the view of the new bridge when he'd

found her on the rooftop. He thought taking her somewhere with a view of the bridge would be a good way to show that he cared to learn more about her than just how to please her sexually (though he was definitely doing well in that regard already).

Callum decided to wear loose-fitting jeans, Doc Martens, and an Aerosmith t-shirt he'd owned since high school. Having checked the weather to see that it would be a balmy eighty-four degrees out today, he decided to pull his shoulder-length hair into a messy bun.

Ready to go, he grabbed his keys and headed out the door to pick Rosie up. Logistically, it would have made more sense for Rosie to meet Callum at his apartment since her apartment in Summerville was in the opposite direction of downtown from his, but he was happy to spend the extra time with her in the car.

He'd spent his evening last night curating the perfect playlist for their drive. He'd included everything from classic rock, some indie alternative, and even Harry Styles because he knew Rosie loved him. He had one chance to show Rosie that he was serious about pursuing something between them, and he wanted everything to be perfect.

Callum pulled into Rosie's apartment complex right at ten. Normally, he would text whoever he was picking up to let them know that he was there, but not today. He parked his Jeep and walked up the three flights of stairs to her door, knocking to let her know that he was there. Rosie opened the door, revealing her outfit: a floral midi skirt, a cropped tank top, and Doc Martens. Noticing that Callum was also wearing Docs, Rosie rolled her eyes.

"Nope. We're not matching. Sit on the couch while I change my shoes."

Callum grabbed her arm, stopping her from going back into her apartment to change, "What's wrong with us both wearing Docs?"

"It's coupley."

"They're practical shoes. We're going to be walking a lot. And last time I checked, this *was* a date?"

"I didn't even like matching with Justin, and we dated for years," Rosie tried to pull her arm out of Callum's grasp.

"Good thing I'm not Justin," Callum's eyes grazed down her body, then back up to meet her eyes. "Keep the Docs—you look hot in them."

"Fine," she returned the gaze, eyes trailing down Callum's body then back up, then smirked. "So do you. So, where are we going?"

"If you'd stop complaining about my shoe choice long enough to get in the Jeep, you'd know," Callum responded sarcastically. "You look beautiful by the way."

"Thank you," she blushed, avoiding eye contact with him.

Rosie clearly wasn't used to this side of him, and, Callum had to admit, he liked seeing her ruffled.

"So do you," she replied. "Not beautiful, but—you look hot. Handsome. Ugh, you know what I mean."

"Hot handsome, huh?" Callum smirked at her.

"Shut up. Can we go now?" Rosie asked.

"Just waiting on you to lock your door, sweetheart."

He'd added the 'sweetheart' out of curiosity.

She blushed about four shades darker than she had when he'd called her beautiful, information Callum decided to hold on to for later use. Rosie locked her door and they walked down the stairs to his Jeep.

Making their way out of Rosie's apartment complex, she again asked, "*now* do I get to know where we're going?"

"Nope."

"Is this how you usually treat girls on a date?" Rosie pretended to be offended.

"I've never cared enough about a girl to plan an elaborate date with a surprise location," Callum answered. "Until you, that is."

He could tell that Rosie was still a little hesitant to be vulnerable with him, so he'd tried to keep the conversation a happy mix of sarcastic and heartfelt. He hoped that, after today, that would change.

As they drove down I-26, Rosie perked up upon hearing the familiar guitar riff of the live version of Landslide.

"As much of a dick as Lindsey Buckingham might be, he's easily one of the best guitarists to walk the Earth," Rosie commented. "I've always preferred this version."

"So have I. *The Dance* is arguably just as iconic of an album as *Rumours*," Callum added.

"Ooh, can we listen to Silver Springs, too?" Rosie looked at Callum hopefully.

"Way ahead of you, sweetheart."

He threw the nickname out there again with hopes that Rosie would blush just as deeply as she had when he'd called her sweetheart earlier. Much to his delight, she did. Callum decided then and there that he was going to make it a point to work it into every conversation they had for the rest of the day.

"Silver Springs is on this playlist. And, before you ask, yes it's also the '97 version."

Several songs later, Rosie looked over at Callum with a giant smirk spreading across her face.

"Callum Costello," she smiled at him appreciatively. "Did you make a date playlist?"

"Maybe," he halfway admitted. "Depends whether you find it sweet or creepy."

As Callum pulled up to the light off the exit ramp onto King Street, Rosie leaned over and kissed his cheek.

"Definitely sweet," she beamed up at him.

Suddenly it was his turn to blush.

Callum parked in a deck across from Marion Square, only a short walk from the local bookstore. When Rosie tried to open her door, he clicked the lock button on the driver's side door.

"Am I not allowed to get out of the car?" Rosie asked sarcastically.

"You're allowed to wait five seconds for me to walk around and open your door for you," he answered, just as sarcastically.

Before she could argue, he got out of the Jeep and walked around to the passenger side.

"Thank you," she told him as he opened her door.

"You're welcome," he winked.

As they walked out of the parking deck and onto the sidewalk, Callum grabbed her hand, lacing their fingers together. She didn't object. They walked down the street at a leisurely pace. Callum loved walking downtown—he loved the architecture, the trees, the bustling energy. He'd learned a lot about the history behind the buildings downtown from Lilah over the years, which had made him appreciate it all the more.

They were almost to the bookstore, so Callum decided to lead into his plans for their date, "so, I have a few things planned for today—all downtown," he told Rosie.

"Well, we're on King, so I'm guessing the first thing involves shopping of some kind."

"You'd be correct," Callum replied, still not giving away the bookstore plan.

"I don't have money to buy new clothes right now," Rosie went on.

"First of all, you won't be paying for anything today—I'm taking *you* on a date. Secondly, we aren't shopping for clothes," he told her.

"Then what are we shopping for?"

Oh, Rosie had *definitely* underestimated Callum's ability to plan a date.

"We're going to a bookstore."

"You don't read."

"You're right, I don't. But you do," he beamed.

That wasn't entirely true considering his little dip into the world of romance novels. He'd actually ended up finishing the book he'd started reading at the beach house—he couldn't stop himself. And, yes, he had needed to stroke himself to release, not just one, but two additional times before finishing the book. He'd been in a perpetual state of arousal the entire time. How did women survive like that?

"Callum, I have never been more serious about anything in my life: do *not* let me leave the store with more than four books."

"Did you miss the part where I said you wouldn't be paying for anything on this date?" Callum shoved her with his shoulder jokingly. "You will get as many books as you want, and I will be paying for all of them."

"I think you're severely underestimating how many books I can pick up in a single trip to the bookstore."

"Nah, I'm not. I've seen your bookshelves."

"You're not serious."

"So very," he teased.

He led her into the bookstore, which was a lot bigger inside than it looked from the street. Callum hadn't ever been inside before today, but he'd researched the best local bookstores in downtown and every single website he'd been to had pointed him here.

Opening the door for Rosie, he explained what he thought would be her favorite part of the date, "We can browse for as long as you want, but I do have one requirement before we leave."

Rosie raised her eyebrows in question.

Callum continued, "we each pick out a book for the other to read. You choose a book that's important to you, and I'll do the same."

Rosie stopped walking, turned to face Callum, then stared at him without speaking.

"What are you doing?" he asked her.

"Processing the fact that *Callum Costello* just told me he's going to read a book."

"Ouch, Rose," he shoved her arm jokingly.

"I haven't ever seen you read a book in the decade and a half that I've known you—excuse me for being shocked," she shoved him back and laughed.

"Well, people can change. That's sort of the whole point I'm trying to prove here."

Callum's tone was a little more serious then. He was still trying to find the right balance between lighthearted and vulnerable with Rosie. He didn't want to be too much, too soon, and scare her away.

She'd agreed to this date, and that changed everything between them. He had to give her time to adjust to the new reality between the two of them—a reality in which Callum wouldn't have to watch Rosie walk out the door after they'd slept together, a reality in which she would stay, a reality in which he was allowed to hold her simply because he wanted to feel her warmth.

"Besides, I'll have you know," his fingers danced across various book spines in the romance section until he found the one he was looking for, "I read this one just a few weeks ago."

Smugly, so smugly, he held out the paperback edition of the book he'd downloaded at the beach house.

Rosie full-on cackled for a few seconds until she realized that Callum was serious. Then, her mouth abruptly dropped open.

"You…" she just stared. "So when you said you'd Googled the books I'd been reading…" She trailed off, eyes bouncing between the book in Callum's hand and his eyes.

"I didn't intend on reading it, at least at first," he explained. "But after looking up the synopsis," Callum looked Rosie straight in the eyes, one arm braced on the bookshelf behind her head, "*and* reading your review, I was so intrigued that I figured 'why the fuck not?'"

Callum had never seen Rosie at a complete and total loss for words in the entire decade and few odd years he'd known her. It was intoxicatingly satisfying.

"My—," Rosie breathed. "My review?"

"Yeah, turns out there's this cool app, Goodreads, that's like Instagram for book reviews. I actually read several reviews, but yours was *by far* my favorite," Callum smirked.

Having apparently regained enough sense to flirt back, Rosie leaned in slightly and muttered, "And? What did you think?"

"About the book? Or your review?"

"Mmm," Rosie placed a hand on Callum's hip, "both?"

"Well, I learned a lot," he offered, bracing the hand of his that wasn't holding the book on the shelf behind Rosie's head.

"Such as?"

He leaned in to whisper against the shell of her ear, "what a one-hand book is."

He could have sworn Rosie arched into him, just slightly enough to be perceptible. Remembering both that they were in a bookstore and that he had vowed not to let anything inherently sexual happen between them until he could prove himself to Rosie, he took a step back.

Noting the confusion in her eyes, he quickly justified his actions.

"Not that I haven't previously enjoyed acts of public indecency with you, but I told you that I want this to be about starting from the beginning, learning all the sides of you that I never had the privilege of seeing until now."

"Am I at least allowed to kiss you? Because I might die if you tell me I can't even do that," Rosie smiled softly.

"Yes, Rosie," Callum said, pressing a kiss to her forehead. "You're allowed to kiss me."

The fact that Rosie *wanted* to kiss him, even knowing it wouldn't lead to anything more, made Callum's heart flutter far more than he knew what to do with.

Every fifteen minutes or so, Rosie would glance back at Callum as if she were ensuring that he was still content to let her browse. As far as Callum was concerned, he would happily watch her peruse the shelves for the rest of the afternoon if that's what she wanted. He was just grateful to be in her presence, that she had chosen to spend today with him. Even so, he was bothered by the fact that Rosie seemed to expect him to grow bored of this.

"Is there a reason you keep looking at me like you're

waiting for me to drag you out of here?" he asked, hoping that it came across as casual rather than invasive.

"I..." Rosie hesitated. "I don't want this to come across as me drawing any comparisons between you and Justin, so please don't take it that way," she grabbed Callum's hand gently as if to emphasize the fact. "But he never wanted to go with me to bookstores, and, on the rare occasion that I managed to convince him, he just spent the entire time complaining about how long I was taking. His favorite complaint was 'you can't possibly tell me you don't have books at home that you haven't read yet when half of your apartment space is taken up by your books.'"

"I could watch you look at books all day, Rosemary June," Callum gently squeezed her hand. "Don't spend another second worrying about me. I'm just happy to be here with you. Though I do wish you wouldn't insist on carrying all of those books by yourself when I have two perfectly useful arms right here," he gestured to the stack of six (seven?) books that Rosie had picked up.

"Aren't you supposed to be picking one for me to read?" Rosie questioned.

"Aren't *you* supposed to be picking one for *me*?" Callum retorted. "All I see are smutty, and, yes, smutty is now a word in my vocabulary, romance novels in that stack."

"Who says I haven't picked yours yet?" Rosie smirked playfully up at him.

"Touché," Callum laughed and continued to follow her deeper into the stacks and stacks of books.

Every time Callum thought they had reached the end of the store, another tiny room would magically appear. He was honestly a little worried that they'd get lost in here.

He already knew which book he planned to give Rosie—he just hoped she didn't laugh at him for it.

After they'd browsed for the better half of the morning, Rosie decided that she was content with her stack and was ready to check out.

"Alright, hand them over," Callum extended his arms for all of the books Rosie had picked out.

"As sweet as that is," Rosie maintained her grip on her stack, "I can't let you pay for all of these."

"You can," Callum took a step toward her, arms reaching out to grab the books. "And you will. Buying you something that makes you happy makes *me* happy."

"Okay, you can buy all of them except the one I picked for you. I want it to be a surprise," Rosie insisted.

"Deal," Callum agreed. "We can surprise each other with our picks at the next stop on this date."

28

FOUND FAMILY, BEST FAMILY

Rosie:

Rosie had been so content strolling down King Street, her fingers intertwined with Callum's that she forgot she was supposed to be guessing where their next stop was going to be. She realized though, the second they took a right onto Beaufain Street.

"Lowcountry Coffee Roasters is stop two," Rosie declared proudly.

She didn't even bother to frame it as a question.

Lowcountry was a favorite among locals and was far enough off King Street that hardly any tourists ever stopped in. It used to be a small, two-room house but was converted into a coffee shop a few years back. It still felt homey, and the wall that faced the street was made up almost entirely of windows so that customers could see out into the beauty of downtown. It had the allure of sitting on a grand, wrap-around porch.

"Fuck you very much for ruining my surprise," Callum

teased, sounding significantly less annoyed than the statement implied.

As they walked down Beaufain, they passed the old elementary school on the right.

"Growing up, I always wished I was districted for a school in downtown," Rosie thought aloud.

"You think they stop and get ice cream on King on their walk home?"

"I hope so," Rosie sighed. "I miss it."

"It wasn't part of the plan for today, but I'll happily buy you ice cream on King Street if that's what you want," Callum offered.

The thought was so sweet, so genuine. But not quite what Rosie had meant. What she missed wasn't necessarily the ice cream itself, but the simplicity of being a child and feeling as though a scoop of ice cream might just be enough to fix all of your problems. Rosie wasn't quite sure how to relay such a niche sense of nostalgia to Callum, so instead, she just squeezed his hand and smiled up at him.

As they neared the front door of Lowcountry, Callum turned to her and tipped her chin up toward him with his pointer finger as if he needed her to hear his next words clearly.

"This is nice," he said softly. "Being here, with you, is... really nice."

Rosie couldn't help her smile, nor the blush that spread to her cheeks at having all of Callum's attention directed solely at her as if she were the only thing he cared about at this moment. Leaning just slightly onto her tiptoes, Rosie laced her hands together behind Callum's neck.

"It is. Nice, I mean. Lovely, even."

Callum made no move to break their embrace, hands

finding her waist now. He looked gently, adoringly down at Rosie.

"What?" she asked.

"For the first time in a long time, I'm just genuinely content to be somewhere. I'm always thinking about the next thing, never fully embracing the present moments—but not today," Callum pressed his forehead to Rosie's. "Not with you. Never with you. When I'm with you, I don't want to think about what comes next. I just want to exist with you, for as long as you're willing to let me."

Before she could stop herself, Rosie pressed her lips to Callum's. It was a gentle kiss. A kiss that would lead to nothing further—a rarity between the two of them. A kiss solely intended to convey just how happy, safe, and *seen* she felt with Callum too.

How had she missed it for all these years? Or had she? Had she just let herself live in willful ignorance, afraid to feel anything more than physical attraction to Callum? Afraid that, if things didn't work out, she'd lose more than her friendship with Callum? Afraid that she'd lose her relationship with Elena and the rest of the Costellos, too?

Callum smiled down at Rosie and gestured toward the front entrance of Lowcountry, "c'mon, let me buy you a coffee."

Most of Lowcountry's windows were lined with wall-to-wall planks of wood that served as table space with various bar stools to maximize seating in the small interior. The open space in the middle of the room was filled with two long refectory tables. The only isolated seating in the entire coffee shop were three small tables where people could sit across from one another, yet even one side of those shared a wall-to-wall bench. That was what Rosie loved most about Lowcountry—they fostered a sense of community. After they had both ordered, Rosie her usual black Americano and Callum a drip coffee with one scoop of sugar, they sat at one of the isolated tables with a view of the street.

Rosie had been to Lowcountry more times than she could count but could count on one hand the number of times she'd been here on a date. Even in the two years she'd dated Justin, they had seldom gone to a coffee shop together. He always reasoned that it was cheaper to make coffee and read at home than at a coffee shop; being here now with Callum made Rosie realize that Justin had simply cared more about staying at home and playing video games than he had about doing things that would have required them to actually talk to each other.

"Ready to swap books?" Callum asked, drawing Rosie from her thoughts.

"Sure, I'll go first," Rosie offered.

She was extremely confident in her book-recommending ability—her entire life revolved around books, after all—and she was excited to give Callum the book she'd chosen.

"That's a back-handed offer. What if mine sucks?" Callum teased. "And then I have to follow your pick for me, which I have no doubt will be perfect considering the amount of time you spend with your nose stuck in a book."

Rosie really had no idea what to expect from Callum. She'd had a dozen ideas swirling around in her head for Callum, but she was also the kind of person who read sixty-plus books a year. When was the last time Callum had even read *a* book? Choosing books for each other had been his idea though, so he must have done his research.

"Do *you* want to go first, then?" she teased back.

"Nah, I'm just messing with you. I'm pretty proud of my choice, actually," Callum smiled.

The only requirement that Callum had given her was that the book she chose had to be important to her. Important in what manner, Callum hadn't specified. The first thing that came to mind was *Gatsby*, but that didn't feel right since they'd all read that in high school. After nearly thirty minutes of perusing, she found her choice.

She reached into her tote bag to grab the book, then placed it on the table between them.

"*The Perks of Being a Wallflower* by Stephen Chbosky," she stated.

Callum picked up the paperback, looking it over. "Isn't this book incredibly sad?" he asked.

"That depends on the lens you view it through," Rosie offered.

"Tell me, then. What's your lens?" Callum asked genuinely.

Justin would never have asked something like that. He wouldn't have asked about a book Rosie was reading in general, especially not such an intimate question. She knew she shouldn't be spending so much of this date reflecting on her relationship with Justin, yet she couldn't help but notice all of the ways in which Callum was simply *more*. More thoughtful, more vulnerable, more considerate, more supportive... just *more*.

"Well, as you know, I came out during high school. After I came out, people I had known since kindergarten suddenly just stopped talking to me, and..." Rosie hesitated.

Though she was in a far better place mentally than she had been during high school, it was still hard to talk about sometimes. People she'd known for years suddenly treated her like a disease that they didn't want to get too close to for fear of being plagued by it themselves. But queerness wasn't a disease; it wasn't a choice. She understood now that their behavior said much more about them than it ever did about her. People tended to be afraid of what they didn't understand because it was easier than being willing to admit that their worldview might not be perfect. Sure, she'd had Noah and Elena, but that didn't erase the pain entirely.

"I would smile at them in the hallways, and they would just keep walking. It was like they saw right through me, like I was invisible. That, or they would pull their cardigans closed or their necklines higher whenever I was nearby. As if I was a predator..."

Callum's leg brushed against hers under the table, a silent encouragement that *he* saw her. That she was safe here, with him.

Rosie cleared her throat to keep from crying, "Um, so, yeah, that sucked ass. But, then I found *Perks*. And it saved me. It was the first time I read a book and truly saw myself in one of the characters. The book starts during Charlie's first year of high school, and it's all written in a series of letters to the reader. He talks about feeling ostracized by his peers, feeling like an outcast, and not knowing what he was doing wrong, or why people didn't want to talk to him anymore. And then..."

"And then?" Callum mirrored her smile.

His eyes hadn't left hers the entire time she'd started talking. She knew she had his full attention.

"And then, Charlie meets Patrick and Sam," Rosie closed her eyes, seeing the scene in her head: Charlie sitting down at the football game and meeting Patrick, being utterly fascinated by Sam and suddenly feeling like maybe the world doesn't suck so much. "And I realized that I had my own

Patrick and Sam: Noah and Elena. And suddenly the world didn't suck so much.

"It's the book that made me fall in love with the found family trope, the book that taught me that the right people will appreciate and love me just as I am and everyone else can fuck off. In the last letter of the book, Charlie thanks the reader for making him feel less alone, but the ironic thing is that Charlie made *me* feel less alone. It was the first time I'd ever felt like a book had been written just for me."

Callum didn't say anything, just stared at her in awe from across the table.

"What?" Rosie asked softly.

"I could listen to you talk about the things you love forever," Callum smiled. "And I love that I'm now getting to learn things about you because you *want* me to know."

Rosie couldn't help but remember what Callum had said at Waffle House the week before.

"I've known pieces of you for over a decade. I've known what you've shown me as Elena's brother. I want to know you, Rosie. I want to be someone you know about by choice, not someone you have to know about because of proximity."

She hoped he realized that the only reason she was showing him so much of herself was because he'd made her feel safe enough to do so.

"So, what book did you pick for me?" Rosie inquired.

"You have to promise not to laugh at me," Callum muttered, almost shyly.

Callum was not a shy person. Especially not with her.

Rosie gently brushed her hand against his across the table, "I promise."

Rosie and Callum's relationship had been built on a foundation of teasing each other, and she still wasn't quite sure how to be soft with Callum without any trace of humor, so she added, "unless you pull out *Fifty Shades of Grey* or Dr. Seuss, in which case I would definitely laugh at you."

"Despite my recent realization that women are really just reading porn out in public, no I did not buy you *Fifty Shades of Grey*," Callum laughed.

Callum gently slid A. A. Milne's *Winnie-the-Pooh* across the table. It was a beautiful collector's edition, bound in emerald green. Rosie had no idea why Callum had chosen it, but she felt a tiny pang in her heart thinking about Mrs. Pammy and Mr. Mark reading this to a baby Callum.

"Tell me, Callum, why are we going on a trip to the Hundred Acre Woods?"

"Growing up, you know, my family moved around constantly for dad's job. It wasn't until the eighth grade, when I met Lilah, and... well, *you* that I truly felt like I belonged somewhere," Callum began.

Perhaps she and Callum were more alike than she'd ever realized. Callum didn't feel like he had a place to call home, while Rosie felt like she didn't belong in the only home she'd ever known.

"I don't know if my parents ever realized, but I would read Winnie-the-Pooh before bed every night when I was in middle school. Even if I met people at school that I thought I could become good friends with, I was scared to get too close. I knew that we could just move again, and, if I never had close friends, I couldn't lose them. So, instead, I traveled to the Hundred Acre Woods every night. The only place I allowed myself to belong because it couldn't be taken from me whenever we inevitably moved again," Callum sighed. "I know probably that sounds childish and silly, but—"

"It sounds honest," Rosie cut him off because she couldn't stand to see Callum minimize his own childhood like that.

Society tended to brush off children's emotions as if they somehow mattered less just because children lacked autonomy. But that wasn't true at all—children felt the same complex emotions that adults did; they just didn't have all the tools to express them yet. What they did have, however, were actions: actions like reading Winnie-the-Pooh to themselves every night to feel a little less lost and alone in the world.

"I understand. The inhabitants of the Hundred Acre Wood were your found family like Charlie, Sam, and Patrick were mine," Rosie smiled endearingly.

29

AMANDA BYNES WAS RIGHT ABOUT GOUDA CHEESE

Rosie:

Like their first date, Callum had refused to tell Rosie what he had planned for their second official date. The only information he'd given her was to 'dress comfortably,' so she guessed that they would be doing something outside given that the late summer weather was especially nice today. She'd had just enough time to change when she got home from work before Callum texted that he was on the way to pick her up.

Callum wore a pair of off-white athletic shorts, what appeared to be a vintage Bowie t-shirt, and sneakers. The only thing on the floorboard of his Jeep was a backpack, which didn't provide Rosie with any helpful insight about his plans for this date. When they'd crossed the new bridge into Mount Pleasant, she'd jokingly asked if he was taking her back to work.

Eventually, they turned into the Palmetto Islands County Park. After weaving through several miles worth of dirt roads amidst palmetto trees, live oaks, magnolias, and crepe myrtles, they parked near what appeared to be a meadow. Remembering Callum's demand that she wait for him to open her door for her on their last date, Rosie unbuckled her seatbelt but stayed put. Callum grabbed the backpack from the back of his Jeep, then rounded the front to let her out.

"This is beautiful," Rosie appraised her surroundings as she emerged from the vehicle.

If it weren't for the lack of a basket, Rosie would have guessed that the plan for this date was a sunset picnic. When Callum steered her down a dirt path that diverted to the right of the meadow, she grew even more doubtful.

"You know, if this were a first date, this is the part where I would start to wonder if the person was a serial killer," Rosie joked.

"And here I was thinking I was being romantic," Callum answered sarcastically, lacing their fingers together.

"The fact that we're the only ones in this part of the park isn't exactly helping."

"It's a lot busier on the weekends—the park closes at sunset, so the drive isn't worth it for most people by the time they're off work during the week."

As they reached the end of the dirt path, an old, wooden observation tower emerged from the canopy of rich green foliage.

"Aside from Shem Creek, this is my favorite place to watch the sunset," Callum explained. "And I know that you love the silhouette of the new bridge against the sunset, but seeing the colors of the sunset reflected in the marsh is just as beautiful."

"How many stories is this thing?" Rosie squinted up toward the top of the massive structure.

"Four," Callum laughed. "Hence the dress code for the date."

"And you're sure this thing is sturdy?" Rosie shook the railing as she climbed the first flight of stairs as if she could assess its safety by doing so. "It looks like it was built in the 1800s."

"Shouldn't you of all people know not to judge a book, or, well, an observation tower, by its cover—er—lack of a paint job?" Callum sighed in defeat. "That was a mess, but you know what I mean."

"Watch it, Costello, or I might push you off," Rosie quipped. "Let a woman fear for her life in peace."

Callum abruptly halted mid-step to turn around and face her.

"You're safe with me. At least, I hope you feel that way," Callum exhaled heavily. "I just—hope you know that I wouldn't do anything to hurt you, Rosie."

She'd always felt safe with Callum; it was impossible for two people to have such an intimate physical relationship without trust. Yet Rosie couldn't shake off the feeling that Callum was alluding to much more than her physical safety.

Did she trust him emotionally? Rosie wasn't entirely sure she did yet, but she knew that she *wanted* to. The shift in the dynamic between them was still so new that she didn't quite know what to make of it. Was her hesitation because of Callum's history of fucking around? Or was it because she was so petrified by the idea of things not working out between them... and what that could mean for her and Elena? Wasn't that the whole reason she'd asked Callum if they could hold off on telling his family, specifically Elena, about the dates? If things between them went to shit, it would mean losing far more than Callum, which was something Rosie wouldn't let herself think about.

Not sure how to convey any of that to Callum when she barely understood how she felt herself, she settled on light-heartedly acknowledging the weight of Callum's words.

"And I hope that *you* know I wouldn't actually push you off this tower. We can't exactly have another date if you're dead."

"Planning ahead are we?" Callum asked in a tone Rosie thought was intended to sound sarcastic but sounded hopeful instead, as they resumed climbing up their stairs.

And *seriously*, how many goddamn stairs were attached to this fucking thing? Rosie didn't exactly work out, but she wasn't out of shape. The view had better damn well be worth it. She distracted herself from stair after incessant stair by staring at Callum's ass as he walked just slightly ahead of her. The ass she loved grabbing as he drove into her...

"Rosie?" Callum prompted her.

Right, he'd asked her a question.

"Hm?" she asked, trying her best to sound innocent.

She wasn't fooling anyone.

"Enjoying the view?" he snorted.

"Oh, shut up. It's not my fault you have a nice ass," Rosie defended. "It's distracting."

"I could say the same about you," Callum chuckled, glancing longingly at Rosie over his shoulder.

As they rounded the fourth and final set of stairs, Rosie surmised that this date must be Callum's version of a picnic. Instead of a basket, Callum had packed everything in his backpack; and, instead of a picnic blanket, Callum laid down an oversized beach towel.

Among the contents of his backpack was a mini bottle of Pinot Grigio (Rosie's favorite), a can of Island Coastal (his favorite local lager), a Ziploc bag of whole strawberries and green grapes, a bag of pepperonis and a block of gouda cheese.

"Gouda?"

"You quote *She's the Man* so often that I figured it would have been a missed opportunity otherwise," Callum snorted. "I don't even know if Gouda is good. I just saw it in the store and couldn't pass it up."

"I love Gouda," Rosie chuckled. "Will you hand me the knife?"

"What knife?" Callum asked, sounding genuinely confused.

"The knife to cut the cheese?" Rosie clarified.

"Shit. I..." Callum ran his hands through his hair, one of his tells that he was stressed, "have obviously never been on a picnic."

"Yeah, I can tell," she laughed. "My teeth work just fine—I'll just bite a piece off," she tried to reassure him as she took the cheese and bit it enthusiastically.

Maybe that would show him how little it bothered her. Callum's demeanor only shifted from stressed to embarrassed. Had she said something wrong? She'd only been joking with him. Why did he suddenly seem so sullen? Like he'd shrunk into a smaller version of himself.

"Callum," Rosie muttered softly, gently turning his face toward hers with the palm of her hand. "I was just teasing," she tried to assure him. "You know that right?"

"Yeah," Callum sighed. "Yeah, I know."

"Seriously—you've put more effort into these two dates than Justin put into our entire relationship. I'm having a great time," Rosie encouraged him.

She wasn't sure that drawing a comparison between him and Justin was the best idea, especially given how clearly Lilah had warned her against it. But she needed Callum to know that she recognized everything that he'd done to make these dates special. And that she appreciated the effort.

"Talk to me. Where's your head at?"

"Honestly? I'm worried that, because I managed to fuck up something as simple as packing utensils for a goddamn picnic, I won't ever be enough for you," Callum avoided Rosie's eyes.

He didn't shove her hand away though, just kept his eyes on the ground. Rosie kept quiet, silently urging him to continue talking to her.

"It's just... I know what everyone thinks of me, what you thought of me only a week ago, and I'm absolutely petrified that I will never be able to do enough to prove otherwise. I don't know how to do this," he gestured between them. "How to be in a relationship, how to voice my feelings, how to prove to you just how desperately I'm trying to be the kind of man that you deserve, and I—"

Rosie cut him off with a kiss. It was a kiss through which she desperately hoped to convey just how wrong every word coming out of Callum's mouth was. He wasn't just some guy that fucked around without regard for others. She saw the emotions he hid from most of the world. From himself. She saw that he was already enough, that he had nothing to prove to her. She saw *him*. And that scared the shit out of her.

Pulling back, she held his face between her hands and forced him to meet her eyes.

"I'm sorry that it took me so long to see it, to see you," she forced the words out. "But you don't have to prove anything to me. You're already enough."

Callum smiled coyly, leaning into her touch to rest his cheek in her palm. Though Rosie had seen, kissed, and tasted her way across every inch of Callum's body more times than she could begin to count over the years, the gentle touch that now passed between them somehow felt more intimate than any before. Ever since that night at Waffle House, when Callum had admitted his feelings for Rosie, every touch that had passed between them had borne an undeniable weight. Though not a bad one.

For the first time, in the nearly decade and a half they'd known each other, intimacy didn't automatically equate to sex. For the first time, Rosie yearned to touch Callum just to feel close to him, not because she knew it would inevitably lead to more. She didn't need it to become more. This was enough. He was enough.

Rosie felt as if she should say something, ask something. How many more dates did she get with Callum? What were they to each other now that they'd crossed over the line of being just friends with benefits? When was she allowed to sleep with him again?

As far as she was concerned, Callum had more than proven that this thing between them was far more than a good fuck; she thought she'd been attracted to Callum before, and yet that was nothing compared to the way she felt now that feelings were involved. She wanted to ask all of these questions that had been swirling around her mind, but then she remembered what Callum had said on their last date.

For the first time in a long time, I'm just genuinely happy and content to be somewhere... When I'm with you, I don't want to think about what comes next. I just want to exist with you, for as long as you're willing to let me.

The time for questions would come later. Right now, Rosie would exist in this moment with Callum. She still wanted to feel wrapped up in him, if only in a different way.

Rosie placed her hands on his knees and began to move them apart from one another.

"What are you..." Callum began to ask.

"Will you," she hesitated, "will you hold me?"

The look in Callum's eyes conveyed such yearning that it threatened to fracture a piece of Rosie's heart.

"I've never... no one has ever wanted me for this—" Callum offered as an explanation, "like I make them feel safe."

In answer, Rosie fitted her back to his chest. Callum's arms instinctively wrapped around her. She laced their fingers together, nuzzling back into his warmth. They stayed that way, content to be wrapped up in one another, as they watched the sun melt from the sky in vibrant explosions of tangerine, vermilion, and gold.

I do. *In your arms, I feel safe.*

30

SPECIAL DELIVERY FOR ROSEMARY JUNE

Rosie:

Rosie had spent many weekends curled up with a book, perfectly content to remain alone and unbothered. This past weekend, however, was different; every time she'd tried to pick up a romcom, she thought about Callum. It wasn't that she wished she was with him because she'd reached a level of horniness she didn't realize was possible; she wanted to hear his laugh, wanted to joke with him, wanted to see the look on his face when he talked about the things he loved. She just missed *him*, which was a terrifying realization considering they weren't even officially together.

Rosie attempted to shed the complicated web of emotions that was currently being spun in her mind as she took the elevator up to her office Monday morning. She'd set her stuff down, check her calendar, and hopefully have time to grab an Americano from the espresso bar before her first meeting of the day.

"You look happier than I've seen you in weeks," Isla sing-songed as Rosie reached her desk. "Would this have anything to do with Elena's hot as fuck brother? *Please* tell me you're hooking up with him."

Today, Isla was wearing a coastal blue sweater with white, linen trousers. Her eyeliner, matching as always, looked like little blue waves flowing away from the current of Isla's eyes.

"Good morning to you too, Is," Rosie laughed.

Rosie and Callum had agreed not to tell Elena and the rest of his family that they were dating, but they hadn't said anything about work friends, right?

"That wasn't an answer to my question," Isla smirked.

"Maybe it does," Rosie smirked back.

"I'd say you could tell me about it in line for coffee, but we have a title and cover design meeting in thirty minutes."

"Has anyone ever told you that your omniscient-like knowledge of the calendar is unsettling?" Rosie rolled her eyes and started unpacking her bag. "Which manuscript is the meeting for?"

"I'll have you know that *some* people find it helpful," Isla teased, feigning offense. "And it's for that sapphic enemies-to-lovers one where they have to plan a wedding together."

"I thought we approved the cover design for that last month? A cartoon-style cover?"

"We did, but the author had feedback about a few things. Something about one of them not looking masc enough, I think," Isla explained.

"Ah. Well, I'm gonna get set up and try to reply to a few emails before we have to be there."

"You're telling me to go away? Rude, honestly," Isla gave her best attempt at a puppy dog face, which looked more sarcastic than sad.

Isla had a very intimidating demeanor, which often meant that her facial expressions didn't translate the way she thought they did. It was one of Rosie's favorite things about her.

"I'll see you in thirty minutes," Rosie chuckled. "You'll survive."

"Not that you deserve it now, but here," Isla held a coffee cup out to her. Rosie had assumed it was full of whatever concoction Nolan had made for Isla this morning. "I got you an Americano when I was down at the espresso bar since I figured you wouldn't have time to get it before the meeting. Which, by the way, I wouldn't have known to do had I not checked the calendar..."

Rosie graciously accepted, "have I told you that I love you this morning?"

"Yeah, yeah. I love you too, my dearest work wife," Isla rolled her eyes and walked back to her desk.

Upon opening her inbox, Rosie was inundated with emails about potential manuscripts, questions and concerns from some of her authors, and updated drafts of manuscripts based on her editing feedback. Potential and updated manuscripts would have to wait, but she could get started on replying to some of the questions her authors had asked.

One was worried that her female main character was more developed than her male main character, one wanted to know if it would be a copyright issue to name-drop a store in the real town where her story takes place, and one of her newly acquired authors wanted to ensure that Rosie knew her manuscript 'contained *many* instances of graphic sexually explicit content.' Oh, if only she knew. Rosie often liked to joke that she got paid to consume porn on a daily basis, which was at least a little bit true. Rosie responded to let her know the more smut, the merrier.

Before she knew it, Rosie only had five minutes until her

meeting; answering emails was like being in a vacuum where time ceased to exist.

The title and cover meeting had flown by—the team agreed with the author that the cover needed an update to better indicate the nature of the story. Rosie had just sat back down at her desk and was contemplating going down to see Nolan and grab another Americano when she got a call from Nora at the front desk.

"Hey Nora, what's up?"

"Hey, honey, I've got a man down here who says he's got a delivery for you. You expecting anything today?"

"Not that I can think of?" Rosie wondered aloud. However, she did sometimes receive ARCs from other publishing houses that didn't have her home address. That was probably it. "But you can go ahead and send him up anyway."

"Alrighty, hun," Nora said, hanging up.

Checking her calendar to see that she didn't have any other meetings until this afternoon, Rosie decided to take the next few hours to work on editing a manuscript that was set to come out this fall.

"Excuse me? Rosemary Dawson?" a man stepping off the elevator called.

He was carrying an open box in his arms that was at least two feet tall.

"That's me," Rosie answered.

The box was definitely too big to be an ARC or two, and she had racked her brain trying, unsuccessfully, to remember placing any recent orders. Rosie scrambled to clear a space off on her desk for the package as the man approached.

"I don't actually know what I ordered—do I owe you?" Rosie asked.

"You didn't order these," the delivery man laughed as he set the box down; it came across as amused rather than rude like he knew something Rosie didn't. "These are from, uh," the man paused, pulling a slip of paper out of his pocket, "a Callum Costello."

Before Rosie could react, he was reaching into the box and carefully removing a vase full of the most beautiful bouquet Rosie had ever seen. It was a perfect blend of zinnias, peonies, Russian sage, and various greenery.

"You don't owe anything, darling, but I do need a signature that you accept the delivery," the man explained as if Rosie's heart wasn't running a marathon right now.

She was pretty sure it might beat right out of her chest.

Rosie signed off, staring in shock over the fact that *Callum Costello* had sent not just flowers, but probably insanely expensive flowers, to her work. Justin hadn't ever sent flowers to Rosie's work, not even one time in the two years they'd spent together. Yet Callum had. On a random Monday. When they weren't even dating officially.

Rosie leaned in to smell the bouquet, inhaling what could only be described as the scent of pure summer. As she did, she realized that there was a small card attached to the vase. Her heart fluttered far too much as she opened it.

Rosemary June,
I've been reading The Perks of Being a Wallflower since our bookstore date, and I hope

you know that you deserve more. These flowers are a start.

-C

On their last date, Rosie had risked opening up about her relationship with Justin, despite Lilah's warnings, as a way of showing Callum that he was more than enough. That he had, in a matter of weeks, done more for her than Justin had in the two years they'd been together. The flowers were evidence that Callum had genuinely listened. And had gone out of his way to continue to show up for her.

Rosie was not going to cry at work. Nope. Absolutely not. No matter how thoughtful the flowers were, no matter how seen she felt by Callum's note. Thankfully, Isla was running toward Rosie's desk before the tears could start falling.

"No *fucking* way are those from hot brother," Isla whisper-screamed.

Rosie just nodded, clearly flushed and biting her lip to try to keep from grinning.

"Oh my god?!" Isla exclaimed. "Oh my god, oh my GOD!"

"Shh, I'm not trying to attract the attention of the entire office," Rosie whispered-screamed back.

"Babe, be real. The entire office can see them from across the room. That's gotta be, what, at least an eighty-dollar bouquet?"

"You're fucking with me," Rosie had no idea how much flowers cost.

She would much rather spend her money on a new book, thank you very much. There was no way Callum had dropped close to a hundred dollars on *flowers*.

"At least. Honestly," Isla spun the vase around to look more closely, "these might be closer to a hundred."

One hundred fucking dollars. Rosie didn't know how to even begin to thank Callum. Opening her text thread with Callum, she started by stating the obvious.

> Rosie: You sent me flowers??

> Callum: I'm hoping this means you like them?

> Rosie: Are you fucking kidding me?! They're beautiful.

> Callum: Good, though they don't stand a chance next to you.

"Ooh, I know that face. What's lover boy saying?" Isla asked, attempting to snatch Rosie's phone from her hand.

Rosie playfully swatted Isla's hand away.

"Nosy much?" Rosie teased. "Ask nicely and I'll show you."

It's not like she could show Elena or Noah—not yet at least; though Rosie was starting to not like keeping this a secret anymore.

"Fine. Can I *pretty please with lover-boy on top* see the texts that have you smiling at your phone like an idiot?"

"I don't think insulting the person you're trying to get something from is the best tactic," Rosie rolled her eyes. "Here," she relented, passing the phone to Isla.

Rosie watched her amused reaction as she read through the texts.

"Oh, he is *so* in love with you," Isla boldly declared as she handed the phone back to Rosie.

Why did hearing that set Rosie's heart beating out of her chest? It wasn't like it was true. Did she *want* it to be true?

"We've been on two dates," Rosie tried to rationalize.

"Yeah, maybe, but you don't need that many dates to realize that you love someone when they've been in your life for over a decade."

Rosie's cheeks heated. Not that she would ever admit it, but Isla had a damn good point. She had very few memories since high school that didn't involve Callum in some capacity. When Rosie remained silent, Isla left her with a parting comment: "just think about it."

Rosie would. Whether she wanted to or not.

Before returning to her work, Rosie sent one last text to Callum, this one she didn't plan on showing to Isla.

> Rosie: Thank you, Callum. I love them.

I love you, the voice in her head whispered.

> Callum: Good. Did the barista bring your Americano up yet?

As his text came through, the elevator dinged. Nolan stepped out holding a coffee cup and headed in her direction.

31

ITALIAN—THE LANGUAGE OF ROMANCE

Rosie:

Rosie stood in her bedroom, contemplating how to reply to the text she'd just received from Noah.

> Noah: Babe, we both know 'busy' just means you plan to sit on your couch all night with a book and a glass of wine.

Rosie had been evading plans with Noah and Elena for the last few weeks, ever since her first date with Callum. Elena was still trying to set her up with people, and Rosie didn't know how to explain to her that she wasn't interested without telling her about dating Callum. Which she still wasn't ready to do. More accurately, *still didn't know* how *to do*.

Things were going really well between them, and she didn't want to jeopardize that by adding the pressure of outside opinions. She hadn't told Noah either, not wanting to put Noah in the position of having to keep a secret from Elena. She knew she should just be honest with both of them, but the little voice in the back of her mind kept whispering.

What if this doesn't work out? You don't want to lose your best friend too, do you? You don't want to lose the only family you've ever felt whole with, do you?

> Rosie: Actually, I'm still catching up on reading submissions for potential manuscripts. Been playing catch-up ever since Elena's wedding.

That wasn't an outright lie. Rosie *was* behind on submissions, she just didn't plan to catch up on them tonight. Tonight, she and Callum had plans to make lasagna together and watch a movie at his apartment. Knowing Callum, they would be making the pasta from scratch.

Though Rosie had never done anything besides boil the pre-made pasta that came in a box, she was fairly certain that the process would involve a lot of flour. With that in mind, she dressed in sweatpants and an old t-shirt that she wouldn't mind getting dirty. Callum had seen her dressed to the nines, looking like an actual trainwreck, and in every state between over the last decade; he wouldn't lose sleep over the fact that she was essentially wearing pajamas on a date. Double-checking that she had everything—keys, wallet, emotional support book, and a bottle of wine to drink with dinner—she headed down her apartment complex's stairs.

Given that this date would offer her and Callum more privacy than the others they'd been on, she figured it would be a good time to have a conversation about physical intimacy. She understood and had been more than supportive of Callum's reasoning for wanting to refrain from anything sexual for a while. But if Rosie and Callum were going to continue dating—and she hoped that they would, because Rosie had thoroughly enjoyed these last few weeks with Callum—she needed to be clear with him about her wants and needs. Physical intimacy was a way to build trust, a way to deepen the connection between two people.

She would respect Callum's boundaries, but she also knew he was holding back as a way of proving to her that he was pursuing her for more than sex. Rosie had seen that to be true time and time again over the last few weeks, and she was ready to take the next step with him. But only if he was, too. Hence the conversation she hoped to have.

Callum:

The last time Rosie had been in Callum's kitchen, he'd knelt between her spread legs until she came against his tongue. Though that had *definitely* been enjoyable, he was having just as much fun making homemade pasta with her tonight.

Callum stood, arms wrapped around Rosie from behind, 'helping' her knead the dough for the pasta.

"I didn't know you could be so domestic," Rosie smirked up at him.

"Rosie, my Nonna would roll over in her grave if she knew I paid actual US dollars for pre-made noodles, let alone if I boiled those noodles and proceeded to feed them to my girlfriend."

The words were out of his mouth before he could stop himself.

Rosie whirled around to face him, still wrapped in Callum's arms because he had clung to the dough in his hands in a panic.

"What did you just call me?" she asked, staring up at him intently.

Nothing on her face betrayed how she felt about his little slip-up, and he had no idea what to do with that.

Shit.

If Callum repeated himself, would he scare Rosie off? If he pretended he hadn't said anything, would that ruin his chances with her? Would she again think he wasn't capable of commitment?

"Um, well, I," Callum hesitated. "I mean, we're dating, right? I mean, we've gone on dates," he tried to correct himself but felt like he was making things worse every time he opened his mouth.

"Is this your way of asking me to be your girlfriend?" Rosie smiled softly.

Smiling. She was *smiling*. That had to be a good sign, right?

Fuck it.

"Yeah," Callum smiled back shyly. "Yeah, I think I am."

"My *boyfriend*, Callum Costello," Rosie turned the words over in her mouth. "I like it."

"Yeah?" Callum realized he liked hearing Rosie call him her boyfriend far, far more than he probably should.

"Yeah," she laced her hands together behind his neck and leaned up to kiss him.

"Rosemary June, my girlfriend," he whispered against her lips.

Evidently, Rosie liked hearing those words just as much as he did, because she brought their bodies closer together, pulling Callum down to her by the neck. For weeks, all Callum had allowed himself were soft, innocent kisses. Right now, as Rosie's hands roamed freely across his chest, down to his ass, as she arched into him... he was having a very fucking hard time stopping this kiss from escalating into something more.

"The dough—" Callum tried to get the words out.

"What about it?" Rosie muttered against his lips.

"We have to keep kneading it," his breath was ragged, "or it won't turn out."

Rosie let out a noise that sounded like a disappointed moan but pressed one final kiss to Callum's lips and conceded.

"Only if you promise to finish what you started later," she muttered as she swept her thumb across Callum's bottom lip.

Fucking hell on earth.

"What *I* started?" The question came out as an exasperated plea.

Without answering, Rosie simply turned around to continue kneading the dough.

"How do you know when it's kneaded enough?" Rosie asked.

Callum's Nonna had first 'taught' him how to make pasta from scratch when he was just seven years old. She'd attempted to teach all of his siblings at one point or another, but some of them hadn't taken to it so quickly. By the time Callum was eleven, he knew the recipe by heart and could navigate the process with little to no help.

"Um, I don't really know how to quantify that in words. It's more so understanding how the dough should *feel*," Callum tried to explain. "For instance, ours feels a little too wet, so we can add a bit more semolina to bring it to a better consistency."

"*Feel* the dough? Not *wet* enough? Is this what people mean when they say that Italian is the language of romance?" Rosie snorted.

Callum leaned down so that his lips brushed the shell of Rosie's ear, "making pasta with you is proving rather difficult. Your questions are quite distracting."

Callum could feel Rosie shudder against him.

"Fine," she crossed her arms and looked up at him over her shoulder. "I'll ask a real question. What is the difference between regular flour and semo... sema... sema-whatever-the-fuck?"

"Semo*lina*," Callum laughed. "It's a specific type of flour that has a higher concentration of protein."

"And that's important because?"

"Well, more protein means more gluten, which is what helps give the dough its structure," Callum explained.

"Oh, that actually makes a lot of sense. I've never had homemade pasta before."

"Well, lucky for you, you have a handsome new boyfriend with Italian grandparents who taught him to make pasta before he had any business being near a boiling pot of water."

"I'm lucky for more reasons than your ability to make pasta," Rosie said softly.

Over her shoulder, Callum could see Rosie's lips turn up into a smile. He couldn't stop his own lips from following suit.

32

SO CALLUM JAMES DID

Callum:

CUDDLING ON THE COUCH, empty plates cast to the side, Rosie and Callum laughed until their stomachs hurt as Amanda Bynes impersonated her brother in *She's the Man* so that she could play soccer. Rosie had begged Callum to watch it with her ever since he'd brought the gouda cheese on their last date. He had agreed on the premise that he would say yes to anything Rosie asked if it made her happy.

"Is this really what guys are like when they're interested in someone?" Rosie asked with a laugh as the male lead stumbled over his words at a carnival kissing booth.

"Do we all turn into blabbering, nervous, idiots, you mean?" Callum snorted.

"In so many words."

Callum could feel the rumble of Rosie's laugh against his chest.

"Hmm, you tell me," he traced his fingers up and down Rosie's arm. "Have *I* acted like a babbling, nervous idiot these past few weeks?"

Rosie flipped over so that, rather than lying with her back to his chest, her chest now rested against his, Rosie's body tucked perfectly between Callum's legs. He'd noticed earlier that Rosie hadn't been wearing a bra, but now he could *feel* that she wasn't. A sensation that wasn't doing much for his self-control.

"Nervous and babbling?" she smiled softly as if trying to hide a smirk, "a little. Idiot? No." Her pointer finger traced the neckline of his t-shirt. "I still can't believe the first time you watched this movie was in college. You grew up with four sisters."

"Listen, I thought I was proving my masculinity by avoiding rom-coms like the plague, okay? High school's a bitch," Callum reasoned.

"Touché," Rosie conceded. "Thank God you went to college."

"Excuse me, let's not forget that you were always *quite* interested in me. Even before college."

"Um, no. *You* were interested in *me*," Rosie braced her forearms on either side of Callum, pushing her weight up to stare at him more fully.

"Do you need a reminder of how things started between us?"

"I'll tell you what I do remember," Rosie rolled her eyes sarcastically.

He loved it when Rosie rolled her eyes, especially when she was rolling them in response to his fingers, his tongue... *Shit*. This was not the time to be thinking about touching Rosie. Especially not now that she'd shifted ever so slightly in his arms so that their hips were perfectly aligned. She would definitely feel his cock hardening. *Shit shit shit.*

"I remember you *spilling*—" Rosie held up air quotes at the word spilling, "a glass of water on the floor to distract

Liam long enough for me to sneak down the stairs to your room in the middle of the night."

"You're forgetting the part where you texted me from Elena's room complaining about the fact that she was asleep and you were '*oh so bored*,'" Callum's hands found Rosie's hips underneath her oversized t-shirt and squeezed.

"Well *excuse me* for finding you more entertaining than sleep," Rosie huffed.

The tension that had been building between them suddenly dissipated. Though Callum knew she was joking, something about hearing Rosie refer to him as merely entertainment stung. He'd been intrigued by her since the day he first set eyes on her at their neighborhood basketball court. Had rearranged his plans to be home whenever Elena had invited Rosie over on the off chance that he got to talk to her.

"You know, you weren't just entertainment to me," Callum admitted. "You were the only one of Elena's friends that I ever bothered to pay any attention to, and I went out of my way to be close to you. You didn't *really* think I just liked hanging out with my big sister *that* much, did you?" Callum smirked.

Callum assumed Rosie had seen the hurt in his eyes that he'd tried to hide with humor because she quickly amended her earlier statement.

"That was a poor choice of words. You aren't just entertainment to me either, Callum James."

No one called him Callum James. Except Rosie apparently.

"You have no idea how much I like hearing you say my name like that," Callum admitted, a bit coy.

"Like what?"

"Like..." Callum struggled to find the right words. "Like I'm someone you plan to keep."

"I do—" Rosie leaned up to kiss him lightly, "plan to keep you, that is."

He was still getting used to being so vulnerable with someone. All of these feelings might not have been new, but Callum had been denying them for so long that they *felt* new. He found himself treasuring every new piece of Rosie, clinging to them as if he could make up for the decade and some of wasted time. Time that he could have spent with Rosie like this.

Callum leaned forward to press his forehead to Rosie's, "I want to know about all of it."

"About what?"

"Everything I missed out on because I was too much of a dumbass to realize that I'd been harboring feelings for you for a decade. Everything I missed when you went off to college. All of it," Callum elaborated.

Rosie smiled, settling herself between Callum's legs on the couch.

"College was better I guess? I mean, freshman year sucked ass. That's the year Noah came out; people reacted largely the way they did to me in high school, and having communal dorms didn't help," she sighed.

Rosie tended to do that, to talk about the hate she'd faced as if it wasn't a big deal. Callum couldn't help but think of Lilah then; Lilah, who had faced just as much hatred, who went about her life as if the spiteful comments didn't leave a lasting mark. But Callum knew they did. And he fucking hated it.

"I'm sorry, Rosie."

"What do you have to be sorry for?"

"No one deserves to be ostracized for who they are,"

Callum said bluntly. "And I know that I will never fully understand what that feels like, being straight, but I did spend years holding Lilah whenever someone said something particularly fucked up to her. Most of the time, she shook things off, and fed me some version of 'it is what it is.' I had to watch her internalize interaction after interaction until it boiled over into tears. And I wanted to hurt everyone that had ever hurt her, to make them feel ten times worse, to shake them and ask how the fuck they could justify causing someone so much pain over something they couldn't change about themselves, even if they wanted to."

"I've always admired that about you," Rosie laced her fingers with Callum's. "How fiercely protective you are of the people you care about. And I feel incredibly lucky to be one of those people now."

With his other hand, Callum traced encouraging circles across the small of her back, silently urging her to continue. Reminding her that he was listening, that he wanted to continue learning about her life.

"Sophomore year, things were a lot better. Noah and I shared an apartment free of ignorant bitches. Then I transferred to NYU to finish my degree, which you knew, and, yeah, that's pretty much it."

"I knew you went, but, like I said at Waffle House, I've only known pieces of your life, Rosie. I want to know everything. You were a barista for a few years, right? Tell me about that."

He didn't care if he sounded desperate. He'd never cared about the minute details of anyone's life before, but damn if he didn't want to know everything there was to know about Rosemary June Dawson. He wanted to know what kind of toothpaste she used, what her favorite cereal was, if she preferred even or odd numbers. Any and every detail that made her who she was.

"God, I fucking loved it. Well, aside from the usual bullshit that comes with any job in the food service industry that is," Rosie laughed. "This probably sounds absolutely ridiculous, but I genuinely miss frothing milk. And the aroma of a fresh espresso shot being pulled."

Callum gently turned her face toward his with his right hand, "It doesn't sound ridiculous. And I understand. I always work at least one bartending shift a week—partly because I don't want to forget what it's like to be in the trenches, but also because I just genuinely love the job. Though I do get tired of making vodka sodas," he snorted. "And lemon drop shots."

"Don't shit on lemon drop shots! I love those," Rosie put a hand to her chest, feigning offense.

"Did you love them while you were hurling them into Noah's toilet the morning after Elena's bachelorette party?" Callum smirked.

"In my defense, I drank those on top of an entire fish bowl of who knows how many different liquors! And besides, Noah ordered them, not me."

"Fair enough. But c'mon, you can't tell me there isn't a specific drink you hated making."

"It wasn't a specific drink necessarily, just people generally not understanding that what they were ordering wasn't what they actually wanted, and then trying to tell me I was doing my job wrong. Like damn, if you know so much more than me come steam the fucking milk yourself."

"What I'm learning from this conversation is that baristas and bartenders have a lot in common," Callum laughed.

"God, there was this one bitch who ordered a vanilla

latte with coconut milk. Just take one guess as to what coconut milk tastes like."

"Gonna really go out on a limb here and say coconut milk probably tastes like coconut."

"You'd be correct. See? Not that hard of a concept to grasp. Anyway, the bitch ordered the vanilla latte with coconut milk and then complained that it tasted like, and I fucking quote, 'vanilla and some other weird flavor.'"

"And then you told her to fuck off?" Callum snorted.

"I wanted to, but I wanted to keep my job more," Rosie sighed. "So I just explained to her that the other flavor she was tasting was the coconut from the *coconut* milk with as little condescension as I could manage."

"Maybe baristas and bartenders don't have as much in common as I thought. I can just kick anyone out if they give us shit."

"Yes, but you're the manager," Rosie raised her eyebrows dramatically. "My boyfriend, the manager of Lafayette's," she rolled the words over in her mouth, "has a nice ring to it."

Callum hadn't told many people about his plans to buy Lafayette's. He wasn't a fan of unsolicited advice, which tended to come with the territory of discussing future plans. He'd told Lilah, of course, and his parents. For the first time, he found himself wanting to tell someone else, too.

"Actually, I plan to put my double majors to use and take over ownership whenever Hank is ready to retire. Already talked it over with him and everything—he's just not quite ready to let go yet."

"What the hell? That's fucking amazing, Callum, why didn't you ever tell me?"

"I guess I just didn't think it really mattered to anyone." At the hurt in Rosie's eyes, Callum quickly amended, "I mean, I don't think that anymore. I just... I know you used to see me like most everyone else did: the permanent bachelor who would never achieve anything of substance, who would always be okay with his life being 'just good enough.'"

"First of all, there's nothing wrong with being content with where you're at in life, not needing some grand plan to be happy. Secondly, I'm so sorry that I ever made you feel that way. I'm sorry that I never took the time to look beyond the facade you let people project onto you. But I see you now, Callum, and I want you," Rosie maneuvered herself so that she was now straddling Callum rather than just laying on him. "I want all of you."

Slowly, without breaking eye contact with Callum, she brought his hands to her hips. An invitation. One that Callum really, really didn't want to deny.

"And I know you don't need this. I don't either, but I *want* this. More than I've wanted anything. More than I've wanted *anyone*," Rosie said, almost a plea.

"I won't be able to stop myself, Rose," Callum said as a last line of defense for his self-control.

He was desperate to touch her, but he had to be sure she understood that it wasn't just sex. Not anymore. If they crossed this line, he would be ruined for anyone else. Hell, he already was.

"I didn't plan on asking you to," Rosie leaned down to whisper against Callum's lips, the movement punctuating her words. "But if we're really doing this," her right hand traced a path up the column of his neck. "If we're committing to a real relationship," her tongue traced the path where her hand had just been, "then I want every part of a real relationship with you, including physical," she kissed the skin under his ear, practically humming, "especially physical."

Rosie leaned back just enough to look into Callum's eyes. He wasn't sure he was breathing. He *was* sure, however, that he had never been harder in his goddamned life.

"I need *you*, Callum, not just a good fuck," Rosie said earnestly.

No one had ever needed him. Ever. They might have needed the release he could *offer* them, but never *him*. He had no words for the relief he felt at hearing Rosie offer him what it had taken him over two decades to realize he'd been craving.

Callum shifted his hands to cup the sides of Rosie's face, desperately needing her to understand the gravity of his next words.

"I need *you* too, Rose. It's always been you. And I'm sorry it took me this long to realize that. But now that I have you, I intend to do everything in my power to keep you. Because you're it for me, Rosemary June. I need you to know that before... before anything else," he admitted nervously.

Rosie smiled then. And the relief Callum had felt minutes ago swelled.

"You're it for me too, Callum James," Rosie whispered his words back to him.

There it was again: *Callum James*. A reminder and a promise that this thing between them was real. Even if it scared the shit out of him.

Callum pulled her to him, kissing her desperately. His hands found her hips. Her hands found the waistband of his sweatpants. They tugged gently.

"Let me show you how much I need you, Callum," Rosie breathed. A plea. A promise. "Please."

Finding himself beyond the point of words, Callum nodded his encouragement as he glanced down his torso to where Rosie's hands lingered.

"Thank God," Rosie breathed as she pulled his sweatpants and underwear down in one swift motion.

She glanced from the hard length of his cock up to meet Callum's eyes with what seemed to be a mix of hunger and adoration in her eyes.

"Perfect," Rosie whispered as she slid her hand up his shaft without a trace of hesitation.

Nothing had ever felt so good in Callum's entire life. He had never mixed sex and emotion like this, never allowed himself to be so vulnerable with someone. Until now. Until Rosie. And it changed everything, made every touch that much more gratifying.

"How are you real?" Callum muttered.

It definitely wasn't the sexiest thing he'd ever said to Rosie. He was usually much better at dirty talk. But this wasn't like any previous time with Rosie; this was new and different and everything he never knew he wanted.

She only laughed as she lowered her mouth to his cock. She traced her tongue up the length of him, swirling around the head of his cock before sucking him lightly into her mouth. Callum thought that he might be content to watch Rosie's perfect lips wrap around him, to watch her cheeks hollow as she gave him the pressure he sought, for the rest of his life. He'd never seen something so beautiful.

Instinctively, he pushed the copper strands of her hair back from her face and held them behind her head, both giving her better access and himself a better view.

Usually, it was all brash movements, moans, and force between them. Not that that hadn't been great too, but this was infinitely better. This was the first time Callum had truly let himself *watch* as Rosie pleasured him. The way that she seemed to enjoy the feel of his cock in her perfect mouth as much as Callum did filled him with an overwhelming sense of euphoria.

Rosie picked up her pace then, moving one of the hands that had been resting on Callum's thigh around the base of his cock. That he was too big to fit into her mouth entirely did nothing to stop Rosie from trying.

"Holy fuck, Rose," Callum groaned. "God this is everything... you're everything."

She hummed her approval, and Callum felt the sound reverberate along his cock. He wasn't going to last much longer, and he desperately wanted to be inside of her when he came.

"I'm close, baby," Callum breathed out as if to convey to Rosie that she could stop, that they could have sex instead.

That he wanted her to feel just as much pleasure as she'd been causing him to feel. It was then that Callum noticed the absence of Rosie's other hand. He followed the shape of her arm to where it was currently moving between Rosie's thighs.

Jesus. Fucking. Christ. Rosie was touching herself to the feel of Callum's cock in her mouth. If he hadn't already been close to release, that alone would have done him in.

"Rose, baby," Callum moaned. "Fuck I'm going to come."

Staring directly into Callum's eyes, Rosie sucked him harder, pumped him faster. He could see the frantic movement of the hand between her thighs as well. She gave him a look that said *if you even try to take your cock out of my mouth, you lose your hand.*

His last thought before he came was that he fully intended to return the pleasure she'd given him. Evidently finding release herself, Rosie moaned against his cock, taking everything he gave. Swallowed it all without breaking eye contact for even a second.

Yeah, Callum was entirely ruined for anyone but Rosie. She was it for him. Would always be it for him. *Had* always been it for him.

"I don't even—" Callum started. "That was... fucking hell, Rosie."

She moved, carefully, up his body to kiss him, "Yeah, I know."

"I'm *definitely* not complaining, but you didn't have to swa—"

She cut him off with a kiss. Callum tasted himself on her tongue and could already feel himself hardening again beneath Rosie's body.

"I didn't do anything I didn't want to do," Rosie smirked. "I came too, in case you missed that."

"Are you fucking kidding me? I don't think anything has made me that hard in my life."

"Hard enough to go again?" Rosie ground her hips against his now fully-hardened cock. "I haven't felt you inside me in nearly two months, and my vibrator is a pathetic substitute. I might lose it if you don't tell me you'll fuck me tonight."

Suddenly, Callum was reminded of the night of Elena and Cole's wedding. When he could have sworn he heard a vibrator through the door to Rosie's room in the beach house.

"Actually, speaking of vibrators..." Callum smirked at the blush that immediately painted itself across Rosie's cheeks. "The night of Elena and Cole's wedding, I heard you from the kitchen."

"I..." Rosie paused, looking up at Callum through her lashes and smiling coyly. "I wanted you to hear me. I don't think I've ever been as horny as I was walking away from you in the hallway earlier that night. I wanted you to walk back through my door and fuck me instead. That's what I thought about while I fucked myself."

"I fucked my fist to the thought of you being one door away and riding that damn vibrator instead of me," Callum admitted.

Rosie rolled her hips against him again, earning a breathy groan from Callum.

"*Please* tell me that noise means you'll fuck me," Rosie said.

"Only if you ask nicely," Callum dragged one of his hands up from her hip to tease Rosie's nipple under her shirt.

He fucking loved that *she* loved having her tits played with.

"Callum Costello, will you please do me the honor of sliding your cock inside me until I'm screaming your name so loud your neighbors know who you are?" Rosie asked.

And so Callum did.

33

JUST FUCKING AROUND

Rosie:

Though they had been together earlier that afternoon, Rosie and Callum drove separately to the Costello's for family dinner night. Things had been going really well for the past month; they'd been going perfectly if Rosie was being honest. Even so, a small part of her couldn't help but wonder when the shit would hit the fan.

She hadn't mentioned this to Callum because she knew it was unfair to project her trust issues onto her relationship with him, especially given that he'd done nothing but treat her right since that first date a month ago. It had been nearly three months since Rosie and Justin had broken up, which was enough time for Rosie to recognize that her anxieties stemmed solely from the betrayal she'd felt in finding out that he'd been cheating on her for a year. And that had nothing to do with Callum.

Whenever she started to spiral into that train of thought, she tried to remind herself of the declaration Callum had made the night they'd finally had sex again since admitting to having feelings for each other.

Now that I have you, I intend to do everything in my power to keep you. Because you're it for me, Rosemary June. I need you to know that.

Thoughts of Callum aside, Rosie was excited about family dinner tonight. Noah would be there, and it would be the first time in a few weeks that Rosie, Noah, and Elena had all been together. Elena had jumped into home decor projects after getting back from her honeymoon, Noah had taken on an apprentice at the tattoo studio she worked at, and Rosie had been 'catching up on manuscript submissions' (read: hanging out with Callum constantly).

As far as Noah was aware, nothing had happened between Rosie and Callum since the night of her shitty date at Lafayette's. That did nothing, however, to stop her from casting dramatic gestures between the two of them that Rosie thought were intended to be taken as 'I could cut the sexual tension with a knife.' Which was more than true.

If she was being honest with herself, she was dying to tell Noah the truth about her and Callum: that they were in a committed relationship. But she refused to put Noah in a bad position with Elena. So, she would remain quiet, even if it was killing her slowly not to be able to talk to her best friend.

"I'm gonna grab a few beers from the fridge in the garage," Callum announced to no one in particular.

Rosie took this as her cue to follow. Since they still hadn't told anyone else in his family about the two of them, Rosie had been stealing every little moment she could to be alone with Callum at these Costello family events. Ever since they'd had sex again, Rosie couldn't get enough of Callum. She wanted to touch him constantly; not just sexually, though that was certainly also true, but she'd begun to crave his casual gestures of affection.

As she headed toward the garage, she nonchalantly mentioned that she "was going to grab a few more seltzers and did Noah or Elena want another too?"

"Yeah, watermelon kiwi if we have any left! Thanks!" Elena happily answered, oblivious to Rosie's ulterior motives.

Before Rosie could get away, Noah grabbed her arm and blocked her in the empty laundry room.

"Callum can grab drinks, you can tell me what the fuck is up between the two of you. He went down on you on the fucking *rooftop* of the bar he manages, which by the way is quite frankly the hottest thing I've heard in my entire life and I cannot believe actually happened to you, and then suddenly you have no further updates? I don't buy it."

Rosie was about to lose her window to get a few minutes alone with Callum. Noah already assumed they were fucking, so what was the harm in leaning into that enough that Noah would let pass?

"If you let me go 'help Callum with the drinks,'" Rosie threw up air quotes around help, "I might actually have something to spill."

"You sneaky bitch," Noah whisper-yelled, playfully hitting Rosie's arm.

Thankfully, this seemed to be enough to satisfy Noah for the meantime because she moved out of the doorframe to let Rosie pass. Rosie slipped down the hallway off the kitchen that led to the garage. Callum's head snapped up at the sound of the door opening, but he visibly relaxed when he realized it was her.

"I was hoping you'd follow me," Callum immediately moved toward her.

"I would hope that an editor would know to read between the lines," Rosie smiled as she laced her fingers together at the nape of Callum's neck.

Any other words they might have said would have to be uttered against each other's lips as they crashed together, Callum backing Rosie into the fridge to press himself even closer to her. She imagined that he too felt that intrinsic need to be as close to her as possible.

As Callum ran a hand gently, teasingly up her thigh, lifting so that one of her legs was wrapped around Callum's waist, the garage door opened.

"Fuck, sorry!" Elena frantically squeaked. "Wait, what the fuck?!" she added as she realized what she was looking at.

It wasn't as if Elena and Callum's entire family didn't know their history. Elena wouldn't be upset that they were hooking up, but she might very well be upset that Rosie hadn't told her about it. *Shit.* Before Rosie could say anything, Elena started rambling to explain herself, as if she was the one who'd been caught making out with her best friend's brother in the garage.

"You had been gone for a while, so I came to check if you needed any help carrying the drinks in... and..." Elena trailed off, eyes bouncing between Rosie and Callum. Neither of them had even a single drink in hand. "And clearly you don't need help."

"Elena, I'm sorry," Rosie tried. "I know you're upset that I didn't tell you, but..."

"But we're just fucking around, Elena," Callum quickly added. "It's not like there was really anything to tell."

As soon as the words were out of Callum's mouth, Rosie realized just how much she hated hearing Callum refer to things between them as if they meant nothing. As if *she* meant nothing. Rosie recognized that he only said it out of respect for her, out of respect for the fact that she'd asked him to hold off on telling his family for a while. It made her feel sick to her stomach nonetheless.

"Okay, relax, it's not like I didn't see it coming," Elena held up her hands in surrender. "You two were *all* over each other at the wedding, but, it's just—do you really have to mess around *here*? In our *parent's garage*?" Elena raised her eyebrows in Callum's direction.

"Fair," Rosie conceded, freeing herself from Callum's arms.

"Both of you had better bring in two arm-fulls of drinks unless you want Mom to start gossiping," Elena snorted.

"Knowing Mom, she and Lydia placed bets on how long it would take the second Rosie followed me out here," Callum teased with a wink in Rosie's direction.

"Ew, just grab some drinks and hurry the fuck up."

And with that, Elena left them alone.

34

THE WICKED WITCH OF WEST BAY

Rosie:

NOAH WASTED no time in switching the subject back to Rosie and Callum the second they were in her car headed to Lafayette's for drinks. Callum obviously wasn't working tonight, and Rosie had already spent the entire day with him, and she *really did* owe it to Noah to go out.

She hadn't meant to be, but Rosie had been a shit friend recently. She didn't know how else to keep things with Callum a secret other than making up excuses about being busy every time Noah had asked. And Noah never made excuses to get out of plans with Rosie. Noah was always there for her, even in the middle of the goddamn night. Yeah, she owed Noah a girl's night. And an apology.

"Okay, so tell me what the hell is going on."

"We're just fucking around? Same as always?" Rosie deflected.

She was still trying to stop her brain from replaying Callum's earlier words on a loop.

We're just fucking around, Elena. It's not like there was anything to tell.

Rosie knew she had absolutely no right to be upset with Callum for having said it when she was the one who asked to keep things between them for now. But she couldn't shake the gnawing feeling in her gut at hearing him dismiss her like she didn't matter. Because Callum mattered a hell of a lot to her. Frankly, he mattered to her more than almost anyone.

"As I said earlier, I don't buy it. But you've never pushed me to talk about things before I was ready, so I guess I can extend the same courtesy to you. Just know I'm here, okay babe?"

"I love you—for a lot of reasons, but especially for that," Rosie laced her fingers with Noah's as they walked down the sidewalk to the bar.

"Tell me one thing though—is it good?" Noah raised her eyebrows dramatically.

Noah could always make Rosie laugh. God Rosie was lucky to have a best friend like her.

"He made me come on a rooftop, Noh," Rosie could feel her cheeks heat at the memory.

"Ugh, when is it *my* turn to come on a rooftop?" Noah asked dramatically. A couple on the sidewalk turned their heads and stared as they passed. "Too loud?"

"Maybe a bit," Rosie laughed, "but to answer your question, it could be your turn, like yesterday, if you would let go of your guilt and try to talk to Lilah."

Talking about Noah's problems was a welcome distraction.

"Rosie, you know it's not that ea—"

Rosie grabbed Noah's shoulders, bringing them to a halt

in the middle of the busy sidewalk, "Noah. Lilah is queer, which means that she went through that realization at some point too. Just talk to her. She'll understand."

"I tried. She didn't."

"So try again. Maybe a little liquid courage will help?" Rosie pulled Noah through the front door and straight toward the bar rather than their regular table.

"Two lemon drop shots please," Noah told the bartender.

Rosie recognized him—Carter maybe? He'd been working the night she was on that god-awful date with Cole's coworker.

As the bartender set their shots on the wood countertop in front of them, Rosie held out her card, "keep it open, please."

Noah held her shot glass up, "to liquid courage."

Clinking her glass against Noah's, Rosie repeated back, "to liquid courage."

In unison, they touched the glasses to the counter, then downed them. Rosie licked the sugar off the rim; she didn't care that it made her look underage. It was tasty.

"I'll be back in a sec. Gotta pee," Noah announced, sliding off the barstool.

"Want me to order you a Rosé?"

"Eh, surprise me—but only one! I'm driving, remember?" Noah called as she walked in the direction of the bathrooms leaving Rosie alone with her thoughts once again.

Rosie twirled her empty shot glass as her thoughts drifted back to that moment in the garage with Callum. She was already feeling the lemon drop, given that she'd had a few drinks at the Costellos before getting into the car with Noah.

She'd thought she was doing the right thing by waiting to tell Elena and the rest of the family until she was sure things would work out long-term with Callum, but maybe that had been the wrong decision. Maybe, Rosie worried, the time to tell her had passed. Would Elena be pissed at her for keeping it a secret for a month? Would she feel betrayed? Would Mrs. Pammy and Mr. Mark even take their relationship seriously after they'd fucked around for all these years?

"What else can I get for you?" Carter (maybe?) asked, interrupting Rosie's thoughts before she could enter a full-on spiral.

"Two Cosmos, please," Rosie ordered.

Rosie decided that Noah, logically, had to like a Cosmo because she liked Rosé. Rosé was pink and so was a Cosmo. It was sound logic. Or maybe she was a bit more tipsy than she'd originally thought. Oh well. Noah was driving, and she could get her car from the Costello's tomorrow.

Next to Rosie, two girls whose appearances, no offense, screamed tourist sidled up to the bar. They stared dramatically from one end to the other, seemingly looking for someone.

"He's not here," the one closest to Rosie whined.

"Maybe he got a new job," the other shrugged.

"But he was *just* here," the whiny one said, flailing her hands dramatically.

Thank god they hadn't ordered drinks yet, or one of them would definitely be wearing it right now. Rosie made a mental note to watch her back whenever they did order.

"Spring break wasn't that long ago. Why would he get a new job that fast?" the whiny one continued.

Rosie figured they couldn't have been much over twenty-one, and they had to be talking about one of the bartenders. Rosie was attempting to recall Callum's workers' names. It couldn't be *maybe Carter* as Rosie had decided to refer to him, still not sure that was actually his name.

"I don't know," Tourist Two, Rosie decided to call her, sighed.

"Where else are we supposed to find a hot, flirty, probably down to fuck bartender?" the whiny one continued.

Probably down to fuck? Jesus. These women were no better than a man, objectifying whoever the fuck this bartender was like that. Rosie took a big gulp of her Cosmo.

As they continued to describe this mystery bartender, the realization sunk in, "*and* he had tattoos and long, curly hair. He's, like, a rarity."

They were talking about Callum. *Her* Callum. Oh *fuck* no. In one sip, she downed the rest of her Cosmo and signaled to maybe Carter for another.

Rosie understood that flirting was part of being a bartender; more flirting, more tips. The math was simple. But still—how often was Callum flirting with random women at work for them to come to Lafayette's with the sole intent of sleeping with him? Could she ever expect Callum not to grow tired of her if he even has this much of a reputation with random women at the bar? Whether or not things worked out with her and Callum, she wasn't about to let these bitches try their luck.

"Hey," Rosie plastered the biggest, fakest smile she could muster across her face and leaned down the bar to Whiny and Tourist Two. "Not to eavesdrop, but I totally just saw a guy like that at the bar down the street." She reached out to touch Whiny's arm in mock sincerity. "I don't know if he's the mystery man you're talking about, but he was definitely flirty. I would totally have tried to fuck him if I wasn't taken," Rosie continued with a wink.

"Oh my god!!! You're like, the best stranger I've ever met," Whiny squealed. "Please tell me you remember where the bar was."

"I don't remember the name... I'm a *little* bit tipsy," Rosie's voice went up an octave on 'little,' really trying to sell her intoxication, which wasn't all that difficult since she genuinely was a bit tipsy. If she pretended not to know the name, these bitches wouldn't be able to look up this non-existent bar. "But, I remember it was *that* way," Rosie pointed left out the front door. "On *West* Bay Street. Cute little dessert bar place."

Whiny jumped off the barstool and threw her arms around Rosie, "girl, you totally just saved this vacation. Thank you!!!"

"No problem," Rosie smiled.

To Whiny and Tourist Two—complete strangers—it seemed genuine, but anyone who knew Rosie would be able to read the mischief behind the smile.

"Uh, why did you just direct those random girls to West Bay? There is no West Bay?" Noah asked, back from the bathroom.

"Exactly."

Noah simply raised her eyebrows at Rosie, clearly waiting for more of an explanation.

"Fine. The little bitches came in here looking for Callum, talking about how he was 'probably down to fuck' because he's just sooooo flirty. Which," Rosie held up one finger in Noah's face, "first of all, is fucked up." She now held up two fingers, "and second of all, he's taken."

Shit. Rosie hadn't meant to say that last part out loud.

"Oh, he's taken, is he? We're talking about this now?"

"There's nothing to talk about."

"Oh, so you're *not* jealous and defensive right now because you're in love with Callum?" Noah dead-panned.

Rosie's mouth dropped open. She was not *in love* with Callum Costello. Sure, she felt safe with him and loved being around him. Sure, Callum always made her laugh. And, yeah, maybe he treated her better than anyone ever had, paid attention to the little things, and surprised her with flowers and coffee at work 'just because.' But that didn't mean she was in *love* with him... unless it did.

Oh shit. That was exactly what that meant.

She was in love with Callum.

Noah reached out to wipe a tear Rosie hadn't even realized slid down her cheek. Why was she crying? Fuck, this is not how this night was supposed to go.

"Talk to me," Noah pleaded. "Please. I don't know how to help you if I don't know what's going on."

"But I don't want you to have to be a bad friend," Rosie sniffled.

"Why would I be a bad friend for caring about whatever shit you're going through?"

"Because I didn't tell Elena. And I didn't tell you because I didn't want you to have to keep secrets from her because you're her best friend too. I wanted to tell you so bad, so, so bad, but I was scared and now I don't know what to do because what if it's not worth it and everything blows up in my face and I lose everyone I've ever cared about?" Rosie let it all out in one breath because she was pretty sure she'd start full-on sobbing if she stopped talking even for a second.

"What did you wish you could tell me? Tell me now," Noah said gently.

"I'm with Callum," was all Rosie could get out.

"Well, yeah, I kinda gathered that much."

"No. I mean I'm *with* Callum. Callum is my partner," Rosie avoided Noah's eyes, scared of her reaction.

Scared that Noah would be mad that Rosie hadn't told her. Scared that Noah wouldn't take it seriously, scared that no one would ever take their relationship seriously, that all they'd see was a fuck boy and a sad girl on the hunt for a rebound. Rosie didn't know which scenario frightened her the most.

"Since when?" Noah asked.

Rosie wished she would say more. That she would give any indication of how she was feeling.

"A month ago. He was acting weird after the rooftop and when I wouldn't leave him alone about it, he admitted that he had feelings for me. We've been going on dates in secret since then."

"Well, that explains why you've been so busy lately," Noah held up air quotes around the word 'busy.' "Why didn't you tell anyone?"

"Because I was scared."

"Of?"

"What makes me so different from every other girl Callum has lost interest in over the years? And then there's also the fact that I haven't been out of a relationship for that long and what if no one believes that I'm really in love with him? What if everything gets fucked up and I lose Elena too? And the rest of the Costellos. Not just Callum... I—if that happens I don't want you to have to choose between us. I can't lose you guys. I just... can't," Rosie laid everything bare like she'd always been able to do with Noah.

Noah didn't say anything. Instead, she wrapped Rosie in a hug and whispered in her ear, "You will *never* lose me. *Ever*. Do you understand me?"

Rosie nodded.

"So you admit that you're in love with him?" Noah smiled.

"Out of everything I just said, that's what you're stuck on?"

Noah just shrugged.

"Are you mad?" Rosie asked, barely audible.

Noah grabbed Rosie by the shoulders, forcing Rosie's attention on her, "only because you let yourself believe that you deserved to carry this alone when I'm right here."

"I don't deserve you," Rosie pulled Noah back into her arms to hug her again.

"It isn't about deserve, babe. You're my family. I will love you no matter what happens in our lives."

"Wait, did you text Lilah?" Rosie asked, untangling her body from Noah's abruptly.

"No," Noah laughed, "I've been a little busy," she continued, waving a hand in Rosie's direction.

"Well, are you going to?"

"Are you going to give things with Callum a genuine chance?"

Rosie could have said yes, but that would have been a lie. The truth was, she didn't know. She was still so scared.

"Well, for what it's worth, no relationship can survive without vulnerability. Giving your heart to someone else and trusting them to care for it... there's always a risk. But you've made a career out of helping people tell genuine stories about love, so you should know better than anyone that the risk is what makes a relationship worth it."

"And do you?" Rosie paused. "Think a chance at true love is worth the risk of losing the family I found for myself?"

"I can't make that decision for you, but you chose the

Costellos as your family for a reason. And Callum chose *you* for a reason. Have a little more faith in them."

Rosie knew that Noah was right, but that didn't change the fact that she was absolutely petrified by the thought of losing everyone she loved.

35

JUST FRIENDS

Callum:

After getting back from his parents' house, Callum settled in to watch a few episodes of *Shameless (U.S.)*. He'd seen the show all the way through at least seven times, so it was a comfort show for him at this point. Netflix had just asked if he wanted to continue watching when there was a knock on his front door. He couldn't imagine who it would be. Rosie was out with Noah while Elena and Cole had gone straight home after family dinner. It could have been Lilah, but she had to report to the job site by six AM, so there was no chance she'd be knocking on his door at—Callum checked the time on his phone—eleven fourteen at night.

Looking through the peephole, he realized the person knocking was Rosie. And she'd been crying. Callum flung the door open so swiftly that it ricocheted off the wall and nearly closed itself again.

"Hi," Rosie squeaked out. "I'm sorry for just showing up."

Why was she sorry? She could show up anytime she

wanted as far as Callum was concerned. Hell, he'd even considered giving her a key.

"What's wrong, sweetheart?" Callum asked.

"I have to talk to you, but I don't want you to hate me."

Fuck. Fuck, fuck fuck. No one ever led a conversation with 'we need to talk' unless it was bad. And how on earth did Rosie think Callum could ever hate her? His heart was pounding as he guided them to the couch. It felt like the moments before going through a haunted house—the scary thing had yet to happen, but the anticipation was enough to make you feel like you'd just had the wind knocked out of you.

"What's going on, Rosemary June?" Callum asked, trying to be as gentle as possible even though he was sure his heart was seconds from leaping straight out of his chest.

"Hearing you tell Elena earlier that we were 'just fucking around' felt like a gut punch," Rosie started.

Callum gently tipped Rosie's face up toward his.

He needed her to see the sincerity in his eyes when he said, "the *only* reason I said that is because you didn't want everyone to know about us yet. It killed me to say it, because you are everything to me, Rosemary. *Everything*."

I love you, he realized he wanted to say. But now wasn't the time.

"I know. And I don't fault you for that, but..." she hesitated.

"But?" Callum whispered.

"But hearing you say it cracked a piece of my heart open anyway. And if that's how much it hurts *knowing* you didn't mean it... I... I can't risk you meaning it one day..."

Callum just stared at her, speechless. He felt a tear roll down his cheek and made no attempt to wipe it. Everything he'd done, everything he'd tried to prove for her wasn't enough. *He* wasn't enough. His greatest insecurity was coming true, and there was nothing he could do to stop it.

When Callum didn't say anything, Rosie continued, "I just don't want anyone to get hurt."

Too damn late, Callum thought. *He* was hurt. More than he'd ever been. Because he'd never let someone in like this before. Everything about Rosie was new, including the immense pain that was now creeping its way through Callum's veins.

This is why you like to fuck around, a little voice in Callum's head whispered to him. *If you never bother to give a shit about anyone, they can't make you hurt like this,* it said.

"I just can't lose my family. And that includes *you*, Callum. You've been as much a part of my life as Elena and Noah have for the last decade, and I can't lose that... because as much as I wish there was, there is no way to guarantee that this," she grabbed his hand and squeezed, "will last. And I just... I can't lose Elena's friendship, and I can't lose yours either..."

"So what are you saying?"

He needed to hear her voice it clearly, even if it killed the last shred of hope in his body.

"I'm saying, if we stay friends... *just* friends, then I don't lose anyone. And that has to be enough."

"I can't be just your friend, Rosie..."

"Callum," Rosie pleaded.

They were both crying now.

"You mean too much for me to pretend otherwise," Callum muttered through sobs.

Without another word, Rosie leaned up on her tippy toes to kiss Callum's forehead. And with that, the love of Callum's life walked out his front door.

Rosie:

Rosie didn't allow herself to turn around as the door swung shut behind her, not even when she'd heard Callum whisper that one word. *Stay*.

Months ago, the night Callum had gotten shitfaced, called Rosie to drive him home and almost admitted his feelings to her, he'd whispered the very same thing. *Stay*. The sense of deja vu was nearly enough to knock her off her feet. Was nearly enough to make her turn around. Nearly, but not quite.

Rosie felt the absence of Callum before she even reached Noah's car like someone had ripped a vital organ from her body and then sewn her shut. Rosie had always seen herself as confident, a risk-taker, but when it came down to something that really mattered—some*one* that really mattered—she was just a timid, emotionally stunted excuse for a grown woman.

Had she made a mistake? She wasn't sure.

Would she regret her decision? Also unsure.

All she knew in the twenty minutes it took for Noah to drive her home was that the pain she thought ending things with Callum would alleviate was more prevalent than before. And it was screaming for Rosie to let it envelop her, to pull her into oblivion. She decided then and there that she would greet it like an old friend.

36

BEST LAID PLANS

Rosie:

NOAH AND ROSIE had gotten back to her apartment late Friday night. Or had it technically been Saturday morning? Rosie had lost all sense of time to the hurt that had burrowed itself deep inside her chest. Either way, Noah had put the car in park, and declared that she was staying the night.

Rosie had been too drained to do anything other than pass a spare hoodie to Noah for her to sleep in. Noah had accepted the hoodie and crawled into bed next to Rosie, wasting no time in pulling Rosie into her arms. They had always been that way—able to communicate their emotions without the need for words. It was a tender gesture between a friend who was petrified of falling apart and another who was determined to hold her together.

She cried softly in Noah's arms for several hours until she'd exhausted herself enough to surrender to sleep. When she woke up the next morning, it was to the smell of freshly brewed coffee drifting down the hall and Noah's side of the bed empty.

She mustered up the strength to walk down the hall, bypassing a trip to the bathroom—she wasn't ready to look herself in the eyes yet. She didn't think she'd ever looked worse than she did right now given that she hadn't taken her makeup off last night even after she'd sobbed uncontrollably for what felt like hours. All that the mirror was likely to yield was a picture of herself as a raccoon that had just been hit by a bus. She definitely needed a cup of coffee before she was ready to deal with that.

Rounding the corner into the kitchen, she heard Noah speaking softly. When she came into full view, Rosie realized Noah was on the phone.

"Yeah, she's awake," Noah told whoever was on the other end of the call. "Let me ask."

"Ask me what? Who is that?" Rosie asked.

"Elena," Noah stated. "She's asking to talk to you," she continued, "if you're feeling up to it that is."

"She knows," Rosie stated.

It wasn't a question.

"She knows," Noah admitted.

"Because you told her?" Rosie wasn't sure if she was angry or relieved that someone else had relayed things to Elena—maybe a bit of both.

She'd wanted to be the one to tell Elena herself, to ensure that the narrative didn't spin itself into anything it wasn't. Yet, at the same time, she couldn't deny the slight loosening in her chest.

"Sort of?" Noah shrugged. "Lilah called Elena, who called me when she couldn't get ahold of Callum."

"What are you talking about? It's not even light outside yet? He's probably just asleep."

"Babe," Noah turned her phone around to show Rosie the time: seven thirty-four PM.

"Holy shit," Rosie mumbled. "No wonder I have to piss so bad."

"Yeah... you've kinda been asleep for sixteen hours."

"And you stayed here? This whole time?" Rosie was afraid she might start to cry again.

However, maybe that was just the insane amount of water in her body fighting to free itself. She really needed to brave the mirror if only to relieve herself.

"Of course I did," Noah shrugged as if it were nothing. As if Rosie wasn't the luckiest person alive to have a friend like Noah. "Go clean yourself up, then we'll talk."

Rosie started to reach for the pot of coffee, but Noah spun her in the direction of the bathroom.

"I'll pour you a cup and bring it in. Go," she instructed gently.

As she walked down the hall, she heard Noah telling Elena that she'd call back in an hour or so. Rosie was in so much shock from realizing that she'd slept for almost an entire day that she'd forgotten that Elena was still on the phone.

A much-needed shower and a change of clothes later, Rosie sat on her bed with a mug of warm coffee in her hand and Noah at her side.

"So, since I evidently checked out of existence for an entire day, wanna fill me in on whatever the hell I missed?" Rosie asked.

She took a sip of the coffee. Black.

"Long story short: Callum wasn't answering his phone,

so Lilah called Lafayette's and they told her that he called out of his shift like an hour before it started, which is super unlike him. So then Lilah called Elena because she was worried about him. And when you didn't answer your phone either, Elena called me to see if I knew where either of you were, thinking maybe you'd hooked up and stayed the night together or something and that's why Callum had called out of work."

Rosie was quiet as she processed.

"I told her that I didn't know where Callum was, but that I was with you and that you were fine, just sleeping after a rough night, and..." Noah hesitated to continue.

"And?" Rosie prompted her to keep going.

"And, given that Callum also hadn't replied to anyone for almost a full day, she put two and two together and figured something had happened between you guys."

"How much does she know?"

"I didn't give her all the details—I figured you'd want to tell her yourself. But she knows that you broke things off with Callum. She just doesn't know exactly what 'things' encompasses."

"And..." Rosie squeezed her eyes shut in an effort not to let another tear fall. "And, Callum?"

"What about Callum?"

"Is he... is he, um, okay?"

It killed her that she felt like she no longer had the right to know the answer to that question.

"I haven't talked to him, but it seems like he's doing about as well as you are," Noah gestured to the tangle of dirty clothes and blankets where Rosie's bedroom floor should have been.

"Like shit then," Rosie laughed.

It was a weak laugh. And she wasn't quite sure why it

had even come out. Maybe she'd cried out all of her tears and there just weren't any left. Maybe she was laughing at the absurdity of it all. This *had* been her doing. She had only herself to blame for the way she felt in the aftermath.

Had she fucked things up so irrevocably with Callum that there wasn't a shot in hell he'd want to hear from her even if she somehow found the courage to try to fix things? Rosie was pretty sure the answer to that question was a resounding yes. The hurt in his eyes as she'd left his apartment was evidence enough of that.

She'd thought she was making the right decision—the only decision that would allow each of them to make it out of this whole mess unscathed. Yet here they were, both of them somehow more hurt than she had thought possible.

"Well, you can't live like this for the rest of your life," Noah gestured around the room. "And if you stay catatonic for much longer you're going to need an IV. No offense to you, but I much prefer to use needles to turn people into art, not to play nursemaid. So, what are you gonna do about it?"

"Any chance you think Elena would be willing to have a girl's night tomorrow night? I need to fix things with her before I can even begin to think about Callum," Rosie sighed heavily.

37

WALLOWING NEVER HELPED ANYONE

Callum:

CALLUM HAD ALLOWED himself twenty-four hours to wallow. Except that it had now been thirty-seven hours and he'd still only gotten up long enough to pee and grab more tissues. He'd called out of his shift on Saturday, which technically wasn't even a thing he could do as general manager. Really he'd just texted the staff to say that he wouldn't be coming in that evening and that it was no one's business why. Oh well. Fuck the inventory and fuck everything else too.

He hadn't told Lilah what happened yet because saying it aloud was too painful: he was in love with a girl who had no faith in him. And just what the fuck was he supposed to do with that?

He wished he could be angry. Surely this would be a lot easier to deal with if he were, but he understood why Rosie had done it. On their date to Lowcountry Coffee Roasters, Rosie had told Callum how it felt to come out as bisexual in high school. Callum had known that girls had stopped inviting her places, but he hadn't known that they'd started treating her like a predator. As if being attracted to the female gender somehow meant that she was attracted to *all* women. She'd been alone. Except for Noah and Elena.

Her own parents didn't even acknowledge her sexuality, but his did. Elena, Noah, and his family... they were the only people in her corner for so long. So yes, Callum understood why she'd run away from him, but that did absolutely nothing to alleviate the pain. Because Rosie had every right to feel the way she did, even if it meant that his own heart got trampled in the process.

He couldn't cook himself dinner without thinking about teaching Rosie to make his Nonna's pasta. He couldn't go to work without anticipating Rosie at one of the barstools teasing him while he mixed drinks. Couldn't open Spotify without seeing the playlist he'd made for their first date, couldn't watch the sunset without thinking of the night he took her to watch it from the observation tower, couldn't order a cup of coffee without the subconscious thought to order a black Americano for Rosie too. She'd carved her way into every aspect of Callum's life.

Hell, he couldn't even go to another family dinner without the fear of having to see her and act like it didn't absolutely gut him to know that she didn't reciprocate the love he felt for her. How would Rosie act toward him the next time they saw each other? Or would she just avoid him altogether? Callum thought that might be worse.

Sitting up to grab the glass of water on his end table, Callum felt a twinge of pain shoot down his lower back. Evidently, sleeping on the couch the previous night hadn't been the best idea; he decided he could wallow more comfortably in his bed. Slowly, he dragged himself from the cushions and tracked down the hallway into his bedroom.

His head had barely hit the pillow before Callum passed out again.

Callum woke up the next morning, still sad, but in less physical pain. Moving to the bed had been a good idea. He realized he should probably text Lilah, given that he'd basically dropped off the face of the earth for two and a half days and she would definitely be worried about him. He padded back down the hall to find his phone in whatever crevice of his couch it had fallen into.

Callum let himself relive the conversation with Rosie fully. She had been crying just as hard as Callum had, which meant that clearly she was hurting too, despite thinking she was making the right decision. What was it that she had said about losing family?

You've been as much a part of my life as Elena and Noah have for the last decade, and I can't lose that...

I can't lose Elena's friendship, and I can't lose yours either...

And finally, the part that had hurt Callum the most:

I'm saying, if we stay friends... just friends, then I don't lose anyone. That has to be enough.

A friendship with Callum 'had to be enough'? Meaning Rosie *did* want more than friendship with him, but was too scared to let herself have it? Would things have been different if Callum had told Rosie he loved her? Would that have been enough to make her stay?

Callum knew what he had to do then, and it was a much better use of his time than wallowing was. Even if it didn't work... then at least he'd know he did everything he could. At least he would have told her that he loved her. Then maybe he could try to move on in peace.

Finally, he found his phone, the battery life at a meager six percent, and with seventeen missed calls from Lilah and a few from Elena. Shit.

He decided to return Elena's call before Lilah's; best to do the scarier of the two first.

She picked up on the first ring, "Callum?"

"Hi."

"Oh, thank god, are you okay?" Elena asked, concern shredding her voice.

"Not really, no," Callum admitted.

"What happened? I haven't heard from you in nearly forty-eight hours, and Noah told me Rosie isn't doing well but she won't talk to me either," Elena explained, exasperation punctuated by worry.

"Yeah, um..." he started, not sure how much he could explain. Rosie had wanted to be the one to tell Elena about them; even in his anguish, he refused to take that away from her.

"Please," Elena begged. "Please just talk to me. Tell me something."

"I'll tell you my hand in things, but I won't take that right away from Rosie, either. This isn't just my story to tell," Callum sighed, trying his best to convey how much he respected her.

"Go ahead then."

Callum couldn't read her tone. He had no idea if she was angry with him. He wished he could see her face right now.

"I realized a little over a month ago that I had feelings for Rosie," he began.

"I'm sorry, you what?" Elena asked in disbelief.

"I have feelings for her, Elena," Callum repeated. "And I told her. I told her that I wanted to be with her—not just physically, but that I wanted to be her partner. That I wanted more than this stupid fucking game we've been playing for all these years."

"What makes her different from any other girlfriend you've kept for a month or two and then abandoned?" Elena asked, a bit of defense creeping into her tone.

Somehow, in that moment, he loved his sister more for being so protective of her best friend. For being so protective of the very person Callum cared so deeply for.

He understood her hesitation. The revelation that he had been subconsciously comparing every woman he'd ever dated to Rosie had shocked him, too.

"None of them were her. None of them could ever *be* her. I could never commit to those women because, in the back of my mind, a little voice kept whispering to me, telling me that Rosie was the best thing that would ever happen to me.

"And I never got the chance to tell her that. So now, I'm sitting here, feeling bad for myself and wondering if things would have ended differently if I'd have just told her that I loved her. If it would have been enough to make her stay," Callum finished.

This was the first time he'd said it aloud. He'd never told anyone—except his family—that he loved them. Callum had expected to be afraid as the words left him; instead, he just felt relief. Whether or not she loved him back—whether or not she ever would—he didn't have to hold it in anymore.

"You—you love her?" Elena sounded beyond incredulous.

"I do," Callum admitted. "And I know that you probably don't believe me and that you're probably not very happy about us being togeth—"

"So why didn't she stay?" Elena asked, cutting him off. "If you love her. Why wouldn't she stay?"

"That's her part of the story to tell. I respect her too much to speak for her," Callum answered plainly.

"I'm sorry."

"For?"

"Several things. For starters, I'm sorry that you're hurting. And also for ever making you feel like I wouldn't support you. Because I do. Both of you. And I know I don't know the whole story, but I want you to know that I will do everything I can to help fix things. I love both of you. So stupidly fucking much. And I just want you both to be happy. Even if that's with each other. Especially if that's with each other," Elena declared.

"Thank you, Elena. I love you too," Callum told her.

"So what are you gonna do?" she asked.

"I'm not exactly sure yet," Callum admitted.

"Let me know when you figure it out."

With that, Elena ended the call, leaving Callum to face the repercussions of his wallowing. He really needed to get it together, starting with charging his phone, calling Lilah back, and taking a goddamn shower.

Though Callum might have been new to romance books, he knew one thing for sure: when shit hit the fan, a grand gesture could always save the day. He just needed to figure out what the right gesture was.

38

THERE ARE FEW THINGS THAT GIRL'S NIGHT AND PEANUT BUTTER ICE CREAM CAN'T FIX

Rosie:

IF SHE WAS BEING honest with herself, Rosie was more than a little surprised when Elena had actually shown up at her doorstep for her proposed "girl's night." Immediately, Rosie flung her body around Elena's.

"Oof, hi," Elena said into Rosie's hair, wrapping her arms around her in return.

God, she didn't deserve to be hugged. She had been such a shitty friend when all she'd wanted to do was keep the people she loved from getting hurt. She owed so many people an apology, starting with Elena.

"I'm sorry," Rosie muttered through tears that had already started to fall again. "Can we talk inside?"

"Yeah," Elena agreed, following Rosie to her living room.

Taking a seat on the couch and facing Elena, Rosie jumped straight into her explanation. She'd held it in for so long and all that had accomplished was hurting everyone she cared about.

"Um, so I'm sure you've already figured some of this out.

But Callum and I are sort of together. Like, *together* together. For a month and a half now. At least we were until two nights ago when I fucked everything up because I was scared," Rosie wiped a tear from her cheek.

"What were you so scared of?" Elena asked.

"Losing him," Rosie hesitated on her next words. "Losing you. Losing my family."

"Fear of losing him, I understand. No relationship is ever guaranteed, and you went through some shit with Justin. But what I don't understand is why the hell you thought being with him would cause you to lose *me*?" Elena's words came out more as a question than a statement. "Don't you know me better than that?"

Elena wiped a tear from her own cheek as she'd said the last sentence. Rosie deserved every bit of guilt that swept over her body at that. She wanted so badly to reach out and take Elena's hand, but she forced herself to endure the pain she'd caused Elena.

"At first, I was worried that no one would take things seriously between us. Everyone always talks about how much of a bachelor Callum is, how he 'isn't a commitment type of guy,' and I was afraid that we'd constantly have to justify things before we even had the chance to explore our feelings for each other. So, I asked him not to say anything to you at first...

"And I realize now that that put him in an awful position. But by that point, I'd started to worry that, if things didn't work out, that you'd feel like you had to choose between us. And by the time I'd worked through *that* fear, I felt like it had been too *long* to tell you, and that you'd be upset with me for keeping it from you in the first place. So I did the only thing I thought I could do that would prevent everyone from getting hurt: I ran.

"I fucking showed up to his doorstep and crushed his heart in my hand because I was too selfish to face my fears and just fucking talk to you. I looked the man I love in the eye and told him that I couldn't be anything more than his friend. And when he looked at me and told me that he couldn't—wouldn't—do that, I walked away from him.

"And you have *every* right to be mad at me for the way I treated you. Because I have been an exceptionally shitty friend. And you didn't deserve a second of it. I'm so fucking sorry, Elena."

"You're right," Elena said. "I am angry. I would never abandon you just because things didn't work out between you and Callum. I'm a better friend than that."

"I know you are," Rosie choked out. "Is there anything at all that I can do to make it up to you?" Rosie asked, her tears coming full force now.

"You might not deserve it right now," Elena began, and Rosie's heart sank. "But part of being a good friend means that I refuse to leave you to deal with this alone, even though you hurt me by not telling me. Besides, I promised Callum I'd do what I could to help fix things between the two of you."

"You talked to him? Is he, um, is he doing okay?" she asked hesitantly.

As if she had the right to know.

"He misses you," is all Elena said.

"He told you that?" Rosie couldn't believe what she was hearing.

She'd taken the heart he'd laid so bare before her and smashed it into a million pieces. Why on Earth would he be missing her? He should want nothing to do with her. In fact, he had every right to never speak to her again.

"I'll tell you the same thing he told me," Elena smiled softly. "That's not my part of the story to tell."

Rosie jumped at the sound of a bang on her front door. Suspiciously, Elena did not.

"What was that?" Rosie asked.

"Backup," Elena smiled, walking across the room to open the door.

"I thought this might be a peanut butter ice cream kind of night," Noah shrugged in the doorway, a grocery bag looped over one of her arms.

An hour and half a pint of peanut butter ice cream later, the weight of the world had stopped feeling so heavy because Rosie had finally allowed her best friends to help her shoulder it. Which is what she should have been doing all along. She knew that now, and she'd never make the mistake of trying to carry everything alone again.

Knowing it was Rosie's comfort movie, Elena had suggested they watch *She's the Man,* but Rosie didn't feel like explaining that it wasn't her comfort movie anymore because the mention of gouda cheese was liable to make her cry. So, she'd instead suggested that they browse the romcom sections of the streaming services they had combined access to. Eventually, they'd landed on *The Proposal*, because who didn't love Betty White?

"Did Justin ever say anything about the screenshots from Isabella's Instagram?" Noah asked without looking away from the TV screen.

"Nope. He did, however, tell me to 'call off my man' the night Callum punched the fuck out of his face," Rosie answered. "Didn't even acknowledge the screenshots."

"Do you think she knows?" Elena chimed in.

"That he was cheating on us both?"

"Yeah," Elena said.

"I have no idea," Rosie thought aloud. "Not really my problem though."

If she was being honest with herself, she would rather not know than find out that Isabella *had* known. To find out that Justin had chosen *her* over Rosie. She already felt like shit for everything that had gone down with Callum, Elena, and Noah. She didn't have it in her to suffer the feeling of inferiority on top of it all.

"What if you reached out to her?" Elena suggested. "And hear me out before you say no. Doesn't she deserve to know, too?"

"What if she already does?" Rosie argued.

She knew she was being dismissive, but she was just so emotionally exhausted.

"I mean, you'd get closure either way," Noah shrugged, agreeing with Elena.

Rosie knew they were right, but she didn't know if she was ready to face it. If she ever would be.

"I'm saying this because I love you," Elena started, "but you clearly still need to work through the fact that Justin cheated on you. I don't think you would have walked away from Callum like you did if you'd dealt with things instead of brushing it under the rug."

It hurt to hear it voiced aloud, to know that her biggest insecurities were so painfully obvious to everyone else. But Rosie knew Elena was right, and that she of all people had the right to call her on her shit right now.

"Look babe," Noah said, setting a hand on Rosie's shoulder for emphasis, "either she already knew, and she's just as shitty as Justin. Or... she's just another woman who's been played by a man and deserves to know the truth. And even *if*—emphasis on if because I really don't think she knows—she did know and was going along with it, the whole stigma around 'the other woman' has never made sense to me. The other woman isn't the one who's supposed to be in a committed relationship. I just don't get why women are always the ones at fault."

"Noh has a good point," Elena agreed.

"Either way," Noah continued, "you can't heal from it without closure. And we both know you aren't going to get that from Justin. You should talk to her," Noah stated definitively.

Rosie hadn't realized that while Noah was busy giving her speech, Elena had unlocked her phone, pulled up Isabella's profile, and opened a direct message thread. She placed Rosie's phone in her hand in silent encouragement. Rosie had to do this herself, but she was not alone. She would never be alone again.

Rosie began typing...

I know you probably don't know who I am, but I know who you are because we've kinda sorta been dating the same guy... I know it might be weird to ask, but would you be willing to maybe grab a coffee and talk?

39

PHALLIC-SHAPED GLITTER

Rosie:

THOUGH SHE WAS FEELING a shit ton better than she was at the start of the weekend, Rosie was grateful that she'd preemptively taken Monday off of work as she currently found herself sitting across from Isabella at a coffee shop.

"I'm really glad you reached out to me," Isabella began. "I thought something was up with Justin last month, but he kept assuring me that we were fine. If you hadn't reached out... I don't think I would have known he was cheating on me with you. And on you with me. On us? Sorry... I tend to ramble when I'm nervous," she said, avoiding eye contact with Rosie.

"What do you mean you knew something was up?" Rosie asked, curious.

She had been too blind to see the signs, and it filled her with a fucked up sense of relief to know she wasn't the only one.

"Well, he had a broken nose after going out with his friends one night."

Oh, Rosie knew all about that broken nose and the man that had been the cause of it. Her heart sank a bit at the thought of Callum.

"When I asked him what happened, he fed me some bullshit story about how his friend had accidentally elbowed him because they'd been drinking, but I didn't buy it. His nose was too fucked up for it to have been an accident. I realized someone had to have been really *really* pissed off at him to do something like that, which is when I really started to worry... I wondered who he could have made *that* angry that he wouldn't tell me about..." Isabella explained. "I think that's when I knew, but I didn't want to be right, so I didn't ask. I was too comfortable in the relationship, and I was scared of who I would be without it."

"My best friend's brother is the one who broke his nose," Rosie explained.

She couldn't hide the smirk that tugged at her lips.

"Oh my god," Isabella raised her eyebrows in shock. "Why? Are you two together?"

"No," Rosie said, her smirk fading fast. "I mean, we were, but..."

Isabella sat patiently, giving Rosie the space to decide whether or not she wanted to talk about it. Whether or not she wanted to offer up a vulnerability of her own. Rosie appreciated it far more than Isabella would ever know.

"I fucked things up for us. I didn't tell Elena—my best friend—" Rosie clarified, "because I was worried that if things didn't last with me and him she'd feel like she had to choose between us. So I ran, and I broke his heart, and part of me has this lingering hope that somehow we could fix things, but..." Rosie trailed off.

When Isabella didn't say anything, Rosie admitted, "I think I was too proud to acknowledge that Justin cheating actually affected me. He fucking sucks, and I wanted to just move on, but... I kinda just projected my newfound insecurity onto Callum—Elena's brother—and that fucked everything up."

Isabella looked at her, truly looked. And it wasn't a look of judgment, but one of understanding. Because she, too, had been cheated on. She, too, knew what it was to feel like she wasn't enough.

"I just can't believe we both wasted so much of our lives on him," Isabella groaned into her cup of coffee.

"*I* can't believe *I* thought he was going to propose."

Rosie couldn't stop the laugh that escaped her, the idea of a marriage with Justin seeming entirely preposterous to her now.

"God, men are the worst," Isabella returned Rosie's laughter.

Rosie knew, like her, that, while it probably still hurt, laughing was better than crying. Was better than giving Justin another second of her energy. Noah had been right about women always being the ones to take the blame, though it was rarely their fault. And if talking to Isabella was the first step in breaking that stigma, Rosie was glad for it.

"I'm really happy that we got the chance to talk," Rosie smiled.

"I couldn't agree more," Isabella answered. "Thank you again for reaching out to me. I know it couldn't have been easy. And I want you to know that it wasn't for nothing. Talking to you has given me the bravery to finally confront him."

"You can thank them for that, actually," Rosie explained, pointing to the table on the other side of the room where

Noah and Elena sat, trying and failing to look inconspicuous.

They'd insisted on coming. *For moral support,* they'd claimed. Elena had taken Monday off work too in support of Rosie, and Noah didn't go into work until noon because the tattoo shop she worked at didn't open until one PM.

Rosie hadn't wanted the conversation with Isabella to feel like an interrogation; so, they'd compromised and agreed to sit far enough away to be out of earshot, but close enough to step in if needed.

At Isabella's confusion, Rosie explained, "Noah and Elena: my best friends. They were with me the night I found out about Justin's cheating. They encouraged me to reach out to you on the grounds that you deserved to know too."

Rosie and Isabella let out a simultaneous laugh as they glanced toward Noah and Elena, who both turned their heads away at the same time, making it very obvious that they were trying to overhear the conversation.

"They seem like great friends," Isabella said.

"They are," Rosie couldn't help but smile. "And I'm sure they're dying to come talk to you."

"Wh—why?" Isabella asked, seemingly nervous.

"Elena to know that it went okay, and Noah because she's just straight up nosy," Rosie laughed again, causing Isabella to visibly relax.

"Okay, sure, invite them over."

Noah hadn't even fully reached the table before she started talking, "okay, so I'm assuming you *didn't* know Justin was cheating if the two of you are over here laughing together."

Rosie shot her a look that said, *way to make it obvious that you were eavesdropping.* She merely rolled her eyes.

"Wait, so does Justin know that you know?" Noah asked, glancing between Rosie and Isabella for answers.

"No," Isabella confirmed. "Not yet, at least."

"Keep it that way, at least for another few days," Noah said, crossing her arms. "So, what's the plan?"

"The plan for what?"

"Uh, the plan to ensure that Justin gets his karma?" Noah answered like it should have been obvious. "I believe in the universe, but it can't hurt to speed her along."

"What, you think we should egg his car or something?" Isabella raised her eyebrows in Noah's direction.

"You're thinking too small," Noah smiled deviously.

"Seems like you already have a plan, Noh," Elena chuckled.

"Step one: acquire the materials," Noah said in answer.

"Do I want to know why you just so happen to have these?" Rosie asked as Noah handed her and Elena each a black ski mask to put on before they got out of the car.

Noah merely shrugged.

Rosie pulled her phone out of her pocket when she felt it vibrate.

> Isabella: Got the keys.

Phase one of their—really Noah's—grand revenge plan had officially commenced. As far as Justin knew, things were fine between him and Isabella; the women had decided to use that to their advantage. Isabella's job was to swipe his spare car key from the hook on her way out of his apartment tonight and bring it back to the group.

From there, Noah would knock on his door and rip into Justin about the fact that he not only had cheated on Rosie, but he'd also not even bothered to acknowledge the fact. While Justin was distracted by Noah, Rosie, Elena, and Isabella would use the car key Isabella had swiped to fill Justin's car with several pounds of tiny, dick-shaped glitter.

Then, Isabella would run back up and apologize for 'accidentally' grabbing Justin's keys instead of her own on the way out the door. Justin, hopefully suffering from the emotional whiplash of having Noah turn up on his doorstep so close to the time Isabella had left, would be none the wiser until he opened his car door to go to work the next morning.

"You're up, Noh." Rosie flashed her phone's screen in Noah's direction.

"I'm about to deliver a grammy-award-winning performance," Noah teased as she headed toward Justin's apartment building.

"Where the fuck did you guys even find glitter this shape?" Isabella asked as she rounded Justin's car, clicking the unlock button on his key.

"That's a Noah question," Elena laughed as she tore open the first of several bags of the phallic glitter.

Noah had purchased an array of colors—pink, purple, orange, and blue—because, apparently, people didn't just want their dick-shaped glitter in one color. Rosie, Elena, and Isabella each ripped a bag open and started hastily dumping it across every surface of Justin's car.

Rosie's phone vibrated again.

"Noah's headed back down," she told Isabella. "That's your cue to head back up."

Rosie and Elena quickly finished spreading the glitter while Isabella ascended the steps to Justin's building. Rosie had just clicked the lock on the car door when Noah made it back down.

"Wait," Noah paused, grabbing the left-over glitter from Rosie, "let's give him one last surprise."

Noah dumped the rest in the space between Justin's windshield and his wipers so that, the next time he turned them on, it would rain dicks. Literally.

"Isn't that dangerous? We want to get revenge, not to indirectly kill him," Elena asked, ever the voice of reason.

"Nah, there's not enough to obstruct his view, just enough to be a really fucking annoying cherry on top," Noah answered.

"Alright, now let's go before he looks out the window," Rosie urged.

Given how loud they were laughing as they ran toward Elena's car, Rosie thought that their ski masks probably weren't that effective at all.

40

WORDS I SHOULD HAVE SAID

Callum:

FRIDAY MORNING CAME, and Callum found himself on the phone with Isla.

"We're all set?" Callum asked Isla over the phone.

"Yep. She should be here any minute, and everything is set up on her desk," Isla's voice confirmed through the line.

"I can't thank you enough."

"Don't mention it. Seriously," Isla laughed. "What kind of person employed by a romance publishing house *doesn't* believe in the power of a grand gesture?"

"Fair enough," Callum found himself laughing too. It felt good to laugh, especially after a week of misery twined with a kernel of hope. "Seriously though, thank you Isla."

"You can thank me by inviting me to the wedding. Crediting me in your 'how we fell in love' speech wouldn't hurt either," Isla snorted.

"Let's not get carried away," Callum sighed. "I have to win her back first."

"You will."

"How can you be so sure?"

"Because I've seen her practically float into work everyday for the past month. I've seen her giggle while texting you from her desk when she doesn't think anyone is watching. I've seen the way her cheeks turn bright red whenever I ask how her weekend was. She never acted like that—not once—in the entire two years that she was with her asshole ex. Because the way she's acted since the two of you started your secret whatever-the-fuck is how you act when you're head over heels in love with someone. Because the two of you have the kind of love for each other that people write stories about."

Callum was pretty sure he'd stopped breathing. That kernel of hope he'd buried away multiplied, spreading through every vein in his body. He'd meant it when he'd told Rosie that she was it for him. So either this plan of his went the way he wanted it to, or he would resign himself to the fate of watching Rosie's life from the sidelines.

All Callum managed to say before hanging up the phone was "let's hope Rosie feels the same way."

If the agony of this past week hadn't killed him, the anticipation of waiting for Rosie's reaction might just do it. Even so, he waited. For her, he would always wait.

Rosie:

Rosie had called in sick on Monday and Tuesday, which wasn't technically a lie. She *had* been sick, just more in the 'too depressed to leave her bed' kind of way rather than the 'fever and runny nose' kind of way. Isla had called last night to ask if she was coming in today, which had effectively made Rosie contemplate calling out again.

She dreaded the impending conversation she knew would soon unfold with Isla all the way up the elevator. It wasn't that she didn't want to talk to Isla. It was just that she knew Isla was going to ask about 'Elena's hot brother' and she was afraid she might lose it. Again.

As she stepped off the elevator in the direction of her desk, she glanced across the office space.

No Isla. *Huh*. That was odd.

Rosie was about to sign into her computer to check the staff-wide calendar when she noticed a book-sized box on her desk. Figuring it was PR or an ARC, she went to open it and realized there was no shipping label. That meant that it was internal mail of some kind. In that case, why had someone wasted time on wrapping it?

Too impatient to ask around the office for an answer to the question, she ripped at the wrapping. When she had successfully worked the brown butcher paper off and removed the lid from the box, she saw what appeared to be a *very* old, cloth-bound book. Lifting it out of the box to get a better look at the title that was embossed into the cover, she nearly dropped the book in pure, unadulterated shock.

There was absolutely no fucking way in hell or on earth that she was holding what she suspected this to be. Because, if it was, then Rosie was holding a book worth several *thousand* dollars... A first edition that she, as an editor and lifelong reader had always longed to have in her possession, but could never justify the cost of purchasing.

Yet there, embossed into the faded green cloth, the title stared back at her: *The Great Gatsby*.

Who the hell would have given her a gift like this? She would have never spent this much money on herself... Rosie fought every intuitive sense that told her she knew *exactly* who cared enough to do something like this for her. Because she really, really didn't deserve his kindness after all she'd done to him.

Rosie moved the box to the side to set the book on her desk and examine it more carefully. Gently turning the front cover open, she revealed a certificate of authenticity that noted the following information:

***The Great Gatsby.* Fitzgerald, F. Scott.**
Scribner's 1925. First Edition and First Printing
Original cloth-binding with blind embossing on cover and gilt to spine (gilt slightly faded).

All four main first printing issues points present: 1) pg. 60, line 16 "chatter" 2) pg. 119, line 22 "northern" 3) pg. 205, lines 9-10 "sick in tired" 4) pg. 211, lines 7-8 "Union Street station."

First edition, first printings of *The Great Gatsby* started around two thousand dollars... Rosie had once seen a copy sell for as high as nearly nine thousand dollars. Which was absolutely insane and also the reason why she'd never actually attempted to acquire a copy herself. She didn't exactly have a few grand lying around for rare, collector's edition books. Yet here she was, somehow in possession of one.

Realizing there was something else hiding underneath the first-edition *Gatsby*, Rosie gently set her now most prized possession to the side to unpack the rest of the box. What she found somehow managed to be even more astonishing than the rare book had been.

It was a manuscript: *Words I Should Have Said* by Callum

James Costello. The cover of the manuscript was a photo she didn't realize had even been taken— a candid picture of Rosie and Callum from Elena's wedding. Callum had grabbed her by the waist in the ocean and spun her around as if he'd been planning on dunking her under the water.

The sunset in the background of the image cast them in a partial silhouette, but there was enough brightness to the image that you could just barely make out the details of her and Callum's faces. They looked... happy. *Rosie* looked happy. And if she were being completely honest, the expression on Rosie's face made it seem as if looking at Callum caused the rest of the world to cease to exist. It almost seemed as if Callum himself made up the entirety of her world.

It was a beautiful picture. The kind of picture that people kept in shoeboxes in the back of a closet somewhere, until decades later when their kids asked what their lives had been like when they were younger. The thought of showing that picture to her future kids had Rosie's stomach twisting itself into knots—partially because of the sheer intimacy of the photo, and partially because she realized in that moment that she imagined those future kids to be Callum's.

Picking up the manuscript, Rosie felt that it was not very long, maybe a chapter or two. Had Callum written this himself? And if this was from Callum, did that mean that he really was the one who had purchased the first-edition *Gatsby* for her too? It was the only explanation that made sense, despite how little sense it made after the way she'd treated him.

Callum *had* made an ordeal about the fact that he knew Rosie's favorite book was *The Great Gatsby* when she'd been on that atrocious blind date over a month ago. But he did *not* have a spare few thousand dollars to spend on a gift like that. Hell, maybe he did, but that was beside the point given that it was still far more money than Rosie would have ever even *considered* spending on a gift like that for herself. It was too much. *Way* too fucking much.

With shaking hands, she picked up the manuscript and began to read...

Words I Should Have Said
by Callum James Costello

CHAPTER 1: WHERE THINGS FELL APART

I was close to passing out on my couch with Shameless still playing on Netflix when I heard a knock on my front door. Rosie had gone out with Noah, Elena, and Cole had gone home, and Lih had to report to the job site by six AM, so there was nearly no chance she'd be knocking on my door so late.

Looking through the peephole of my front door to see a sobbing Rosie was the last thing I expected. I nearly knocked my door from its hinges, ripping it open to let her inside. I had no idea what was wrong but I felt some long-dormant part of me awaken with the urgency to take her pain away. To protect her from whatever—or whoever—had made her feel this way. And then she'd had the audacity to apologize for 'showing up so late.' As if I would ever turn her away.

"What's wrong, sweetheart?" I asked.

"I have to talk to you, and I don't want you to hate me."

I didn't know how to tell her that there wasn't anything she could possibly ever do that would make me hate her—at least not without throwing too much emotion at her too soon. That was something you said to someone you were in love with, but it was too soon to tell Rosie. And this certainly wasn't the time for me to confess.

So instead, I just asked her what was going on. My heart was in my ass, and I was trying desperately to hold my shit together, to be something solid for her to hold onto.

"Hearing you tell Elena earlier that we were 'just fucking around' felt like a gut punch," *Rosie started to tell me.*

I grabbed her face and tilted it up, trying to get her to meet my eyes.

"The *only* reason *I said that is because you didn't want everyone to know about us yet. It killed me to say it, because you are everything to me, Rosemary.* Everything," *I told her.*

And then she halted my world with one small, seemingly insignificant word.

"But..."

But... I don't love you.

But... you aren't enough.

But... you will never be deserving of my love.

I stood, stunned in silence, as I watched her descend the stairs of my apartment complex.

CHAPTER 2: WHERE THINGS GET PUT BACK TOGETHER

It took me all of a minute to realize that I couldn't let her leave like this. Even if it wasn't enough, even if she still walked away, I had to tell her that I loved her.

I flew down the stairs, sprinting for the parking lot where I saw her closing the passenger side door to Noah's car. As relieved as I was to know that she wouldn't be driving herself home while crying that hard, I refused to let her go.

I refused to be too late.

I refused to lose the best thing that had ever happened to me.

I didn't think as I bolted into the road in front of the moving vehicle. Noah screeched to a halt, staring at me in disbelief. The second I knew I wasn't going to be run over, I moved to the passenger-side door and pulled the handle.

"I just need to say something," I pleaded with her. "And if it doesn't change anything, if it's still not enough, then you can leave, and I promise I'll do my best to stay out of your way. But, please, Rosemary, please just let me say this one thing."

"I'm listening," she whispered softly.

"I love you. I am so completely and hopelessly in love *with you. And I know you're scared, but—"*

"You love me?" she asked, shocked.

"How could I not?" I sighed, not sure how else to make her understand that she was everything I never knew I needed. "And I promise, if you just take the leap of faith and get out of the car, I will be here every step of the way for whatever comes next. You're not alone. I'm here. I will continue to be here—for as long as you'll allow me."

Slowly, so slowly, she grabbed her bag from the floor of Noah's car and laced her fingers with mine.

"Okay," she said. "I'll stay."

CHAPTER 3: WHERE WE GO FROM HERE

I was hoping that maybe... maybe there's a chance we could write this chapter together?

41

SOMETIMES YOU JUST NEED A MOM

Rosie:

Rosie closed the manuscript and placed it back on her desk. She stared at it in shock.

Rosie couldn't call Noah, because she couldn't stand to hear 'I told you so,' no matter how well intended. And Noah *had* told her so. Rosie had just been too skittish to listen. She had no one to blame but herself.

Calling Elena didn't feel right either—Rosie wanted to talk to someone who understood the situation but was a bit more emotionally objective.

She decided to call Mrs. Pammy. Before she could psych herself out of it, she dialed.

"Rosie, sweetheart, what's wrong?" Mrs. Pammy's voice asked from the other end of the line.

Rosie could barely get the words out through her choked sobs, "I fucked everything up."

"Baby, I have no idea what you're talking about, but I'm sure, whatever it is, you'll find your way. You always do."

"I'm not so sure this time," Rosie sighed, regaining some sense of self upon hearing the voice of the woman who had been like a mother to her for all these years.

"You wanna tell me what happened?"

"You'll think it's crazy."

"Try me, honey," Mrs. Pammy encouraged.

"I've uh..." Rosie hesitated. "I've been, um, seeing someone."

"What part of that was supposed to be crazy? You deserve to find happiness with someone new after that the way that shithead Justin treated you. You know, my offer to slash his tires—"

"Oookay, Mrs. Pammy," Rosie laughed—a soggy-sounding laugh through all of the tears, but a laugh nonetheless. "Calm down—you sound like Noah."

"I love Noah."

"Me too, but I don't particularly want either of you to get arrested, which is why you will not be slashing anyone's tires on my behalf. Besides—this has nothing to do with Justin."

"Okay, okay. But if you change your mind..."

"You'll be the first person I call," Rosie conceded. "Well, you and Noah."

"Good, now get to the part of this story that's supposed to be crazy."

"It's the person I've been seeing."

Rosie wasn't sure how to frame things. Would she understand? Or would she still see their relationship as an on-again-off-again fling that would never be anything more?

Rosie shook her head as if to force those thoughts from her mind. That line of thinking was what had landed her in this mess in the first place. She had been too afraid—of other people's opinions on her and Callum's relationship, of whether or not Callum would grow bored of her, of whether or not she was ready to be in another relationship, of how Elena would react to the fact that Rosie had kept a secret from her for so long...

Her fear had fucked everything up, and she needed to let go of it, once and for all, if she had any chance of possibly repairing the damage she'd caused.

"It's Callum, isn't it?" Mrs. Pammy asked, simply.

As if she'd expected it. As if she already knew.

"How—" Rosie stammered. "How did you know?"

"Now, he doesn't know that I know this, and he just might disown me for telling you, but one of the first weekends you ever came to stay with us, I had gone outside to take the trash out when your mom pulled into the driveway to pick you up. He and Lilah had been playing basketball in the driveway and he walked right over to your mom and announced that he was going to marry you one day," his mother laughed, as if her statement hadn't just shaken Rosie's entire world.

"He—he what?"

"He said, and I quote, 'I'm Callum, the one that's going to marry Rosie one day.'"

Rosie was, for what felt like the millionth time that morning, entirely speechless.

"Baby, I don't think the idea of you and Callum is crazy. I think it makes all the sense in the world." Rosie let that thought settle over her. "And for what it's worth, the way I've seen that boy look at you over the years is all the evidence I need to say that there is nothing you could do that would fuck things up bad enough to lose him forever. And nothing would make me happier than officially making you a part of this family. Lord knows we already love you just as much as the rest of the kids."

Rosie knew Mrs. Pammy was no stranger to the word 'fuck'—she'd seen her bookshelf—but it was still funny to hear it coming from her mouth, which made Rosie laugh.

"There's the Rosemary I know," Rosie could hear the shape of Mrs. Pammy's smile around her name. "Now, tell me what happened that supposedly ruined everything."

Rosie relayed everything that had happened over the last few months: hooking up with Callum, swearing off any future hookups with Callum and ultimately failing in that endeavor, how blissfully happy she'd been while secretly dating Callum, the night that she'd gotten drunk and scared and fucked it all, and the events of this morning that had led to her call: the first-edition Gatsby and the manuscript.

"I can't think of a single person who would go to all that trouble for a person they weren't absolutely head-over-heels in love with," was all his mom had to say.

The fact that Mrs. Pammy was a romance reader was really working in Rosie's favor right now. It was hard to scandalize someone who read that much smut. When Rosie didn't say anything in return, Mrs. Pammy asked *the* question.

"Do you love him?"

Did she love Callum James Costello? The Callum she'd known since childhood, the Callum that had never failed to make her laugh, the Callum who accepted and defended every facet of her being, the Callum that had allowed her to see the most vulnerable parts of himself, the Callum that had proven how much he cared about her time and time over, the Callum that had proven to be the single most thoughtful person she knew, *her* Callum? Did she love him?

"Yeah," she finally let herself admit out loud. "Yes, I love him."

"Then go tell him, baby," Mrs. Pammy said definitely before ending the call as if it were truly just that simple.

Maybe it was.

42

WHERE WE GO FROM HERE (FOR REAL THIS TIME)

Callum:

THE RINGING of Callum's phone broke the silence he'd been anxiously sitting in. It was Lilah.

"Hey," he answered a bit grumpily.

"Good morning to you too," Lilah joked.

"Sorry—sorry. I was just hoping you were Isla with an update," he explained.

He and Lilah had spent the past two days working out every detail of what they'd decided to call 'Plan Grand Gesture'.

When he'd finally answered the absurd amount of missed calls and texts Lilah had sent, she'd called him an asshole. Which he deserved. Then she said she was on her way over to comfort his 'sorry ass.'

After explaining everything that had happened, he'd told Lilah that his biggest regret was the words he didn't say; he hadn't told Rosie that he loved her. He'd just let her walk away. Lilah had encouraged him to write down everything he had felt at the moment to better organize his thoughts.

After he'd done what Lilah suggested, they'd sat down to figure out how to win Rosie back.

"You need to find a way to meet her where she is," Lilah had said.

"She doesn't want to talk to me, and I want to respect that."

Rifling through the notes Callum had made, Lilah had smirked up at him and said, "maybe you don't need to talk to her. Maybe you should write to her."

Thus, his jumbled mess of emotions became *Words I Should Have Said* by Callum James Costello.

He'd already had the first edition copy of *The Great Gatsby*. He'd planned to give it to Rosie for her birthday in the spring but didn't want to have to keep looking at the damn thing and reliving the pain in the case that the manuscript wasn't enough to fix things between them. So, he'd decided to wrap it up with the manuscript.

Callum had called Rosie's office and asked for Isla. Technically, Lilah had called in an effort to be less suspicious. He'd explained Plan Grand Gesture to Isla, and everything had fallen into place from there. Now, here he was: sitting on his couch waiting for a call from Isla.

"Damn, I was calling to see if you'd heard from Rosie yet," Lilah sighed.

"She has to have opened it by now, right? She gets to work at nine, and it's ten thirty. Lilah said they didn't have any meetings until noon, so—"

"Calm down, Bolton," Lilah teased him. "Maybe something came up. Give her time."

Before Callum could say anything else, there was a knock on his door.

Callum quickly put Lilah on speakerphone to check for a text from Isla. Nothing. Nothing from Rosie either.

"Fuck, fuck, fuck..." Callum rambled, unsure what to do.

"What's going on?" Lilah asked.

"Someone's at the door."

"So open it?"

"What if it's her? What if she's here to tell me that it's still not enough? That *I'm* still not enough?"

"What if she came to tell you that you *are*?" Lilah countered.

God, Callum was lucky to have her in his life. He let Lilah's confidence in him give him the strength to stand up and walk, one foot in front of the other, to his front door. Slowly, he turned the knob and opened it.

Rosie stood in front of him, clutching the box he'd wrapped the copy of The Great Gatsby and his own manuscript in. Callum just stared back at her, stunned.

Without a word, she handed him his manuscript and flipped open to chapter three. Underneath his own handwriting, he could see Rosie's scrawled across the page. She nodded at him to read what she'd written. With shaking hands, he took the pages from her steady ones.

I was hoping that maybe... maybe we could write this chapter together?

This chapter, and every chapter after.

If I'm not too late, I want to be with you. And I want everyone to know. Because I would be the luckiest person in the world to be loved by you. You think you're the one who is undeserving, but you couldn't be more wrong. I'm the one who doesn't deserve you—not after how I hurt you. Not after I let my own selfish fears get in the way. But I want to try to become someone that deserves your love.

I'm sorry I was too afraid to say it until now, but I love you, Callum James. You're it for me too.

"You love me?" Callum asked gently, afraid he would somehow break whatever spell had brought her back to him.

"I love you," Rosie admitted. "I am so completely and hopelessly in love with you," she continued, repeating his own words from the manuscript back to him.

"Oh, thank God," Callum muttered, dropping the manuscript and his phone on the kitchen floor and threading his hands in her hair.

He kissed her like a starved man. She kissed him back just as hungrily.

Ever so faintly, they could hear Lilah's cheer emanating from the floor. Callum had evidently forgotten to hang up. Oh well.

"I love you, Rosemary June Dawson," he whispered against her lips. "Completely," he kissed her cheekbone, "and hopelessly," he kissed the shell of her ear, "in love with you," he kissed her neck.

"I love you too, Callum James Costello," Rosie whispered back, tilting her neck to give him more of herself.

Moving to intertwine his fingers with hers, Callum remembered that she was still holding the box. He grabbed it from her.

"Just gonna set this where it will be safe."

"Yeah, actually, what the fuck were you thinking when you bought this?" Rosie asked, sounding entirely exasperated.

"I was thinking that I'm in love with you and that I wanted to give you something that would make you as happy as you make me," Callum answered sheepishly.

"You didn't need to buy me a gift that costs several *thousand* dollars to make me happy, Callum." It was her turn to look sheepish, "You did that just by being you."

"I wanted to spoil you," he argued. "And right now, I want to spoil you in lots of other ways instead of arguing about how much money I'm allowed to spend on you. Which, for the record, is however much I want," he smirked at her.

"We're talking about this again later," Rosie said, walking in the direction of the hallway.

"Oh? And what exactly are we doing right now?" Callum teased, following her down the hallway that ended with his bedroom door.

"You said you wanted to spoil me, didn't you?" she teased back.

"I don't *just* want to spoil you. I want to worship every inch of your body, Rose."

"Then come here," Rosie sat innocently on the edge of Callum's bed, leaning back on her hands.

Callum stood in front of her, planted a gentle kiss on her forehead, then dropped to his knees. Spreading her legs so that he could settle between them, he flicked the material of her pants.

"I don't like these—they're in my way."

"Then take them off," Rosie stated, smirking down at him.

"Bossy," Callum hummed. "I like it."

Sliding his hands up the inside of her pant legs, Callum pulled the Doc Martens from Rosie's feet. As he slid farther up to undo the button of her slacks, he felt Rosie shudder.

"Everything okay, baby?" he teased.

"You're taking too long," she complained, feigning annoyance.

"Lift your hips and help me out then," Callum replied in the tone of a man who had all the time in the world.

Honestly, he deserved a medal. He wanted inside of her so badly, but not until he'd shown her how happy he was that she'd come back to him. In every way he knew how to express. Starting with his mouth.

Rosie lifted her hips to let Callum slide her slacks down and off, but she didn't stop there. She reached up and pulled her shirt over her head, revealing the absence of a bra. The woman Callum loved—who, for some unfathomable reason, loved him back—was sitting, naked on his bed waiting for him to touch her. He didn't know how the hell he'd gotten so lucky.

Callum's hands found her hips to move her higher up on the bed. "Lie back," he instructed.

She did as she was told.

Reaching around her, Callum grabbed a spare pillow

and placed it under the small of Rosie's back, then settled between her legs, looking up at her.

"Have I mentioned that I love you?" Callum asked, not that he hadn't just told her five minutes ago.

The excitement of being able to say it was just too great to hold it in for any longer than that.

"Only a few times," Rosie laughed. "I love you too, just in case you forgot."

"Good—just checking. Have I mentioned that I also love your pussy?" Callum gently kissed the inside of Rosie's thigh.

She grabbed Callum by his hair and pulled him closer to where she clearly wanted him. "Callum, please," she begged.

God, he loved when she begged. Almost as much as he loved the sounds she made when she came. Which would be at least ten times tonight if Callum had absolutely anything to say about it.

"Mmm, not so bossy now, huh? Tell me, sweetheart, what exactly do you want?"

"You."

Callum could have teased her further, but he was equally desperate for the taste of her on his tongue. He brushed a kiss ever so lightly against her clit, then dragged his tongue across the length of her cunt. She moaned, and his cock strained against his boxers.

"Fuck, I missed you," Rosie said breathily.

"It's only been four days," Callum laughed against her skin.

"Yeah, well, I spent those four days thinking I'd lost you forever, sooooOH fuck, that feels amazing. *You* feel amazing."

"You could never..." Callum slid two fingers inside her.

"...lose me forever," he whispered, curling his fingers for emphasis.

The hands Rosie had threaded through his hair pulled his mouth back to her. Callum really fucking liked when she was bossy and demanding. And he would happily give her whatever she wanted.

He picked up his pace, pumping his fingers in and out of her throbbing core as he ran his tongue greedily over her clit. She writhed against him, seeking release. Her heels dug deliciously into Callum's back, a sign of just how much Rosie was enjoying this.

"Louder, baby," Callum instructed. "Let me hear you."

His comment had been meant to push Rosie toward her own orgasm but had effectively made Callum so painfully hard that he found himself seeking friction against the mattress. Rosie liked to play at being bossy, but Callum knew that what she really loved was pretending to be the one in charge only to have control taken from her. There was bliss to be found in giving up control.

Rosie pulled at his hair so hard Callum thought he might have a bald spot, but he didn't mind. Not as she screamed his name with her release.

43

EVERY CHAPTER AFTER

Rosie:

IF ROSIE HAD to choose a favorite body part of Callum's, it would be his tongue. Though that might just be her post-orgasm brain talking. She should probably take his pants off to see how his cock competed with his tongue.

In the time it had taken her breathing to return to normal, Callum had found his way up to bed to lay next to her; he was trailing gentle kisses across her shoulder. Maybe Callum's lips were Rosie's favorite body part. There was just so much of him to love—it was impossible to choose.

The feel of his t-shirt against her skin reminded Rosie that Callum was still, much to her dismay, fully clothed. She wanted the feel of his bare skin against hers, not these stupid clothes. She wanted to be as close to him as physically possible, with nothing in her way.

She rolled so that she was leaning over him on the bed and tugged at his shirt, "off, please."

"Yes, ma'am," Callum answered with a smirk, sitting up to pull the shirt over his head.

He tossed it mindlessly to the floor. Curling her fingers between the band of his boxers and his hip bone, Rosie pulled at his pants next.

"These too."

Callum eagerly lifted his hips to help her pull them off.

"What now, sweetheart?" Callum asked sensuously.

She'd been so bossy earlier, and he was letting her take charge now. The smirk on his face combined with the sight of his hard, waiting cock sent a pulse to her core. But that would have to wait. It was her turn to make Callum scream with pleasure.

"Lay down," Rosie instructed him, pushing him by his shoulders.

He did as he was told, even going as far as to tuck his arms behind his head and stare from his cock and up to Rosie with an expectant grin on his face. Oh, if Callum wanted to play, she would play.

She straddled his body, kissing his neck while teasing her bare pussy against his cock. His head tipped back with a moan. Slowly, so painfully slowly, she trailed kisses down to his collarbone, then to his stomach, still not giving his lower half the direct attention he wanted.

She kissed his hip bone, sucking just enough to leave a mark. Heat flared in his eyes when he realized. So, he liked being marked by her. *Interesting.*

She moved to his other hip bone, sucking harder, the mark she left this time darker and more obvious. A claiming. The hunger in Callum's eyes flooded through Rosie and took control of her next words.

She ran her tongue up the length of him, "Whose cock is this?"

"Yours," Callum breathed out, every muscle in his body

tightening as his right hand instinctively threaded into her hair and pulled.

Hard.

Holy fuck. Rosie had never spoken to Callum like this, but the safety she felt in knowing he was hers had her shedding all her inhibitions and giving into her every desire. And if Callum's throbbing cock was any evidence, he was enjoying it just as much as she was.

"Say it again," Rosie demanded just before taking him into her mouth.

His answer was barely discernible through the moan he let out then, "Yours, yours, yours."

She took him fast and deep. Her right hand echoed her mouth, pumping him with just enough pressure to drive him crazy. With her left hand, she reached down to lightly squeeze his balls. At this, Callum's fingers tightened in her hair. She didn't need to check to know that she was wet again. Feeling Callum physically react to the pleasure she was eliciting from him was more of a turn-on than anything. She loved knowing how much he loved her mouth on his cock.

She broke her pace to slowly circle the tip of him, eyes flitting up to his. Rosie loved seeing Callum like this. Undone. She could see the desperation in his eyes, the longing.

"Louder, baby," she parroted his earlier words back to him. "I want to hear how much you like fucking my mouth."

She'd barely wrapped her lips around him again before he was thrusting up into her mouth.

"Fuck, baby... about to come," he managed through uneven breaths. "Swallow me, Rose."

His next thrust into her mouth was his undoing. Rosie

took everything he had to give, not moving her lips from his length until he had relaxed into the mattress.

The way they'd settled, one of Callum's thighs was nestled between Rosie's. She knew he could feel how much she still needed him.

"I *really* fucking hope you have the energy to go again," Rosie teased. "Not that that wasn't great, but I need to feel you inside of me, Callum."

His cock hardened beneath her in answer, "roll over."

He grinned and wound his arms around her waist.

"Mmm, actually..." she traced a path up his neck with her tongue as she moved to straddle him fully. "I was thinking..."

"Whatever you're thinking," Callum let out something between a sigh and a groan. "I think it's a *great* idea."

"You haven't even *heard* my idea yet," she laughed against his skin.

"The love of my life is sitting naked on top of me—the only thing that could make this better is if you were sitting on my face instead," Callum said simply.

His hands found her hips, and he guided her to move against him.

She reached for his cock beneath her and positioned him at her entrance.

"I love you too," Rosie laughed joyfully and lowered herself in one quick motion.

"What's wrong, baby?" Callum asked an hour later from his position as big spoon to Rosie's little.

"I didn't say anything was wrong," Rosie answered.

"No, but I can feel your heart, and it's beating faster than usual," Callum pointed out.

Damn him and his stupidly perfect powers of observation. She didn't want to ruin the absolutely perfect day they were having by bringing up the fact the conversation they still needed to have with Elena.

"We have to talk to Elena now that we're really doing this," Rosie breathed out.

"You're still worried about that?" Callum asked. Rosie could hear the fear in his voice as he asked. He wouldn't say it aloud, but she was sure a part of him was worried that she'd run off again, scared.

"I'm not going anywhere this time. I promise."

At that, Rosie could physically feel his arms relax around her.

She turned around, still cocooned in his embrace, to look him in the eyes as she said, "I won't make that mistake again. I knew before the door to your apartment even closed that I had just lost the love of my life... but I didn't turn around because..."

A few tears trailed down her cheeks at the memory.

"I didn't turn around because I was scared. But I know with absolute certainty that a life without you is far worse than anything I could have imagined. I love you. I want a life with you. And I won't let anything, including my own stupid brain get in the way of that."

The tears were falling more heavily now, and Callum just held her closer, giving her the safety she needed to let go of everything and just be in this moment with him.

"I love you, Rosemary June," he said over and over as he traced soothing circles down her back, up her arms. "We'll tell her together. You don't have to do anything alone—not anymore."

Rosie kissed the inside of Callum's arm that was wrapped around her, finding herself brave enough to ask something she'd always wanted to know.

"I always wondered about the meaning behind this tattoo," Rosie traced the shape of Icarus inked into Callum's skin.

Callum sighed, unwrapping his arm from Rosie's body to look down at the piece.

"We don't have to talk about it if—"

"No, it's not that," Callum explained. "It's just not a very happy explanation."

"Will you tell me anyway?"

Rosie knew the myth of Icarus—had studied plenty of mythology in college—but wanted to hear why Callum had chosen to bear a permanent image of his fall.

"I'll tell you anything you want to know about me," Callum kissed her forehead. "I don't know if you paid attention to the order of when I got my tattoos, but this was the first tattoo I ever got," Callum began.

"Oh, believe me, I noticed," Rosie laughed, burying her face in Callum's chest. "I thought you were hot before, and then you went and got a tattoo and I thought I was going to die. And then you just *kept* getting them."

"I'm glad you like them so much," Callum laughed. "Do you remember the night we made pasta, when I told you about my plans to buy Lafayette's from Hank?"

"Of course," Rosie answered.

"And I told you that the reason I never mentioned it to anyone was because I felt like all people thought of me was that I would be a bachelor forever content to just get by?"

Rosie found Callum's hand and laced their fingers together, a silent gesture to convey that she knew he was more than that. She saw him for the person he truly was.

"That expectation started back in high school. A lot of people found me attractive, and I was surrounded by a lot of women because of my sisters and Lih, and along with that came the assumption that I got around. At first, I tried to defend myself against the notion, but I learned very quickly that it's much easier to prove people right than it is to prove them wrong...

"So, I just leaned into the image. I let people think I was just a player who bounced around from girl to girl. And I convinced myself that it was fine, that I was happy because the only person I ever really wanted was off limits," he continued.

"Me," Rosie looked up at him, tears threatening to fall.

"You," he confirmed, smiling sadly.

"And if I couldn't have you, then what was the point in trying to make a relationship work with someone else? By the time I realized how miserable it felt to be the bachelor, the fuck boy, the player—you name it, I've been called it—I felt like it was too late to convince anyone that I would ever amount to anything else," Callum sighed.

Rosie clung to him, squeezing him tightly as if she could hold him together by the sheer force of her will, "I'm sorry it took me so long to see through the facade."

"I didn't want you to," Callum squeezed her back reassuringly. "At least not at first."

Rosie pressed a soft kiss to his bare chest and cuddled closer to him.

"We had that mythology unit in tenth grade, which was when I learned about the myth of Icarus. I saw a part of myself in his story. A man reaching for the sun, for something great, but never being able to touch it, and, instead, falling to his death. So, the day I turned eighteen I went and got the tattoo. A visual reminder that, no matter what I did, I always seemed to fall short. That I would never reach the sun."

The level of vulnerability Callum was offering Rosie at this moment was enough to make her start crying again.

"Shh," Callum whispered, stroking the hair back from her face to look her in the eyes. "There's no reason to cry. That was a long time ago. Besides, unlike Icarus, I found my sun." He smiled down at Rosie, "And I'm keeping her."

If she hadn't already been crying, that would have done it.

"I hope you know how proud I am of you," Rosie said softly. "And how proud I am to call you mine."

"Likewise," Callum answered, kissing her brow softly before wrapping her up in his arms once again.

They fell asleep like that, wrapped up in one another.

Safe. Happy. Warm.

At peace.

44

SOMETIMES, THINGS WORK OUT

Callum:

THE NEXT WEEKEND, Callum and Rosie walked hand-in-hand toward the front doors of Over Easy. Having finally sorted through their own problems, it was time to talk to Elena. Again. Together this time. Callum could feel the anxiety emanating from Rosie; he would do just about anything to take it from her.

"Hey, look at me," Callum said gently, moving his free hand to turn Rosie's head in his direction. "She's your best friend, who loves you unconditionally, and she just wants you to be happy. Everything is going to be okay." He kissed her forehead, "promise."

"I know, I guess I'm just nervous that she's still a little mad at me," Rosie sighed.

"The fact you were willing to make yourself miserable for the sake of protecting her emotions is the very reason she won't be, baby."

Callum knew how much Elena loved Rosie. They were each other's chosen family. And the idea of Callum and

Rosie together wasn't even new to Elena, given that she knew about their history. The only thing that had changed was the fact that they were now emotionally involved rather than just physically. Though, if Callum were being honest with himself, they had always been emotionally involved even if he'd been too blind to see it.

Despite knowing that everything would ultimately end up okay, Callum squeezed Rosie's hand without saying another word. Just because he wasn't worried didn't mean that he would minimize her emotions.

Elena had texted them both to say that she'd gone ahead and grabbed a table.

"Hey, my sister is already here, brunette, short," Callum told the hostess.

"Yep, head straight back and to the right," she directed them.

As they walked toward the table, Rosie tried to pull her hand away, but Callum didn't let her.

"Together, Rosie. No more hiding."

"You're right. No more hiding."

As they approached the table, Elena noticed their intertwined hands. Before either of them could say a word, Elena laughed.

"It's about time you two lovesick idiots worked your shit out. I've been waiting to hear what happened for a week. I'm dying here."

"Turns out, I am *great* with grand gestures," Callum declared proudly.

"You can tell me all about it once we order some coffee," Elena gestured for them to sit.

"So... you're not even a little bit weirded out? Or still upset?" Rosie asked incredulously.

"Well, I mean you can save the sex details for Noah, but other than that, nope," Elena said definitively.

Callum had to fight back a smirk.

"I know now that the only reason you kept it from me was because you didn't want to lose me," Elena continued. "And, like I told you a week ago, that never would have happened. But I understand that you were scared.

"You're my best friend, Rosie. All I want is for you to find as much happiness as I have with Cole. Who gives a fuck if you found that happiness with my brother? You're happy. I've quite literally *never* seen Callum so happy. What kind of a best friend or sister would I be to stand in the way of that?"

Under the table, Callum squeezed the hand that was still holding Rosie's, "I told you it would be okay, baby."

Rosie glanced up at him, then back to Elena, still looking a bit unsure, "you're absolutely sure?"

"I'm absolutely sure," Elena repeated simply. "I love you, Rosie."

"I love you too," Rosie let out a sigh of relief. Callum could feel her relax next to him.

"Honestly, this is kind of ideal for me," Elena continued. "This just means you'll legally be my sister one day."

"Woah, slow down. We've only been officially dating for like two months," Rosie laughed. "And honestly do they even count since no one even knew we were together?"

"Considering I was wildly in love with you the entire time," Callum pressed a kiss to her forehead, "I think they count."

"Wow, baby bro. When did you become such a sap?" Elena teased.

Honestly, the idea of being married to Rosie didn't sound even the least bit crazy to Callum. It sounded like exactly what he wanted the rest of his life to look like. But he could wait a while to tell her that.

Rosie:

"What do you think you're doing?" Rosie asked Callum as he reached for the front passenger door handle.

"Getting in the car?" he asked, confused.

"Not shotgun, you're not. Girls only," Rosie smiled as she shoved him backward.

She was more than aware that the only reason Callum actually moved toward the back door was because he'd allowed it. He was far too strong to be pushed around by Rosie if he didn't want to be.

"Be my guest," Callum told Elena as she squeezed past him to open the front door.

After they had all gotten into the car, Rosie asked, "So, where to?"

"I think we should—" Callum started.

"Wasn't talking to you, babe," Rosie cut him off.

"Bookstore?" Elena suggested.

"Always," Rosie said at the same time that Callum said, "ooh, you can pick out another smutty romance for me!"

"Should've seen that one coming," Elena groaned. "You're a bad influence," she added, turning to Rosie.

"Hey, I discovered smut all on my own, thank you very much," Callum argued from the backseat.

"I'm not sure I want to hear that story," Elena laughed.

"So, we're at the beach house, right? The night of your wedding…" Callum began recounting his experience.

Elena and Callum's sibling bickering faded to the background as Rosie thought about just how truly lucky she was. She sighed, contentedly. Two of her favorite people in the world, two of the people she loved the most. And she got to keep them both, forever.

"I could get used to this," Rosie said to herself.

EPILOGUE: ONE YEAR LATER

Callum:

"Needs more semolina," Callum's Nonna pointed out from her place at the kitchen table.

"Nonna," Callum groaned. "I know Rosie's a bit of a mess, but have some faith in me at least. You taught me yourself," Callum muttered as he begrudgingly added a bit of semolina to the dough.

Though he wouldn't admit it to Nonna, he hadn't noticed that the consistency was a bit off. He was more than a little sidetracked with his plans to propose while they were visiting his grandparents in Italy. Callum had had the ring for a while now, but proposing in Italy had much more allure than proposing in South Carolina. So, he'd waited.

They had taken the ferry from Anzio to Ponza, the small island where his grandparents lived, yesterday afternoon.

"You leave that pretty girlfriend of yours alone," Nonna scolded him, pulling him from his thoughts. "I'm still not quite sure what she sees in you."

Callum scoffed. Rosie snorted.

That was Nonna—always giving him a hard time. It was her way of showing affection, and Callum loved her for it.

"Eh," Rosie shrugged in Nonna's direction, "he's pretty handsome."

The two of them shared a conspiratorial glance. It should come as no surprise to Callum that Rosie fit right in with his family—she had come into his life as his sister's best friend, after all. Even so, a sense of pride flared in his chest at the sight of Rosie and his Nonna giggling together, even if it was at his expense.

"That he is," Nonna agreed with Rosie.

Callum returned his attention to kneading the dough for their dinner, silently thankful for the task to distract from the panic that threatened to creep in whenever his thoughts drifted to the ring that was carefully hidden at the bottom of his duffle bag. If everything went according to plan, Callum would set out tomorrow with a girlfriend and come back with a fiancé, the happiest man alive.

Rosie:

Rosie was pretty sure her insides were 90% pasta after two days with Callum's grandparents. She'd been stupidly nervous when Callum proposed the trip to visit them, wanting desperately for them to like her.

All her fears, however, had been eliminated the second that they got off the ferry and his Nonna had fussed at Callum about 'not letting that pretty girl of yours carry her own bags' and insisting that 'he'd been taught better.' By dinner, they were sharing laughs and Rosie had learned every embarrassing thing Callum had ever done as a child, which was apparently a lot.

"How far of a hike did you say this was again?" Rosie asked, worried that she was too full of pasta to make it the rest of the way without falling off the side of the island.

"Not too much further," Callum laughed. "In my defense, I tried to tell you that a second helping was a bad idea."

"I want your Nonna to like me! I was not about to deny her offer for another serving," Rosie argued. "And, to be fair, I assumed a hike meant like a nice trail, not step-like structures carved into the side of a literal cliff."

"One, I'm pretty sure my Nonna likes you more than me. And two, we're on the coast of an island. Where the fuck did you think we would find a flat trail?" Callum snorted.

"Delusional hope?" Rosie sighed, defeated.

"We're almost there," Callum laughed again. "It'll be worth it, I promise."

After a few more minutes, they reached the last descent of the cliff. The path couldn't even be considered step-like anymore—just a steep, rocky terrain. The only thing separating them from falling to their death was a sad-looking fence that came up to Rosie's mid-thigh with a stanchion-esque rope to hold onto. However, Rosie seriously doubted that it would support her weight should she stumble.

"Let me go first so that you can grab onto me if you slip," Callum directed Rosie behind him.

"You're sure this is safe?"

"I've been a few times before and I'm still alive aren't I?"

Slowly, carefully, they made it to sea level with their limbs still intact.

"Welcome to Grotta della Maga Circe," Callum said proudly, gesturing to the fenced-off cavern behind him.

"Circe, as in Homer's *Odyssey* Circe?" Rosie asked.

"*Exactly* as in Homer's *Odyssey*," Callum answered. "Legend has it that Ponza is actually the island of Aeaea from Homer's *Odyssey*. According to mythology, the sorceress Circe dwelled in this very cave during the winter months," Callum further explained.

"Holy fuck?" Rosie said in disbelief. "That's cool as shit."

"Told you the hike would be worth it." Callum smiled proudly.

"How did you know I liked mythology?"

"You majored in English," Callum deadpanned as if no further explanation were needed.

To be fair, none was. Every English major went through a Greek Mythology phase.

"Can we go inside?" Rosie asked, hopeful that the gate could be unlocked.

Much to her delight, Callum pushed a lever, and the gate swung open. Rosie walked deeper into the cave, absolutely in awe of the historical value of the place. The cavern ceiling had to be at least thirty feet high.

"How did you find out about this place?" Rosie asked, thinking Callum was still right behind her.

When she didn't hear his answer, she spun to see where he'd gone. What Rosie saw when she turned around was better than any view Italy—or any country for that matter—could offer her. Callum was down on one knee, holding a small, velvet box and smiling at her like he'd never seen anything so beautiful.

"Rosemary June Dawson, will you marry me?" Callum asked nervously.

Speechless, she crossed the space between them. He had a habit of making her speechless, she realized.

"Yes," she answered, kissing him. "Yes, yes, fucking *yes*, I will marry you, Callum James Costello."

"Thank God," Callum smiled. "I was really worried there for a second when you didn't say anything."

"I was in shock!"

"Why would it shock you that I'd want to marry you?!"

"Just shut up and put the ring on my finger," Rosie laughed with pure, unadulterated joy in her heart.

ACKNOWLEDGMENTS

I want to begin by thanking my parents, who knew from a very young age that my life would revolve around literature in some capacity. My childhood nickname was Belle, after the Disney princess, as my adolescence was merely a series of being told to 'kindly put the book down and come eat dinner with the rest of my family.' Not only did my parents recognize the tether between me and the written word, but they fostered it; they read to me every night all the way into middle school, and praised the short stories I wrote. As an adult, my dad mentioned casually to my mom that I should write a book. My mom informed him that I had, in fact, done just that, but hadn't told him about it because it was really, really smutty. Thanks for being proud of me anyway, Dad. I love you both immensely.

My sister, for being a constant in my life, and for always supporting my endeavors. I love you. I am forever grateful to have a best friend in you.

Emma, who is the reason this book exists in the first place. Thank you for sitting across from me each and every Wednesday without fail for over a year while I wrote Rosie and Callum's story. Without you, this book would still be an idea drifting around in my mind. Thank you for smacking me upside the head with the notion that the only person with the power to stop me from bringing this story to fruition was me. You believed in me even when I didn't believe in myself.

To my middle name twin—meeting you was like looking into a mirror. You made me feel seen and reminded me that I wasn't alone during one of the hardest years of my life. Growing up with you will always be one of my greatest blessings. Thank you for being my Sam and Patrick.

Amy, for answering my incessant number of questions, for telling me honestly if something was cringey and needed to go, and for always bothering her husband to ask for his opinion on whether or not a man would actually do/say something. (I suppose I owe a thank you to her husband too.)

My childhood best friend, who inspired everyone's favorite character: Noah. I'm eternally glad that middle school me met you at camp. (And I'll try not to take offense that everyone likes you more than my FMC).

To my spice girls–you know who you are. Thank you for encouraging me every step of the way.

My beta readers, who read the earliest—and shittiest—version of this story. Thank you for being invested in this journey with me, and for all of your feedback along the way. I hope this final draft was worth the wait.

To my editor, Sabrina Grimaldi. Writing my first novel felt incredibly daunting until you stepped into the process. Thank you for helping me tell Rosie and Callum's story and for loving them as much as I do. Having you as my editor has been the biggest blessing, and I can't wait to work with you again.

My cover artist, Annie, who brought the essence of this story to life in a way that exceeded my wildest dreams. One of the perks of being an indie author is having full say in your cover design, and I truly couldn't have chosen a better person for the job. Thank you for bearing with me as I tried to convey my ideas to you without any of the proper vocabulary.

And lastly, to you, the reader. Thank you for giving my little found family a chance. I hope that reading this story made you feel seen. I hope it made you feel a little less alone for a little while. I hope it made you laugh. I hope it made you feel wistful. I hope, simply, that it made you feel human.

Thank you, thank you, thank you.

ABOUT THE AUTHOR

Stephanie Lynn Bellis is a part-time indie author. *Words I Should Have Said* is her debut novel. She loves romance & fantasy novels, Noah Kahan, Guinness, black coffee, and Halloween. In her spare time, you will likely find her at a bookstore, a coffee shop, or a concert.

 instagram.com/writingbyslbellis

Printed in the USA
CPSIA information can be obtained
at www.ICGtesting.com
LVHW040047140624
782912LV00005B/381

9 798218 417703